PASSION'S SURRENDER

Hawk reached out a hand and took her gently by the wrist. "Come lie down with me. I'll warm you."

She sank to her knees, unable to stand, and her face was almost level with his. He smiled at her, a quick, almost uncertain smile, and Deborah's tension eased slightly.

"I don't know what to do," she said simply. He nodded.

"I know. We'll do what comes naturally. You'll see."

Could this be Hawk? This almost gentle man with promise burning in his eyes and a tender touch? This new perception of him battled with how she'd seen him previously, the fierce, brutal warrior filled with anger.

Then there was no more time for abstract thought, because he was pulling her to him, his arms holding her in a tight, possessive embrace.

"Kiss me," he coaxed, tilting her face with a finger beneath her chin. His voice lowered to a rasping whisper. "Kiss me."

As he set his mouth on hers, Deborah closed her eyes. The kiss was smothering, consuming, and she felt dizzy from it. Her hands moved to hold his upper arms to keep from falling, and she felt the smooth, powerful flex of his muscles beneath her fingers. A moan vibrated in the back of her throat, and when she opened her mouth to gasp for air, he took immediate advantage . . .

VIRGINIA BROWN

COMANCHE MOON

ZEBRA BOOKS
KENSINGTON PUBLISHING CORP.

ZEBRA BOOKS

are published by

Kensington Publishing Corp.
475 Park Avenue South
New York, NY 10016

First Printing: May, 1993

Printed in the United States of America

To Marlene Monroe—who loves romance and handsome heroes as much as I do. This one's for you, Marlene.

Book I

The race is not to the swift nor the battle to the strong . . .

Old Testament

Prologue

Presidio County, Texas 1859

"I don't know who did it," the boy said. He met his father's angry gaze calmly. "I only know it wasn't me."

"*Some*body left that damned gate open, Zack, and now my prize mare's running loose." Daniel Miles glared down at him with hot rage glittering in his pale eyes. Shadows flirted with sunlight in the dusty barn, and a shaft of light threw a wavering square across the floor. Zack shifted warily, and a hot glare struck his eyes.

"It wasn't me," he repeated in a monotone, blinking at the bright light.

Fury reverberated in every syllable as Daniel Miles ground out, "You're lying, Zack. If your brother didn't leave that corral gate open, and you didn't do it, then I guess you want me to believe that it just blew open."

Zack's eyes narrowed fractionally, and he stepped out of the light. He sensed what was coming, and knew that it wasn't the open gate that fueled his father's rage. Zack flicked a wary glance toward his older brother. Sixteen-year-old Danny stood as still as a fence post, his face as white as buttermilk beneath his tan. Zack instinctively knew that Danny was the guilty one, and he

3

also knew that Danny was too frightened by their father to admit it. Mentally squaring his shoulders, Zack waited silently.

"Don't stand there just looking at me!" Miles bellowed. His big hands curled into fists, and his beefy face creased into furious lines. "I want to hear you admit it for once."

When there was no reply, no indication that Zack had even heard him, Miles swung a heavy hand in a backstroke that caught the boy on the left side of his face. Zack reeled but did not fall, his dark hair lashing into his eyes as he quickly regained his balance and stood upright again. A small trickle of blood formed at one side of his mouth, but other than that, he gave no sign that he'd even felt his father's blow.

As Zack steeled himself for the next blow that he knew would fall, he glimpsed his brother's wince and almost felt sorry for him. It didn't matter if he was taking the blame for Danny. Not anymore. It had ceased to matter months before. This scene was becoming increasingly frequent, and he didn't even know why. All he knew was that for some reason, his father had begun to hate him.

For over two years he'd done what he could to appease his father's rage, but it had been useless. Now he just accepted the unrelenting hatred and resentment without comment.

He didn't know what to expect next.

Daniel Miles didn't leave him wondering long. With his face still contorted in rage, he reached for the buggy whip hanging on the barn wall. His expression altered to grim satisfaction at seeing some reaction from Zack at last.

Taking two quick steps backward, Zack heard his

own voice crack with uncertainty. "What are you going to do with that?"

"Teach you some responsibility," Miles growled. He gave the whip a snap, and it cracked loudly in the air.

"I won't be whipped," Zack said in the flat, emotionless tone that always seemed to enrage his father. "I'm not an animal."

"You're an insolent whelp, and you'll do as you're told by God, or I'll skin you with this!" The whip snaked forward before Zack could move out of the way, catching him across his chest and slicing through his shirt and skin as easily as if they were only warm butter.

Zack looked up in disbelief. Then pure, murderous fury welled inside him. He was ready when the whip lashed toward him again, and caught it with one fist. The frayed tip coiled around his arm, cutting red marks into his brown skin.

"I won't take this!" he spat angrily, and gave a jerk that yanked the whip from Miles's hand. The butt-end skidded along the hay-strewn floor of the barn, stirring up chaff. Swinging the whip by the end, Zack threw it across the barn where it curled against a post and fell in a tangled heap. His chest heaved with anger, pain, and sorrow. He furiously blinked back tears as he faced his father.

The words he wanted to say wouldn't come. He didn't know how to ask *why*. He didn't even know what questions to ask. He was only fourteen. All he knew was how to resist.

Daniel Miles started toward Zack with all the force and power of an enraged bull, his big hands reaching out to grab him. His fingers barely caught Zack's shirt as he dodged in an agile twist, and there was a rending sound of tearing material. Zack was already tall for his age, but without the brawn of a man. He was wiry, not muscled, and certainly no match for the bigger, stronger fury that pounded at him.

When Amelia Miles reached the barn, running at the heels of her eldest son's urgent summons, her husband was out of control. He'd managed to back the boy into a corner and had retrieved the whip, and he was using it with vicious force. Not a sound came from the corner where Zack crouched with his arms over his head, just the whining crack of the whip against flesh.

Shocked to the core of her reserved English nature, Amelia reacted immediately. "My God!" she cried, rushing forward to grab her husband's arm as he lifted it again. "What are you doing to Zachary?"

Panting, his eyes wild, Daniel turned toward his wife. He winced silently at the stark censure in the blue eyes so much like Zack's, and Daniel slowly lowered his arm as he gazed at Amelia. The whip hung limply in his hand.

"I will not tolerate this," Amelia said sharply, and pushed past him to go to Zack. The boy was huddled in a bloody heap on the barn floor, his face turned to the wall. His arms were still over his head in a futile effort to deflect some of the blows. He didn't make a sound when his mother spoke gently to him. She put her hand under his arm to lift him.

"Danny," Amelia said over her shoulder to the anxious youth hovering in the background, "go and put some water on the stove. Get out the salve and clean cloths. Your brother will need them."

Zack lifted his head at last to look at his mother. There was no anger in his eyes now, only a bewildered pain that cut at her more harshly than any words he could have uttered. A gash streaked his cheek with blood, and his blue eyes met hers.

"I don't understand," he said simply, in that calm,

toneless voice that she'd become accustomed to hearing. "I just don't understand."

Her heart aching, Amelia walked him past her husband, only pausing when Miles said harshly, "I don't want that half-breed bastard here another day. I can't stand looking at him."

Amelia felt Zack stiffen beneath her hand, and knew the time had come to tell him the truth, to admit the truth to herself.

"Why didn't you tell me?" A fine paleness tinged his dark face as Zack looked at his mother with accusing eyes. "All these years . . ."

"I wasn't certain, Zachary. And neither was your fath—was Daniel. It was so close in time, and we both hoped that you were . . . were his child." Amelia's voice broke.

"And now you tell me that my real father is some Comanche in New Mexico Territory, a damn renegade who kidnapped you and—and—oh God."

Zack couldn't continue. His customary impassivity was no protection against the cutting pain that sliced through him now. He sucked in a deep, steadying breath.

"At least now I understand why Pa—Daniel—hates me," he said after a moment of choked silence. He winced against the pain of the cuts and welts on his back, chest, and arms as he reached for a clean shirt.

"As you grew older," Amelia said into the silence, "it became more obvious that you were not his. When you were small, with your blue eyes and dark hair like mine, you could still have been his child. We prayed for it to be so."

7

"Tell me about him," Zack said abruptly, and Amelia did not have to ask whom he meant.

She straightened, a characteristic gesture that Zack had always associated with English gentlewomen. The years had not altered her cultured English accent, and it lent a fine clip to her words as she lifted her chin and met Zack's gaze.

"We lived in New Mexico Territory then. My father had been deeded a land grant by the governor in Louisiana, and he gave it to Daniel and me for a wedding present. The land was not as populated then, though Indians sometimes raided. When your brother was only a few months old, one of the Comanche who came to buy beef from us saw me out riding. He'd seen me before, and always stared at me."

Amelia paused and looked down at her delicate hands, folded in her lap like small flowers. Zack stared at them, and thought of her stroking him as a child, those small, fragile hands always busy and comforting. The lamp on the table flickered briefly as shadows outside the rambling frame house deepened into dusk.

Listening as his mother related how the young Comanche had stolen her that day, kidnapped her, and taken her as his wife, Zack began to understand a great many things. He had always looked different from his father and brother. They were both light-skinned and blond, while his mother had dark brown hair, blue eyes, and pale skin. Not Zack. His hair was darker, more coarse and thick, and his skin turned a deep bronze in the sun. Now it all made sense. It also left him virtually homeless. He couldn't stay when Daniel hated him so badly.

When his mother had finished, her voice trailing into silence, Zack stirred at last. "I have to go."

Her eyes flew to his. "Go where?" she whispered

8

in a pained voice. "How will you live? You're so young ..."

"I don't know where. I have my rifle, and I'm a good shot. I'll get by." His words sounded heavy and tortured even to his own ears, and Amelia buried her face in her palms. "I'll be all right, Mother," he said softly, emotion quivering in his voice for the first time. "And I can't stay here. Not anymore. You know that."

Amelia Banning Miles rose as slowly from her chair as if she'd just aged twenty years. She crossed to the cherry cabinet she'd brought with her from England and opened a drawer. Fumbling inside it for a moment, she withdrew a cloth bundle and turned back to her son.

"This was ... was his. He gave it to me when he set me free. He said he didn't want to let me go, that I was a good wife." A faint smile touched the corners of her lips. "I think, in his way, he loved me. But Daniel had roused most of New Mexico Territory, and the soldiers were so close that he knew he was endangering everyone in his tribe for a white captive. So he took me back. Daniel insisted that we sell our land and come to Texas. None of us knew about you at the time ..." She paused to clear her throat. "Then I found out, and thought— since there was a chance you might be Daniel's child after all—" She jerked to a halt and thrust the cloth-wrapped bundle into Zack's hands. "Your father gave me this and told me if I ever needed him, I was to show it. Any Comanche who saw this would know I was not to be harmed, and would take me to him. You may want to use it someday."

Zack took the bundle without unwrapping it. He felt nothing inside. No pain, no anger, nothing. Only a dull acceptance of what his mother had told him.

He left that night, and a full moon shed bright light across the Texas plains as he rode his horse at a brisk

9

trot. A Comanche moon, he'd heard it called, and he almost smiled at the irony. Life had a certain justice, he supposed.

Chapter 1

Sirocco, Texas—1871

A wedding is always a happy time. Or at least, that is
what Deborah Hamilton had always believed. Yet somehow, her own wedding had left her exhausted, and she
had to force herself to smile and nod at the well-wishers
attending the grand wedding reception. It had to be just
the strain of all the preparations that left her drawn and
weary.

Her father had been planning this for months. All the
important guests he'd wanted to impress with his im-
proved circumstances were at the Velazquez hacienda
for Deborah's marriage to the heir of the Spanish
fortune—except John Hamilton himself. But Deborah
hadn't expected her father to attend her wedding to
Miguel.

Miguel. Deborah slid her gaze toward him and attempted to smile. The wedding festivities had left many
men drunk, and her new groom was no exception. He
swayed at her side with the effort to stand, and his lustrous dark eyes skimmed the crowd of dancers errati-
cally. Deborah bit back a sigh. She'd had to deal with
inebriated men before, but never one that was her husband.

"Don Miguel," she whispered when he staggered and she had to grab his arm to steady him, "perhaps you should sit down beside me for a while."

His gaze sought hers, and his mouth split in a grin as he hugged her clumsily. "You are anxious to lie with me, *sí?* And I thought my pale little bride would have to be coaxed into playing the part of a wife!"

She winced at his crudity, but kept a polite, trained smile on her face as the young men with him laughed and made vulgar jokes. At twenty-three, Miguel was only three years older than she was, and she supposed she should feel fortunate. Her best friend in Natchez had married a man thirty years her senior, and had considered herself lucky that he still had most of his teeth. Suitable men were scarce after the conflict between the states had ended.

Though the war had ended over six years before, it had left behind too many widows. Yes, Deborah Hamilton counted herself fortunate that her father had not married her to some impoverished gentleman with impeccable antecedents and empty pockets. Of course, that would not have been John Hamilton's style. He appreciated money, and all the benefits that went along with it. He also appreciated the increased business his firm would receive with the Velazquez fortune as one of his investors.

Miles of the Velazquez rancho spread along the border between Texas and Mexico, and had once been a part of Mexico. Since 1847, it had been within the boundaries of Texas, thus losing some of its vast acreage after the peace treaty had set the Rio Grande as the southern boundary. But it was still a considerable size, and would make a formidable inheritance for the children she and Don Miguel would have. As her husband, Miguel would be able to lay claim to American citizen-

12

ship, as would any child from their union, thus ensuring the future of the Velàzquez rancho. Military rule in Texas had ended the year before, and now the years of uncertainty and battle with the American government would end. Yes, it all worked out wonderfully for everyone. Even Deborah.

She was reasonably content. Miguel was young, and if a bit crude and immature, he was handsome and courteous. It could have been much worse, especially for a well-bred young lady from Mississippi. Her lot in life should improve dramatically.

Deborah slid a glance toward her cousin Judith, who had accompanied her to Texas. An orphan, Judith had left nothing or no one behind. Perhaps Judith would find a husband soon, too. She was certainly pretty enough, with pale gold hair and bright eyes as blue as the wildflowers strewn across the wild Texas hills. Deborah prayed the move to Texas would be good for her.

A faint smile curved Deborah's mouth as she saw her cousin flirt with a handsome young *caballero,* who bent over her hand with a gallant flourish. There was a world of difference between her and Judith. Judith was ebullient and vivacious, where Deborah was quiet and reserved, betraying her mother's English heritage. Deborah even spoke in the same soft, cultured tones her mother had used, with a trace of the English accent that Elizabeth Hamilton had kept until the day she died. Deborah's quiet gentility often seemed at odds with the brilliant mane of russet hair she'd inherited from her father, and the soft brown eyes that could regard the world with a hint of mischief.

That gentility had made her acceptable to Miguel Velazquez, she knew. Ordinarily, he would have wed a woman of his own class, who'd grown up in the strictures of Spanish life.

Miguel wrapped a heavy arm around Deborah and leaned close to whisper in her ear. His breath was spiced with tequila, and she turned her face slightly away as he said, "The night drags on, *amanté,* and I grow anxious for you. Come—let us hide from the others for a while."

A pang of nervous fear shot through Deborah, and she looked at him with glazed eyes. No one had told her exactly what happened on a girl's wedding night. All she knew, was that it involved extreme intimacy, and that little fact she'd overheard from one of the servants. Only her innate dignity kept her voice cool and steady.

"It would be an insult to leave our guests, Don Miguel. They expect us to lead the dancing shortly."

Loud music filled the air; guitars throbbed and horns soared while brightly attired guests whirled across the stone tiles of the huge patio lit with colorful lanterns.

"There are to be fireworks before the customary dance," Miguel coaxed softly. His dark eyes flared with hot lights that made her quiver. "We can rejoin them then, and no one will even know we have been gone."

Deborah suppressed the urge to refuse, pressing her lips tightly together as she stared at him in dismay. Miguel was her husband. If he insisted, she must obey. It was what she'd been taught from childhood, what she expected.

Yet she had not expected that he would lead her to the shady arbor where grapevines curled tightly on wooden frames. It was remote and private, but she had thought he would take her to their elegant bedchamber.

"Don Miguel—here?" she murmured doubtfully as he stopped and pulled her close. Her head began to ache, and fear pounded through her even harder. She had thought there would be a maid to help her undress, to brush out her long russet hair and tie pretty ribbons in it. Then she would don the lovely nightdress she'd brought with her from Natchez. But this—this was so sordid, so demeaning.

"*Sí,*" he was muttering thickly as he pushed her up against the wall of the arbor. His hand tugged clumsily at the bodice of her elaborate gown. "Here is just as good as anywhere else, my lovely wife. And we don't have to wait for everyone to pay us compliments first. Or for the endless toasts that will be drunk before we can find our pleasure in bed."

Deborah tried to reconcile herself to the fact that he would not be dissuaded, but couldn't keep from stiffening as he pawed at her. His hands pushed impatiently at her gown, ripping it in his haste and tearing off the intricate roses sewn onto the bodice and sleeves. She ground her teeth together and tried to think of anything but the moment and what he was doing.

Her lovely gown with seed pearls and silk roses adorning the skirt in tiers was pushed up around her waist, bunched in looping folds over her many petticoats. Miguel swore softly in Spanish, and his motions grew rougher and more impatient.

"All these clothes—*Madre Díos!* Take them off now."

"But Miguel—" Deborah gasped when he jerked at the laces holding her soft cotton drawers around her waist, and heard the rip of material. His fist closed around a wad of cloth as he tugged it free.

When his hand seared across the bare, quivering flesh of her stomach, Deborah closed her eyes. She barely felt his mouth on her lips, her cheek, and the arch of her throat as he tilted back her head. Night air whisked over her shrinking flesh when he pulled down the bodice of her gown, ripping the exquisite embroidery in the process. Miguel's mouth traced hot, wet trails over her skin, and Deborah shuddered at the invasion, wondering how much worse it could get.

Even as her mind screamed *No!,* she knew that the worst was yet to come. She heard Miguel fumble with the buttons of his trousers, heard his panting breath as he swore softly at the delay. Then the hot, rigid press of his flesh against her bare thighs made her jump. Revulsion shot through her, and despite her vow not to protest, not to plead, she shoved hard at him with the heels of her hands.

"Miguel! Stop that—you must stop at once, *please.* Listen—the fireworks have begun. They will be looking for us to lead the dance . . ."

He groaned. "Not yet, not yet. I go too fast . . . and you are not ready for me. . . . I understand. Let me kiss you, so that you will be ready for me . . ."

Not understanding what he meant, Deborah knew only that he wanted to kiss her, and she lifted her lips with a kind of desperation. That much she did not mind. A kiss, after all, was proper between a husband and wife. Miguel's mouth was wet, and his kiss searching as he held her close, her bare breasts crushed against his ruffled shirt front. Gold buttons on his vest dug painfully into her skin, and she tried to ease the sting by twisting away.

That only made Miguel hold her more tightly, his hands closing cruelly around her upper arms. He ground his hips against her, and reached down with one hand to lift up her skirts and stroke the downy triangle between her legs. When she shuddered, he grew more excited. Ignoring her cry of horror, he slid a finger into the soft heat of her body.

Never had Deborah imagined such shocking pain. It shot through her like a flame, and her nails dug into Miguel so hard she should have brought blood. He

16

didn't seem to notice it. He was panting, and dear God—he was trying to push his swollen organ into her, shoving her up against the wall of the arbor so hard she couldn't move or even draw a breath.

As he strained against her, Deborah tried to remove herself from time and place. She heard Miguel curse vaguely, the words mixing with the loud pops of fireworks that Don Francisco, Miguel's uncle, had bought for the evening's festivities. They sounded faraway, muffled by the harsh rasp of Miguel's breathing and her own smothered cries. Delighted screams rose in the distance as the fireworks exploded, and she felt a detached sense of dismay that she was not there to see the display.

The dark shadows in the arbor grew lighter, and she could see Miguel's face now, taut and straining as he tried to plunge his rigid staff between her thighs and into her body. Her flesh resisted, her nails dug more deeply into his back as he shoved against her, and she heard him swear again.

Half-sobbing, Deborah saw Miguel lift his head, his dark eyes focusing on her face.

"Díos," he muttered, "I am sorry to hurt you." He put up a hand to cup her cheek in a soft caress. She gave a moan that made him flinch.

Deborah saw his mouth open, but no words came out. He looked faintly surprised, a little puzzled, and then he was sliding limply toward the floor of the arbor. She stared numbly, not quite able to comprehend the swiftness of this change, unable to understand the small, neat hole just above his left ear. Blood spurted from it, dripping down Miguel's face as his body sagged uselessly against her legs. She stared at him stupidly.

"Miguel . . . ?"

Fireworks exploded again, a rattling firestorm that

popped and popped. Screams pierced the night more loudly, and this time Deborah understood.

They were not the screams of delight she'd thought, but screams of terror and pain. As Deborah crouched, frozen in the darkness of the arbor with her wedding gown still hanging from her bared breasts, she saw a shadow silhouetted against the bright background of rising flames and death.

Terror stilled her voice, and she sat paralyzed as a painted, half-naked warrior stepped into the opening and looked down at her. Smoke filled the air and stung her eyes, and Deborah heard the jubilant yells of the raiding warriors rise high above the screams of death.

Chapter 2

The nightmare went on and on. Deborah Hamilton Velazquez was numb with exhaustion and fear. She was not alone. There were others who were captives, mostly women, and a few small children. All of them had passed the point of screams or protests in the past days, and simply endured. It was enough for the moment that they were alive.

Judith was tied on a horse just in front of her, and looked back as they rode along single file. Her blue eyes were dazed when she whispered hoarsely, "They'll kill us, you know. Or worse. Oh God, Deborah, what can we do?"

Forcing the words past dry, stiff lips, Deborah murmured, "Be brave. And pray. I don't think hysteria will help us now."

When Judith nodded numbly, Deborah turned her weary thoughts to her questionable future. In the space of a few minutes, her entire life had changed. Gone was her husband, dead in a grape arbor, and gone, too, were most of the men attending the wedding fiesta. She'd glimpsed the bodies sprawled like broken dolls on the hacienda grounds. Then the descent into pure terror had erased everything from her mind but the need to survive.

That survival instinct kept her going now, in the face of exhaustion, hunger and cold. Fear had been relegated to the background. More important needs had surfaced.

Chestnut strands of her hair hung limp and tangled in her eyes, masking her vision as she tried to keep up with the steady pace set by the men she'd heard one of the other captives call Comanche. Her legs were sore and aching, and her body bruised from several falls. Only the driving certainty that soldiers would give pursuit kept her from surrendering to despair at times. Surely, there had been at least one survivor from that night to alert the Army.

By the time the Comanche warriors rode their horses down into a pine-choked valley, it was almost a relief. Even if death awaited them at the journey's end, it had to be better than this nightmare of bruising travel and constant threats in a language none of the captives understood.

They were dragged from their horses and bunched together in the center of a village of tall, hide-covered tents. The captives huddled miserably. The returning warriors whooped as they greeted their families, and the air was filled with noise. Comanche children ran and squealed and dogs barked while the white captives waited, kneeling in the dirt, some with tears, some with dry sobs, some shivering with apprehension.

In the ensuing melee, Deborah stood with her head held high, too numb to react. The tatters of her lacy wedding dress hung in folds from her slender frame. Her eyes focused on a spot far distant from the chaotic village. Bright streamers of her hair draped loosely over her shoulders, and her face was calm and composed as she seemed not to notice those around her. She alone stood stiffly upright.

That was how Hawk first saw her.

Seated beside the chief, he watched as those who had gone on the raid returned victorious. They laughed and boasted of their prowess, the easy victory they had enjoyed. The men had been drunk, the raid almost too easy.

Hawk's gaze swung inevitably toward the captives. As was common on such a foray, only some women and a few children had been brought back. Most of the women were dark-haired, which was as expected. Not many whites had settled in the area where the war party had gone to steal horses; the raiders' target had been a huge Spanish hacienda on the border.

Yet, one of the women had bright tresses the color of the sun. And the woman who stood so quietly in the center of the captives had richly hued hair of a deep auburn. It was unusual, and caught Hawk's attention. His gaze grew sharper as he noted the elegant dress clinging in stained white satin to her slender curves. It had once been beautiful, but was now torn and dirty. The skirt hung limply, and Hawk knew enough about the clothes such women wore to see that the many petticoats she'd once worn had been discarded; whether by necessity or accident was pure conjecture.

He allowed none of his thoughts to show on his face. It remained expressionless, eyes fathomless, his mouth set in a straight line of indifference. Hawk felt no sympathy. It was simply the way of things. Life and death were an unending cycle, and it didn't matter where a person lived, but how a person lived. Happiness was an abstract emotion, something he hadn't thought about since he was a young boy. He was a man now, and thought as a man. A man was not to think of only personal satisfaction, but of the good of his people, his father said, and he followed that advice.

21

Yet Hawk's gaze returned repeatedly to the young woman standing stiffly with her chin tilted and her eyes grave. There was something about her that arrested his attention. Perhaps it was that she showed no fear. Nothing showed in her face, no reaction at all. The rest of the women were sniveling and weeping, but that one slender girl stared straight ahead in an unblinking gaze.

Night fell, and the village celebration went on. Fires leaped high, and the raiders danced and bragged beneath the sky. Deborah had ceased to think. She'd ceased to feel. Her arms were numb where the ropes had been tied too tightly on her wrists, cutting off circulation. Some of the women had fallen asleep, yielding to exhausted fear. The children who had been captured were taken from the group by some of the Comanche women.

Deborah's head turned, and she called softly, "Be brave, little ones."

It had not escaped her notice that the children were treated kindly for the most part, with the women touching their small heads and crooning to them in soft voices. Maybe the children would be allowed to live, perhaps even adopted. Deborah harbored no such hope for herself or her cousin, who drifted into exhausted slumber with the others. The other women were Mexican, some of them servants, some of them guests who had come to attend her wedding.

Her wedding. That seemed like years ago, not days. Why had she never considered that something like this might happen to her? It had seemed so farfetched then, even when her friend LuEmma had warned her about the hostiles in Texas. Of course, having lived in Natchez all her life, LuEmma considered any other part of the world primitive and uncivilized. Now Deborah was inclined to agree.

She shifted position, her legs aching with the strain of remaining upright. She didn't sleep for the simple reason that she was too frightened. Fires punctuated the darkness of the camp, red-gold flames lighting the camp and the figures of the dancers. It was a scene she'd never imagined, and Deborah felt fear prickle up her spine with malicious swiftness.

Gathering her fortitude, Deborah remained erect and watchful. Her eyes widened slightly when she saw a man approaching the captives. He walked with a lithe, powerful stride, and her throat tightened when she realized he was looking directly at her.

He looked so fierce, with jet-black hair worn long and loose. A feather dangled from a small braid over one ear and the rest of his hair brushed against his shoulders. His face was dark and coppery and he was tall, much taller than the others, she noted distractedly. Like the others, however, he wore only a large square of cloth between his legs, tied at his waist, leaving his broad chest bare. Knee-high moccasins clung to his calves, and he wore some kind of amulet on a rawhide thong around his neck.

Deborah was frighteningly aware of his presence, of the danger evident in his loose, fluid stride. When the Comanche stopped only a few feet away, she refused to avert her gaze. She met him stare for stare, her chin lifting in that quick gesture of pride that was inborn in the Hamiltons.

His eyes were clear and cold, his expression so indifferent that she almost lost her nerve. Fear pulsed through her nerves in singing waves, and her knees began to quiver.

It took all her self-control to keep calm, but Deborah

felt that if she revealed the depth of her fear, it would only hasten the inevitable. Smoke from the campfire stung her eyes and nose, and there was an indefinable odor in the air that she couldn't identify. She tried to concentrate on anything but the predatory gaze of the Comanche only a few feet away. He stood watching her without speaking for several moments, seeming to assess her, then turned and walked away. Deborah felt a wave of relief wash over her. Perhaps he would leave her alone, at least for a while.

But then she knew she had erred, for he returned with a buckskin-clad woman in tow. The woman looked to be Mexican, but he spoke to her swiftly in the deep guttural language Deborah had come to recognize as Comanche, and the woman nodded. She turned toward Deborah.

"That one wishes to know your name," she said in halting English that Deborah had difficulty understanding. The woman had to repeat it twice before she was understood, and her voice grew sharp with irritation.

Deborah's chin lifted slightly. "My name is Deborah Hamilton. May I ask what is to be done with us?"

The words were out before she realized she should have given her married name. It was only natural, she supposed, as she had been wed and widowed in a matter of hours. If she was to be ransomed, she needed to give her married name, and she opened her mouth to correct her mistake, but the woman had turned back to the cold-eyed Comanche.

At the man's prompting she asked Deborah, "Where is your husband?"

"Dead."

No emotion betrayed her, not by the slightest quiver of her voice. It did not seem like an odd reaction, not considering the other incredible events that had so dras-

24

tically changed her life in such a short time. Her gaze focused on the Comanche. She deliberately met his steady stare again, and was struck by a difference she hadn't noted before.

"You—you have blue eyes," she blurted, startled at the discovery. She hadn't thought about a Comanche having blue eyes, but it was obvious some of them did. At least, this one did. Flames reflected from a blue so intense as to be almost indigo, and the blue eyes in such a dark face were both frightening and familiar. She didn't realize she was staring until he spoke, his voice a harsh, rasping growl.

"Haa. Keta tekwaaru. Kima habi-ki."

Her perusal was quickly ended by the Comanche's harsh comment. She didn't understand the words, but the tone was easily translated. A faint shiver prickled her bare arms with gooseflesh, and she looked away without speaking.

Hawk saw her faint shiver, and noted with appreciation her quick recovery. Her voice was soft, with a trace of an accent he recognized as English. He was glad she had a soft voice instead of an annoying screech, as many white women had.

With a wave of one hand, Hawk dismissed the Mexican woman and stepped closer to Deborah Hamilton. His gaze raked her from the top of her tousled russet hair to the tattered hem of her gown, pausing with deliberate inspection at the full thrust of her breasts. The torn bodice of her gown revealed more than it hid, and the creamy skin he saw beneath the ragged edges of material was enticing. Slender hips curved beneath the heavy skirt, and there was a flash of bare leg that piqued his interest.

Hawk allowed himself a moment's speculation as to the exact nature of the body beneath the gown, then

25

shifted his attention to her face again. Aristocratic bones sculpted an exquisite face, from her wide, gold-flecked brown eyes and thick dark lashes to her high, delicate cheekbones and the fragile sweep of her jaw. Her lips were full, with the top lip slightly shorter than the bottom, giving her the appearance of a sultry Madonna.

Even tousled and tangled, her hair beckoned him to put his hands in it. Thick auburn tresses waved around her shoulders, spilling over her breasts and back in shining curls. In daylight, it had caught the sun in fiery splinters; at night, it gleamed with a deep coppery beauty that reflected the firelight in elusive glimmers.

Desire hit him then, swift and hard, giving a name to the lure that had drawn him closer to her. This woman reminded him of the more pleasant things in life, before harsh reality had intruded, before he'd turned his back on that way of life.

Hawk's gaze caught hers again, and he saw the quick widening of her eyes, the lifting of her lashes as she recognized something in his face. It gave him an unsettling feeling.

Pivoting on his heel, he walked away.

"She belongs to Spotted Pony. He is the one who reached her first." White Eagle peered closely at Hawk. "Do you want her, my *tua?*"

Hawk did not answer his father. No answer was necessary. White Eagle knew that he wanted her, and that Spotted Pony would demand a huge ransom or a fight as payment. Neither one mattered to Hawk. He would just as soon do one as the other.

Plenty of ponies wore his halter, and he would not miss any for a ransom. And if the truth be known, he was restless and in the mood for a good fight.

He looked toward the center of the camp again. The fires had burned low. Deborah Hamilton had yielded to exhaustion and sat on the ground beside the blonde girl, her head tilted back and her eyes half-closed. She had to be bone-tired, yet she refused to relinquish her vigil. Hawk's eyes narrowed slightly.

When he looked at his father, White Eagle's face was turned toward the captives. There was a stark elegance to the older man's features, a purity of line and bone that would have been called aristocratic if he were white. A faint smile curved Hawk's mouth. As a Comanche, White Eagle was called anything by the white man but aristocratic.

Hawk hadn't known what to expect from White Eagle ten years before, nor did he really expect anything from him now. There was an unspoken understanding between them that allowed Hawk to travel his own path without question, coming and going from the Comanche camp whenever he pleased.

Nothing was asked about his life away from the camp in the mountains stretching from Texas into New Mexico; it was as if he didn't exist once he left *Numunuu* behind. *Numunuu*, Comanche for The Comanche People, had given him a vague sense of belonging, after years of aimless wandering.

Those lonely years made him appreciate the sense of family he had now. White Eagle made him welcome. *Kwihne tosabitu*, White Eagle, had been glad to see his son come home. He never said, but Hawk often wondered if his father disliked seeing him leave to go back to the white man's world. This time, he'd decided to stay. He would do his best to fit in, to live, raid, even think as one of the People. There was nothing for him in the world he'd left behind, nothing but a sharp sense of failure.

27

Each time he joined *Numunuu,* Hawk stayed longer and longer. That made his young half-sister, *Ohayaa,* happy. Sunflower was a lovely, shy girl of thirteen, almost old enough to marry, but still too young to have a household of her own. She stayed in her widowed father's tipi with her maternal grandmother, caring for him and her half-brother.

Hawk's attention drifted back to the woman. She was still awake, still watchful, still hiding her fear. He felt a faint stirring of admiration, and was surprised by it. He normally felt nothing for the captives brought in. This one was different, and he didn't know why. It disturbed him. It left him feeling vulnerable, and he didn't like that.

Rising to his feet in a swift, lithe motion, Hawk felt White Eagle's appraising gaze on him as he strode from the camp to the silence of the woods beyond.

Chapter 3

Morning came in chilly streaks of rose and blue, barely rimming the sky at first, making the tall pines around the village look like dark lace against the growing light. Deborah watched; her back was stiff and aching, her legs numb. She'd slept fitfully. Each small noise had jerked her awake, certain that doom was at hand. No one had bothered with the women, however. They'd been left in the center of the camp to dread their futures.

When the camp began to stir, she could hear faint voices, murmured laughter, the sounds of human beings rising to face the new day. Realization knifed through her that to the Comanche, she and the others were unimportant matters to be disposed of at leisure. It was as if they were no more important than the cattle they'd brought back, or the horses. And to the Comanche, she supposed, they weren't. Women were dispensable, especially captive women.

With her head tilted back and the sun behind her, Deborah saw the man who'd spoken to her the night before leave a cone-shaped tent decorated with strange drawings on the exterior. He ducked out the lowered flap and tied it back, then turned and stretched lazily. Her breath caught.

He was a magnificent animal, she had to admit that, radiating power and confidence and muscled fitness. There was a strange beauty about him that made her feel queer inside, a warm sort of breathlessness that she couldn't explain. It wasn't exactly unpleasant, but neither was it welcome. It was too disturbing.

She'd stared at him too long, because he looked up and saw her. A faint smile slanted his harsh mouth into a replica of humor, but Deborah thought that this man must rarely laugh. He looked every inch the brutal, savage warrior she'd heard roamed the western plains. Even the name *Comanche* struck fear into the hearts of those who heard it. LuEmma had been right. She should have listened to her.

Deborah turned her head away, her chin still held high. The rough wooden post behind her dug painfully against her spine, and she shifted to a more comfortable position. The other captive women began to stir, waking slowly, some sobbing as they realized it had not been a horrible nightmare after all.

Hawk saw her turn her head in a disdainful, haughty gesture. A faint smile tucked the corners of his eyes for a moment, but his lips quickly settled into a straight line. He pivoted on his heel and strode toward the ribbon of water that lay just to the east of the camp.

He stripped and plunged into the icy stream, then rubbed vigorously at his body with a handful of grass to scrub his skin. When he left, dripping on the grassy banks, he shook his head as a dog would do, flinging water in all directions. His long hair lay wet and cool on his shoulders. It was invigorating. Cooking smells wafted on the breeze from the village, and he tied his breechcloth on again, tucking his longknife into the sheath at his lean waist.

When he walked back into the village, Hawk saw that the girl was gone. With an unhurried stride, he switched his direction toward Spotted Pony's tipi. The girl was there, her body rigid with revulsion, her eyes wide with numb fear, and her face as pale as mountain snow. She was quiet; no sound passed her lips, but Hawk could see her mouth ever so slightly quivering with a suppressed scream.

Spotted Pony turned from his scrutiny of the girl as Hawk approached, and the glitter in his black eyes indicated he knew why he'd come. Slightly shorter than Hawk, the warrior was well muscled, with long legs and arms, his torso powerful. He had many battle scars flecking his dark skin. Spotted Pony was a powerful adversary, but so was Hawk. He nodded.

"Ahó. I am honored that you visit me," Spotted Pony said in greeting, and Hawk nodded back.

He could see the slight greed gathering in Spotted Pony's eyes, and knew immediately that he understood the reason for his visit. Hawk came straight to the point.

"How many horses for the white woman?"

Spotted Pony pretended surprise. "You want her?" he asked with a wide-eyed expression of amazement. "But I stole her, and planned to keep her. In spite of such skinny arms, she might be useful. At least she does not chatter like a crow."

"Horses are more useful." Hawk did not look at the white woman. He kept his gaze on Spotted Pony, his tone flat and disinterested. "My sister could use help with the cooking. Another woman would be of better help than the horses I have."

Spotted Pony narrowed his eyes as if considering the

31

oblique offer. Both men were aware that the more reluctant the seller, the higher the price. Spotted Pony gave a doubtful shake of his head.

"I don't know if I need more horses," he said slowly, and flicked a gaze toward the pale, quiet woman who stood as stiff as a young oak tree beside him. She must have sensed they were talking about her; her eyes grew even wider, the pupils dilated with gold light. Spotted Pony looked back at Hawk. "Maybe I need another wife to help with the cooking and scraping of hides."

"You need more horses to hunt buffalo to feed the wife you already have," Hawk said. "Another empty belly to fill would crowd your lodge."

As the men conversed in their rough language, Deborah's gaze jumped from one to the other. She didn't know if she was more frightened by the man who had taken her from the Velazquez hacienda, or the hard-eyed man who was still wet from an apparent swim. She didn't like the way he'd looked at her the night before, speculatively, as if she were his next meal. Yet she had no doubt that she would be treated in the same manner by the man who had abducted her; she'd seen his flat, cruel eyes, and he'd handled her roughly. If she had to choose—and she realized she had no choice—she would choose death over the horror that awaited her.

Survival had seemed so important earlier, but now she thought that perhaps there were worse things than death. If the furtive, fearful look in the eyes of some of the Mexican women she'd seen slinking through the camp was any indication, she would prefer a quick ending. Deborah wished she understood Spanish, so she could ask some of the women who had been taken captive with her what was planned for them. They seemed to know; Judith had gasped with shock and fear when the warrior had approached and cut Deborah loose from

32

the others. One of the Mexican women had moaned in a mixture of Spanish and English that, "It has begun."

What had begun? And dear God, what was about to happen to her now? The Comanche men had apparently finished their discussion, and with a gesture of hands, taken leave of one another. She didn't know what to expect. The tall, blue-eyed Comanche turned on his bare heel and strode away without even glancing at her. Not once had he looked directly at her, nor indicated by any word or action that he was aware of her, yet she knew that he was.

Deborah waited. Time passed, and the odors from nearby cooking pots tantalized her. She still stood with her hands tied in front of her, her back stiff and straight as the Comanche kept her beside him. He sat cross-legged in front of his hide-covered tent, smoking a pipe after he'd eaten from a bowl. No food or water had been offered to any of the white captives. Deborah's stomach growled a protest, but she gave no other indication of her need.

A pressing need to go into the bushes was her most urgent thought, and she held herself upright with a quiet desperation. A woman in a beaded buckskin dress served the man, offering a word now and then as she scurried about, bringing him a smoldering stick from the fire to light his pipe, or a water pouch, or following some growled command. Deborah had made up her mind to try and communicate the urgency of her need to the woman, when she saw from one corner of her eye that the blue-eyed Comanche had returned.

He was leading five horses. They were splendid animals. Straight legs and thick necks gleamed in the sunlight, and they pranced with high spirits as he led them forward and tied them to the post beside the lodge.

Turning, he pulled a bundle from the back of one of the horses, and held it out.

Her captor rose slowly as if still thinking, but a gleam of satisfaction shone in his black eyes. He flashed a glance at Deborah, then took the bundle held out to him. He flipped back the edge of the woven blanket, smiling when he saw a rifle shining dully in the folds. For him, it seemed as if the bargain was sealed.

Deborah watched tensely, saw the blue-eyed Comanche turn toward her, his eyes glittering with hot lights. She knew in that instant what had happened. A protest at being sold as casually as that welled up in her throat. There was no time to voice it before he said something in the rough, growling language they used.

When she shrank back, her captor shoved her forward again, speaking sharply and leaving her in no doubt that she was being given away. Bargained for, she corrected silently, watching as the rifle and horses were examined by the buckskin-clad woman who must be his wife.

What did it really matter? She wondered wearily in the next instant. One captor was much like another. And perhaps this one would at least feed her, and allow her to tend her needs.

Fear, exhaustion, and deprivation had left her strangely compliant. She offered no more protest or resistance as the blue-eyed Comanche curled a hard hand around her still-bound wrists and took her with him. He was firm, but not rough, not like the other had been. And he led her to a tent set back apart from the others. It was larger, with painted figures on the cone-shaped exterior. Tall poles rose from the center where the smoke from a fire curled upward. Deborah could smell something cooking in the pot outside the lodge, and a young girl looked at her curiously as she was pulled forward.

After a brief exchange of words between the young girl and her new captor, Deborah's bound wrists were placed in her custody. The girl spoke softly, smiling somewhat shyly, and motioned that she was to follow. It was the first time she'd been offered any choice instead of pushed or pulled one way or the other, and Deborah went willingly.

Then she was glad she had. The girl took her to a clump of bushes some distance from the camp, and indicated she was to tend to any private needs. It was difficult with her bound hands, but Deborah managed to lift her skirts. As her fine cotton drawers had been removed that night in the arbor with Miguel, her skirts and a single petticoat were all she wore.

When she stepped out from behind the bushes, she gave the girl a smile of gratitude at her tact. The girl nodded gravely as she beckoned her forward again. Deborah was led to the edge of a swiftly running stream, and would have bent down to drink if the girl had not stopped her. Dark hair swung in two neat plaits over her shoulders as she shook her head and said something in Comanche. Then the sharp blade of a knife slashed upward, slicing the tight ropes around Deborah's wrists.

Deborah couldn't help a gasp of pain as blood flowed through her constricted veins back into her abused flesh; the girl replaced the knife in the sheath at her side before taking Deborah's wrists between her small, callused palms and rubbing them briskly to restore circulation. Then she indicated with a smile that Deborah was to wash herself.

The water was icy but clear, and felt good on her dry skin. Hitching her skirts up as high as she dared, Deborah waded out into the shallows, letting the water swirl around her bare calves.

She knelt and cupped her hands, drinking deeply of the cool water, letting it slide down her parched throat and wet the front of her dress. She didn't care. It seemed like days since she'd had her fill of water. Finally she felt the girl touch her shoulder and shake her head, motioning for her to drink more slowly.

After she'd quenched her thirst and washed every place she could reach without totally disrobing, Deborah waded back to the muddy bank and stepped up on the grass beside the silently watching girl. She dried her hands on her damp skirts.

"May I take some water to the others?" she asked, pantomiming drinking and pointing toward the village.

A quick shake of the girl's head was disappointing, but not unexpected. Poor Judith. Deborah's distress mounted. If she could only manage to converse with her new captor, perhaps she could ask him to buy Judith as well. Her fears for her cousin were as strong as her fears for herself, but together they might draw some comfort from one another.

Refreshed, but still frightened, Deborah walked silently beside the girl back to the tall tent. She surveyed the tent drawings she'd seen earlier more closely. Figures representing men and horses at war were scattered across the hide, and odd squiggles that looked like insects formed a neat row. She counted seventeen before the girl motioned that she was to go inside.

Deborah was surprised at the size of the interior. It was much bigger than it looked from the outside, and neat in spite of the dirt floor and crude furnishings. Soaring poles braced the stitched animal-hide cover, and the structure was tilted slightly toward the front, giving more headroom in the rear. It was roughly oval, with a stone-ringed fire just off-center. Only embers glowed red and gray between the stones. It looked as if all cooking was being done outside in the warm weather.

Rather shyly, her pretty companion motioned for Deborah to be seated on a pallet of hides and blankets; then she ducked back out the open flap of the tent. As Deborah knelt slowly on the pallet, she wondered what would happen to her now, and where her new captor had gone. He was not inside, nor had she seen him outside as they'd approached from the stream.

Nervous and afraid, she waited. Insects buzzed annoyingly close, and she swatted at them. Children laughed outside, sounding like children anywhere. Deborah smiled at the thought. She shifted position when her feet began to grow numb from kneeling, and sat down with her legs drawn up in front of her chest.

Something brushed along the back of her neck, and she half-turned, squinting at the unfamiliar drifts of fur hanging from the framework. It was vari-colored, in different shades of brown and black, some of it long, some short. The strips seemed to be attached to ovals of hide that dangled from a thin, bent-willow circle.

Deborah stared until an uneasy feeling crept over her, and she began to feel a tightness grow in her chest. Those fur strips—they were too long to belong to an animal. Not any animal she'd ever seen. Her mind refused to accept the logical explanation, and all the color drained from her face as she tried to find a more acceptable interpretation of what her eyes told her she was seeing.

Scalps. Dear God, she was looking at human scalps. The long, silky strands of some of the hair was unmistakable, and she bent her head and gasped, fighting nausea. As the nausea receded, panic blossomed, and she had to curb her desire to run screaming from the tent out into the camp. That would do her no good. And it would only attract unwanted attention. She closed her eyes until the faintness passed, and wished she'd never come West.

Not that wishes did much good. If they did, she would be at home in Natchez and sitting on the porch sipping cold lemonade from an elegant glass. The air would be thick with the sweet fragrance of magnolias and honeysuckle instead of the stench of burning meat. And she would not be terrified that her own hair would soon hang from a pole in one of these odd-looking tents.

Deborah closed her eyes again and recited Bible passages from memory. If God was listening, He needed to do something quickly, she thought, then chastised herself for her hasty prayers. She should have learned patience as well as humility.

Time passed, and Deborah's reluctant survey of her surroundings grew more curious. There were no more grisly discoveries, though she did not search very hard. Mostly, she sat and waited. And tried to repair her garments. Her torn gown gaped open revealingly. She tried to tie the torn edges of her bodice together. It was no use. It covered her, but only barely.

Light slowly filled the interior as the sun rose higher, and Deborah looked around her with interest. A variety of items were stacked neatly at the sides. Blankets were folded in an orderly manner, and gourd vessels sat in tidy rows. A few wooden bowls, scoured clean, were wedged in among carved cups and loosely woven baskets filled with some kind of berries. Her stomach growled at the visual reminder of food. Would they ever think to feed her? And what about her cousin and the others? Were they to be starved, too?

Deborah tucked strands of her tangled hair behind her ears as she struggled for composure. It wouldn't help to grow upset. She would need all her self-possession to get through this ordeal.

Footsteps sounded in the dirt outside the opened flap, and Deborah steeled herself. Relief made her almost weak when the slender girl entered, and she sighed.

The girl looked up and smiled, as if she knew how Deborah must feel. *"Ihka puni tuihu,"* she said in a soft voice, her smile widening when Deborah just stared at her. She lifted the bowl in her hands, and a curl of tantalizing steam rose in the air. *"Kuhtsu?maru."*

The unfamiliar words were simply gibberish, but the girl's meaning was clear as she held out the bowl. Deborah took it gratefully. There was no spoon, just a bowl of some sort of stew. Chunks of meat and vaguely familiar vegetables bobbed in a thick, fragrant gravy, and with a sigh between pleasure and dismay, Deborah dipped her fingers tentatively into the bowl.

A soft giggle made her look up. Mischief danced in the young girl's eyes, and she held out a shallow spoon carved from bone. It had a rough wooden handle. Deborah smiled at the look of delight on the girl's face as she reached for the spoon. She forced herself to eat slowly instead of wolfing down the food, but it was difficult. When the bowl was half-empty, she looked back up at the watching girl.

"Thank you," she said softly.

Kneeling, the girl looked at Deborah with her head tilted to one side like a small, interested bird. Her thick shiny hair gleamed in the soft light, and a smile curved her lips.

"Ura." When Deborah looked mystified, she repeated in a slow, hesitant voice, *"Ura*—thank you."

"Do you speak English?" Deborah asked immediately, but the girl only stared at her without answering. Well, it was too much to hope that she'd know more than a phrase or two of English, she supposed. Probably learned from a trading post. At least the girl was friendly, and seemed to like her. She cleared her throat.

"Wura," she said in an effort to mimic her, and that sent the girl into peals of soft laughter. Deborah laughed, too, wondering what she'd said. *"Uruu?"* she tried again, and more laughter greeted her effort.

When she'd finished the stew, the girl took the bowl and gave her a gourd of cool water to drink. With her basic needs satisfied for the moment, Deborah studied the Comanche girl, wondering if they could possibly communicate successfully. It would be helpful to have a sympathetic ally in camp, especially when she recalled a pair of hard blue eyes and an even harder face.

Deborah smiled, and the girl smiled back, obviously ready to cooperate in the business of making friends.

Putting her palm against her chest, Deborah said, "Deborah." Then she reached out to indicate the girl, tilting her head to one side and lifting her shoulders questioningly.

A smile curved her mouth as the girl chirruped, *"Ohayaa."* She put her hand on her chest and repeated, *"Ohayaa."*

Deborah repeated it several times until the girl was satisfied, and felt a sense of accomplishment. Then *Ohayaa* pointed a finger up toward the patch of sky visible through the smoke hole. Pantomiming, she spent several minutes translating her name into English for Deborah, pointing to the sun, mimicking the role of a plant, until finally Deborah exclaimed, "Sunflower!" and the girl nodded eagerly.

"Sunflower," she said, smiling at Deborah in triumph. A shy gleam lit her eyes, and she leaned close, her voice a soft whisper. *"Haitsi."*

"Haitsi—what does it mean?" Deborah asked, then

said strongly when it became apparent that Sunflower was saying she was a friend, *"Haitsi.* Yes, we are friends."

Sunflower nodded wisely, and there was a gentleness in her that tugged at Deborah. "Friends, *haa.* Friends."

A harsh voice intruded suddenly, and both Deborah and Sunflower looked up in alarm as the flap to the tent was thrust aside. The blue-eyed Comanche was briefly outlined against the sunlight as he ducked in, and it was obvious he wasn't pleased.

"Miaru," he said again, more harshly than before, and Sunflower looked unhappy as she scrambled to her feet. There was a brief exchange, in which it was apparent to Deborah that he was berating her for being too friendly with his captive, then Sunflower left without glancing back.

Deborah's hand clenched in her lap, and she sat in stiff, apprehensive silence as her new captor hunkered down on his heels next to her. His eyes were cold and hard, and she tried to study him without being obvious.

His knee-high moccasins had long fringe hanging from the cuff and along the sides; the wide strip of cloth belted around his waist and hanging loose in the front and back looked clean. The bare expanse of his chest was smooth and dark, gleaming a dull bronze in the dim light, and his long legs were hard and muscled.

He was much too briefly clad, and she looked away from him, feeling the heat rise to her face. She'd not been this close to a man so scantily clad before, except for the brief moments with her original captor. It was unnerving.

Even more unnerving was the cold blue gaze directed at her, studying her closely. Deborah flushed as his gaze dropped to the expanse of skin visible beneath her torn bodice, and her hand rose involuntarily to cover her

41

breast. He reached out with a leisurely motion, and captured her wrist in his strong, hard fingers.

"Keta."

When she stared at him uncomprehendingly, he met her eyes with the suggestion of a smile and released her arm. Then he reached behind him and lowered the flap to the opening. It fell in a soft rustle, blocking out bright light and the world, leaving them alone in the tent.

Deborah stared at him with growing comprehension. When his gaze drifted down her body again, then back up to her face, she instantly knew what he intended.

Chapter 4

"No!" Deborah tried to back away, but Hawk's hands flashed out to grasp her wrists. He held them in one hand, slowly pulling her to him, enjoying the feel of her soft skin beneath his fingers. She was so soft, her skin as smooth and rich as butter, gliding beneath his hand when he slid his palm up one arm.

He could well understand the man who had taken her in a grape arbor, knew that a soft, lovely woman such as this one would tempt a man to impetuous action. Spotted Pony had told him how he'd found her in the arbor with a man, that they'd not heard his approach or understood the commotion because they were making love.

Hawk also understood that this woman would not have instigated it. There was an innate dignity to her that would have submitted to a husband, but not initiated the act in so public a place.

The tipi was private, and Hawk intended to take this woman, to taste her sweetness for himself. There would be no shame involved, only pleasure. He would treat her gently, but she would lie with him.

"Kima habiki," he murmured softly. He wanted her to lie down with him willingly, and his tone of voice was

gentle. A faint tremor shook her, and he forced himself to go slowly.

She was frightened, and he knew he should probably speak to her in the language she understood, but he didn't. There was an unwillingness to admit to being anything but Comanche, even in this girl's eyes. He had come back to his father's camp with the intention of staying *usúni*—forever. He'd spent too long living a lie in the white man's world, a world that he had tried to make his own. He'd never felt comfortable there, no more than he did here. There were too many slurs thrown at him, slurs that had made him too quick with a gun, too quick to retaliate. Maybe here, in his father's camp, he could find the peace that had been denied him in his mother's world. He'd walked a shaky line between them for so long it had begun to seem natural.

The year he'd spent riding with the Pony Express had given him a keen instinct for survival and made him expert with a sidearm. He didn't regret the experience, though it had left him with more scars and a healthy respect for the Apache and Comanche. That experience had been what decided him to find his father, to seek acceptance.

There would be no more living in two worlds. Not any longer. No, he would make this shivering girl understand him with actions, not familiar words.

Hawk's gaze shifted from the girl's wide eyes and fear-stretched mouth to the soft mound of her breasts. They were warm, like heated velvet, a miracle of pink and ivory with only a suggestion of blue veins just beneath the translucent skin. Small rosy nipples hardened to tight buds when he pushed aside the torn material of her gown, and Hawk's mouth curled in a faint smile.

"No," she whispered again, desperation making her

voice thick when he reached out to cup a firm, round breast in his palm.

Hawk ignored her. Soon he would make her want him as he wanted her, once he got past her initial resistance. It was inevitable that she feel resistance, just as it was inevitable she lie with some man. Being a captive entailed certain duties, and for a woman, lying with a man was one of them if she was comely.

"Kima," he said again, urging her toward the pallet on the floor of the tipi.

She began to struggle, panic flaring in her eyes as he pushed her gently but firmly backward. With a show of strength he did not expect from so delicate a woman, Deborah fought him furiously. She kicked at him, making him grunt with irritation as her feet struck his shins. Fortunately, her long skirts hampered her movements, and he was able to shift her to one side, sliding an arm around her waist to hold her up against his hip and thigh. Her legs flailed harmlessly, occasionally brushing against the back of his leg but doing no damage.

No novice at subduing an opponent, though admittedly it was usually an angry male, Hawk put a deft foot behind her ankle and jerked. Deborah sank rapidly backward, and he used his weight to carry her to the ground. His movement did not deter her in the least from her struggle; indeed, it grew more violent in intensity as he lay atop her.

She began kicking again, her legs freed as her skirts were tossed up around her thighs. Panting with effort, she managed to land a blow to his inner thigh, and he grunted with pain this time.

"Puaru. . ." he muttered harshly, not finishing his sentence as she managed to free one hand. It came up in a slashing blow that caught him on one cheek. His head snapped back with the force of it, and he caught

45

her hand again in a cruel grip. Pulling her arms up, he pinned her to the floor.

He glared down at her. Her hair was in wild tangles in her eyes and across the pallet of blankets and soft robes, a bright contrast against the dark fur. Her face was pale with fear and desperation, and her eyes blazed up at him with a look so condemning he was startled. Didn't she understand that she would be taken by some man in the camp? It should make little difference to her who. At least he would be gentle with her, if she would allow it.

She kicked and twisted beneath him, trying to get away. Hawk subdued her easily, with her hands pinned over her head and his body weighing her down. He shifted so that his legs controlled hers, his thighs clamping hers together. Then he waited for her to tire.

When she finally paused in her struggle, panting for breath with soft sounds of distress coming from her throat, he eased his grip on her wrists. His body fit against her curves from hip to breast, and he knew she had to be aware of his erection nudging her soft belly. Her movements had made it impossible for him not to react, and the slide of female flesh against his brought the inevitable results.

She grew very still. Her long, curved lashes flew up and she gazed at him with fear and something else, a look almost of confusion. Hawk stared back at her. She had been a married woman, and she had to know what came next.

Slowly, so slowly that he felt the tension grow between them, Hawk lowered his head to kiss her. She accepted the kiss, but did not return it as his lips brushed lightly over her mouth. First, he kissed the corners of her mouth with light, fluttering caresses, then touched the tip of his tongue to the swell of her upper lip. Her breath came in shuddering gasps for air.

"Pihnákamaru," he murmured. It was an understatement. She was more than sweet. The teasing satin of her mouth lured him farther, and his tongue gently washed the outline of her lips in quick strokes that sent a flash of heat through him. Her breath quickened, and she squirmed under him.

Desire speared him when she moved, and he shifted so that his thighs wedged between her clenched legs. He felt her resistance, saw the protest well in her eyes, and bent his head again to kiss it away.

Murmuring low, reassuring words that he knew she could not understand, Hawk nuzzled the side of her neck below her ear. She smelled like woodsmoke and warm woman, and he clung to his restraint. The touch of his mouth against her neck made her jump under him, and he soothed her when she cried out and twisted her head away.

It took all his self-control not to remove his breechcloth and just take her, but Hawk did not want a screaming, struggling woman on his robes. He wanted her willing and warm and wrapped around him like a soft cocoon, opening body and mind to him.

Hawk shifted control of her wrists to his other hand, then cupped Deborah's chin in his palm and lifted her head to look at him. Her eyes were glazed with fright, a warm honey color with golden specks that absorbed the sunlight coming through the smoke hole of the tipi. He smiled with appreciation of her courage in the face of fear, and rotated the pad of his thumb in a gentle, caressing motion against her cheekbone.

Then, slowly, he drew his hand down over the arch of her throat to her collarbone, his fingers tracing a light pattern in the delicate scoop between the bones. His

47

hand moved downward, to that tempting valley between her breasts, the silky skin luxuriant and pliable beneath his fingers.

He levered his body to a slant, still holding her down with his weight on her, his hand moving to cup her breast. She shuddered, and he felt an exquisite tightness in his groin.

Hawk brushed his thumb across the tight rosebud that looked delicious and fragile and oh so sweet and felt her vibrate with reaction. He concentrated on that tiny nub, dragging his fingers over it in teasing flicks that made her squirm. Her breath came quickly now, and not from exertion. There was a flushed, dazed expression on her face that turned to shock when he bent to draw her nipple into his mouth.

She cried out, arching upward as if seeking the source. Hawk flicked his tongue around her nipple, listening to her distressed whimpers with growing anticipation. Her hips moved, and he wedged her legs farther apart, fitting himself into the notch of her thighs.

He shifted his attention to her other breast, giving it the same washing with his tongue and lips, and felt the awkward motion of her hips beneath him. She gave another soft cry, and it made him shudder with desire for her. She was almost ready for him, almost to the point where she'd open willingly.

Hawk slid one hand down to her belly, sliding his palm beneath the torn material of her gown, gathering her skirts up around her waist. She was heated silk beneath his fingers, hot and damp with need, and he dragged his hand through the tight nest of curls that hid her from him.

Crying out, she bucked and heaved with renewed panic, and he caught her mouth with his and kissed her deeply, his tongue mimicking the sex act as she strained

48

against him. When she was limp and quivering, he lifted his head to stare down at her with a raging need he couldn't remember feeling so intensely before.

Caught in a snare of her long hair and his hands, Deborah tried to interpret that steady gaze. His eyes had changed to the color of smoke, hot and gray as raw steel. New emotions raged inside her, battling with shock and fear.

Somehow, her first resistance had melded into something else. Never had she dreamed he would make her feel anything but fear or revulsion, yet there had been a response to his touch that she couldn't deny. Disbelief rendered her momentarily motionless. She lay still and helpless, watching his eyes—cold, clear eyes beneath a fan of thick, spiky lashes.

What he was doing was similar to what Miguel had done, but there was a vast difference in how she responded. It was baffling. It was terrifying.

He moved, and she felt the quick, cold slice of a knife whisper over her skin, then her gown just fell away from her in limp folds. Deborah couldn't move. She felt his intent gaze on her, studying her naked body. A flush warmed her skin from her stomach to her eyebrows, and she knew that this was only the beginning of her humiliation. There was no compromise in the icy eyes watching her.

A haze of tears mercifully blurred her vision when he rose to his knees over her and untied the leather thong that held his brief garment around his waist. Deborah closed her eyes as it fell away. That one brief glimpse was enough to acknowledge her worst fears, making her doubt that she would survive what he intended to do to her.

For a moment she considered going for his knife, to use on him or herself. But she knew she couldn't. Her situation had been reduced to the basics. She wanted to live, however badly he hurt her. An instinct stronger than herself and older than time made her lie still for him.

Muttering something in the low, rough language that made no sense to her, he lowered his body back over her and spread her thighs apart with his knees. Deborah willed herself to remain limp. Perhaps it would make him gentle.

But when he put his hand on her, raking his fingers through the tight nest of red-gold curls at the juncture of her thighs, she couldn't help a sudden jerk. Oddly, his voice sounded almost tender when he said something to her again, and Deborah shuddered as he stroked her intimately. Would this never end? She felt helpless, exposed, humiliated.

A choked sob caught in the back of her throat, and her body arched helplessly when his hand pressed inside her. It was like a knife-thrust, and her eyes flew open to stare up at him accusingly.

There was an odd expression on her tormentor's face, almost one of shock, and Deborah had the fleeting impression that she'd somehow surprised him before he withdrew his hand and sat back on his heels. He stared down at her without speaking, his chiseled features impassive again. She wished she dared cover herself; there was something so tense about him, almost as if he were uncertain, that she dared not move at all.

Light caught in his dark hair, glittering in the sleek strands like trapped sunbeams, and Deborah saw his lashes flicker for a moment, brushing down over his eyes as if to hide his thoughts. Then he looked down at her again, growled something she was glad she didn't understand, and rose in a swift, lithe motion.

Deborah was caught by the stark beauty of his muscled body, the play of bronze skin and power as he moved to pick up his brief garment. She watched silently. His long hair swung forward in a gleaming fall that hid his face, and when he straightened, she flushed at the look he gave her. A faint half-smile touched the corners of his hard mouth.

"Sua yurahpitu." He said the words slowly, distinctly, as if to reassure her, and for some reason, Deborah's fears began to fade. Maybe he wouldn't harm her now. She wasn't certain why he'd stopped, but gratitude made her nod slowly in reply to the questioning look he gave her.

He bent, grasped a blanket from the neat stack at one side, and flung it over her. She grabbed it gratefully. He tied the strip of cloth around his waist again, picked up his knife, and left.

Deborah stared after him. Her body ached from their struggle and his brief invasion of her, but she knew that there was much he could have done. Had wanted to do. Why had he stopped?

Hawk wondered that himself. Why had he stopped? Because she was still untouched there, still a virgin? He'd been too startled to react at first. Spotted Pony was obviously wrong about what he'd seen. That didn't surprise him. In the chaos of a raid, many things could be misinterpreted. But she had said her husband was dead, and he knew that Deborah Hamilton was not the kind of woman to lie without reason. Perhaps she'd thought he would not hurt her if she could gain his sympathy, but that idea was as farfetched as the notion that she could be a married virgin.

He didn't understand it.

And more—he didn't understand why it had made a

51

difference to him. Maybe he wasn't as callous as he thought. Maybe there was a part of him that remembered the early lessons his mother had taught him long ago. Oh, so long ago. Too long to remember, he'd thought until today.

Twelve years. Twelve years of riding, looking, running, and riding again. The only respite had been here, in the camp of his father, where he'd gained some acceptance at last. It had meant putting his white blood behind him, forgetting what he'd done and who he'd been, but he'd managed to do it. Not many in the camp had been inclined to challenge White Eagle's son to prove himself, though there had been those warriors who had tested his strength. Tested his prowess as a man and the son of the chief. So far, he'd managed to prove himself.

Yet even here, lost in the cool mountains of New Mexico, where no white man could find their camp, Hawk often questioned his own motives. Why was he here? He had another life in the white man's world, one that had earned him a certain notoriety. But it had not eased that restless yearning inside him, that need for something that he couldn't even name. Here, at least, he was not constantly badgered with choices.

Until now.

Until this one woman had come into his life and presented him with an unexpected choice.

Hawk walked upstream, stripped, and went for a swim in the icy waters of the stream.

"If you want her, my *tua*, take her." White Eagle looked at his only son with a trace of amusement glittering in his dark eyes. "A man should not deny himself the comfort of a woman's company. Especially that of a captive."

"If she were—" Hawk stopped and looked away.

"If she were not white?" His father laughed softly. "You have strange requirements, *Tosa Nakaai.*"

Hawk flinched. His father had used his name, a very personal, private thing to do. No Comanche would presume to use his name thusly, so White Eagle must be trying to make a point of the differences between their cultures. He looked away when his father spoke again.

"Would you feel better if she were *wia?*"

Hawk's mouth tightened. The Mexican-Comanche women were available to all, unless taken to wife. No, his father knew very well that he would not feel better if Deborah were one of those women.

"Kee!" he spat, and White Eagle shrugged.

"Then take her. Make yourself feel better. It is only because of your past that you do not do so. If she were *wia* you would have already taken her." He looked off toward the ridge of the mountain peaks gnawing at the darkening sky. "This one is weary of having you growl like the bear these past two days. Take her, and ease my ears."

The small branch he was whittling into a flute broke between his fingers, and Hawk tossed it aside. "She has never known a man."

"Aiie."

There was a wealth of comments in that one exclamation, and Hawk almost smiled. White Eagle was not the most verbal of men. For him to offer this much advice, was beyond his normal practice.

"The woman is only a captive," White Eagle said after a long moment of silence, and Hawk stiffened.

That was true. For him to deny it would give her a

more important status. For him to agree, would keep her such. He said nothing, and felt his father's disapproval.

Wind blew through the pines, and they swayed with a majestic dignity that only old trees exhibit, gently, as if caressed by the wind. Hawk closed his eyes, and let the music of the pines seep inside him.

"A long time ago," his father began, "I took a white woman from her husband. It was not meant to be. I did not see what I was shown, or hear what was said. Many died. There was much trouble. *Subetu.*"

Hawk opened his eyes. He knew what his father meant. It would cause trouble if he kept her and did not use her. There were others in the camp who watched her, young men who did not find her pale skin and hair of dark fire to be ugly. He saw them, and he knew what they would say if he did not make the woman his. Damn. His desire for Deborah grew more complicated every day, and it was frustrating and irritating at the same time.

He resisted an angry reaction, knowing White Eagle would be disappointed in him. It wasn't the Comanche way to reveal that kind of emotion, especially not over a captive woman.

His eyes shifted to his tipi, where Sunflower visited with Deborah. He should end that friendship before it went too far. There would be no good come of it, but he hated to deny his young sister anything that pleased her. And he saw the faint gratitude in Deborah's eyes when she glanced at him, and knew that if anyone could ease her stay in the camp, it was Sunflower.

But it was unfair. Things would not stay the same, and he knew that. And he must be the one to change them.

Hawk rose to his feet in a smooth motion that gained

his father's attention, and their eyes briefly met. Then he strode in the direction of the tipi where Deborah waited.

Chapter 5

Afternoon light spilled through the triangular opening onto the hard-packed dirt floor, and Deborah gazed idly at the tiny dust motes swimming in the trapped sunbeams. She'd smoothed blankets and furs, hung clothes that she assumed were *his* from the poles, examined baskets lined along the walls, and braided her hair. Time still dragged in a slow pull that seemed like eternity.

Sunflower had gone, and Deborah had the feeling that she had been forbidden to linger. There was a sweet shyness about the girl that made her wish they could be friends, but it was obvious that had been forbidden.

Her thoughts drifted frequently to her arrogant jailer, and she found herself wondering about him. He'd not come back since that first afternoon, and she wondered why. She was grateful to be left alone, but curious as to the reason. Why were her emotions so contradictory? There was a perversity in her nature, she thought wryly, that she should definitely not cultivate at this time in her life. It could be more dangerous than she'd ever dreamed.

Deborah smoothed the folds of skirt she wore, and felt the soft material drift through her fingers. Sunflower had brought her new garments, shyly, as if expecting to be rebuked. The bright cotton skirt and loose blouse had been accepted gratefully, and she had done her best to convey her appreciation to the girl.

It felt strange to wear nothing but a skirt and blouse; none of the familiar underclothing hindered her movements, and she felt slightly guilty for enjoying the freedom. Though her freedom was restricted by being captive, she'd found surprising respite in the unusual state of leisure. She sat idly most of the time.

Accustomed to being constantly busy, whether with sewing or mending or the supervision of household tasks, Deborah had first welcomed the cessation of activity. Now, however, it was beginning to pall. She was left with too much time to think, too much time to dread what she felt must be the inevitable.

He would come again, would seek her out, and she would be helpless to refuse whatever he wished from her. His first actions remained indelibly etched in her memory, and when she caught glances of him from a distance, she flushed. He had not approached her again, but obviously chose to stay in another lodge. Tipis, they were called. There was another name for the dwellings, too, something like *kahni,* but it had been too hard for her to recall and so they'd settled on tipi. Sunflower had conveyed that to her, as well as several other terms she could understand. Being able to interpret her captors' words would be a blessing, but most of their language still eluded her.

Even more elusive was the man Sunflower had referred to as *Tosa Nakaai.* Deborah had no idea what it meant, or indeed, if it meant anything. Sunflower had endeavored to act it out for her, and she knew it had something to do with the sky and a bird, but she wasn't certain what. Several choices had occurred to her, none of them particularly flattering.

57

The arrogant blue-eyed Comanche had invaded more than her body that night, with his brief touch. He had invaded her mind, and was constantly intruding when she tried to concentrate on the more important hope of escape for her and Judith.

She'd seen Judith once, from afar, and had not noticed any sign of abuse. Hopefully, her cousin was faring well. She prayed she would get to speak with her soon, so that she could find out for herself how she was doing.

Deborah glanced at the opening of the tipi again, and saw—as she'd become accustomed to seeing—the passing of others outside. Children shrieked with laughter; dogs barked and growled, and she could hear the muffled laughter of women at work. Comanche women seemed to work constantly, scraping hides, cooking, gathering firewood, and tending children. She was certain there were many other duties as well. The men, she'd noticed, seemed to spend their time fashioning new weapons, telling stories, and probably planning new raids. They hunted, of course; plenty of meat drying on wooden racks attested to that. Comanche society seemed structured and well ordered to those born to it. To a frightened captive, that structure was menacing.

Slaves were for the menial tasks, and worked hard. The glimpse of her cousin bent low under huge bundles of firewood, her face dirty, her hair loose and tangled, had hurt. Judith did not look otherwise mistreated, but Deborah had no doubt that every person in the camp must have a function.

Which meant that *Tosa Nakaai* would have a duty in mind for her, too.

She shuddered. She could imagine what that duty would be. There had been a fierce hunger in his eyes that night, a hot fire that had burned her wherever his gaze touched. In the long night hours, she remembered it, remembered how he'd sparked an answering fire in her. The memories were as disturbing as the reality. And her body had burned and ached with an unfamiliar restlessness that made her wonder if the recent events had not deranged her in some way.

When she closed her eyes at night, she kept remembering him as she'd last seen him, that magnificent body so overwhelmingly male and powerful and frightening, his eyes beneath the thick brush of his lashes taking her breath away. The contradiction of her thoughts bewildered her, and she knew that she was in danger of losing sight of her goal.

Daylight still brightened the tree-studded valley when Deborah saw a shadow darken the opened flap of the tipi. She froze in the act of trying to re-weave a fraying reed basket. Her hands shook slightly as she recognized her visitor.

Tosa Nakaai bent, and ducked into the tipi. When he stood, his height made the interior suddenly seem much smaller. Indeed, his intimidating presence made the roomy tipi seem entirely too small for both of them.

Deborah kept her gaze on the basket, afraid to look up at him. She sensed his gaze on her. She could almost feel the heat of him so close, and there was the slight scent of fresh air and woodsmoke that penetrated her frozen senses as she tried to ignore him.

"Kima," he said, and when she kept her head bent, he reached out to touch her lightly on the head. *"Nu kwuhupu."*

Deborah inhaled deeply for courage, and looked up at him as he towered over her. His face was shadowed by the light behind him, and she had an impression of an-

59

ger mixed with uncertainty, which was confusing. Did she puzzle him as much as he did her?

"Kima," he said again, and tugged at her shoulder.

She rose to her feet, knowing that to resist him would be useless and possibly dangerous.

"I assume you want me to come with you," she said in a calm tone. Perhaps if she exhibited no fear, he would be more likely to treat her gently.

He backed to the flap and held it open, repeating, *"Kima."*

Frightened but determined, Deborah stepped out of the tipi and into the sunlight. She blinked at the glare, and felt his hand on the small of her back.

"Mia ranu," he said roughly, which she assumed meant she was to walk. She cast him a quick glance.

"Where?" Shrugging her shoulders to indicate doubt, she half-turned to face him, but he caught her by one shoulder and turned her back around. He gave her another push, and a spurt of anger made her incautious. "Idiot," she mumbled as she began to walk, wincing at the rocks cutting into her bare feet. "How am I supposed to understand your language? You sound like two tomcats in a fight when you talk—oh!"

His hard hand seized her by the nape of the neck, and he growled, *"Keta tekwaaru,"* so harshly that she knew he must mean for her to be quiet.

Deborah's quick, rebellious anger subsided as swiftly as it had risen, and she remained silent as her captor walked her through the camp. Tall grasses waved in patches, and she could see the glittering ribbon of water where Sunflower took her to bathe in the morning and evening. Trees shifted in the constant wind, whispering leaves rustling like secrets on the air currents. People stared curiously as she passed them, and Deborah kept her gaze steady and outwardly calm, though she was raging with uncertainty inside.

Did he mean to harm her? Perhaps he wanted to take her out of the camp so that he could rape her without being seen, but then she reasoned that he probably didn't need to hide anything like that. She had the distinct impression that captives were dispensable, and could be dealt with any way the captor chose. Her throat tightened, and she managed to walk without stumbling only by sheer determination.

"Tobo-ihupiitu," he said finally, pulling on the back of her blouse to indicate that he wanted her to stop. She did, and couldn't help a sudden shiver.

They were in a remote, wooded copse, with the camp far behind them. Water splashed and gurgled over muddy banks and smooth stones only a few feet away. Tall pines swayed with a loud, swishing noise that made her think of taffeta skirts rustling in church. Deborah closed her eyes, and shivered again.

"Nakaru-karu," he muttered, his hand pressing her down to a thick tuft of grass. *"Kahtu."*

She was grateful. Her knees had grown weak, and her legs too flimsy to support her much longer. This man terrified her; there was no evidence of any emotion in his stark features, no hint that he might be gentle in any way. If not for that fleeting impression of uncertainty she'd had earlier, Deborah would have thought him as unemotional as the pine trees shading them. That brief hint that he might be human was heartening, though not very comforting.

Tosa Nakaai knelt down beside her, and she felt his gaze burning into her. She felt unclothed without the armor of her undergarments, and briefly regretted their loss as much as she had recently enjoyed her new freedom. It felt as if he could see through the thin material

61

covering her, and she resisted the impulse to rearrange her clothing.

Deborah tried not to look at him, but the pull of his eyes finally drew her reluctant gaze. They were so blue, so cold and yet so warm, with the fire she'd seen before lighting them with a need so strong she almost felt it. Deborah swallowed her dismay. He seemed to sense her response, a quick flutter of her pulses when she met his eyes that she couldn't explain.

"Please," she whispered when he reached out to touch her, one finger stroking along the sweep of her jaw, "don't do this."

Ridiculous, of course, to bother pleading with him. Even if he could understand her, he would do what his nature dictated. He was a Comanche, and they were savages, were they not? She'd heard tales, but had not believed how true they were until lately.

And now—now, the Comanche who'd bought her was stroking her face. His features were taut with purpose, his voice soft and raspy.

"Keta? nu kuya?a-ku-tu."

His dark head slowly bent, and he kissed her above the bronze curve of his hand. His mouth was warm, soft, and she shook with reaction. When his lips grazed her own, barely brushing over them in a whisper as light as the touch of the wind, Deborah closed her eyes.

He murmured something and tilted her head back. She opened her eyes to look at him.

"Muhraipu," he said softly. *"Muhraipu."*

Deborah stared at him. He wanted something; she saw the expectation in his eyes.

"I don't know what you want," she began, but his fingers tightened slightly, not painfully, and he gave her head a slight shake.

"Muhraipu." He kissed her again, more firmly this

time, his mouth lingering over her lips before he drew back. His voice was a husky whisper. *"Muhraipu."*

Deborah was shaking, but she thought she understood. "Kiss? Is that what you're saying? *Muhraipu.* Kiss."

He smiled, a faint curving of his hard mouth that held a hint of good humor. *"Haa. Muhraipu. Kiss."* His hand drifted down to cup her chin in his palm, and Deborah felt the subtle shift of his muscles as he leaned forward again, was not surprised when his other hand moved behind her to cradle her head.

This kiss was different from the others; there was no driving passion, or hesitancy, but a gentleness that amazed her. So, this hard-faced savage with hostile eyes and harsh manners could be tender when he wished to be. It was a startling revelation to her.

Deborah did not try to avoid his kiss, but she did not participate. Rather, she allowed him to tease her mouth with his tongue and lips, testing the limits of her endurance as if he knew how he made her pulse race. Surely, he couldn't tell. Surely, this man could not sense that his touch destroyed many of her preconceptions about him. If he could be this tender, this kind, then perhaps he could not be the rough, fierce captor she'd thought him until now. And perhaps he would not make her ease that driving hunger that vibrated just below his surface.

He broke off the kiss abruptly, his brick-brown chest moving in a brisk tempo as he stared at her, and Deborah saw the male hunger in his eyes again. Despite his gentleness, there was still that to contend with, that masculine need that stood between them as palpably as if it was carved in rock. She swallowed her dismay, her faint protest, and knew that it would do no good to protest against a force as strong as the desire of a man to mate with a woman.

63

A drift of wind lifted a curl of her hair from her forehead so that it teased her nose, and she brushed it away. Tosa Nakaai watched, then took her hand in his. It was dwarfed by his large hand, his long, blunt fingers and rough palm, and somehow made her feel more helpless than anything he had yet done.

There was an odd expression on his austere face, a faint shifting of facial muscles that gave the impression he was remembering something or someone else. Perhaps it was the way he held her hand, cradling it gently in his broad palm as if he held a small, live creature. He began to stroke the heel of her palm in light touches, tracing along her slender fingers in feathery caresses that made Deborah catch her breath. She felt oddly drawn to him, although he was a Comanche, and he would very likely force her to do things she'd never dreamed existed until recently.

Yet, somehow, she didn't mind.

He looked up at her, his gaze riveted on her face. What he saw there must have prompted him to action, because he took her hand and drew it to his face. She was trembling. Her fingers shook as he touched the tips to his mouth, and there was a soft huskiness in his voice.

"Tuupe." He dragged her fingertips over his mouth and repeated, *"Tuupe."*

"Tuupe." Her voice shook slightly. "Mouth—*tuupe.*"

He watched her as he slid her fingers up his face. *"Koobe."* He raked her hand over his face. He was warm, his skin rough and soft at the same time.

"Koobe," she whispered. "Face."

"Pui." He touched her hand to his eye. *Ka-ibuhu* was his eyebrow, *puitusii* his eyelashes. *Muubi,* his nose. He gave her a lesson in Comanche anatomy, and Deborah forgot to be afraid.

64

Until he sat back on his heels, his eyes holding her smiling gaze, and reached out to put his hand on her breast.

"Pitsii."

Paralyzed, Deborah could not force the echo past her lips. His palm felt suddenly too hot against her skin, and he caressed her breast while he watched her. When she sucked in a deep breath, the motion pushed her breast into his palm, and she saw the starburst of reaction in his eyes. There was a quick flare, like a shooting star, then his lashes lowered to hide his eyes.

Quivering, Deborah felt trapped. The lowering sun took with it the warmth of earlier, and there was a loud, piercing cry overhead that drew Tosa Nakaai's attention. He glanced up, then sat back on his heels.

"Tosa Nakaai," he said softly, and pointed.

Deborah looked up, and saw a huge hawk circling gracefully overhead. Its wings were outspread, and it seemed to just glide on the wind currents, almost as if suspended. The setting sun gilded the wingtips with lucid light. There was a lethal beauty to it that left her admiring and frightened at the same time, and she realized suddenly that this man had the same effect as the bird for which he had been named.

"Tosa Nakaai," she whispered, startling him. "Hawk. We call that a hawk in English. They're lovely. And deadly, just like you are. Hawk. The name fits you. You're a predator, just as that bird of prey is a predator, and I'm afraid of you."

He was looking at her coldly, and Deborah tried to speak but couldn't. There was no anger in his eyes, but she was suddenly afraid she had said too much. Maybe he understood her tone, and she had somehow betrayed her fear and inexplicable longing. It was not a combination of emotions that would leave any woman comfortable, and the fact that she was this Comanche's captive did not help.

Tosa Nakaai—Hawk—looked away from her. His profile was etched against the fading light like a cameo, pristine, pure, sharply defined. Shining black hair framed his face. The single braid and dangling feather brushed the muscled curve of his shoulder when he finally turned back to face her, and Deborah was startled by his frustrated expression.

"*Kekunabeniitu*," he said in a growl that left her in no doubt that she'd somehow touched a nerve. He rose in a fluid motion that made her cringe back toward the rough trunk of the pine tree.

He bent, grabbed her wrist, and pulled her to her feet in a swift move that made her gasp with fright. But he did not try to hurt her, only turned her around and took her with him back down the grassy slope to the camp.

When he left her at the entrance to his tipi, Deborah looked at Sunflower and wondered why. What had she done that had made him change so swiftly?

Chapter 6

Hawk caught his swiftest horse and vaulted astride the broad back, drumming his heels against its sides. The animal snorted, huge hooves digging into the earth and sending up thick clods as it broke into a run.

Both seemed to feel the need for a run, and the ragged edges of the moon offered plenty of light across the prairie as they flew like loosed arrows. There was a fierce, exultant pleasure in the run, the release of pent-up energies and frustrations.

The night smells were familiar. Sharp-scented sage, the brisk fragrance of spruce, the hot smell of dust, all filled his nostrils and heightened his senses.

Deborah.

Her name was the driving beat of his horse's hooves against the earth. *De-bor-ah, De-bor-ah, De-bor-ah,* the rhythm grew faster and faster, her name echoing in his mind with each strike of hoof, each fluid stroke of leg. Names were powerful; all Comanche knew that a person's name had a special meaning, a special power all its own. That was why it was considered bad form to use a person's name, an invasion of their privacy, or a way of lessening their power.

Hawk wasn't that superstitious. A result of his earlier

upbringing, no doubt. Yet, when she'd said his name, both in Comanche and in English, she'd somehow touched a part of him that no woman had yet glimpsed.

And he hadn't taken her.

He'd meant to. After all, that was why he had taken her from the tipi up to the privacy of that slope, so that if she resisted, no one would hear. To resist was not shameful, but he'd not wanted others to hear her cries.

And he hadn't taken her.

He wasn't sure why not. He knew how to play the game of courtship, teasing, touching, and he knew enough about white women to know what made them respond. Yet, he had not been able to finish what he'd begun. Somehow, her words had formed a wall around her that he could not bridge. It would have shamed him.

Was there more to his attraction to her than just her delicate beauty? He wondered. For a moment, holding her small hand in his, marveling at the fragile delicacy of her bones and soft, creamy skin, he'd been reminded of his mother. Her hands had not been soft; hard work had roughened them through the years. Yet she had taken care of them, had rubbed them with ointment and cream and sometimes cried at the calluses marring palms and fingers.

It had been a searing memory, long-buried and presumed forgotten. Until Deborah Hamilton had dredged it up for him, like a ghost from his past.

He'd thought he could run from the memories, run from the things he did not want to confront, but he was wrong. He could not run from himself, and all the yesterdays had formed his todays.

Resentment flared in him, that he could cope with the brutal way of life, yet flinched at childhood disappointments. It made him feel less a man, and weak.

Reining his horse to a slow trot, Hawk knew that he

68

would have to come to terms with the woman. She could not be allowed to affect him.

Deborah wiped at her damp forehead with the back of her hand. She was helping Sunflower with the never-ending tasks, and found it much more difficult than chores in Natchez. Of course, in Natchez there had been modern conveniences to ease the backbreaking labor involved in washing clothes. Paddle-boards and huge tubs, and even a machine that could be turned by use of a large crank made life easier at home.

But, washing clothes against rocks in a swift-moving stream was almost as effective. The soap was some sort of combination of animal fat and plant roots.

They were far downstream from where the drinking water was drawn, and today, Deborah caught a glimpse of her cousin not far away. Her heart pounded fiercely, and she felt a surge of excitement. Had Judith seen her?

She had, and slowly, trying to disguise their intentions, the two managed to work their way toward one another.

"Judith," Deborah whispered when they were close; she was bent over and pretending to concentrate on scrubbing a square of cotton. "Are you all right?"

"I'm surviving." Judith's bright hair was combed, but looked dark with dirt. Her face was pale, and there were scratches and bruises on her arms and face. "That she-wolf who keeps me close likes to pinch, but that's the extent of my injuries. So far."

"No, don't look at me," Deborah warned softly when her cousin started to turn toward her. "Pretend to drop something and we can both bend again."

"How are you faring?" Judith whispered. "I saw that tall Comanche drag you from camp one afternoon."

How did she explain? Deborah hesitated. "He hasn't hurt me. Not like . . . like he could, I suppose. I mean, he only tries to talk to me, but he sounds so fierce, that he scares me at times."

Shuddering, Judith murmured, "He looks so savage that he scares me just looking at him!"

"I don't think he's that savage," Deborah said, then could have laughed at her words. Was she defending him? The strange look Judith threw her made her flush and try to explain. "He's been kind at times, though I know that sounds odd."

"Somehow, I thought he was . . . uh, taken with you. I mean, I've seen him looking at you so intently."

Deborah pushed at a wave of hair blocking her vision, and slanted a glance at her cousin. Judith looked concerned and puzzled, and she had to laugh ruefully.

"I have no idea what's in his mind. All I know, is that he has not harmed me. Yet." A frown furrowed her brow. "At times, when I wake up, there are unexpected gifts. A hairbrush, for instance. Moccasins when my shoes fell apart. Two satin ribbons for my hair. I know he brought them. No one else would. Yet I know he's waiting for something."

"We need to escape before something happens to you," Judith said. She glanced around cautiously. "So far, we've been lucky."

"Let's try to meet again soon. Can you get close to me at the stream tomorrow morning?"

"I'll try. But we have to be careful. If one of them notices us talking together, they'll be more watchful."

With a quick, soft good-bye, the cousins moved apart in an aimless motion. To a casual observer, it would have seemed innocent.

To the man standing up on the hill, it was a forewarning.

* * *

Sunflower studied the toes of her moccasins, and Hawk watched the pouting curve of her lower lip as she reflected. Her head lifted, dark eyes appraising him.

"But why can't I practice my English on her? It could do no harm."

"I do not wish it."

"It would make things easier."

"Easy is not always the best way." Hawk felt a surge of impatience. Normally, he was quite patient with his young sister. It surprised him that he suddenly felt like boxing her ears. "Do not disobey me," he warned when the girl gave a heavy sigh and looked away from him. Her startled reply was evidence that she was aware of his tension.

"I would not do so."

"You like her."

Sunflower nodded. *"Haa."* She seemed to struggle for words, then said, "She is *kesósooru*—very gentle. And she does not screech, or whine, or complain like others I have known. She is different."

"Yes. She is different. Do not allow your sympathy to make trouble for her. I have not hurt her."

Sunflower looked suddenly very adult, and flashed him a sly glance. "But you want her in your robes."

Making his voice stern, Hawk growled, "It is not seemly for a young maiden to speak of such things. Shall I tell old grandmother and have her take a switch to you?"

Sunflower laughed, mischief dancing in her dark, liquid eyes. "She would have to catch me first."

"I could catch you for her."

Sobering, Sunflower said uncertainly, "You would not do that."

71

"Do you wish to test me?"

She shook her head, disappointment shadowing her pretty face. "I do not think so. You look very fierce when you speak of *Eka-paapi.*"

Hawk stared at her. *Eka-paapi.* Red head. It was appropriate enough, but he would not have given her a Comanche name. It was too personal. Too permanent. Irritation made his voice harsher than usual, and Sunflower backed away from him when he spoke to her.

"Go back to my tipi and stay with her. Do not let her from your sight. It will go bad for you if she leaves here and you could have stopped her."

Sunflower paused. "That is why you are so angry? Do you think she will leave you?"

"This is not a matter to discuss with children," Hawk said stiffly, and saw the hurt flare in his sister's eyes. He said nothing to ease it. She must believe that he would be very angry with her if Deborah escaped the village. That would make her doubly vigilant.

Hawk watched as Sunflower stomped toward his tipi. It was set slightly apart from the others, and those in the village had come to accept his strangeness. He did not stay with his father, sister, and the old mother of his father's late wife, but had always kept his own lodge. He liked his privacy, liked being alone. Since Deborah had come to the camp, however, he'd spent his nights in his father's lodge, or outside on a robe beneath the stars.

If he went into his own lodge to sleep, he would not be able to resist pulling her beneath his robes, and he had to prove to himself that he could stay away from her. A faint, wry smile slanted his mouth. It had come to this, then, that he would allow a woman to dictate his habits. And she didn't even try. In fact, she would be astonished if she had any idea that her presence disturbed him to the extent that he avoided her.

A hard knot coiled in his belly, and Hawk fought a surge of anger at himself and the woman who governed his actions without knowing it. She was a sickness, and he would ease himself on another. That would blunt the edge of his need, and put him in control again. Yes. That is what he would do. There were women in camp who found him favorable.

Sunflower thrust a basket at Deborah. *"Kima."*

By now, Deborah knew that meant to come. She nodded, and slid her feet into the soft deerhide moccasins she'd been given. Hawk had brought them to her, shoving them into her hands without a word, his face set and hard. Only Sunflower's muffled giggle had alerted her to the fact that his thoughtfulness meant more than just protecting her feet. It was thought-provoking.

"Panatsayaa," Sunflower said when Deborah rose to her feet and took the empty basket.

Blackberries. Or raspberries. Deborah grew confused at the similarity of names. She assumed it would be blackberries they were to pick. And she was never certain when one of her attempts to mimic Sunflower's Comanche language would send the girl into peals of laughter. Sometimes, she was able to understand what she'd said wrong—as in *wura* for "thank you" when it really meant mountain lion. It would be easy to get into real trouble in a conversation, she could see that.

The sun beat down fiercely, and Deborah wondered with a sigh why Sunflower had chosen such a hot morning to search for berries. Late afternoon would have been better. It was cooler then. Insects buzzed annoyingly close, and she was grateful for the cool clothes she wore. If she'd still been clad in petticoats, drawers, chemise, and high-necked dress, she would have fainted from the heat. There were some things that the women she'd known could benefit from, and that was the comparative freedom of dress the Comanche women enjoyed.

But Deborah's simple skirt, blouse, and moccasins kept her much cooler, and allowed her to walk through the high grasses. The blackberry bushes ranged along a crest overlooking the camp. To get there, they had to cross the stream and pass the meadow where the horses roamed.

Deborah watched curiously as young boys played in the tall grass, pretending to be warriors, she supposed. They had small bows and arrows, and gave chillingly realistic whoops that reminded her of that night at the Velazquez hacienda. Some of the horses snorted and shied away, and a man shouted angrily at the boys as they played too near.

Ropes trailed from many of the animals, and Deborah watched as the man caught one of the horses by the end of the braided leather. It seemed that the horses most often used were haltered with a rope and allowed to roam free, while the others grazed in the high, lush grass. It gave Deborah an idea that was both startling and terrifying.

She was still lost in thought when they reached the prickly line of bushes atop the crest, and paused to sink down on a flat stone. Sunflower sat down and removed her moccasin, frowning at a stone she shook out. She muttered something in Comanche, and slid her foot back into the shoe. Then she looked up at Deborah.

"I'm ready," Deborah said slowly, and saw the comprehension in the girl's face. Sunflower could understand some English, she'd decided. She wasn't certain how much, but there were times Deborah had made herself well understood.

74

"Kima." Sunflower rose, dusted off her skirt with one hand, and picked up her basket.

They walked carefully down the line of bushes. Some of the limbs were so heavy with fruit they brushed along the ground. Laughing, both of them ate almost as many berries as they picked. Sweet, sticky juice smeared their hands and mouths, and stained their clothes. It was a satisfying morning, with the heat of the sun and the delicious taste of berries on her tongue.

Deborah grew drowsy, her eyelids drooping. She saw that Sunflower was sleepy also, and they sat down in the shade of a cottonwood to rest. Birds sang loudly overhead, and the wind cooled clothes that had grown damp with perspiration. Deborah loosened her hair, as it had become tangled in the long thorns of the blackberry bushes and pulled loose from the neat braid. She lifted it from her neck and closed her eyes for a moment, heavy strands spilling over her hands and arms in a light, tickling wave.

"It's beautiful out here," she said softly, not knowing if Sunflower could understand all her words but compelled to offer conversation. "I understand why people would want to live so simply. Before, it was always a mystery to me. I'm afraid that my people consider Indians—*all* Indians—to be little more than savages. They're wrong."

She curled her arms around her drawn-up knees and smiled at the listening girl. *"Haitsi. Haa?"*

Sunflower smiled back at her. *"Haitsíi—haa."*

She'd made some sort of distinction in the word, and it had taken on a different meaning, Deborah realized. Sunflower's sweet smile and soft eyes conveyed only friendship, so she knew it had been a pleasant difference.

"Ura. Thank you."

75

Sunflower looked away from her, back toward the valley where the tipis were scattered beside the cool waters of the stream. Deborah sensed that she was troubled, and wished the language barrier could be bridged.

"I don't know what is the matter," she began hesitantly, "but I wish I could help. You are very pretty, and very nice to me, and I do not like to see you sad."

Sunflower flashed her a startled glance. Surging to her feet, the girl seemed about to say something, her mouth quivering slightly. Then she gave a shake of her head, and the long, dark tails of hair over each shoulder swung violently.

"*Yaa,*" she muttered. There was confusion in her eyes, and Deborah lapsed into silence.

She wondered how it would affect this girl when she and Judith managed to escape. She prayed that escape was possible, prayed that no one would be hurt. A lingering doubt jabbed at her, the doubt that they would even be able to find the way back to civilization. Surely, by now soldiers should have been able to find them. Had any been alerted? Was anyone still looking for them? It had only been three weeks since they'd been taken from the Velazquez hacienda, and rescuers could not have given up yet.

Though not quite certain where they were, Deborah knew they were within a few days ride of Texas. Probably in New Mexico. If she and Judith managed to escape and went south, they could possibly find a main trade route. But if they were caught—the possibilities were frightening. Deborah had no illusions about her captor. He may not have treated her as harshly as he could, but there was a steely core to him that would not endure an escape attempt.

When they made their attempt, she and Judith would

have to be ready to accept whatever fate might bring them, and not turn back. The reprisals would be harsh.

Sunflower handed Deborah a skin of water, and she drank deeply. It was best, she'd discovered, not to examine some of the containers and even the food too closely. Suspicious differences from what she had been used to would have rendered her unable to eat anything, and so she simply took what was offered without close examination. The water skin, for instance, reminded her of an animal intestine, and she dared not look too closely. She gave it back, and Sunflower took it without comment.

Some of the easy companionship of the morning was gone, and Deborah wasn't sure why. Perhaps her words had somehow disturbed Sunflower.

"Kima," the girl murmured, and Deborah followed her back into the blackberry bushes.

Now the sun was directly overhead, burning down with a fierce intensity. Even the birds had quieted, and the droning of the insects seemed louder than before. Soft rustlings in the tall grasses seemed furtive, though Deborah thought it must be only the wind.

She plucked a particularly juicy berry, dropping it atop the others in her basket. Her fingers were stained a purple so dark as to be almost black, and her hands and arms were scratched in dozens of places by the thorns. Her skirt snagged on a vicious thorn, and she turned, muttering softly about the inconvenience.

A low rumble made her head snap up, and she'd opened her mouth to speak when Sunflower put a warning hand on her arm. The girl was stiff and tense, radiating a sense of urgency and fear.

Deborah trembled. She'd seen the Comanche return with women from another tribe, and knew that the tribes often warred against one another, stealing women and

77

horses with utter disregard. It would not be unheard of for a warring tribe to do the same here.

Her heart pounded fiercely in her chest, and her knees went weak with fright. She hadn't realized it, but her hand was on Sunflower's arm, her fingers digging deeply into the girl's skin. Sunflower tugged silently at her, and Deborah eased her grip.

The rumble came again, and this time it was discernible as a male voice, deep and husky. It sounded amused, and there was a soft, feminine squeal. Deborah felt faint. Had an enemy caught someone unawares? Were there many of them? She followed Sunflower's example, and sank slowly to the ground as noiselessly as possible. Thick berry branches hid them from sight of a casual observer and she prayed no one would know to look for them.

Crouched under the thorns and fruit, they waited, and it seemed as if the voice grew nearer. Deborah sliced a glance at Sunflower, and saw her eyes widen with sudden recognition. She gave Deborah a startled glance, then put a finger to her lips in warning.

Puzzled, Deborah could not imagine the reason.

Until the man came into view, and she saw Hawk. He was with a woman, one of the Mexican-Comanche women, and they did not seem to be fighting, as she'd first thought. Instead, Hawk had an arm around the woman's waist, and she was giggling. Deborah stiffened.

There was an unmistakable meaning to their actions. Even before she saw Hawk pull the woman's loose blouse away, his hands dark and bold against her plump curves, she knew what he was doing. The memory flashed through her mind of the afternoon he'd touched her similarly, and how he had sparked a fire in her.

He was lighting fires in this woman now. Deborah

closed her eyes, but she could not block out the sounds. They crashed against her ears like thunder, the woman's giggles turning to groans, then gasps, and Hawk's growling voice sounding strained and labored. It seemed to go on forever. Then he made a rough sound that grew into a panting groan, and the woman cried out loudly. Silence fell.

This silence was more deafening than the first. It lay in thick clouds over her, until finally she opened her eyes. To her surprise, tears streaked her cheeks.

She could not imagine why.

Chapter 7

Hawk swore softly under his breath, startling the woman beneath him. She stared up at him with wide brown eyes full of fear, and he touched her cheek with a gentle hand. It was all the assurance he was in the mood to offer.

A slight sound in the bushes just beyond the grassy knoll where he'd chosen to lie with the woman had alerted him to another's presence. His sharp eyes had caught the bright motion of a cotton skirt, and he'd known, then, who hid in the bushes.

Though he wasn't quite certain why it should bother him if Deborah and his sister saw him with the woman, it did. He waited until the two crept away, then rose to his feet, readjusting his breechcloth. His partner looked up at him, her blouse still down around her waist and tangled with the hem of her skirt. The bare brown curves that had excited him only minutes before, left him cold now.

Growling at her to dress, Hawk pivoted on his heel and strode down the slope toward the village. He didn't wait on the woman, but left her to follow him. She would be used to such brusque behavior. Her tipi was at the edge of the village, and saw many men come and go.

Hawk thought of Deborah, her wide hazel eyes and soft white skin, and found that his spent passion had left him more on edge than before. He should not have tried to replace one need with another. It wasn't just that he wanted to lie with a woman. He wanted Deborah.

Ahead of him, almost at the village now, he saw her, her bright hair streaming behind her as she ran. Sunflower's dark head was close beside her. Hawk swore again, an oath in English, low and vicious. There was no comparison in Comanche, nothing vile enough.

His mood worsened, and when his foot struck something in the tall grasses, he looked down and saw an abandoned basket. Ripe, gleaming berries spilled across the ground in a narrow stream.

Hawk paused. Now he knew why Deborah and Sunflower had been in the bushes, and it eased his anger. He bent to retrieve the basket with the few berries still in it, then continued down the slope and into the village.

The hot sun beat down, and sharp shadows cut across the bare earth. Dust lay in a heated haze along the ground, stirred up by passing feet. Someone called out to him as he passed their lodge, but he didn't bother to reply.

When he reached his tipi, he ducked inside and paused, tossing the berry basket to the floor. Deborah stared up at him, but when he reached out for her, she shrank back.

Anger spurred him, drowning out his first surprise at her reaction. Uttering a sharp comment, he slapped a hand on her wrist and yanked her to her feet, jerking her up against his chest. He could feel the rapid thunder of her pulse under his fingertips, the surge of fear in her trembling body.

Their eyes met, and he wondered what she saw in his face that made her react violently. She lunged sideways to escape, but he kept his hard grip on her wrist, and his hold swung her around.

Her small, berry-stained hand came up as she was swept back, and before he could move, her palm smacked against his cheek with a loud crack. Stunned into immobility, Hawk just stared down at Deborah with shock.

Her lips were parted, her breath quick and tortured, and her wide eyes were glazed with tears. Russet strands of hair framed her pale face in a tangle, and he could feel her brace herself.

No one spoke. Beyond a small gasp from Sunflower, no sound was made. The silence was heavy and fraught with tension. Hawk felt a muscle leap in his jaw with the strain of holding back, and it took him a moment to regain control.

Then he moved in a swift motion, lifting Deborah and tossing her over his shoulder. He bent, ducked out the open flap of the tipi, and strode back through the village.

Deborah had the good sense to remain still. If she had made a noise, fought him, he would have lost his tenuous grip on restraint. But she lay limp over his shoulder, and no one dared call out to him as he carried her back up the grassy slope he'd just traveled.

Fury made him rougher than usual, and he didn't care if she was terrified. She should be. No woman should dare strike a man, especially a captive woman. If any but Sunflower had seen her, his pride would have demanded immediate and harsh retaliation. As it was, her blow had pushed him to the very limits of his control.

Now, he just wanted to force her to lie with him, to put himself inside her and erase all the memories. He wanted to hear *her* voice in his ear, whispering soft words of encouragement, hear her cries of pleasure.

The need was growing stronger every day, and he wondered if his father was not right when he'd said he should take her. She was a captive. *Pu kwuhupu*—his captive. And she should learn that lesson well.

But Deborah Hamilton was also a lady. She had dignity and courage and compassion, and those were rare qualities in one woman. He wanted to hold her to him, let her come to know him slowly. He wanted time, yet time pressed him hard. He wanted—Deborah. Yet he did not trust her not to find a way to escape the village. He'd seen her talk to the golden-haired woman, knew that was her cousin. And he knew that Deborah Hamilton had the courage to defy the odds and try to leave this remote camp in the mountains. It would be just like her to go with no thought to the consequences.

Hawk knew all of that. Just as he knew that the sharp press of his desire for her would launch him into something he might regret. But he couldn't go back. He'd seen her, he'd bought her, and he wanted her. There was no denying any of that, no forgetting it now.

When he stood beneath the shade of a grove of pines, Hawk swung her to the ground. One hand curled around her upper arm to steady her. She flung back her hair with a proud, defiant gesture and met his heated gaze with angry eyes.

Her anger amazed him. She should be terrified. He'd been rough with her, yet she glared up at him as if he was not twice as large and much stronger.

"I suppose now you'll rape me," she said in a cold, caustic tone that made his jaw clench. "It's to be expected, I assume. After all, that is what you've wanted to do since you first saw me. Shall I lie down for you?"

When he said nothing, but stared down at her through hot, narrowed eyes, she seemed to lose some of her bravado. Her small, round chin quivered slightly, and he

83

saw the quick, nervous flutter of her hands. Yet she would not look away from him. Her soft brown eyes, hiding sparks of gold in the centers, held his gaze as if challenging him.

"Kwabitu?" she said, jerking a hand toward the ground, her pronunciation mangled but understandable. "Do you want me to lie down for you?"

There was such an expression of angry contempt in her tone and eyes that Hawk felt a surge of shame. It was quickly followed by anger. She should not provoke him. She was not sitting in an elegant drawing room somewhere, but was his captive. If he were any other man, he would throw her down and toss up her skirts as she was challenging him to do. Did she think her contempt made her safe?

Slowly, deliberately, he drew her to him. Her eyes grew large and dilated, but she refused to look away. Good. He wanted her to see his anger, see what he could do if she was foolish enough to continue.

With the same deliberation, he began to pull away her blouse, baring her creamy skin. There were faint red patches on her body above the neck. Sunburn. Sunflower should not have taken such a fair-skinned woman into the heat of the day without adequate protection. Hawk hesitated, but Deborah made the mistake of trying to pull away and he renewed his determination.

"Puaru" he growled when she tugged harder. His hand tangled in her hair to hold her, while his other hand began the methodical stripping away of her garments. If she wanted to resist, she was given the opportunity.

But she went still and quiet, closing her eyes as he peeled off her clothing, her lips quivering with suppressed screams. Somehow, it was not quite the victory

84

Hawk had envisioned. There was no satisfaction in subduing a compliant antagonist.

He released her hair and stepped back, watching her through narrowed eyes as she stood with her arms at her sides and her eyes closed. The wind lifted her hair in a drift of dark fire strands, curling one around the peak of her breast. Hawk watched her nipples tighten into small, pebbled buds.

She was so beautiful. He'd never dreamed she would be so perfectly formed. There was nothing to hide her from his view now, no shredded clothing or shadows. Sunlight gilded her pale body with light, made it gleam dully like unpolished marble.

Small, firm breasts tilted impudently, and her narrow waist flared into gently curving hips. Slender thighs and shapely calves narrowed into slim ankles, and her bare feet were small and delicate. She was so finely made, so fragile and patrician, that she made him feel clumsy and coarse. And she renewed the desire he'd thought stemmed for the moment.

Despite Hawk's recent release, he felt the surge of lust hit him again, as strong and hard as if he had not been with a woman in months. He swallowed, and wondered if he had not chosen the wrong vengeance.

"Nananisuyake," he muttered in a voice so hoarse he almost didn't recognize it as his own. Pretty. No, she was more than that.

He looked up at her face again, her still, white face and closed eyes. Heat was rising in him, undeniable and strong, yet he felt strangely reluctant to force her now. There was a rather pathetic courage about her rigid stance and refusal to plead. She waited. And he burned for her.

Knowing he was pushing himself to the limits, Hawk took a step closer and touched her. His hand rested on the curve of her breast, and he felt her flinch. His thumb dragged over the tempting bud of her nipple, sun-warmed and deliciously pink. He had wanted to punish Deborah for daring to strike him when he had only come to comfort her, but now he found that his vengeance had turned on him.

It was he who was in torment, he who suffered the most. She had not known a man, and did not know the ache of denial as he did. And it occurred to him again that he did not need to deny himself what he wanted when it stood before him in lush, naked surrender.

But that was not the way he wanted her surrender, not with grief and resistance. No, he wanted her willing and warm and arching into his touch, not shrinking away from it. There were embers of passion glowing in her; all it would take was the right spark to ignite them into flames, and he wanted to be that spark.

Hawk curled a finger under her chin, his thumb brushing over her skin lightly. *"Punitu nue,"* he muttered, and tapped her cheek with a soft flick that made her open her eyes. When she was looking at him, he bent his head and kissed her, his mouth gentle. Her lips were sweet, juicy, the taste faintly familiar. He lifted his head and a slight smile slanted his mouth. *"Panatsa-yaa."*

She blinked, then flushed. "Yes ... blackberries ... we were eating them earlier." She was shaking so badly he put one arm around her back to hold her close, so that she fit him from breast to knee.

That was torture. Her skin was satiny beneath his palm, soft and warm, luxuriant to the touch. He let his hand drift down to the small of her back, then spread his fingers over the curve of her buttocks. He pressed, and her belly rubbed against his almost painful erection.

86

It was exquisite torment. He fit her close to him, his breath coming in harsh, ragged pants for air.

He'd thought his release on the Mexican-Comanche woman would ease his need, but knew now he'd only been fooling himself. There would be no release, no satisfaction, until he eased himself inside Deborah.

He slid his hands down her arms to grasp her wrists, then he lifted her hands and put them on his chest. Her palms were cold, surprising him. He felt shivers rack her entire body, and saw the telltale quiver of her lower lip.

Hawk glanced up. The sun was bright and searing, heating his skin, yet Deborah was shaking as if chilled. Why was it he felt on fire, yet she was shivering?

Tucking her into him, he lowered his body to the ground in a smooth motion. Deborah lay beneath him, cushioned on a lush tuft of grass, her hair fanned out in a silky dark fire over the ground. Hawk levered his torso up on one arm, his hand spread on the grass. Slowly, slowly, he drew his other hand down over her body, caressing her.

"You don't have to do this," she whispered when he met her gaze again, and Hawk grew still. "Oh, God—if you can understand me at all, please . . . *keta!*"

Keta. Don't.

Hawk sat frozen in place. His gaze was caught by the pleading in her eyes, the soft hazel pools that caught sunlight in splinters and reflected his own face.

Deborah lifted her hand, touched his face with a tentative finger. Her hand was shaking, and she could see the indecision in his stark blue eyes as he looked down at her. It was almost too much to hope that he would not do what it was obvious he intended. She could feel the hard thrust of him against her thighs, the tension in his muscled frame.

He shifted slightly, and his face moved into shadow, with the sun behind him. The curve of his shoulder gleamed a dull bronze, slick and powerful and intimidating. She tried to hold to her resolve, but it was growing noticeably weaker the more she was around him.

What was it about this man that lured her at the same time it repelled her? She should be horrified, terrified, yet she sometimes found herself wondering about him. After hearing him with that other woman, hearing the primitive sounds that were shocking and arousing at the same time, she had run just as much from herself as from him.

His touch kindled a flame in her she couldn't deny. She wanted to. She wanted to pretend herself inviolable, but she knew she wasn't. He could have her. It would be easy. All he had to do, was kiss her and caress her, and talk to her in that soft, husky tone he'd used before.

The unfamiliar words could vibrate all the way to her toes, coupled with the intense, shimmering blue ice of his eyes. She felt enveloped by him, absorbed, as if she was inside him, as if her skin was heated bronze and muscle. The air she breathed smelled of him, of wind and leather and the now-familiar musk of his skin, warm and arousing.

But she wasn't ready, didn't know if she could survive the yielding of body and soul to this man who filled her days with seduction and her nights with dreams. What had been so brief and frightening with Miguel was different with Hawk, was intense and arousing and potentially devastating. It was strange, the way he made her feel, as if she should cling to him, as if she should allow him the freedom of her body without protest. There was a fevered pleasure in his caresses, in the sweet torment of his touch.

Odd, but she had always thought there had to be a basis of love and friendship between a man and a woman for there to be this intense an attraction. It was obvious she was wrong. All her long-held standards crumbled in the face of his desire and her response.

Her only defense now was surrender.

And it worked. Hawk held her gaze for a long time, his eyes shadowed by his lashes, his mouth a straight, harsh line. Then he rose in a lithe motion and gestured for her to dress.

While she did, he walked a little away from her and stood with his back to her, as if he could not watch. She slid him a quick glance as she hurriedly dressed, and saw that his back was rigid, his muscles taut with strain. The black silk of his hair brushed against his broad shoulders in a light, swinging motion. She thought of the hawk she'd seen, and how its wings had swung in lazy motions as it flew overhead.

She smoothed the folds of her skirt over her legs with trembling fingers, then cleared her throat. Hawk turned. His hard gaze swept over her, and a faint, sardonic smile curved the erotic line of his mouth.

"Kima."

Come. Yes. She supposed she would have to follow him. She had no other choice. If not for his unexpected mercy, she might have much more to worry about than being commanded to follow like a pet dog. It would, Deborah thought as she picked her way down the grassy slope in Hawk's footsteps, be unnerving to see how much longer she could hold off his determined assault on her senses.

Chapter 8

A week passed, dragging dusty heels of time so slowly that Deborah despaired. Since the day she'd struck Hawk, he had not approached her again. He came to his tipi to eat, and to speak with his sister, but he said nothing to her.

She felt his gaze on her, though, even when he was a distance from her. It burned into her, hot and blue and searing, making her ache with some nameless emotion. Just when she thought it was fear, her feelings had turned into something entirely different.

When he was near, even ignoring her, she trembled. A hot flush rose inside her, and her legs grew weak. Hawk invaded her dreams more vividly now, and sometimes—God help her—when she dreamed, she dreamed that she was the woman beneath him on a grassy slope. The moans were hers, the soft cries and gasps came from her lips.

He had awakened something inside her, some demon that made her wonder what it would be like to be possessed by him.

Judith was appalled.

"You can't mean it," she whispered one morning when they were washing wooden bowls in the stream.

Their watchers were not far away, and the noise of the rushing water caused their voices to rise a bit to be heard.

Deborah flushed. "But I do. He's not as bad as I'd first thought."

"For God's sake, Deborah! I admit he is handsome, as Indians go, but he's a ruthless savage! How can you even think he might be gentle, or kind, or even decent? Haven't you seen how many captives there are in this camp? And we're part of them . . ."

"Judith, he could have done to me what he wanted, yet he listened to me and did not."

"Listened to you!" Judith's blue eyes were wide with amazement and shock. "How could he even understand you? None of these savages can understand English."

Deborah swished a wooden bowl through the water. "I wonder. Sometimes, I think they understand more than we guess. Yet, if they did, I suppose they would speak to us. It becomes quite inconvenient at times for them to try and give orders in a language we don't understand." Her smile was faintly wry. "Even Sunflower gets frustrated."

"You're very fond of that girl."

Judith's voice was accusing, and Deborah forgot that she was supposed to be more discreet and looked up at her cousin. "Yes, I am. She's sweet, and full of life and fun. If she were white, she—"

"But she's not white." Judith's motions were abrupt and irritated, and Deborah sighed.

"No, she's not."

"I hope you haven't grown so enamored of your captors that you no longer want to escape," Judith said a few moments later.

"No. I haven't. In fact, I think I have a plan."

For the first time, Judith's voice was eager and full of hope. "Tell me!"

Deborah glanced around. The other women were busy with washing and chattering, and Sunflower sat on a flat rock with reeds she was soaking to make more pliable. The girl seemed entirely engrossed in what she was doing.

"The horses are kept in a meadow just beyond camp. I've gone through there to gather berries. Do you know where I mean?"

Judith nodded. Her head was bent so that her hair hung down in golden streamers, hiding her face. "Yes. I've seen them when I've been out looking for firewood." She splashed some water over her bare, scratched arms. "I've also noticed that many of the men keep their horses tethered close to their tents."

"Only the favorite ones, I think." Deborah paused. It was true. Even Hawk had his favorite horse, a huge gray stallion with black mane and tail, and a thickly muscled chest. She'd seen him brushing it, talking to it, feeding it as if it were a pet. "But that's only at night. The others are left free to roam."

"Yes, I saw a lot of them grazing in the high grass."

"Then maybe you noticed that they run free except for a rope halter. If we could manage to catch two of them, we'd be able to ride out of here."

Judith was silent for a moment. "How would we do that? We're both watched too closely. Your handsome admirer never takes his eyes off you, and when he's away, that girl is your keeper."

"There will come an opportunity. We just have to be ready when it presents itself." Deborah glanced up and saw that Sunflower had waded nearer, bending in the stream to soak the green reeds she used to weave baskets.

She edged away from her cousin, and tried to appear as if she was engrossed in washing bowls. After a moment, she whispered loudly enough for Judith to hear, "Gather as many things as you can for a long journey. Hide them. Be ready. I will do what I can, also. Perhaps the time will come soon."

Judith flung her long hair back from her eyes, and cast Deborah a quick look. "I will. We'd better move apart now."

They did so as unobtrusively as possible.

The women began to straggle back to camp slowly, bearing washed garments in woven baskets. Deborah saw Judith not far ahead of her, her back bent under a heavy load. It was frustrating, not being able to help her cousin. She wished she knew enough Comanche to plead with Hawk to purchase her cousin. Life couldn't be kind to her, not with the bruises she'd seen on Judith's fair skin.

A loud cry caught Deborah's attention, and she glanced up to see her cousin being yanked along by a tall brave she didn't recognize. Judith was trying to resist, but her blond hair was caught in a brown fist. The man laughed cruelly, and made a crude gesture that provoked laughter from others watching. Deborah started forward, but Sunflower grabbed her arm and shook her head.

"I have to help her!" Deborah snapped, and pushed the girl's hand away. She'd gone no more than three steps before a stout woman barred her way, dark eyes glittering with a threat Deborah didn't like. She paused and said calmly, "Get out of my way," but the woman didn't budge.

Sunflower began chattering, obviously pleading for her, and by the time Deborah managed to look for Judith again, her cousin had disappeared. There was no sign of the man who had been tormenting her, and she stood helplessly.

After a moment, the surly Comanche woman walked away, and Sunflower plucked anxiously at Deborah's sleeve. She made signs to reassure her, but her obvious wish to ease Deborah's mind helped only slightly. She felt helpless to assist her cousin, helpless to assist herself. What could she do but make things worse for both of them?

She could only pray for Judith, pray that she was not being used roughly.

When they returned to the camp, Sunflower ducked into the tipi and brought out a large bolt of cotton. She knelt down and put it in Deborah's hands. Her dark, liquid gaze would not meet Deborah's as she communicated her wishes. Deborah understood that she was to sew a dress.

The material was soft and pliable, and she threaded a long needle and began working it through the material, punching holes with swift, certain movements. The stitches were small, the seams neat. She'd been taught well in her childhood, but she'd never dreamed those lessons would one day be performed in a Comanche camp. Sunflower had admired her earlier handiwork, and been quick to produce a paper full of silvery needles.

Most of Deborah's days the past week had been spent in sewing, though occasionally Sunflower brought out a game played with sticks and a blanket. The object, Deborah had learned, was to be the first one to move her awl—a sharp, pointed instrument used in piercing thick animal hides—all the way around the blanket. Positions were marked, and sticks were tossed to determine the number of points given. It had taken Deborah nearly three days just to understand the rules, and her dismal showing at the game had elicited much laughter from the other players.

Though the days were not as harsh as they could be, it was the nights that tormented her. Frequently, she caught a glimpse of Hawk nearby. He made no overt effort to avoid her, nor did he seek her out. Yet she knew that he had not forgotten her. He was only waiting.

That night, Deborah sat outside Hawk's lodge with Sunflower. Insects stung her skin, and she slapped at them idly as she watched the men gather in the middle of the camp. There was something going on. Men laughed and talked, and an air of excitement pervaded the entire village.

Hawk stood to one side, his face impassive in the flickering firelight, his features as cold as if carved from stone. Her heart lurched. He was so handsome, and she wondered if she had truly lost her mind as Judith seemed to think. How could she have come to care for a Comanche? A man so far removed from everything in her normal sphere that it was ludicrous to even think of him in any way but as an enemy? Yet she did.

Impossible, of course. He would never fit into her world, and she did not want to fit into his. Though she was truly fond of Sunflower and felt a bewildering lure to Hawk, she knew she could never be content away from everything familiar.

In the past week, the need to flee had grown so strong as to be almost overpowering. Every glance Hawk gave her, every smoldering stare that scorched her soul and left her aching, made her aware that he would not wait much longer. Soon, he would take her. The brief, heated touch of his eyes on her only marked the passing of time.

Beyond the bright fire-glow and leaping shadows, Deborah could see her cousin's bright head. She stood with some of the other captives, idly for once, watching the activity of the camp. Deborah wished she understood more of their language than she did. Then, perhaps she would understand the reason behind the increased activity.

Weapons were brandished, and horses snorted and pranced nervously, tossing manes and heads and stirring up clouds of dust. The men seemed eager, and Deborah caught a few words that she could understand.

"Kwuhupu. Nabitukuru. Sikusaru. The random words were enough to make her shudder. *Captives. War. Steal.* It was evident that the Comanche intended to make another raid on unsuspecting victims. And there was nothing she could do.

Distressed, she rose to her feet, and Sunflower looked up at her with a troubled expression. *"Ni?yusukaitu?"* the girl murmured, and Deborah stared at her blankly. She stood, too, her round, pretty face concerned. As if at a loss, Sunflower put a comforting hand on Deborah's arm and murmured something she couldn't hear.

"I . . . I'm sorry," Deborah said. "I don't understand." She gave a shrug of her shoulders to explain, then looked past Sunflower to the men again. Someone had begun to play the drums, and the pounding rhythm set some of the men to dancing.

They whooped and howled, chanting words that Deborah could not understand at all. An old, stooped man wearing the head of a buffalo came out from behind a tipi and began singing in a high-pitched voice, and everyone grew quiet to listen. Deborah shivered. The old man shook a large rattle made of a gourd, and another made of hide and bone. His chest was bare, but he wore leggings covering his bony legs. Sewn to the leggings were animal heads, rattles from snakes, skins, and claws.

The Comanches treated him respectfully, even with reverence, she noticed. When he had completed a circle of the open area in the middle of the camp, he paused and lifted his shaggy head. His voice sounded eerie coming from a hairy buffalo skull, but Deborah could tell that his words were having a profound affect on the listeners. Some of them cried out, or exclaimed, and were quickly hushed by others.

Even Sunflower, standing next to her, whispered a frightened word that Deborah could not understand. What could he be saying that would silence the entire camp? Or make them afraid?

She sought Hawk, and found that he was looking at her strangely. There was a taut set to his mouth that alarmed her, and she looked away from him.

To her shock, several of the Comanche were staring at her. Not with curiosity. No, the stares were definitely unfriendly. Hostile.

She took a step back, and found Sunflower had left her side. The girl was several feet away, and beckoned to her to come. Deborah did so, not hurrying, but walking with her head held defiantly high. She didn't know what she'd done, but it was obvious that the old man in the buffalo head had said something about her.

"*Kima,*" Sunflower whispered urgently, and Deborah quickened her steps. When they reached the familiar comfort of the tipi they shared, both were obviously relieved. "*Tsaa,*" Sunflower said with a smile.

"*Tsaa.* Good." Deborah managed a faint smile, but kept looking back toward the middle of the camp. The low fire just outside the tipi shed enough light that she could see the slight lines of worry in Sunflower's face, and she sat down uneasily. Something was definitely the matter. There had not been such hostility directed at her before, and it had something to do with the old man in the mask. She wished she knew what.

Sunflower ducked into the tipi, then returned with the unfinished dress. She thrust it into Deborah's hands.

"I am to keep busy, I see," she said ruefully. "To take my mind off whatever was being said about me over there. All right. I can take a hint. Though I wish I knew why everyone suddenly looked at me as if I had done something dreadful."

She'd thought—until tonight—that the other Comanche women accepted her as a friendly, if rather unlearned, part of their camp. Now, it was brought home to her that she was still considered a stranger in their midst.

What on earth had that masked old man said to elicit such reactions from them?

Hawk stood stiffly in the center of the camp, aware of the gazes directed at him. Even his father had glanced at him. To gauge his reaction to Mukwooru's words, no doubt. He felt a flash of irritation. What was he supposed to do? Deny it? No. He couldn't do that.

Deborah was his captive, his white woman, and he, too, was an outsider. Part of him didn't understand that. And part of him did. Somehow, she would not let him forget it, would not let him relax his guard for a moment. She didn't even know it, didn't even realize that she had that effect on him. It was humiliating and dismaying. Would he never be able to belong anywhere? Would he ever feel as if he was one of the People?

He may have come back, but his heart was not here. He'd returned with the intention of living as one of them, going on raids with them, becoming a part of them. He'd failed. His heart was not in the other world, either. *Watsitu Pihi,* old Spirit Talker had called him. Lost Heart. The old man was right. But he had no intention of admitting it to anyone.

And now Mukwooru—Spirit Talker—claimed there were bad omens in the keeping of the white woman by him, that she would bring trouble down on their people. He didn't believe that. But he didn't disbelieve it, either.

Perhaps Deborah herself would not bring the trouble, but the way he felt about her might.

Hawk turned when he saw his father rise from in front of his lodge, saw White Eagle lift his arm for silence.

"This one is sad to hear your words, old wise man," he said gravely into the falling silence. "You speak of my son as if he would bring trouble upon us."

The old man stepped forward, his skinny chest rising and falling from his exertions. Hawk saw every eye trained on him, and knew what Spirit Talker would say.

"I speak what the gods have said, what they have warned. Your son does not fight the good fight with the other warriors. He fights himself, but he does not fight the enemy." Spirit Talker gave a soft shake of his rattle. "A man cannot live in two worlds. It brings death to one, and grief to the other."

Hawk stepped forward now, and saw the shift of eyes toward him. The fire hissed and popped, and somewhere a dog barked.

"I fight when I choose," he said calmly. "I am not a child to be pulled this way and that at the whim of others."

"But you do not go on raids with our young men," Spirit Talker said slyly. "Not unless they raid the Indé, or go beyond *Kwana kuhtsu paa.* Is that not so?"

For a moment, Hawk remained silent. It was true. He did not participate in the raids against the whites. And he only went along if the destination was below the Rio Grande.

White Eagle spoke up somberly. "It is not the time to fight the white men. They are too numerous. You have not forgotten what has befallen those who have left the white man's reservation?"

"They were foolish," someone said. "They allowed the white soldiers to overtake them."

Shaking his head, White Eagle looked over the crowd. It was evident that most of the young warriors were eager to fight. "It is no shame to die, but it is a shame to be starved and made to keep the white man's ways. Do you want to end the same way? A man should live as a man, not be treated as a dog." His voice rose. "When the white man begins to treat the People as if we are subject to his ways, and we allow it, we are no longer warriors but criminals. I say be patient. Wait. See what time brings."

"Another broken treaty? Already hunters come who kill the buffalo to just leave them lie on the prairie," another man said, his voice angry. "They do not respect the Great Spirit that gave us the buffalo for food. They do not keep their promises. I say we should keep ours— kill any who dare to take from us what is ours."

Hawk stood silently, and saw that White Eagle fought a losing battle. The young men were ready to fight. And he would be expected to join them.

"What about our people who were killed?" a tall, scarred warrior demanded. "Only two moons ago, the blue coats rode upon a party of young men out hunting. They did nothing, yet they were killed. And we are to allow that?"

Hawk exchanged a glance with his father. The scarred warrior's only son had been with that party. He'd been just a boy, not a threat. And he'd been slaughtered like the others. People began to murmur agreement, and a loud buzz ran through the crowd. Some of the glances were directed at Hawk.

A flicker of movement made him shift slightly, and he saw a young man step out from the others and point to him.

"I challenge you, as the son of the chief, to prove your manhood," the young man said, and when he turned his face to the light, Hawk recognized him.

Esatai, or Little Wolf. He had long been a rival of Hawk, and resented the way he came and went in the camp. He had made comments before, and once they had fought. It had been a close fight, with longknives, and Hawk had cut him and won. Now Little Wolf swaggered forward, his stance a challenge.

"We go to steal many horses, and if you are not afraid, you will ride with us," Little Wolf said boldly.

Hawk didn't answer for a moment. It wasn't that he was afraid, or even that he disliked raiding. It could be exciting. But he did dislike being cornered, and his voice was harsh.

"Have I not ridden with you to fight the Cheyenne? The Sioux, and the Apache?" he asked. "I have counted coup, and I have taken enemy scalps. My deeds are recorded on the walls of my lodge. I do not need you to question my courage. I have proven it to any who care to ask."

"Perhaps, but I have not seen you fight the white men. Is it that you need a special magic to fight them? Or are you afraid?"

"My reasons are my own." Hawk's eyes narrowed. "I do not need to share them with you."

For a moment no one spoke or moved. The air was still, charged with tension. Hawk could feel Little Wolf's hate and resentment, but did not offer a soothing reply. He felt no need to negotiate for peace when Little Wolf had begun this matter.

"I say you do not dare go," Little Wolf sneered, and glanced around him as if for agreement. A few muttered in accord.

Only one other man dared speak in his defense, and that was his cousin, *Ohawasápe,* or Yellow Bear. Though younger than Hawk by four years, he had no lack of courage. And he had always admired his older cousin.

"I hear the yapping of a coyote instead of the howl of a wolf," Yellow Bear said angrily. "This one thinks that someone here envies my cousin his many ponies and the scalps in his lodge."

Little Wolf glared at him. "I have many ponies of my own! And there are scalps in my lodge . . ."

"Gray scalps, and your ponies are too slow to catch the turtle, much less run with the buffalo," Yellow Bear retorted. His black eyes were narrowed with fury, and Little Wolf took a step forward.

Hawk lifted a hand. "This is my fight, cousin, though I thank you for your words. It is good to hear them." He turned to Little Wolf. "Do you offer me a personal challenge? I will fight you as we did before, if you like. This one does not mind at all."

Little Wolf shifted uneasily from one foot to the other. He still bore a long, thin scar from one eyebrow to his chin, and it was obvious he recalled who had given it to him.

"I will fight you," he said finally, "once you have proven that you are not too afraid for war. I would not like to soil myself with one who trembles at the thought of counting coup on an enemy."

Hawk spat on the ground to show his contempt, and saw Little Wolf's flush. His voice was a growl, and his eyes narrow when he said, "So be it. I will fight you when we return from our raid."

Spirit Talker rattled his gourd, and red feathers shimmied with the movement. "And you must get rid of the white woman," he said in a high, thin voice. "She will bring many troubles upon us if she stays in our camp."

Hawk felt the stares on him, but allowed no emotion or reaction to show on his face.

"No. The white woman is mine. She stays until I tire of her."

Someone gasped at his refusal, and an angry mutter ran though the crowd. Hawk did not move, did not show by the flicker of an eyelash that he heard or cared. An uneasy shuffling of feet in the dust was evidence that his answer had disturbed many of them, but no one else offered a word or protest. It didn't help his mood any to know that he'd already thought everything Spirit Talker had said.

Enough of this. Tomorrow, he would go to Deborah, and he would prove to her that she was meant to be his woman.

A murky gloom lay inside the tipi, though the eastern sky was beginning to lighten with the approach of dawn. The entrance to the tipi faced east; growing light splintered through the cracks in the hide. Deborah stared down in dismay at the stains on her blankets. She had no idea what she was supposed to do about it here, or how to explain it to Sunflower.

Fortunately, Sunflower seemed to know much more about it than she did, and apparently treated her courses as a natural fact of life. Which, Deborah supposed, they were. It was only in her own society that women were forced to pretend such natural functions did not exist.

Here, she was taken to another lodge. The girl led her away from the tipi where she always stayed. On the fringe of the village, on the far side of the camp and almost up against a rock ridge, a shelter made of brush was tucked beneath a huge overhang. Sunflower turned and looked at her shyly.

Deborah stared back at her, uncertain what to say or do. The shelter was small, and stank. Just outside the open doorway, a circle of stones cradled a bed of black, charred ashes.

"Ikaru," Sunflower said, motioning for Deborah to enter the dwelling.

She shuddered, not liking the strong, sharp smell that was evident even from outside.

"I don't understand," she began, but then Sunflower gave her a frustrated glance and gestured. Slowly, with blunt gestures and a few words she didn't understand, Deborah was finally made to comprehend the girl's meaning. Her face colored hotly.

"Tsihhabuhkamaru," Sunflower said frankly.

Though Deborah wasn't certain of the word's meaning, she had understood enough. "I suppose the fact that . . . that my courses are here has upset the natural order of things."

"Nabi?atsikatu," the girl said softly, and Deborah gave a helpless shake of her head.

She thought the word meant forbidden, or taboo, but she wasn't certain. There were so many unfamiliar words that she frequently grew confused. Embarrassment sharpened her voice.

"So, I suppose I am to remain an outcast until this is over with? Not that I mind. I find that some of your primitive rituals are very childish, but harmless."

Ignoring Sunflower's hurt expression, Deborah ducked into the brush shelter. The smell of sage filled the hut with an almost overpowering scent, and cedar and spruce and other plants hung in bundles from the bent poles that formed the ceiling. The roof was thatched, the floor thick with more bundles of tied plants.

When she turned, she saw that Sunflower had knelt and was starting a fire in the stone-ringed pit outside the lodge. She felt a spurt of remorse that she had been so sharp, and sighed.

"I am sorry to have been rude," she said, and Sunflower looked up with a smile. Deborah saw her ready willingness to forgive and forget with dismay. It only added to her guilt for speaking out of turn. She went to the door. *"Haitsíi."*

Dark eyes met hers and Sunflower said softly, *"Haitsíi. Haa."*

Dear friends. Deborah wondered what Sunflower would think when she left without saying good-bye. It would have to be that way, of course, if there was a hope for success.

Just the thought of what she contemplated made her nerves quiver with apprehension. It would be dangerous, and there was little hope they would make it, but they had to try. She and Judith agreed on that.

Judith. Oh heavens, what would she think when Deborah did not go to the stream? The worst, probably. And there was no way to tell her any different.

Smoke rose from the fire that Sunflower had begun, and the girl was motioning her forward. Deborah stepped out of the brush shelter and paused. The smoke was thick and fragrant, smelling of spruce and sage. Sunflower smiled, and beckoned her forward.

Throwing a robe over Deborah's shoulders, she enveloped her briefly in a tent of smoke, then stepped back, taking the robe with her. Deborah understood. It was some kind of ceremony, probably having to do with her time of month. She nodded gravely, and Sunflower seemed pleased.

"It was foolish," Hawk growled, and Sunflower stared down at her toes again, chastened. "She is not one of the People. She does not need our ceremonies."

And, he added silently, he had not wanted to leave without speaking to her again. That was impossible now that Sunflower had taken her to a purification hut. There was nothing he could do. He would have to wait, and speak to her when he returned.

"You will be safe, my brother?" Sunflower asked timidly, and his anger faded at the sight of her forlorn face. She'd meant well.

"I'll bring you something. Would you like that?"

Her face brightened. *"Haa.* Though I like this last gift you have given me very well."

He frowned. "What gift was that, *nu samohpu?"*

"Deborah. She is very nice."

"She is not for you. You know that. And I did not bring her here."

"But you keep her here. That is what Spirit Talker said. He thinks she will bring us bad luck, but I think he is wrong. She tries very hard to please us."

"To please you, maybe," Hawk muttered, then shook his dark head. "You spend too much time with her, my sister. When I return, I will let you go back to our father's lodge. Old Grandmother has been missing your help."

Sunflower stared up at him, and he saw the hurt in her dark eyes. "You are not pleased with me?"

He put a hand on her shoulder, lifting a strand of her silky black hair between his fingers. "I am very pleased

106

with you. I could not have a better sister. You make my heart glad, and I am proud. But the woman will be able to take care of our lodge, and I will once more sleep beneath my own lodge poles."

Sunflower bent her head, and he smiled faintly. The curve of her cheek was still so childlike and soft, her small hands plump as an infant's. Soon, there would be an offer of marriage for her, and she would no longer be a child. It was the way of the world, but he felt a pang of regret that she would change.

"Perhaps I will bring you back some of the hard candy like I brought you before," he said, and she looked up with a smile.

"Bring enough for two. I am sure your woman would want some of her own."

Startled, Hawk only nodded. He wished he had not been so impulsive, and given Deborah into Sunflower's care. His sister would be distraught when the inevitable happened, and he did not want a rift between them.

He looked up and past her, and saw his father watching them. White Eagle looked grave, and Hawk knew he must be thinking about the coming raid.

"Are you certain this is what you wish, my son?" White Eagle asked when Hawk joined him. "I know your feelings about this matter."

After a moment, Hawk said slowly, "I would not shame my father's house by being thought a coward. I do not make war on women and children as Little Wolf does, but I will fight armed men." He shrugged. "I have said to all that my heart is not in it. But I will go, and I will count as many coup as Little Wolf dreams of doing." His voice grew grim. "And when we return, I will meet him with my knife and we will see if he still speaks of my courage in the same way."

"You have met him before."

"And he has forgotten." Hawk met his father's eyes. "I will remind him."

A glint of humor and pride flickered in White Eagle's dark eyes, and he nodded slowly. "It is good. There are some men who learn slowly." He looked past Hawk, his gaze turning to the far ridges of the mountains. "I feel the winds of change blowing down from the mountain passes, and up from the valleys. We will not remain long in this camp."

"So you believe, like Spirit Talker says, about the white captive bringing bad luck?"

White Eagle's lips thinned. "I believe that one day it must end, as do all things. Chief Kwanah has joined with the Kwahari tukhas, and they are making many raids and killing many of the blue coats. White soldiers are angry about the raids, and our young men speak of war when they should speak of peace." His eyes narrowed on the horizon, as if he could see the future. "There is a new chief at the place called Fort Richardson. He trains his men to fight as the Comanche. He is called *Mangomhente* by the People. To the white man, he is known as Mackenzie."

"And you think he will succeed where others have not."

White Eagle shrugged. "That is not for me to say. This I do know—there was a raid on the Salt Creek Prairie, and four of the black men with buffalo-hair were killed. Maman-ti led the raid that time, and took their scalps. There will be more trouble for that deed."

Hawk was certain of it. He knew the white man's world better than he did his father's, and knew that the outrage against the Negroes would not go unavenged.

"You said in the council that they should be patient. It is by your leadership that we are still free instead of on a reservation. Have they forgotten already?"

"Like Little Wolf, some men have short memories." White Eagle's eyes shifted back to his son. "And now, they call you coward when it is me they would like to accuse. It is not just. I am sorry for it."

Hawk shrugged. "I am accustomed to names. For me, they do not have the same power. I have been called many things."

"And that, too, is a fault that must be laid upon my shoulders."

Uncomfortable with the discussion, Hawk shifted restlessly, and White Eagle must have noticed. He sought his son's eyes.

"Spirit Talker was right about one thing—you cannot walk two paths at once. You must choose."

"I have." Hawk found his father's steady gaze compelling. "I came back to the People."

"But your heart still wanders." A gust of wind lifted White Eagle's hair, and the feathers he wore atop his crown fluttered. "I talk too much, like Old Grandmother," he said after a moment. "I, too, forget. Unwanted advice is like throwing feathers into the wind."

Hawk nodded but his father's words stayed with him. He thought of them when he rode away from the camp, painted and dressed for war. And he was glad that Deborah Hamilton could not see him.

Chapter 9

Deborah shivered in the chill of early morning. The days were warm, but when the sun went down, it grew quite cold. She pulled a buffalo robe up to her chin, and glanced over at Sunflower.

The girl lay snuggled deeply in her furs, her long hair fanned out in a careless tangle. Sunflower had shown Deborah how to bind her hair in two long plaits, or wear it with fur clubbing it in two streamers over her shoulders. Since her clothes had become ragged, she now wore a buckskin dress instead of the lighter cotton skirt and blouse.

Traders, or *Comancheros,* furnished the village with any number of items bought from the white man. Brass kettles, rifles, guns, needles, thread, bolts of calico, anything that was traded in a regular trading post, the Comancheros could provide.

Deborah hated the men who had come to the camp, hated their sly grins in her direction. One man, bolder than the rest, stared at her longer and harder than the others. Tall and thin, with lanky blond hair that brushed his shoulders, he gazed at her with hot, lustful eyes that made her feel as if he could see beneath her clothes. He'd tried to talk to her, but she had been quickly rescued by Sunflower, who spoke harshly to the man, saying Hawk's name. That had given him pause, but he'd still stared at her.

Then she'd overheard him talking to White Eagle, and knew from the glances that he was bartering for her.

But White Eagle refused to trade her, though Deborah had the feeling he would have liked to see her leave his camp. In Hawk's absence, he would not consider any offers for her, and she was grateful. She'd seen Sunflower's anxiety, and was more than aware of the hostile glances at her from the others in camp.

It was becoming unbearable.

Even more unbearable, was the knowledge that when Hawk returned from raiding, he would expect her to lie with him in his robes. Her time was running out, and she realized she would have to escape before he returned.

The raiding party had been gone for two weeks now, and should be back any time. Her brief glimpses of Judith had been few and far between, and she resolved that the next time she saw her, she would set a time.

"This is crazy," Judith muttered. Golden strands of long hair cloaked her face as she bent to wash her feet in the swift-moving stream. "We won't get twenty yards before they catch us."

"Do you have another suggestion?" Anxiety made her tone sharp, and Deborah felt Judith's quick glance.

"No."

"Neither do I. We must go tonight. If I don't get away before the men return . . ."

Her voice trailed into silence, but it was obvious what she meant. Judith made a faint sound of distress.

"I thought you liked him. Hawk. Your . . . captor."

"I said he tried to be kind and hadn't yet hurt me." A short silence fell, and the rushing waters washed over her bare calves in an icy flow. Deborah shivered, not entirely from the chill. "He frightens me," she whispered, and knew from Judith's swift glance that she understood. She turned to look at her. "Judith, I saw—I saw a man grab you one day when we left here. No, don't back away from me. Did he hurt you in any way?"

"No! No, he ... not like you mean." Judith shuddered. "I won't let them hurt me like that. I've seen what the men do, and how they treat some captives, and I swore that I would die before that would happen to me." Her gaze was desperate. "Do you believe me? I'm still pure, I tell you, I am!"

"Of course I do." Deborah inhaled deeply. "I didn't mean to distress you. I was only worried. Do you think we can escape tonight?"

"Yes," Judith said. She relaxed slightly, and her voice lowered. "We will go tonight. I'm sorry I'm such a coward. I'll be ready whenever you say."

"Do you have anything stashed away?"

"A little. It's hidden from that wretched old hag who lives to torment me. No slave ever worked harder than I have since I've been here." She flashed Deborah a faint smile. "If all I had to worry about was an overamorous suitor, I'd feel fortunate."

"Maybe I would, too, if it wasn't Hawk." Bending, Deborah washed her hands, afraid she would see comprehension in her cousin's eyes. It was too near the truth. With another man, she may not lose part of herself, that part that no one could touch unless she allowed them. Hawk had come closer than she dreamed possible.

"Tonight, then," Judith said softly, then uttered a soft sound of dismay. "I'd better move along."

Judith moved a little away from her as a Comanche woman came close, berating the captives with a sharp tongue and long stick. Deborah watched helplessly as her cousin suffered several whacks. When the woman moved on, she managed to catch Judith's eye.

"Tonight—when the moon is highest over the valley."

Judith nodded silently.

The hours stretched endlessly. Routine chores seemed to take forever, and Deborah was clumsy at everything she tried to do. Several times, she had to remind herself to take it slow and not get too nervous.

Sunflower watched her curiously. The girl was more quiet than usual, that and the knowledge of what she planned combined to make Deborah's insides quivery with anticipation.

The tension made her more talkative than usual, and her movements were quick and agitated.

"It gets so dusty in here," she chattered, sweeping at the piles of dust drifting over the pallets with a small grass broom. The stiff grass brushed over the hard-packed floor of the tipi in a brisk motion. Deborah coughed at the rising dust, and caught Sunflower's skeptical gaze on her. It made her even more talkative, and she felt as if she was on a helpless tide.

"We haven't really cleaned, not like I used to clean at home. Oh, I know you can't understand most of what I'm saying to you, but I feel so restless tonight. Every spring and fall, we would always take out our carpets and beat them, and air out the draperies over the windows, and clean cupboards and windows. . . . I know you must think me silly, but it's a long-standing tradition where I come from."

Deborah paused, inhaling deeply to calm herself, and

113

managed a smile. Sunflower smiled back, though a bit uncertainly.

"Tsaa nuusakatu?" she asked softly. When Deborah only stared at her, she gave her a bright smile, nodding her head up and down vigorously. *"Tsaa nuusakatu?"* she repeated.

"Ah . . . happy? Am I happy? Is that what you're asking?" Deborah's throat tightened. "How do I make you understand? I can't be happy away from everything I know. Though I admit I have no one who really cares about me in this world, except perhaps Judith, I can never be happy—*tsaa nuusakatu*—here."

Sudden tears stung her eyes, and Deborah looked down at her hands. She was still holding the broom, and she set it down carefully.

"Ke tsaa nuusakatu?" Sunflower said softly. "No happy?"

Deborah gave her a startled glance. "No. No happy."

To her dismay, the girl's eyes filled with tears. Deborah felt awkward and uncertain. She was so gentle, so sweet, so unlike many others she'd known, white or Comanche, that Deborah felt dreadful for having hurt her.

"I'm sorry," she whispered. "But I can't . . . explain."

"Tosa Nakaai—no happy?" the girl said slowly.

"Hawk—he frightens me. He's so fierce, so arrogant, so determined." Agitated, she said in a rush, "I know you don't really understand because I don't myself, but your brother terrifies me though he hasn't hurt me. I can't explain. Oh, how do I make you understand?"

"Tuhupu—Tosa Nakaai?" Sunflower seemed startled.

Deborah didn't understand what she meant, and lifted her hands. Sunflower chewed on her lower lip a moment, as if troubled. Then she looked back at Deborah. *"Ku?e tsasimapu,"* she said, and pointed to the scalps hanging from the lodge pole. *"Aitu?"*

114

Not quite understanding, Deborah said slowly, "Scalps. Bad—oh. Yes. It is bad where I come from to take scalps. *Kee! Aitu.*"

Sunflower nodded understanding at last, and Deborah put out a hand to her. The girl smiled faintly, and whispered, *Haitsíi.* Deborah. Ohayaa. *Haitsíi.*"

"Yes—*haa.* Deborah, Sunflower, dear friends."

This was harder than she'd thought. She'd never dreamed that Sunflower would grow so fond of her. Or that she would grow so fond of Sunflower. For an instant—only an instant—Deborah considered confiding in the girl. Then she knew that she could not. In spite of the language barrier, they could understand one another fairly well. And she knew that Sunflower would feel compelled to stop her from trying to escape. Her farewells would have to remain unsaid.

Stretching and yawning, Deborah made a great show of being sleepy, and crawled into her robes. Beneath the robes, she changed back into her cotton skirt and blouse. She would not take the dress Sunflower had so generously given her. It would be left behind. Her legs brushed against some hide pouches filled with dried meat and vegetables. She had hidden the small store of supplies earlier. They were not much, but if they did not find a fort or homestead or white man within the first few days anyway, they would probably be found or killed.

It was not a comforting thought to consider, and Deborah found it difficult to pretend to sleep as the fire died down and the tipi grew dark. Outside, the wind blew a constant refrain through the trees, and she could hear the unmistakable sounds of the camp preparing for sleep.

Another noise intruded, and for a moment Deborah

115

could not decide what it was. Then the walls of the tipi shuddered and she realized it was raining.

Rain. Dismayed, she lay in the dark and tried to come to a decision. It would be difficult enough to find their way by the light of the moon, but with clouds hiding it, she would be as lost as if in a snowstorm. Rain. After months with only the scarcest amounts, it rained now, when she and Judith were to attempt escape.

Perhaps by midnight it would be gone. There was nothing to do but wait.

Charred stubble was evidence of a recent prairie fire as the armed, painted braves rode leisurely. Over a hundred warriors straddled their favorite war ponies. Kiowa, Comanche, Kiowa-Apache, Arapaho, and Cheyenne rode side by side. Four Kiowa—Satank, Satanta, Addo-etta, and Maman-ti—led the raid. The site for an attack had been carefully chosen.

Hawk had listened silently the night before as Maman-ti made magic for the warriors. After consulting his oracle, the owl, he told them of his prophecies. Maman-ti—meaning Owl Prophet—was very powerful, and had much influence. He had predicted that there would be two parties of whites to pass near them. They must not attack the first group, but allow it to pass unharmed. The second group could be attacked and easily overcome.

Salt Creek Prairie stretched in a wide belt for about three miles, studded with a large hill and bracketed at each end by a thick stand of trees. It was a favorite area for raids, as any party traveling across that open ground would be easy to cut off from the shelter of the timbered groves.

Hawk knew it was a Butterfield Stage trail, and frequently used by wagon trains as well as travelers. A likely route for their purposes. The warriors had waited an entire day the day before, and had allowed one group to pass below them without harm. Recognizing the formation, Hawk had thought it just as well. The column had traveled in the style of soldiers, who would have put up a fierce fight.

Now he waited with the others on a large, flat hill, watching the trail below. The sky was cloudy, promising rain, and a soft wind blew, making feathers dance. Impatient warriors and horses were restive, and the sun rose slowly to the top of the sky. It was early afternoon, and none had yet passed.

Then one of the men made a soft exclamation, and Hawk felt a peculiar twist in his belly. A wagon train came into view, traveling west. They were only a half-mile from the silent, watching raiders.

Hawk counted ten wagons and twelve teamsters. These men had no chance at all, even if more hid in the wagons.

Wind blew, and dark clouds scudded across the sky. No one moved or spoke. It wasn't until Satanta lifted a bugle he kept constantly with him and blew a charge, that the band broke into wild whoops and streamed down the hill toward the surprised wagon train.

Hawk dug his heels into his gray stallion's sides, and rode down with the others. The thunder of hooves and the wild screams made his blood run fast and his heart pound with excitement. Forgotten were his doubts, his mixed emotions about his heritage. Now he thought only of the moment, the thrill of the chase. All his aggressive instincts were given free rein, and he was one of the Comanche, riding with them, surging forward to count coup and take risks.

Shots rang out wildly, and Hawk saw the frantic

117

teamsters try to circle their wagons. There wasn't enough time. Addo-etta and another Kiowa cut off the lead mules, frustrating their attempt. Bullets whizzed past Hawk, but none came close. The teamsters were making desperate efforts to rally, but the outcome was foretold.

Spying Little Wolf on the left flank of the attacking party as he guided his horse toward the wagons, Hawk altered his direction. His big gray pounded over the parched earth. Dust rose in choking clouds. Screams and whoops filled the air, and there was the smell of sulfur and death all around him.

Hawk leaned forward, guiding his mount with his knees, and sent the well-trained animal toward a wagon. The mules had been cut free, but one lay dead in the traces. He leaped his horse over the tongue of the wagon, lifting his coup stick in one hand.

"A-he!" he shouted, touching one of the teamsters with the end of the foot-long stick. The man swerved to fire at him, and Hawk's deft maneuvering sent his horse out of the way. A bullet spat near his ear, singing through a feather in his hair. Hauling back on his reins, Hawk turned his horse, raced toward the wagon again. He could see the man's face, contorted with fear and rage, and reached out to tap him again with the stick. *"A-he!"* he bellowed again, meaning "I claim it!"

The wagon and its spoils would be his after the fight was over. Wheeling his gray stallion, Hawk saw Little Wolf's snarling face, and flashed him a triumphant smile. Then he sped toward another wagon, this one bristling with men and rifles, and rode straight up to it, touching it with his coup stick and shouting *A-he!*

Satisfied that he had acquitted himself admirably, Hawk rode back a few yards and paused. He saw several drivers bolt from the wagons and begin to run. By this time, the other warriors had formed a ragged circle around the wagons, leaving gaps in the ranks. The men burst through one of the gaps and scattered over the prairie. He saw at once that they were headed for the shelter of the timber around the flat-topped mountain.

Several warriors gave chase, and two of the drivers were shot down. One man was hit in the foot, but ignored it as he continued running.

While he watched, Hawk saw the five men make it to the safety of the trees and brush. The warriors gave up and returned to the wagon train. There could be more men inside the wagons, waiting with loaded guns to shoot the first man to approach, and the attackers milled just out of range.

Hawk hung back. He didn't care about the rest of the booty. He had come to make a point, and he'd done so. Even Little Wolf would have to silence his accusations. For a man to ride into a volley of bullets and count coup was considered more courageous than hand-to-hand combat.

His horse pranced nervously beneath him. Gunfire slowed, then stopped completely. The sky had grown even darker. Hawk wheeled his mount back across the prairie, when he heard a final shot. Someone screamed, and he looked back to see one of the young Kiowa warriors pitch to the ground. A surviving man in one of the wagons had shot him in the face when he'd recklessly raced to the wagon to count coup.

After a moment of brief, stunned silence, the other warriors began whooping furiously. They dragged out the hapless driver and chained him face down on one of the wagon tongues, then roasted him over a slow fire. His screams rose to a high-pitched squeal, then finally faded into silence.

Hawk watched silently. Some of the wagons were

burning. The clouds had grown dark and ominous overhead, and the warriors began gathering their prizes from the wagons and scattering the rest over the prairie. To Hawk, the two claims he had made were worthless, but he knew the others would think it strange if he did not claim them.

He rode forward slowly, not looking at the dead driver still smoldering over the fire. The contents of the wagon were sparse, as the wagon train had been hauling corn. He took two rifles, some ammunition, and a pouch of tobacco from under the wagon seat, then leaped to the wagon bed. He caught a glimpse of something bright, and bent down to find a cloth sack filled with hard candy. Remembering his promise to Sunflower, he took it.

They rode away from the burning wagons, herding over forty mules ahead of them and carrying six scalps. As part of the rear guard, Hawk turned to look back at the wreckage of the raid.

A burst of rain fell from the black clouds overhead in a blinding sweep, rushing across the plains in dense sheets. Hawk blinked rain from his lashes, peering at the sputtering fires behind them. The rain would wash away any trail they might leave behind them. The raid had been successful.

Hawk turned his back and nudged his pony into a trot as the rain beat down on him. He would be glad to get back to his own tipi. And, he would be glad to see the woman who visited his dreams every night, her fiery hair framing a pale face.

Even the cold rain could not quench the fire she'd begun in him.

Chapter 10

Hawk stared down at his sister's face. Tears gathered in the corners of her eyes, and she looked drawn. She could not meet his gaze, and his eyes narrowed.

"When did this happen?"

Sunflower hesitated, then said so softly he had to lean close to hear, "Three suns ago."

Stunned, Hawk tried to stem his rising fury. His hands balled into fists, and it was then he recalled the bag of candy he'd carried into his lodge. It hung heavy in his hand. Opening his fingers, he dropped it to the floor, then pivoted on his heel and ducked out the open flap.

Sunlight struck him sharply, and he squinted against it. Deborah and Judith had stolen two horses and left in the night, and no one seemed to have heard them. He didn't believe it for a moment. Someone had to have heard them, yet had done nothing to stop them. They would have been glad to see the white woman go, especially after Spirit Talker's warning.

Someone called out to him as he strode angrily across the camp, and Hawk paused. It was Yellow Bear, his young cousin.

"Your woman has gone," he said when he caught

121

up. Hawk nodded tersely. "I will go with you to get her."

"*Kee*. She may have been taken by the *Indé*. It will be a long ride to find her."

"I tried to follow their trail. It should have been easy after the rain, but a buffalo herd had gone over their tracks."

Hawk's head lifted. So many things could have happened to her. A buffalo stampede was always dangerous, and if the Apache hadn't gotten her, then another band may have. Or the Comanchero. He felt a strong aversion to the men who traded with white and Comanche, and didn't trust them.

"Two women should not be hard to find," Yellow Bear said quietly, and Hawk looked down at him.

"*Haa*, but these two women know nothing about where to go. They could be anywhere."

"And we will find them."

A faint smile curled Hawk's mouth, and he nodded. "It will not be easy."

"But you will not give up."

"*Kee*, I will not stop until she is back in my lodge. And I will make her sorry she dared so much."

"If she is still alive."

Hawk couldn't help the twist in his gut, and hoped it did not show. "And if she has not made it to a fort."

His father was more to the point.

"If she alerts the blue coats, our entire village is in danger."

Hawk looked up from his gear. He had cleaned it, and was readying it to follow Deborah. "Do you think she will do so?"

"Perhaps not willingly." White Eagle sucked on his pipe and regarded his son gravely. "It seems that Spirit Talker's prophecy may come true."

"I wouldn't put it past the old buzzard to have helped her escape just to make sure of that," Hawk said with a grunt.

"There are ways of helping without acting," White Eagle said after a moment of silence.

Hawk knew what he meant. Just turning one's head and not seeing was as effective as putting Deborah on a horse.

"My cousin rides with me." Hawk said. "And there are ten others who have said they wish to go."

"If she has been taken by the Indé, there will be a chance for glory." White Eagle shifted slightly on the balls of his feet, and looked directly into his son's eyes. "If she has been taken by blue coats, there will be a chance for death."

"She must be found before that happens. The risk is great, and no man wishes to see our camp destroyed." Hawk looked away from his father's eyes. He knew what lay beneath the words, the unspoken warning. When and if the soldiers found out that Deborah had been taken by Comanche to this camp, they would come to find them. Their village would no longer be safe. They would have to move to protect the women and children, and leave this spot that offered plenty of forage for the horses and water and game for the people. Spirit Talker was right. He had brought trouble on the camp with his hunger for the white woman.

The wind sang through the trees. The sun was warm and bright. Hawk felt the weight of his decision lean heavily on him, and knew that he would have to leave his father's camp. It was inevitable. He could not risk them all for his own desires. Sadly, he waited for his father to speak. He could see the words he wanted to say, see that events rested heavily on White Eagle.

"Long ago, as you know," White Eagle began softly,

"I had the same need for a woman that you feel now. She was your mother. I thought well of her, and let my heart lead me to risk my people. You are doing the same. Think on it long and hard, my son. What a man does when he follows his heart can have consequences that effect many people."

"I'm not following my heart," Hawk said roughly. "The woman is mine. And she has dared escape. It is my shame that she has done so. I will bring her back to my lodge, and she will not leave me again."

White Eagle looked at him without speaking. Then he nodded. "It is as you say. Perhaps I speak only of what happened to me. My heart lay on the ground for many moons after your mother returned to her people. I did not feel that the Great Spirit smiled upon me again until you came into my camp as a young man. Then I knew that there was a reason for all that had happened. You are that reason, my son. You have learned to walk in both worlds, but have not yet found your way. Perhaps when you do, our people will also find the way to remain free."

Both men looked at one another, awareness shadowing their eyes. Neither had any illusions about the future of the Comanche people, and the truth was hard to bear.

A shrill yip punctuated the hot wind, carrying to where Deborah and Judith rested their horses. They looked up, then exchanged worried glances.

"A coyote," Deborah said after a tense moment passed. "It was only a coyote."

"I hope so." Judith pushed a damp strand of limp blond hair off her forehead. "We've had enough problems without being attacked by wolves. Or worse."

She didn't have to elaborate. The fear of being found

124

by hostiles was a constant nudge in the backs of both their minds. It had been three days, and Deborah worried that they were lost. She'd done her best to guide them by the landmark of the sun, keeping its position fixed firmly in her mind.

They seemed no closer to civilization than they had three days before, though they should have been. It had taken the Comanche raiders only three days to take them from the Velazquez hacienda, so by now, they should have stumbled across at least a remote homestead.

"Are you certain we're not going in circles?" Judith asked after a moment. She dipped her feet into the shallow water of a stream, wincing at the sting of cuts and bruises. "I could have sworn I've seen that hill before."

Deborah gazed glumly at the flat-topped hill thrusting up from a flat expanse. "Me, too. Lord help us, Judith, I'm not certain of anything. Our food is almost gone, and we've not seen anything resembling civilization, and now I'm beginning to wonder if we will. We could be headed in the opposite direction. For all I know, Hawk's village is just over the next hill."

"Wonderful." Judith lifted her dripping feet from the stream and began to shove them back into her tattered shoes. "That should be a heartwarming homecoming. I can just see his delight when you show up again."

"Somehow, I don't think *delight* is the proper word." A spasm of apprehension shot through Deborah. What if he did find them? From the little she'd gleaned while in their camp, she realized that Comanche men did not gladly suffer a woman's rebellion. Sharp words were exchanged, usually ending with the woman's surrender. Resistance, from what she'd observed, was tendered in other, more subtle forms. Flagrant defiance would be dealt with harshly. It was a male-dominated society, largely dependent upon the man's ability to hunt and bring home food. And make war.

Deborah's throat tightened. "Time to ride," she said to banish the frightening thoughts. "We won't get anywhere by sitting here."

"We're not getting anywhere anyway," Judith said in a weary voice, but she rose to her feet. "If I eat one more dried prairie turnip, I think I'll heave it back up."

"It's better than nothing."

"Admitted." Judith smiled suddenly, some of her old spirit flaring. "But not by much. I had to dig so many of those things while slaving for that vicious hag, I can find them blindfolded. If we run out of them, just give me a few minutes to dig some more."

Deborah laughed, her spirits lifted by her cousin's wry humor. "Let's hope that we find rescue soon. I would prefer eating something more familiar."

"Or seeing something familiar." Judith caught her horse by its trailing rope, and led it to a flat rock to mount.

They moved slowly away from the stream, then urged their mounts into a brisk lope. It was quiet. Wind rustled the tall grasses, and an occasional bird called out. There was only the sound of hooves striking the ground, and the swish of their passage through the grass.

Deborah found it more difficult than she'd considered to stay on her horse's broad back without a saddle. Her thighs were raw from rubbing against the bare hide, and her cotton skirt, up around her knees, gave no protection. Judith was in the same shape. The first day had been the worst. By now, she had grown more accustomed to the motion and constant rubbing.

A cry drifted from overhead, and shading her eyes with one hand, Deborah looked up. A hawk wheeled in the sky in lazy circles, regal and dangerous. It was hunt-

126

ing. It drifted on the wind currents for a moment, then with another cry, it swooped earthward like an arrow. There was a thin squeak as some prey met its doom, then nothing. Deborah shivered.

Hawk. Like the bird, he was as predatory, and as determined. And when he found her gone, he would come after her. She knew it. And she knew that he would be furious if he found her. She had to make it to safety, or she would be like that poor doomed creature.

Another yip, shrill and sharp, sounded. It cut through the air like a knife, and Deborah's head snapped around. It was close. Much too close. Her heart began to pound hard and furiously.

"Deborah," Judith began in a trembling voice, but could not finish.

The yip altered to a whoop, and both women turned to see what they'd feared for three days—horsemen. They were riding hard, coming over a far hill at a dead run. Long black hair streamed behind them, and at the front of the line of riders, a familiar figure rode a gray stallion.

"Hawk." Her voice came out hoarse and soft, and Deborah was suddenly seized with panic. She dug her heels into her horse's sides, sending it bounding forward.

The wind whipped her hair loose from the confining braids, lashing it across her face in stinging ribbons. Deborah bent low over her horse's head, urging it on with a desperation borne of terror. *Hawk.* The one, terrifying word reverberated in her head over and over.

Belly-high grass slashed at her bare legs as her mount ran, and stands of post oak and the taller fringe of spruce and cedar soon obscured the line of their pursuers from their vision. Deborah heard Judith beside her, her horse blowing loudly as it tried to keep up.

There was hope, if they'd managed to leave the men behind this quickly, Deborah thought frantically. She turned to glance at Judith, and saw her cousin's frightened face.

"We can make it!" she shouted. "Don't stop!"

For Deborah, the world had narrowed to frantic flight and the thunder of hooves. Wind snagged her clothes, and she could feel the damp heat of the horse between her thighs. A distant sound, like a waterfall, penetrated her terror, and she realized it was the thunder of pursuit. Hawk would have no intention of giving up now, not when he had them in his sight.

The knowledge spurred her to greater effort, and praying she would stay on, she tangled her fingers in the horse's mane and bent low over its neck, as she had seen men do in a race. It seemed to work. The animal's long legs stretched out even farther, and she fairly flew over the uneven ground as if on wings.

As they topped a rise and started down the other side, Deborah glanced at Judith again. She was gamely trying to stay astride her laboring mount. The horse was as lathered as her own, winded and blowing.

Just ahead, the ground dipped to a shallow hollow, then rose again, steeply this time, the ridge high over their heads. Deborah doubted whether they could stay on their horses without saddles, not at that steep angle, but there was no other choice.

"Try it," she urged her cousin over her shoulder, and pressed her mount up the slope. The mare stumbled, regained its balance before Deborah pitched from its back, and managed to gain the top of the ridge. She allowed it to pause a moment, trembling and snorting, and glanced back at Judith.

Her blood froze. Incredibly, the Comanche had gained enough distance so that they were almost upon

128

them. It would be only a matter of moments. Wild whoops and yells rode the air, and Judith's mount struggled up the slope at a slow pace. Deborah's brief glance of their pursuers was imprinted on her mind as she wavered indecisively.

Hawk, his broad muscular frame that seemed a part of the animal he rode, was at the front. She shivered in spite of the hot sun beating down.

Wheeling her horse around in panic, Deborah fought it for a moment before it began the descent. Rocks skittered from beneath the hooves, bouncing. Judith was not far behind her now, and as she forced her horse forward, Deborah caught a glimpse of movement at the bottom of the hill.

There was a flash of blue and yellow, a runnel of sunlight reflected from a rifle barrel. Her heart skipped a beat, then accelerated rapidly as the flash of blue reappeared from behind a stunted grove of mesquite. Cavalry.

"Judith, hurry!" she screamed, pushing at the hair in her eyes and urging her mount to greater speed. "Hallooo!" she called out desperately when it seemed as if the soldiers did not see her. Oh, why couldn't they see or hear her?

She shouted again, and this time the soldiers looked up and saw her. They seemed startled, then switched direction and started up the steep slope. Deborah's heart lurched. There were only three or four of them, not enough to fight the Comanche riding hard in their direction. Neither group of men had seen the other yet, and the two women were caught in between.

Judith's mount struggled down the slope, and Deborah saw that it was almost completely blown. She exchanged a quick, agonized glance with her cousin.

"Go on," Judith urged. "You can make it."

"Not without you." Deborah knew that two women on one horse would be as slow as pushing a winded mount. "Here. Take my horse." She threw a leg over to dismount, but Judith shook her head.

"No, let's try. There's no time."

She was right. The Comanche crested the hill, and saw the soldiers at the same time as the cavalrymen saw them. The charge immediately changed direction, with the Indians now interested in the armed soldiers. The cavalrymen swore loudly; their oaths were accompanied by the clang of sabers and sounds of pistols being drawn.

"Run for it!" one of the soldiers called to Deborah and Judith. "We'll try to cover you!"

Shots rang out, and Deborah squeezed her eyes shut in panic at the same time as she made a decision. Leaning over, she slapped her cousin's horse on the rear, sending it in a leap forward.

"Ride!" she screamed at Judith. "I'll try to divert Hawk . . ."

"Don't be foolish," Judith began, but her words were lost as her horse, panicked, bolted down the slope with the last of its strength.

Deborah swerved her mount to one side, hoping to distract Hawk from her cousin. One saved would be better than neither of them.

She rode at an angle away from her cousin and the soldiers, riding as fast as she could, not daring to look back over her shoulder. The thunder of pursuing hooves drew closer and closer, and a dry sob tore from her throat.

Her fingers tangled in the whipping mane of her horse and her legs slid on the sweaty back of the chestnut as she tried to grip more tightly. Fear was an almost tangible rider, choking her. For some reason, her senses were sharpened to her surroundings; she could hear the rasping efforts of her mare, smelled the sharp scent of horse and sage and heat, felt the slap of tall grasses on her bare legs with almost separate distinction. They all blended, yet remained as sharply distinct as if she was experiencing them separately.

Then she heard the slap of leather against horse, and knew that her pursuer had caught up to her. She glanced back briefly, and saw Hawk.

Astride his huge gray stallion, he looked as fierce and brutal as anything she could have envisioned in her worst nightmares. His long dark hair was caught back with a leather strap around his forehead, whipping in the wind. A hawk feather fluttered over one ear. Paint streaked his bronzed face in jagged smears that lent him an air of savagery, and she had the fleeting thought that he'd hardly needed it to seal that impression.

Hawk leaned from his horse, reaching out for her reins.

One last desperate effort to escape him spurred her to rein her mount in a circle, but she was easily overtaken. Hawk's muscular arm shot out, and coiled around her waist to drag her from the horse in an effortless motion. There was the brief sensation of falling before he caught her to him, and though she struggled, he managed to drag her face-down across his thighs and hold her.

Her legs dangled on one side, her head and arms the other, and she tried to breathe. It was difficult, since her stomach was pressed against his iron-hard legs and the croup of the horse. His firm hand in the middle of her back held her still, and he growled something at her that she was glad she didn't understand. His voice was harsh, angry, rough.

Grass swirled just below her face; she could see the thrust of the horse's hooves, smell the rich scent of sage

131

and animal and man all mingled together. Shouts filled the air, and loud *pop-pop-pops* exploded. Deborah tried to lift her head, but Hawk slammed it back down again.

"Puaru," he snarled, and she recognized the order to stop. Her struggles ceased. It would be dangerous to keep resisting when so much else was going on.

In the chaos, she heard Judith scream, heard a man break into familiar curses. Everything was a blur of time and motion as Hawk kneed his stallion through the tall grass and she bounced head-down. The shooting grew louder, and she felt Hawk shift, saw the brief flash of gunmetal pass her eyes as he brought up his rifle, heard a loud explosion.

"No!" she screamed, trying to lever her body up. "You might hit Judith!"

Uttering a rough comment, Hawk held her down with one hand. She heard him shout something at the others, heard the gunfire slow, then stop. Another scream split the air. A last shot was fired, the whine echoing through her head.

Hawk was wheeling his mount and riding back down the slope at a fast pace. Deborah was afraid to move, afraid she would slide from the horse and be trampled. She curled her hands into the edge of the grass-stuffed pad that was used as a saddle, and clung tightly. The jolting rhythm of the horse settled into a smoother pace, muscles bunching and stretching out, legs moving up and down. Finally, when she thought her ribs must be broken or cracked, Hawk reined his mount to a halt.

She caught glimpses of other horses bunching around them, saw fringed leggings and moccasins, heard the harsh, guttural sounds of the Comanche. Her spirits drooped badly. She fought to breathe, and heard Hawk give a command to the men with him.

132

"Pitsa mia?ru. Notsa?kaaru."

Her eyes closed briefly. She understood *go* and *take*. She shuddered. Not that she'd hoped they would release her. It was just that they'd been so close, so very close. They'd failed. And now they had their angry captors to deal with.

What had seemed to last forever, had taken only a few minutes. Hawk bunched a fistful of her blouse in one hand, and hauled her backward off his lap. He released her, and Deborah plummeted to the ground with a soft cry of alarm.

She sprawled on her hands and knees, but struggled to her feet as quickly as possible. She pushed at the hair in her eyes and tilted back her head to look at Hawk. He was a dark silhouette against the bright, burning sky, and she flinched.

Deborah's heart constricted. Even with his features in shadow and the sun in her eyes, she could see the fury in his face. His eyes were so cold they were almost black, and his mouth was a straight, savage slash across his face that made her shiver with apprehension.

A glance beyond Hawk showed her the other Comanche, and her cousin. Judith struggled and sobbed in front of a lean young brave who held her firmly. He grinned as he ran his hands familiarly over Judith's body, ignoring her frantic efforts to avoid him. One of the men watching said something, and they all laughed. It was ugly laughter, filled with tones that made Deborah shudder.

Judith glanced up, saw Deborah's gaze on her, and bent her head again, drooping in her captor's grasp. There was an air of defeat about her, of hopeless resignation and shame. Deborah felt the sting of tears in her eyes.

All was lost. Lost, lost, lost, and her fate was now in the hands of a cold-eyed man with murder in his stare. Chin lifting, Deborah waited silently.

Chapter 11

"Miaru!"

Deborah stared up at Hawk silently, afraid to move. When he lifted his rifle and pointed it ahead of them, repeating, *"Miaru!"* she reluctantly turned and began to walk. She straightened her spine, refusing to allow him to see how frightened she was as she moved through the tall grass.

The rough edges of the grasses sawed at her hands and arms mercilessly. It even grazed her chin a time or two, but she did not pause. She could hear their horses following, the soft *shunk* of hooves cutting into the soft ground, and a low murmur of voices muffling Judith's faint sobs.

Her throat tightened. The sky was still a bright, hot blue, and the wind bent the grass in places. Perspiration began to trickle down her face, and wet her blouse so that it stuck to her in damply uncomfortable patches. Deborah tried to ignore it, tried to ignore the line of Comanche ranging behind her.

Ruts cut through the slope at an angle, and stones caught at her feet as she trudged through the grass. The soles of her feet in the soft moccasins scraped against sharp edges of the rocks, scrunched dried grass and

135

shifted in the soft earth. She stumbled several times, but managed to keep going.

When she finally began to slow, Hawk rode up close behind her and nudged her with the muzzle of his rifle. By that time, fear and anger was an even mix. Blood pounded in her ears so hot and loud that she could barely hear his growled commands for her to go, hurry.

How *dare* he do this! To pretend to kindness as he had done in the past, then switch so abruptly and confusingly to a man without mercy, was more than she could endure. Not after all the terror and trials she'd been through. Only a finely developed sense of survival kept her from wheeling on him and shouting the few Comanche words she knew.

That sense of survival abruptly deserted her when she stumbled over a dry rut and sprawled headlong in the grass. Hawk merely leaned over and hauled her carelessly to her feet by the back of her blouse and a long strand of hair. The unexpected pain made her gasp, and catapulted her into rage.

As he set her on her feet she whirled, lashing out with one arm and spooking his horse. It reared, squealing, and she had to step back out of the way of the lethal hooves as Hawk reined it back down. His movements were so swift and harsh that the animal almost sat back on its haunches, sleek muscles quivering.

A long, lean leg arched over the horse's back, and Hawk slid to the ground, holding the stallion with one hand and reaching for Deborah with the other. She dodged his grasp and turned to run, but a Comanche warrior cut her off. When she turned another way, she was cut off again by a skilled rider, and jerked to a halt. She would not provide them with sport.

Deborah folded her arms over her chest and waited. She didn't wait long. Hawk gave another terse command, and the men with him nudged their horses into a brisk walk, then to a canter. She saw Judith still struggling against her captor, her golden head bright and tangled, her cries muffled. A feeling of helpless misery welled in her, and Deborah could not answer when her cousin called out to her.

"Deborah!"

That one word held a wealth of emotion.

Hawk seemed not to notice. His eyes had darkened to a blue so deep as to be indigo, and were fastened on her face with such an icy glare that Deborah shivered despite the searing heat of the sun. He must have noticed. A faint smile curled one corner of his mouth into a hateful smirk.

She wanted to hit him then, rage at him and provoke him into getting it over with. Her fate would not be changed by anything she did. It was obvious he'd already decided upon it.

Fear, anger, and despair had wrought havoc with her nerves. They were raw, lacerated with constant strain. Her mood could only be a little less dangerous than his.

"You are nothing more than a savage," she said coldly, injecting as much scorn in her voice as possible. She wanted him to understand the meaning if not her words. "You are beneath contempt. *Aitu!* Evil, mean, cruel—a heathen. Nothing you do to me will make a difference. You can hurt my body but you cannot touch my soul—not without my permission and I will never give that." Her chin lifted so that she met his eyes, saw the flicker in them that told her he recognized her contempt. A mocking smile curled her mouth. "Ah, I see that you can at least understand that. I don't wonder. A man who has no scruples should be accustomed to contempt."

For a long moment he didn't move. The wind lifted

his hair in a slight shifting motion, and the hawk feather spun against the harsh angle of his cheekbone. His gaze stabbed at her with a ferocity that made her wish suddenly she'd not spoken out, and Deborah tried not to tremble.

His proximity was almost like a physical blow; his body radiated raw power, masculinity and hostility, and it took every ounce of determination she possessed to keep from attempting mad flight.

For a moment, Hawk stared at her without reacting. Then before she could move, his hand flashed out to grasp her by one arm. She pulled back, her arm uplifted and between them as she stared at him defiantly, half-daring him to hurt her, half-pleading with him not to. Her heart thudded painfully against her rib cage, and the tightness in her throat seemed to be squeezing it shut.

Slowly, relentlessly, with the hot sun beating down and the wind whispering around them, Hawk drew her to him and held her against his hard body. Deborah could see the rich black flecks in the pitiless blue of his eyes, could distinguish each spiky eyelash. His gaze held her mesmerized; she noted distractedly the faint scars that creased his eyebrow, his cheek, his jawline. She could smell him, smell the musky male scent of him mixed with a hint of tobacco and leather and wind and sun, all combined to throw her senses into disorder.

And, suddenly, she was afraid, terribly afraid. Of him. Of herself. Of all that had brought them to this moment, at this time and place. Death wasn't what she feared, but the searing knowledge of her desire for this man, this hard-faced Comanche who swung from gentleness to brutality as quickly as the wind shifted. It was an inexplicable emotion that left her feeling somehow ashamed of her weakness. But God help her, all she could think of when he held her so close to him was

138

how he'd kissed her and touched her and made her body ache for him in ways she'd never dreamed.

Anger fled, and the terrible weakness remained. Time ceased to exist; only the heat from the sun and his touch filled her now. Dry grasses rustled around them, and his horse stamped its hooves impatiently. Hawk's fingers still cut deeply into the fragile bones of her wrists and his mouth was a straight, taut line in his face.

Without warning, his arm flexed, and he lifted her effortlessly into his arms and tossed her atop his horse. Vaulting up behind her, he reached around her for the reins as the horse started off at a brisk trot. Deborah didn't know whether to be relieved or terrified.

It was obvious he'd come to some kind of decision about her, and she wondered what he meant to do as they caught up with the others.

Nothing was said, no explanation or even a threat as the small band rode hard and fast over the plains and back up into the mountains. The only stops were brief pauses to water and rest the horses, and Deborah and Judith were not allowed close to one another.

It took the Comanche only eight hours to travel the distance it had taken Deborah and Judith three days to cover. At times they traveled in a wide circle, it seemed, as if trying to cover their tracks. They crossed and recrossed their trail several times. Deborah's brief hope that the soldiers would be able to follow them began to fade.

Most of the time, Hawk sat stiffly behind her, his arm coiled around her so tightly that her least movement or struggle cut off her breath. She quickly learned that he felt no compunctions in restricting her breathing, and did not offer more than that first, cursory resistance.

As the familiar valley came into view again and the line of men rode down at a swift pace, the setting sun diffused the jagged peaks of the mountains in a blaze of crimson and deep purple. Night insects had begun their song in the tall grasses, and the rush of the mountain stream grew louder and louder.

Slowly, the weary horses stirred up dust as they rode into the village, threading between the tipis to the growing curiosity of the residents. Deborah saw flaps thrown back, heard hushed voices reporting of their arrival. At the far end, she saw Hawk's lodge, and fastened her gaze on it.

This arrival was different from the last, when the women and children had rushed out in excitement to greet the homecoming raiders. This time, solemn faces stared up as they passed through the staggered lines of tipis. Deborah knew that the punishment for escape would be severe, and she prayed for the courage to face it.

Someone asked Hawk a question as they passed, and his snarling reply made Deborah shudder. There was nothing in his tone to indicate leniency.

Sunflower awaited them in front of her father's lodge, her huge liquid eyes filled with anxiety. She called out as they approached, *"Ahó, samohpu."* Her words were hopeful, but cautious.

Hawk replied in a growl and did not stop there but rode past to his own lodge, where he swung down from his horse and pulled Deborah with him. She stumbled and half-fell, and the quick arm he put around her waist was less than gentle.

"Tahkamuru," he muttered in a savage tone that made her throat close with apprehension. His meaning was clear, and she could feel Sunflower's anxious gaze on her. Deborah did not dare move while he tied his stallion to a sapling by his lodge. She waited quietly, and

140

when he turned back to her, she met his cold gaze steadily.

He grunted something she didn't hear, grasped her by the arm, and shoved her ahead of him into his tipi. With a quick motion, he lowered the flap and tied it. No one would dare enter a man's lodge when the flap was lowered.

As soon as he released her wrist, Deborah took several steps away from him, her eyes fixed on his implacable features. She inhaled deeply, hoping he would understand some of what she said.

"This escape—*kuaru*—was my idea. *Nue*. Uh, no—*nu*." She tried to remember the proper inflections to convey her meaning to him, the right words that would convince him it had all been her idea and not Judith's. The Comanche words would not come, the few she had learned eluding her as she faced him. In a stumbling, halting monologue, Deborah did her best to save her cousin from enduring harsh retribution.

"Hawk—Tosa Nakaai—please ... *keta tsahhuhyaru* ... this was all my fault. Don't ... don't hurt her—"

Her voice broke off abruptly when he made a sharp, impatient sound, and his brows dipped low in a scowl over his eyes. Grabbing her wrist when she began to back away at his fierce expression, Hawk's voice was low and rasping.

"*Subetu*— it is finished, Deborah. You had best plead for yourself instead of your cousin."

Deborah blinked. She stared up at the lustrous velvet of his indigo eyes, the mocking line of his mouth, the primitive masculine beauty of his face. His harsh words made perfect sense, and it took her a moment to realize why. *He'd spoken English!*

She went hot, then cold, then hot again, her face suffusing with color. "You speak English."

"*Haa*—yes. And Comanche, and Spanish, and a bit of Apache and Cheyenne as well as Shoshone." Silky filaments of raven hair swung with the motion of his shaking head. "You have a good grasp of the obvious."

His sneering contempt lashed at her. Deborah's fear for herself and her cousin vanished in a sweep of hot rage. Her small hand curled into a fist, and she saw that he noticed the involuntary reaction. A hard smile slanted his mouth, and he tightened his grip on her wrist.

"Just so you aren't tempted to slap me again," he said softly.

The tension of the past weeks erupted unexpectedly. All her silent admonitions to remain calm evaporated as if never existing. Deborah uttered a shrill scream of rage and launched herself at him, hitting his broad, impervious chest with a solitary fist, scratching him before he could capture her free hand. She kicked, and she bit, and she sobbed every vile name she could think of when he wrestled her to the ground and held her down until she was exhausted. Then he hauled her to her feet again, and Deborah saw that he wasn't even slightly winded by her assault.

"Damn you," she breathed, and saw his brow lift.

"Swearing, Deborah? A proper lady like yourself?"

"I suppose it's the company I've been forced to keep lately."

"So you'd like to think, I'm sure."

She stared at him, a hundred questions crowding her mind. The first one to erupt was, "Who are you?"

"Tosa Nakaai. Hawk. A hunter. A Comanche."

"No, I mean really." She shook her head. "You're one of them, the Comanche, yet . . . yet you aren't."

"You're very observant." He released her wrist with an abrupt motion, giving her a slight shove away from

142

him. "No, I am not full-blooded Comanche, but I thought you'd have guessed that by my eyes. You remarked on it that first day, remember?"

"Yes, I remember. I just thought perhaps you were really one of them."

"No." His voice was bitter, and he began to pace around the small space in quick, restless steps. "I'm not one of anybody. I'm not Comanche, and I'm not white. I'm what's known as a half-breed, and to most people, that's less than human."

Bewildered, both by his bitterness and her own churning emotions, Deborah rubbed idly at her wrist.

"Then why are you here?"

He turned, flashing her a grim smile. "Because it's the closest thing to home I have. Or had."

"Had?"

"Do you think those soldiers will forget about seeing you? No. And when they manage to follow, they won't stop to ask questions. They've been known to kill anything that moves when they ride into an Indian camp."

"I don't believe that. Not—" She stopped, flushing, and he gave her a sardonic look.

"Not white men? Think again. Comanche aren't the only ones who can be ruthless."

"It's hard to convince me of that when I've been your slave for almost two months."

"Have you been mistreated? Beaten? Starved? Raped?"

Deborah's flush deepened, and her chin quivered slightly at his steady regard. "No. Terrorized, though. And no one has a right to enslave another."

"If I'm not mistaken there was a recent war fought over that little fact, right?" Hawk mocked. "And it was between white men."

Her chin tilted higher. "Yes, that's true, but—"

143

"But you're saying that's different. Why? Because no Indians were involved? Or because *you* weren't involved."

"I was involved. Indirectly, perhaps, but my family suffered during the war."

"Suffered? How badly? List your hurts for me, Deborah. I'm interested in hearing them."

Angry, she snapped, "None of this is the issue! You played a horrible trick on me. All this time, you could have spoken to me in a language I understand and made life easier. Yet you chose not to. And since you're half-white, you could have taken me back, released me. If you're part of this village, you could have explained it somehow. After all, you traded for me. You could have done anything you wanted with me."

He looked at her, and his eyes changed, a subtle shift of color and intensity that made her throat close and her pulses race with apprehension.

"Yes," he said softly, "I could have done anything I wanted with you. And almost did. But I still haven't done what I want most. Until now."

"Un . . . until now?" Deborah hated the way her voice came out in a squeak, but there was something so suddenly intense about him, so threatening, that she could barely force the words out. "What do you mean?"

"I mean," he said, reaching out with a leisurely hand to cup her chin, "that I'm going to finish what I started. What I should have done that first day. All this waiting has been for nothing, because I can't risk everyone's lives for my own hunger." His hand fell away. "I'm not waiting any longer. I intend to make you mine."

"No," she said in a choked whisper, "no."

"Yes."

Deborah couldn't move. There was quiet determination that convinced her it would do no good to struggle.

144

Her gaze moved briefly over his slick, naked torso, the smooth muscles and hard bands delineating his chest, rib cage, and belly. She stared, mesmerized, feeling a heated jolt spear through her, then lifted her gaze to his face.

Paralyzed with fear and apprehension, Deborah saw no hint of compassion or mercy in that stark, emotionless visage that gazed back at her. Instead, she saw the end of his waiting in his eyes.

Chapter 12

"Kwabitu," he said softly. "Lie down."

Her daze shattered. Shaking her head, russet strands whipping across her face, she backed away. "No. I won't.

"You don't have a choice," Hawk said coolly. "You can make this easy, or make it hard. That is your only option. I have said I will have you, and I will." He reached out to lift a strand of her hair, threading it between his fingers. "I know you are a virgin. I will be gentle."

"Gentle!" Her eyes were huge and golden, catching the reflected gleam from the low fire in the center of the tipi. "I am supposed to believe that you won't hurt me? You? A man who has treated me as a . . . a possession since I first saw you? This is what you've wanted all along, isn't it?"

His hand fell away. "Of course. Did you think differently? This wanting is what lures men to women, what makes them take risks to have them. I've made no secret of that fact." His broad shoulders lifted in a slight shrug. "I thought once that you might come to me willingly. That is why I waited, why I was patient. Now, my patience and my time have run out."

"Patience! I've been your prisoner for less than two months, yet you expect me to . . . to just lie down with you."

"Yes."

Panic flickered in her eyes, and Hawk knew that he must act swiftly before she did something impulsive. Maybe he should just let her go without this, but he couldn't. He'd waited too long, desired her for too long not to take her. She was a constant ache for him.

His hands flashed out to grab her just as she turned, caught her toe in the rumpled buffalo robe at her feet and began to fall. He let his weight act as an ally, carrying her with him to fall full-length on the cushioning robe.

Hawk half-turned, taking the brunt of the fall on his shoulder and hip. Deborah began to struggle as soon as they hit the robes, her desperate battle making her arch and cry out.

"Screaming won't help you," Hawk warned, "but it will upset my sister. And let everyone else in camp know what we are doing in here."

Deborah grew still, as he'd hoped she might. Her eyes flashed furiously up at him, and Hawk felt a surge of regret. She would hate him for this. Even though he'd seen the longing in her eyes, seen a baffled hunger that she would not admit, she would never forgive him if he took her unwillingly.

"Hawk, please," she said through stiff lips, and he saw what it cost her to plead with him. "Is there nothing I can say that will convince you not to do this?"

"No, *nu tue?tu.*" The endearment slipped out before he could stop it. *My little one.* He hoped she didn't understand it. Shifting position so that his weight didn't hurt her, he brushed back a strand of her hair. "I've wanted you since I first saw you standing there in the middle of

147

camp as if you were a queen and we your subjects. You caught my eye with your dignity and courage."

She swallowed heavily. "And you set about to destroy me."

"Destroy you?" He shook his head. "No. I admire your courage. Just as I admire your beauty."

"If you admire me, then why—?"

"Deborah, a man can admire a woman and still want to make love to her."

"Love!" Her eyes flashed angrily, the silky, gold-tipped brush of her lashes shadowing hot, angry sparks. "You don't know anything about love. All you have in mind is . . . is lust."

"Maybe you're right." Hawk bent his head to brush her mouth with his lips, winding his fingers in her hair to hold her head still when she tried to avoid him. "Open for me," he murmured huskily when she pressed her lips tightly together. "I want to taste you."

"Leave me alone." She tried to twist away, but Hawk held her fast. He kissed her long and hard, until he could feel the slightest trace of a response. He lifted his head to gaze down at her flushed face and the hazy gleam of her eyes. Dust streaked her nose and cheeks, and coated the long sweep of her eyelashes. He felt the tremor of her muscles against him, and relented.

There was a trace of surprise in her face when he rose to his feet, pulling her with him. "You look as if you've been caught in a dust devil," he observed.

"That's hardly my fault!"

His brow lifted. "No," he agreed. "But it was your choice to leave our camp."

"That has nothing to do with it."

He solemnly regarded her dusty dignity, and nodded acceptance. "Take off your clothes," he ordered, but she stood in mute, shocked defiance.

148

A faint smile slanted his hard mouth. He hadn't really expected her to comply. "Fine. We'll do it your way."

A flash of confusion shadowed her eyes, increasing when he untied the flap to the tipi and pulled her outside. It was apparent she thought he intended to publicly humiliate her. Dark had fallen, long shadows were being thrown by the campfires. Her face was half in shadow, half-illuminated, and he saw the agonized indecision in her eyes.

Hawk pulled her with him toward the stream glittering in the light of a nearly full moon. His strides were long and determined, and he ignored her resistance. She hung back as they neared it, perhaps sensing what he intended.

With a swift, merciless swing, Hawk scooped her into his arms and tossed her toward the water, all in the same, smooth motion. She let out a startled cry just before she hit the water. He felt the splash shower over him, and moved forward.

"You were in need of a bath," he said, adding when she sputtered furiously, "I did give you a choice, remember."

"You never said it was for a bath."

"You didn't ask."

She clawed at wet ropes of hair in her eyes, still spitting out water as she glared at him. Hawk felt an odd wave of tenderness for her. It left him feeling strangely uneasy, and his voice grew sharp.

"While you're in the water, clean yourself."

"I suppose you think you smell like a rose?" she shot back. Water splashed loudly, and he knelt to one knee to watch her. Her retort almost made him smile. It did make him think.

When he stood up and stripped out of his breechcloth

149

and leggings, he heard Deborah's soft scream and finally smiled.

"This was your idea," he said coolly when he reached her side and found her frantically trying to get away from him.

"I never meant such a thing!"

"We both need a bath." He caught her arm, hauling her back to him when she waded toward shore. She fell, and he pulled her up out of the water and set her on her feet.

"You're not only cruel," she managed to sputter, "but you're crazy!"

He was faintly relieved to find her more angry and outraged than afraid. It was an uncomfortable feeling to have her shudder with fear at the sight of him.

Holding her firmly, he began to strip away her clothes, the ragged cotton blouse first, then the equally ragged skirt. He felt his way down her legs in spite of her frantic struggle, and found that only one moccasin still clung to her foot.

Deborah's fight had sparked an inevitable fire in him despite the cool water, and she must have felt it. She came to an abrupt halt when he pulled her close against him. His desire rode him hard, and the feel of her wet, slick skin beneath his palms only made it worse.

"Be still, little dove," he whispered huskily, and felt her shiver in his arms.

Night sounds were familiar and soft around them, the shrill of insects, the murmur of birds, and the rush of the water. There was a bittersweet edge to the night as he held her, knowing that there would be only this one night. If he was to love her, he must love her well.

Sliding his hands up the lush curve of her hip, he let his palm rest on the swell in a gentle caress. She was still trembling, her eyes in the dappled moonlight a huge, shining gleam fixed on his face. Hawk realized suddenly that she had surrendered to what he wanted, whether she had admitted it to herself or not. The surrender was there, in her eyes, in the way she let her small hands rest atop the curve of his shoulders in a trusting hold.

Water lapped around her waist, and when he straightened to his full height, it tickled his upper thighs. Her skin glistened. Her hair look almost black with the weight of the water and the shadows, and framed the creamy porcelain of her face.

"Hawk . . ."

He shushed her with his mouth, kissing her, feeling her shivering body as light as a feather in his arms. He resisted the urge to crush her to him, to plunder her sweet mouth with his tongue. Instead, he went slowly, shifting to kiss the corners of her mouth, then her ear, and her throat.

She was a contradiction of heat and chill, her warm skin and the cool water combined in an enticing package. He ran a hand down the gentle curve of her back, his fingers skimming over the bump of her spine, then spreading to cup her buttocks and lift her up and closer to him. She gave a small cry against his mouth, and he kissed her lips again, muffling her cries to moans.

Her breasts pressed against his bare chest, the tight, pebbled surfaces of her nipples raking erotically and making his desire rise higher. Heat was rising in him, mounting so high and so hot he was shaking with the force of it. He was so close now, so close to making her yield, and he was amazed by the fierce need he felt for this one woman above all others. It was a driving ache that had brought him to this point, brought both of them to this trembling urgency.

Deborah rested her forehead against his chest just beneath his throat, her wet hair tickling the underside of his jaw. "Why are you doing this to me?" she whispered. "I don't know what I've done to deserve being raped."

"It won't be rape," Hawk rasped. "You'll see. I can feel your need. We want each other, and it's time we eased that ache."

Her head lifted, and he saw the startled look in her huge hazel eyes. "Ache? Yes. I do ache, but I don't know why."

Her soft admission tore at him, and he had to wait a moment before he responded. "It's natural, that feeling. It's what a man and a woman are supposed to feel for one another."

"We're not exactly your everyday couple." Deborah said bitterly, and he felt her shiver.

"No. I don't know why I want you and no other, but I do."

"I seem to recall your being able to ... function ... with someone else."

Her stiff reminder made him smile against the top of her head. "I found out that no one could replace you as I thought."

"It certainly didn't seem that way."

"Deborah."

She looked up at him, still shivering. There was a soft pleading in her eyes that she didn't voice, and he felt a faint sense of chagrin. Her body wanted him. He just had to drown out her instinctive objections.

"Deborah, you're going to realize how right it is for a man to be with a woman like this," he murmured, caressing the smooth line of her cheek.

"No. We're not married. It isn't right."

"A few words won't make it right." Hawk ignored the inner voice that echoed her words. His mother's early training had left indelible marks, he supposed, but life had managed to blunt the edges. It wasn't as if he was ruining her, not the way he saw it. She'd been married, however briefly, and he would be taking nothing away from her that her husband would not have done given a few more minutes in that arbor. And he would ease the burning fire in him that she'd ignited.

"Deborah," he said roughly when she buried her face against his chest, "You want to go back to your people. But I want this night."

There was a moment of silence, and he could feel her muscles tense. Then she looked up at him again, searching his face in the moonlight.

"I see. What about Judith?"

He hesitated. Judith wasn't his to give, but he didn't want to tell that to Deborah. There was too much hope in her eyes, though she could not know how much her cousin had been through. A rush of anger made him want to refuse, but he knew he could not. No matter what it cost him, he was too white to leave Judith to the fate she'd been suffering since her capture. His mouth thinned into a tight slash.

"Give me this night, and I will help your cousin too."

Maybe it wasn't fair. He had to take them both back whether she yielded willingly or not. But right now, fair didn't matter.

Inhaling deeply, Deborah said so softly the rush of water muffled her words, "All right. I'll . . . lie with you."

She was shaking when Hawk smoothed out his buffalo robes and turned to look at her. Her hair was still wet, her clothes clinging damply to her skin. A fire burned in the ring of stones, but her shivering increased.

153

Hawk reached out a hand and took her gently by the wrist. "Come lie down with me. I'll warm you."

Moving as if in a dream, Deborah took the two steps to his bed of furs and blankets, saw the fire reflected in the deep blue of his eyes, and almost retreated. She couldn't. But she had to. Her freedom and Judith's depended upon it.

And there was something, some nameless yearning inside her—the ache—that urged her forward.

She sank to her knees, unable to stand, and her face was almost level with his. He smiled at her, a quick, almost uncertain smile, and Deborah's tension eased slightly.

"I don't know what to do," she said simply. He nodded.

"I know. We'll do what comes naturally. You'll see."

Could this be Hawk? This almost gentle man with promise burning in his eyes and a tender touch? This new perception of him battled with how she'd seen him previously, the fierce, brutal warrior filled with anger. For a moment, she wondered if she viewed him differently in light of knowing he was only half-Comanche.

Then there was no more time for abstract thought, because he was pulling her to him, his arms holding her in a tight, possessive embrace.

"Kiss me," he coaxed, tilting her face with a finger beneath her chin. His voice lowered to a rasping whisper. "Kiss me."

As he set his mouth over hers, Deborah closed her eyes. The kiss was smothering, consuming, and she felt dizzy from it. Her hands moved to hold his upper arms to keep from falling, and she felt the smooth, powerful flex of his muscles beneath her fingers. A moan vibrated in the back of her throat, and when she opened her mouth to gasp for air, he took immediate advantage.

His tongue slid inside in a smooth thrust that sent a shock wave to her toes.

In spite of her fear, Deborah couldn't help a tremor of response. Hawk must have felt it. He gave a low growl of satisfaction, and deepened the kiss until she was weak and clinging to him with both hands.

Shuddering, her head fell back, and he ran his tongue over the exposed arch of her throat in a trail of sizzling fire that made her moan again. She felt as if she were moving through heated honey, warm and thick beneath his searching hands.

Hawk slid one hand to her buttocks to lift her up and against him, pressing her stomach against the hard bulge at his loins. She shivered again, fully aware of his arousal and frightened by it. And more frightened by the strange reactions taking place in her body. The ache was back, that insistent throbbing between her thighs and the heightened sensitivity of her breasts to his touch.

When he pulled away her blouse, then her skirt, Deborah felt hot instead of cold. She should be chilled, with her still damp hair brushing against her bare back and her clothes gone, but instead she felt that strange, deep heat permeate her entire body.

The strangeness catapulted her into restless motion, and she heard his deep groan when her hips grazed against the heat of his groin.

"You're so sweet," he muttered thickly. "As sweet as I knew you'd be."

"Hawk . . ."

But he wasn't listening. He pushed her gently back to the furs, and his eyes glittered in the dim light with a blue fire that made her breath catch. Desire sharpened his features and made him look fierce and predatory. There was no hint of mercy, only a ruthless need that hurled her into resistance.

155

Fear overpowered her compliance, and she struggled when he stroked a hand down over her body to cup her breast in his palm. He looked faintly surprised.

"Easy, easy," he muttered. "I won't hurt you. You'll see. Don't fight me. Not now. Just relax."

His dark head lowered, the long swing of his hair brushing over her bare shoulder as he kissed her throat, the delicate curve of her collarbone, then lower. Deborah arched upward in mute protest, but his mouth moved to cover her nipple.

Her cry drifted upward, a cry of shock and reaction as his warm, wet mouth seared with exquisitely delicious sensations over her sensitive flesh. The remembered ache intensified, and she half-sobbed. Her nipple felt afire, and his actions increased that sensation as he sucked strongly, his cheeks flexing with the motions. Oddly, there seemed to be a direct connection with what he was doing and that strange, fluttering ache between her thighs.

Writhing, Deborah pushed weakly at him until he lifted his head to stare at her with burning eyes. Slowly, he laced his fingers in hers and drew her arms up and over her head, pressing her hands into the downy softness of the furs.

His action served to thrust her breasts upward in an inviting appeal, and she saw his gaze shift from her face to her breasts.

"Hawk . . ."

The single word drowned in the back of her throat as his mouth covered her nipple again, and she felt him transfer her wrists to one hand as he began to tease the still-damp peak of her other breast. His body fit her from knee to waist, and she could feel his hard maleness against her.

Her breath came in short, tortured gasps for air, and

the heat that he'd begun coiled downward, converging on the burning ache between her legs. She felt the roll of her hips almost as if someone else was rocking her, and knew that she had lost control of her own body. Hawk's caresses and kisses were working a strange magic that made her thighs part when he nudged between them, made her hips arch upward and her body strain toward an unknown release. She was on fire with it, aflame with need.

Uttering a low, harsh sound, Hawk lifted his body from hers for a moment, and jerked loose the string holding the brief garment around his waist. Deborah froze. The memory of his hard body had not faded with time, and the fear she'd felt at her last sight of him returned full-force.

His dark, hard-muscled body held no secrets from her. His desire was plainly revealed in the light of the fire, rising thick and erect from a dusky nest of curls at his groin. He looked formidable, too large, too—male.

"Dear God," she whispered, "I can't do this. I just can't."

A brief smile touched one corner of his mouth. "It won't be as bad as you think. It might hurt this first time, but only for a moment."

Hurt? Her eyes shifted from his face back to his body, then closed. He was wrong. This would kill her.

"Remember," she said tonelessly, "that you promised to take Judith back."

A husky laugh drifted between them, and Hawk lowered his lean frame back over her, nestling between her thighs. She could feel the hot nudge of him against that soft, damp place.

"You'll go with her, I promise."

"Remember," was all she said. She knew that she could not survive the night.

157

"Ah, *notsa?ka*—sweetheart," he muttered thickly. "By the time we come together as meant to be, you'll be ready for me."

She didn't bother arguing with him. It didn't matter. He would do what he wanted, what she'd given him permission to do, whether she agreed or not.

He coaxed her thighs wide for him, his hands gentle and disturbing against the hidden folds of flesh. Deborah tried not to think about what he was doing, but when he began to caress her there, his hands stroking the highly sensitized spot that made her catch her breath, she forgot her fear. Tension built up as he rubbed his thumb against a small nub, making her bite her lip to keep from screaming. He seemed to know it. She could hear his labored breathing, as if it excited him to touch her there.

Caught up in the waves of sensation he created with his hands and his mouth and the husky words he whispered to her as she writhed beneath him, Deborah heard her own moans fill the close air of the tipi. Her thighs fell apart and her hips undulated, and she began to thrash restlessly, seeking an end to the fiery torment he was creating.

Someone was calling his name, and she realized it was her voice, her cries. Her eyes opened, and she saw the hot, glittering fire of his gaze on her, the sensual slant of his mouth. To her utter bewilderment, the tension inside her grew hotter and higher, almost painfully so, and she struggled to keep from exploding with it.

"No, no," she moaned, her head rolling on the cushion of furs, but Hawk paid no attention to her. His hand moved, and his mouth sought her breast, and she shattered as if made of glass, fracturing into a thousand tiny pieces. The explosion made her cry out in shock and de-

158

licious ecstasy, and for a long moment, she felt suspended in time and place.

Hawk was panting as if he'd been running. Turning her head, Deborah buried her face against the slick skin of his shoulder. She could feel the rapid rise and fall of his chest beneath her cheek, smell the musky male scent of him. He turned her head back and kissed her again, his mouth coaxing a response from her stiff lips.

When he settled closer between her thighs, replacing his hand with the rigid thrust of his body, Deborah could not help the small moan that escaped her.

"Shhh," he said, stroking her hair back from her eyes with a gentle hand. *"Sua yurahpitu."*

"Which means?" she mumbled.

"Relax."

"That's easy for *you* to say."

"Have I hurt you yet, *nu tue?tu?"*

Deborah met his eyes. She recognized the last as an endearment, and was strangely comforted. "No."

"Then give me a chance. I don't want to hurt you. I want you to enjoy this."

She didn't reply. Her breasts tingled, and the strange ache between her legs returned while he caressed her. When he began kissing her again, deeply, his tongue teasing a reluctant response from her, Deborah again felt the rise of heat.

In spite of his words, she couldn't relax. Her body felt limp and uncontrollable, opening for him of its own volition. Her breath caught in the back of her throat when he lowered his body on her and held her with his weight, his hand reaching between her legs again to guide himself into her.

Hawk's breath feathered over her cheek in quick pants. A gut-deep groan burst from him, and he muttered. "You're so tight, so very tight." He kissed the

159

curve of her cheek, then her mouth. "You feel so good, so good."

Deborah heard him as if from a distance, heard his soft words turn into groans, then felt him go deep inside her with a single, fierce thrust. She stiffened in surprise, her breath exhaling in a rush.

"That's it, sweetheart. It's over now," he said against her lips. "Only pleasure now, with no surprises. You're so small . . . are you all right?"

Because he sounded so worried, Deborah nodded. "Yes, of course I am."

Resting his weight on his elbows, Hawk levered his body up to look down at her. A frown creased his brow, and he brushed aside damp tendrils of her hair with a fingertip.

Without speaking, he comforted her, his hands soft and gentle and his kisses tender. He kissed the corners of her mouth, the arch of her eyebrow and the tip of her nose.

And as she grew accustomed to the heavy weight of his body impaling her, Deborah's tension eased. He held himself still for a time, but when he finally moved, withdrawing the slightest bit, then thrusting forward again, it was easier. His penetration and withdrawal began slowly, then grew to a faster, fiercer pace, igniting the slow heat into a fire again.

Her response was slow, her body still numbed by the shock of his invasion, but it finally grew inside her, that heat, that thrilling pleasure. The quickening made her hips move under him, actually meeting his thrusts, opening wider for him.

Everything was heightened, his harsh, rasping breaths as he moved inside her, the searing stab of his body, and the friction as he withdrew, the pop of the fire and the smell of his heat, the new scents of their lovemaking.

The mystery was solved for Deborah, that question of *why*. Hawk's possession of her answered her puzzled pondering. Now she knew what made men and women seek each other out for this act, for this ultimate surrender of the body.

With the increase of his movements, the faster, harder tempo of his body slamming into the cradle of her thighs, she felt the increase of tension. It grew, higher and hotter than before, threatening to consume her. She began to whimper, and her eyes opened to see him looking down at her, his features drawn and sharp, intense with passion.

His gaze held hers as he rocked against her, his hard belly scraping against the softer mound of her stomach, his strong arms planted on each side of her, his thighs holding her legs apart as his body moved in that tantalizing rhythm.

"Hawk," she whimpered, not quite knowing what she wanted and hoping he would understand. "Hawk . . . oh Hawk . . ."

His eyes were a blue so dark as to be almost black, his mouth stretched in a taut line, and his throat corded with strain. The powerful flex of his muscles gleamed in the soft firelight, and she heard him groan.

Then, her eyes widening with shock, she felt the waves of release sweep through her in a shattering rush that made her hips arch and her legs lift to lock around his lean waist. His hard, driving thrusts splintered any control she had left, and she cried out again, a high, husky sound that echoed in the night.

With a last, fierce lunge, Hawk thrust forward and went still and taut, his sturdy body arching backward as Deborah dissolved in a convulsing climax. Seconds later, she heard the harsh, guttural groan that signalled his own release.

Chapter 13

It was getting close to sunrise. The interior of the tipi was the smallest bit lighter. Soon, the sun would break over the ridge of the eastern mountains.

Deborah blinked at the gray slits of light filtering through the lowered flap of the tipi. It faced east, as all the lodges did, to greet the rising sun. Part of their religion, she supposed.

Her glance drifted to the man at her side. He lay beneath the robes with her, one muscled arm flung carelessly across her, his thigh wedged between her legs in a still-possessive hold. There was a slight, raw ache down there, and her mouth and breasts felt swollen and tender to the touch.

A faint flush suffused her face as she recalled the things he'd said, and the things she'd done. She wished that he were not beside her, and wondered how she would face him in light of what they'd done.

Did all men and women mate so fiercely? Were the things they'd done—unusual? She wished she knew someone to ask. It didn't seem possible that some of the women she knew had acted with the same wild abandon she had done, giving herself to Hawk so completely.

And worse—if she admitted the truth, she had not

done it only to free herself and her cousin. There had been an underlying attraction to Hawk since that first day, since he'd stared at her so boldly and ignited some response in her. His attempts to seduce her later had only added to the attraction, and she had refused to see it. Now it had been brought forcibly home to her.

Her chest constricted. She'd lain with Hawk, had taken him into her body—and her heart. She loved him.

The realization seared her to the soul, and she quivered at the knowledge. What would she do? She couldn't remain here, not in a Comanche camp. Yet she didn't want to leave him. God help her, she did not want to be free of him after all. Judith would never understand.

She must have made some sound or movement, because when she glanced toward Hawk, she felt him watching her. Pale fingers of light made his eyes glitter; the thick brush of his lashes shuttered them briefly.

"You're awake."

She nodded. "Yes."

"Are you—did I hurt you?"

"Not badly." Her flush felt hot, heating her cheeks so that she couldn't look at him.

His hand drifted from her bare shoulder in a gentle glide, gaining purchase on the rise of her breast and making her breath come faster. His thumb rotated gently on the rapidly puckering bead of her nipple, and Deborah bit back a moan. He stopped immediately.

"Does that hurt, *nu tue?tu?*"

"Hurt?" Her voice came out in a croak, and she cleared her throat. "No. I'm just . . . sensitive."

"Ah."

That one syllable denoted satisfaction, and Deborah lay still as Hawk began to explore her body again. She felt his heavy arousal against her thigh. His body was

163

hot, a mixture of heat and iron-hard muscle as he began kissing her, taking her hands and dragging them over the ridges of his chest.

"Stop!" she hissed when he began drawing her hand toward his groin. Her face flamed. The intimacy was bad enough, but to actually be expected to *touch* him— the searing memory of how he'd washed her the night before, dragging a wet cloth over the most private, intimate areas of her body, was torture enough.

Hawk's hand stilled, folded over her own. She could feel him breathe, the even rise and fall of his chest beneath her palm. He nuzzled her cheek, kissing her.

"Aren't you curious about me?" he asked huskily, his breath tickling her ear. When she didn't reply, he laughed. "I know you are. You're just too much of a proper lady to admit it. It's all right, Deborah. Don't you think we've gone past that by now?"

"Yes," she admitted honestly.

"I agree. Here. Let me. I assure you it will cause me more trouble than it will you." He took her hand from the flat, ridged plane of his belly and moved it lower, catching his breath as her fingers found him. "See," he muttered hoarsely, "you can make me squirm if you want."

"That sounds fair." Her awkward movements became more deft as she stroked him, his hand teaching her the rhythm. It seemed impossible, but he grew larger, his tumescent body straining against the prison of her palm. Deborah's face flushed even hotter, and she felt a strange, unfamiliar breathlessness.

"Enough," Hawk said after a few moments, his voice a harsh croak. His steely grip on her wrist drew her hand away. He was panting for breath, his belly moving in and out with rapid movements.

In the growing light, Deborah could see the sculpted

164

angles and planes of his body, the masculine beauty that had teased her since that first day. He was beautiful, truly magnificent. Why had she not seen that before? Oh, she'd acknowledged his superb body and muscled power, but not the pure line of leonine grace and splendor that was truly Hawk.

Was it because she'd discovered she loved him? Maybe.

She opened for him, her arms accepting when he lay over her and blanketed her body with kisses. His mouth seared across her face, shoulders, breasts, and belly, tasting, teasing, his tongue rasping against her flesh and eliciting moans of delight. He lavished her nipples with hot, wet kisses, lashing them with his tongue until they were tight, rigid peaks. Deborah moved restlessly beneath him, her breath coming in short gasps for air.

This time, there was no urgency in his movements. He took his time, bringing her to pleasure with exquisite slowness. Deborah could not help her response, the cries she gave, or the words she whispered against his throat as he moved over her.

"Hawk, yes, please yes . . ."

He gave a low growl of pleasure, and moved between her thighs with a swift motion. Then he was inside her, his body filling her, rocking against her. Deborah cried out at the scrape of him against still-sensitive flesh, and he went still.

"Are you all right?"

She nodded, unable to speak for the breathtaking mix of pain and pleasure. She ached for him, but the tight friction of his body inside her made her shudder.

He remained still, holding back until she moved in a restless twist of her hips. His gaze was hot and dark with desire as he rasped, "You're sure?"

Deborah lifted up slightly to kiss him, her arms

around the strong column of his neck. Her mouth grazed his throat, his jawline, then his lips.

"I'm sure."

Then her head arched back, soft cries of ecstasy fluttering through the long wings of his hair as he surged forward in a smooth, delicious slide. This was so far outside the realm of anything she'd ever imagined, that she couldn't find the words to explain her reactions to him. Nothing would explain it, she supposed, not this wild, abandoned response he had provoked with his mouth, hands, and body.

It startled them both.

Hawk saw the sensual glaze in her eyes, the parted lips and female awareness denoting the passion that he'd sensed existed in her. Her cool, ladylike exterior had only hidden it. It remained there, deep and quick, like an underground river.

He wanted to take his time, but Deborah's writhing response, her quickened breathing, and the soft cries she gave made him crazy. Her hips undulated beneath him, soft invitations, sending jolts of exquisite sensation all the way to his toes. Their coupling was going too fast—much faster than he'd wanted—but he couldn't slow it down. He hammered into her, her hips rising to meet him, his body answering the urgency that drove them both. He could feel the rising sweep of release, felt her velvet contractions around him and her cries in his ear, and he was lost.

With a low, hoarse groan, he emptied his body into her with explosive force. Her arms clasped convulsively around his neck and held him, and he rested his forehead against hers, too drained to move.

He didn't know how long he lay there, moving only to shift his weight to one side so as not to hurt her. It hit him then, that the *one night* he'd wanted, would not be

166.

enough to satisfy him. He wanted to savor her, to turn over at night and find her in his blankets, her soft body warm and willing, her fiery hair draped over his arm.

But he couldn't.

He had to return Deborah and Judith before the army came for them, came with horses and guns and death riding behind them, came to kill the innocent and the not so innocent. He may not have been responsible for bringing the woman to camp, but he was responsible for keeping her there. He could have, as she'd said, returned her. But he hadn't. He'd wanted her, so he'd kept her. And now he would lose her for good.

For the first time, Hawk wondered what his father had felt when he'd had to return his mother to her people. If it had pained White Eagle half as badly as the pain he felt now, he felt a new understanding and compassion. Some of the resentment at being the product of their union faded, and he knew how easy it was to lose his detachment.

"What are you going to do with me?" Deborah asked softly, startling him. He didn't answer for a moment. The light grew brighter, splintering through the seams of buffalo hide and pouring through the smoke hole at the top. He blinked against it, then shrugged.

"Take you back, I guess."

"Take me back?"

"Isn't that what you want? The promises we traded?" he asked sharply. She made a quick movement that he stilled with his hands, lifting his head to stare at her with narrowed, watchful eyes. "Isn't it?"

"Yes. Of course." She swallowed. "You're hurting me."

He released his grip on her arms and lay back. Staring up at the funneled shape of the tipi, Hawk had the bitter thought that he'd outsmarted himself. If he hadn't taken her, all he'd feel was regret. Not this sharp sense of loss, as if he'd lost something precious. She wasn't precious. He didn't love her. He admired her, savored her beauty, and *wanted* her, but he didn't love her. He knew better than to love anything or anyone. And she obviously didn't love him.

So why was he in such a bad mood?

It was midday before Hawk came for her again. Deborah sat quietly in the tipi, enduring Sunflower's wet glances with wearing fortitude. Finally, the girl said in soft, thick English, "I am sorry that you must go."

Deborah glared at her. "Does everyone in the camp speak English?"

"No." Shaking her head, Sunflower's long hair swished back and forth over her shoulder. "Some speak little. Some none. This one speaks well only because my brother taught me your tongue when I was small.

"Well, I certainly appreciate being tormented these past weeks. It would have helped considerably if someone had been kind enough to speak to me in my own language and explain things."

Deborah's tart tone brought tears to Sunflower's eyes. "I wanted to. My brother would not allow it. This one tried to help you."

Sighing, Deborah said, "I know you did. I'm sorry. I did not mean to hurt your feelings." She glanced at the flap of the tipi, expecting to see Hawk return. "It's just that I'm so confused." The last was said almost inaudibly, a murmured comment, but Sunflower heard it.

"*Unu ohko kamakunu?* Do you love him?"

Deborah stared at her. "Do I love him? Your brother? I cannot answer that."

"Why?"

168

"Because . . . well, because I don't know. He has promised to take me back to my people. It doesn't matter whether I love him or not."

"*Haa*—yes, it does. If you tell him you love him, he will not take you back. You can stay with us, be his—be his *paraiboo?*"

Deborah's brow furrowed. "*Paraiboo?*"

"*Haa.* Chief wife."

"Chief wife."

Nodding, Sunflower said brightly, "Be his chief woman, the first. His other wives would do what you made them."

"Other wives?" Deborah's tone was dangerously mild. Her eyes flashed. She pushed at a strand of hair, then folded her hands in her lap. Her gaze shifted from Sunflower's growing distress to the opened flap. "No, I don't think so."

Sunflower was obviously puzzled. "You would not like to be his chief wife?"

"No, I would not." Deborah stared down at her hands, and unclenched them before she ruined the dress Sunflower had given her. It was soft doeskin, with pretty patterns of beads carefully sewn into the material. She smoothed it back out and glanced up at the quiet girl.

"You do not want to stay in our camp," Sunflower said softly, and Deborah hesitated. How did she hurt this gentle girl by telling the truth? Even if she knew what it was. Which, right now, she didn't. She was confused, so confused, wanting Hawk, facing the realization that she loved him at the same time as she recognized the futility in it. He lived with the Comanche as one of them. She could not.

Finally she said, "No. I miss my own people. Do you understand?"

169

"Yes. I would miss my father and brother." Sunflower's brow creased in another frown. "But my brother does not stay long when he comes. This is the longest he has stayed in our village since I was a *ohna?a?.*"

"Baby?" Deborah guessed, and Sunflower nodded. "I thought he always stayed here."

"*Kee.* He never stays long. He leaves again, goes back to the white man's world." Sunflower toyed with a length of her black hair. "I do not know why he goes where he is not wanted." Her eyes were troubled when she looked up at Deborah with a faint frown. "I do not understand most white men. His father—the man who is married to his mother—sent him away. He still bears the marks of the whip on his back, though they are faint."

Deborah stared at her. "He was whipped?"

"*Haa.* The white husband of his mother was angry because Hawk's father was one of the People. He threw him away, as if he was nothing. He will not talk of it, but I know he thinks of his mother." Sunflower shook her head. "My brother is a good man. He is brave and generous, and in spite of what some of the warriors say, he fears nothing. But he must walk in two worlds, and it leaves him torn."

Deborah closed her eyes at the image of Hawk being driven from his home by hatred. It explained a lot. But it did not excuse his treatment of her.

"He brings me hard candy when he comes back," Sunflower was saying, "but I always miss him. This time, he said he would not leave the People again, but my father said he is torn between two worlds." Her voice dropped. "If you stay, he will not leave us."

"I can't stay for that reason. My cousin and I must go back."

"Can she not go without you?"

"No." Deborah looked away from her sad face, and

saw that Hawk had returned. He ducked into the tipi, his hard face remote and unreadable. Her heart lurched. Was this the same man who had held her in his arms, whispered soft words to her, touched her as no one had touched her before? He looked grim and unapproachable.

She bent her head and began folding a blanket, suddenly shy. Intimate memories would be there between them and she wasn't certain how to act around him now.

So she avoided his eyes. She heard him speak to Sunflower in a soft, patient tone. His husky voice vibrated all the way to her toes. She *felt* it more than heard it, was acutely aware of his proximity.

Sunflower left, and they were alone. Deborah still did not look up at him.

He hunkered down on his heels beside her. "Deborah. Are you trying to avoid me?"

"Yes."

He made a faint, disgruntled sound. "Well, stop it. There is too little time and too much to do to play the grand lady now."

Her head snapped up at that, eyes flashing angrily. "I an not playing a grand lady!"

He met her gaze calmly, dark blue eyes cool and remote. "Aren't you?"

She looked away from that penetrating gaze, and her answer was brutally honest. "I don't know how you want me to act, or how I'm supposed to act after—"

"After what?"

Her voice was faint. "After last night."

"Only last night? Why not this morning, too?" Hawk's fingers were warm when he gripped her chin and turned her to face him. "There is no shame in what we did."

"There never is for a man."

"Deborah." His grip tightened when she tried to turn away. "I know how white women think. It's not that way here. You're not responsible for what happened, if that's what you want to hear."

"Oh yes, well, that changes everything." Her bitter tone made his brow lift. "I can go back and pretend that my life is just as it was before, right? Well, I can't. You know I can't. But you were right about one thing—I'm not responsible. You are."

His mouth tightened, and there was a brief flare in his eyes that made her shiver. He looked furious. Well, she was right, and there was nothing he could do to change that. For an instant Deborah wondered why she felt this compulsion to enrage him. She would never see him again. Soon, he would leave her and it would all be behind her.

And maybe that, after all, was the reason.

Hawk shot to his feet, towering over her. His big hands were curled into fists at his sides, and she could see his struggle for control. She had obviously touched a nerve.

When he reached down to lift her, she trembled but did not back away. What else could he do to her?

"Don't say anymore," he rasped. "I'll keep my promise to you. You and your cousin will be returned. But I won't accept the blame on the other. I'll share it, but you cannot deny what you felt."

Her cheeks flamed. She eased her arm from his grasp and managed to pull the shreds of her dignity around her. "I do not deny that . . . that I felt something. But a man as skilled at seduction as you seem to be, should find it easy to manage that."

A muscle leaped in his jaw, and she waited for him to deny it. What would he say? Would he say she had been different for him, that he really cared about her?

And what, she wondered, would she do if he did?

But she didn't have to worry about that. Hawk said none of those things.

"Subetu," he growled, formal and stiff again, the faint traces of a white man vanished. "It is finished. You will go back to your people."

"And you?"

She saw uncertainty flicker in his eyes for a moment before he hid it with a swift lowering of his lashes. He gave a careless shrug.

"I will do what I must."

"I see." Pain thickened her throat for a moment, and she had to swallow it before she could say calmly, "When do we leave?"

"Miíhtsi. Soon. Be ready."

Deborah stared after him, and the pain seemed almost overwhelming.

It was late the following evening when they reached the outskirts of a fort. Deborah had no idea which one it was, but could plainly see the familiar structure of wooden buildings scattered over a flat expanse. A high, full moon hung in the sky, shedding bright light over the quiet scene.

"Where are we?" she murmured, acutely aware of the tension in the warriors with them. Hawk sat his stallion with an easy grace that belied his brooding expression, and the look he gave her now seethed with intensity.

"Taibo ekusahpana."

"White soldiers. Are we near where I was taken?"

"Kee." His stallion moved restlessly beneath him, and the full moon silvered the jet swing of his hair. In the chalky light, his naked chest gleamed a dull bronze,

173

and there was the quick flash of reflected light from an amulet around his neck.

One of the horses stamped its hoof against the ground and snorted, and was quickly hushed by its rider. There were twenty other men with them, all painted and decked out as if for war. Rifles were loaded and ready, and lances balanced in brown fists.

Deborah realized she was clutching the reins to her horse so tightly her fingers ached from the strain. Nothing seemed to move below in the bright prick of moonlight, no indication that anyone was awake. Yet the Comanche were taking no chances, and remained well out of firing range.

To her left, beyond Hawk, she glimpsed her cousin's blond head. Judith had said hardly a single word the entire time, and the night before when they had camped, she'd remained huddled in a tight ball near one of the men, a young warrior. Deborah had heard Hawk call him cousin, and had thought it fitting that two cousins would return them.

Now that the moment had come for her freedom, she was sad, and amazed by it. In less than two months, she'd come to care about Hawk, and care about his sister.

Sunflower had wept when she'd left, and Deborah had barely been able to hold back her own tears. The girl was heartbroken, and murmured that her heart was laid upon the ground by Deborah's departure.

She thought the description quite apt. That was how she felt at this moment, as if her heart lay exposed for anyone to tread on it. She felt bruised, her chest a tight ball of pain and suppressed emotion. And she wondered if Hawk felt any of what she felt, even the slightest bit. He certainly didn't look as if he did. His face was impassive, his chiseled features as expressionless as carved stone.

Deborah blinked back the sudden sting of tears. Dear God, this was so insane, so beyond anything she should feel at all. He was a savage, a ruthless savage despite the fact that he'd been born into another world. He had frightened her and intimidated her, and if she had not been a virgin, he would have raped her that first night.

Yet, she'd fallen in love with him. It was beyond the realm of her imagination to understand why. Maybe the few, hidden kindnesses he'd offered had only made him seem less brutal to her. Maybe once he was behind her, she would realize how foolish she'd been, that she'd only adapted to her situation to save herself. She hoped so. Because if she hurt later as badly as she hurt now at leaving him, she would not be able to stand it.

Hawk shifted, and she saw him slide from his horse in a smooth, effortless motion. He approached her with that lazy, graceful glide that characterized all his movements, and reached up to lift her from her horse.

She didn't speak, didn't offer a comment as he slid her down the length of his body to stand her on her feet.

"Kima," he growled. He refused to speak English to her in front of his companions, as if it would make him disloyal. She nodded, and followed as he turned and walked several yards away.

Her heart was beating rapidly, and a thousand thoughts chased aimlessly through her head. Was he changing his mind? Did he want to go with her? The question circled repeatedly, even though she knew better.

When he reached the edge of a high ridge overlooking the fort below, Hawk turned. His face was half in shadow, but she could see the wariness in his eyes, those dark blue eyes that could lighten with laughter or

175

turn to a smoldering intensity that made her pulses race and her heart lurch. A light breeze lifted his long hair away from his face. A feather hung from the wide leather band holding his hair out of his eyes, spinning gently against his cheek. A hawk's feather.

On impulse, she reached up to touch it, her fingers grazing lightly against his cheekbone. He caught her hand in a swift grip, stilling her caress. She saw the flex of a muscle in his jaw as he stared down at her.

"*Keta.*"

"You can speak English now. They can't hear."

Hawk's gaze remained riveted on her face. His arms were corded with strain, and he took a deep breath before he released her hand.

"I want to give you something."

Deborah waited, feeling the wind in her hair and cold desolation in her soul. The fringe of her doeskin dress tickled the backs of her bare calves, and the beadwork on the soft moccasins she wore clacked slightly when she shifted position. A coyote howled in the distance, and she could hear the restive shuffle of the horses behind her.

When Hawk moved closer, she caught the scent of tobacco and rawhide, familiar and comforting now instead of frightening as it had once been. Her throat constricted when his hand lifted to touch her face lightly. She tingled where his fingers grazed, then his hand fell away.

With a deft movement, he wrenched something away from his neck and held it out to her. She stared down at it, then looked up at him curiously. He shrugged.

"I want you to wear this."

"What is it?"

"*Ahpu-a tsomo korohko.*"

Bewildered, she shook her head. "I don't understand."

"It was my father's. He left it with my mother should she ever wish to find him. When I was old enough, I searched for him with it. You may do the same if you should ever need me."

A lump made it impossible for her to speak for a moment. She recognized the necklace now. He'd been wearing it the first time she'd seen him. The leather thong was knotted around a small, shiny bone that had carving on it. Feathers had been fastened to the bone and thong, and it was tied again to keep it from coming loose.

"Hawk, I don't know . . . don't know what to say."

"Say nothing. For a change. Just take it and keep it safe."

He pressed the necklace into her hand, and the soft down of the feathers tickled her palm. "Hawk feathers?" she asked softly, but he shook his head with a faint smile.

"*Kee*. Eagle feathers. They are sacred to the Comanche, *Parukaa*. My father is White Eagle—*Kwihne tosabitu*. These are sacred to him, and to any who see them. You will be safe from any of the People who should see this."

"Won't he be upset that you have given away his gift?"

Hawk seemed amused. "No."

"Oh. Well, then, thank you."

He gestured at the sky, where the moon hung bright and heavy, so close Deborah stilled the impulse to reach out and try to touch it. The silvery gleam backlit his ebony hair and gilded his skin with an unearthly glow, and for a moment he seemed mythical, a Greek god stepped down from Olympus.

"When you see the full moon, remember me," Hawk said softly. "It is called by some a Comanche moon."

"Why?"

His grin was white and only slightly mocking. "Because that is when *Parukaa* choose to ride and raid. The night sun gives good light for our warriors to see."

Deborah shuddered at the images his words provoked. She remembered, suddenly, the night of her wedding to Miguel, and how the Comanche had come screaming down to kill and rob and kidnap. The moon had been full and bright, shedding light over the hacienda.

And it was full tonight.

No words would come. She trembled. The necklace draped over her palm, swaying slightly from her movements and the night wind. All her preconceived notions of Comanche as murdering savages had diminished while in their village, and now it seemed as if Hawk deliberately provoked the memories and fears.

"Do you raid with them?" she asked when she knew she shouldn't.

"Yes."

Her eyes closed briefly. "How could you?"

"You'd be surprised at the things I've done." His savage tone snapped her eyes open. "Did you think I'd changed into some kind and gentle playmate because you found out I'm half-white?"

She shook her head. "No. Of course not."

"Just because I wasn't the one who captured you doesn't mean that I haven't done my share of raiding. I have. And when I live in the white man's world, I do what's expected of me there, too."

"I can't imagine it would be as bad as what's expected of you in this world," Deborah returned hotly, indicating the painted warriors with a jab of her hand. The necklace dangled as she swept an arm out to indicate

178

the fort below. "Hawk, there, at least, men aren't expected to slaughter one another for sport or pride."

"They aren't?" His eyes glittered dangerously. "You don't know what you're talking about."

"No, it's true. You know it's true. If you're half-white, then you should come to terms with yourself. You can't deny your heritage. And civilized men don't loot and kill."

"Perhaps not where you come from, but out here, men of all colors kill for whatever reason. Or no reason."

"How can you turn your back on your true heritage?" she asked miserably. "You're half-white!"

Lifting his head to face the wind that blew his hair into silky tangles, Hawk didn't reply for a moment. When he did, instead of being angry or defensive, he sounded tired.

"And I'm half-Comanche. I'm a man divided. *Tuapako-ito*. If I walk the Comanche path, you will hate me. If I walk the white man's path, I will hate myself. A man can live without a woman. A man cannot live without himself."

"Is that why you're here? You chose to turn your back on how you'd been born to live as a Comanche?"

He gave her a half-smile. "No, not really. It wasn't a conscious choice. I simply ran out of room to run."

"What do you mean by that?"

His glance was quick and impatient. "As a white man, I had to make certain decisions, not all of which were popular. Things got—hot for me. I had to hide somewhere, and I thought—hoped—that I could lose myself in the Comanche camp. Or find myself." He shrugged. "Obviously, I didn't do either."

"What can be so bad that you'd choose to raid and ride with Indians?"

There was a flash of savagery in his face that made her swallow, and his voice was rough.

"Let me tell you something you may not want to hear—it's a lot tougher out there in the white man's world than it is in the Comanche's. You think Indians are savages? You ought to get a good look at some of the men I've seen, white men who go to church on Sundays and hire a man to kill the preacher on Monday. No, don't try to tell me any different, because I know better."

For a moment she stared at him, at the white-hot intensity of his face, the cold ice of his eyes. He meant it. And she wondered what had happened in his past to make him so bitter. It was still there, that bitterness, eating at him, tearing him apart. It had made him an outcast wherever he went, left him without a home. For the first time, she caught a glimpse of his other side, the flip side of the coin, the dark side of the mirror. And she didn't know which one was Hawk, which man truly existed. Even his voice changed at times, melding from the clipped, soft tones of the Comanche into a drawling mockery that bespoke another life, another man.

Dear God, what would it be like to lose oneself so completely? She ached for him, but knew he would never accept her sympathy.

"What—what will you do now? Fight with the Comanche until you're killed by soldiers?"

His gaze was brooding, his voice bitter. "No, I can't bring risk to them. I'll help them move to their winter grounds, then ride out."

"But Hawk—where will you go? What will you do?" Anguish made her voice catch, and she saw his mouth curve into a faint smile.

"Whatever I have to do to survive, just like everyone else. Just like you'll do. You'll conform, like the rest. In a few months, you'll forget me. Women have singularly short memories, I've found."

His glance swept Judith, then came back to rest on Deborah. She could feel his withdrawal, his retreat back into the formal, impenetrable shell of a Comanche brave.

Angry tears streaked her cheeks as she gazed up at his silvered profile, the stark lines and harsh angles that formed his features. She wanted to say that it wasn't the same for a woman, for *this* woman. But she couldn't. Her pride had been abused enough, and she could not bring herself to force words of love past her stubborn lips.

Instead, she said calmly, "Thank you for keeping your promise. I will be glad to go home."

"That's Fort Richardson. You're not close to your home, but I don't want to risk my men. There'll be a lot of soldiers out looking for you now." He looked up and past her toward the quiet fort. "It's time for you to go now. Their sentries may not sleep as soundly as usual."

There was a dry sarcasm to his words that made her smile in spite of her pain. She waited a moment, but he did not try to touch her, and she began to feel foolish for waiting on something he obviously didn't want.

There were no words of farewell, nor did he try to kiss her. Hawk turned on his heel. She followed him without comment.

Hawk boosted Deborah back onto her horse. Then he reached up and took the necklace from her hand and tied it around her neck. It lay nestled between the mounds of her breasts, brushing against the intricate beadwork of the doeskin dress. Deborah felt another sting of tears, but lifted her chin to meet Hawk's steady gaze. He smiled, and brushed her cheek with his thumb before turning away.

Hawk motioned for his cousin to bring Judith's mount forward. Yellow Bear transferred the reins to his hand, then Hawk vaulted to his stallion's back. He glanced over at the warriors with him.

"Muu ta-wo-i-a -ka maka-miki!"

Deborah picked out the word gun from his terse command, and felt a chill race up her spine. Did he mean to fire on the fort?

As if he sensed her sudden fright, he turned to look at her, his smile mocking, but his words bitter.

"Keta nu kuya-a-ku-tu."

"I'm not afraid of you," she said, and knew she meant it. No. Not of Hawk. Not really. Of how she felt about him, yes. But not that he would actually harm her. His mouth quirked in a half-grin.

"Tsaa."

Deborah felt Judith's startled gaze on her, and heard her whisper, "You can actually *understand* him?"

Drumming his heels against his horse's sides, Hawk started down the slope, pulling Deborah and Judith with him. The horses half-slid in places, and she had to hold on to the mane with both hands, but Deborah managed to stay on. It wasn't until they reached the bottom that she saw they were hidden in a grove of scrubby trees near a winding stream. Up above them, the fort lay on a flat tableland. Hawk reined to a halt and waited, his lean frame relaxed.

Puzzled, Deborah glanced at Hawk, but he remained still and listening. She exchanged a quick glance with Judith, her heart pounding furiously. For several long minutes nothing happened. Then she heard the first yips break the night silence of wind and insects, and stiffened. Shots shattered the night.

She'd been wrong. Hawk meant to attack the fort!

Her head whipped around, and she heard Judith's

strangled gasp, but Hawk remained still. He seemed to be waiting for something.

Just when she couldn't stand the strain another moment, Hawk nudged the horse up the steep, rocky bank above them, and she had to grasp tightly to keep from falling. A few shots had been exchanged, but after the first spate, they'd stopped. Now she heard voices, and recognized familiar words being shouted back to the Comanche.

Hawk paused on the lip of the bank, jerking their mounts to a halt. Deborah saw soldiers, most half-dressed, all carrying weapons, talking with two of the warriors. Her heart thumped.

"They're discussing the terms of your return," Hawk said when she flashed him a glance.

"You're—*selling*—me?"

"Would you rather I risk them shooting you before they find out you're a white woman?" he asked with an irritable grunt. "And I'm not selling you. I'm trading you back to them."

He tossed her the reins to her mount, then did the same to Judith. Deborah caught them. It was time. She would ride into Fort Richardson and never see him again.

Tears welled again, embarrassing and annoying, and she blinked them back. Fortunately, he didn't notice.

"Then this is good-bye."

Hawk looked at her in the light. He nudged his stallion forward and leaned over to cup her chin in his palm. His hand was warm, and for some reason, she recalled that day under the pine trees when he had held her hand and examined it so gently. She closed her eyes when he kissed her, a light, feathery brush of his mouth across her parted lips.

He deepened the kiss when she leaned into him, and

183

his arm went around her back to keep her from falling off her horse. There was a fierce urgency in the kiss, a desperation that tore at her soul and made her tremble. Her arms wound around his neck, and she kissed him back.

A harsh groan sounded deep in his throat, and he jerked back, his eyes glittering in the press of moonlight.

"I will never forget you," he rasped. "I will think of you always. *Usúni.*"

Wheeling his stallion around, Hawk reached out and slapped her mare on the rump, sending it bounding forward. She gave a startled, anguished cry that echoed in the night, but he was gone.

Dust boiled up behind his stallion's hooves as Hawk rode in the opposite direction. Deborah caught a glimpse of him as she and Judith reached the soldiers, who were eagerly reaching up to grab their horses. He rode between the soldiers and his own men, whooping and yelling like a fiend, and before any of the soldiers could react, the Comanche were gone.

Deborah watched as the last of them were outlined on the rocky ridge. Was it her imagination, or was that Hawk reining back his stallion to its haunches, and lifting his rifle over his head? Then a high-pitched howl rode the wind, and she knew. She knew.

Moonlight sprayed over the scene, a sight she thought she would never forget. Hawk—wild, free, long hair blowing in the wind and looking as if he were a part of his horse. It would be imprinted on her mind forever.

"Ma'am, ma'am," someone was saying, and she looked down blindly. A kind-faced man wearing cavalry pants and a union shirt held her horse. "It's all right, ma'am. They're gone. They won't be back now that they've got what they want."

184

Her horse pranced nervously, and Deborah shifted to keep her balance. "What did they want?"

"Damndest thing—a sack of hard candy. You ever heard of such? You two ladies are lucky, yessir, you are."

Deborah didn't hear the rest of his words. A roar filled her ears, and through the pounding, she heard Hawk's husky voice.

Usúni. Forever.

Book II

Evil is wrought by want of Thought
As well as want of Heart.

—Thomas Hood

Chapter 14

Sirocco, Texas 1872

"It's been over six months for heaven's sake," Judith said irritably. "Are you still thinking about him?"

Deborah turned from the window where she'd been gazing out at the courtyard garden. "About who?"

"About that handsome savage, that's who." Her voice softened. "Oh, Deborah, don't look at me like that. You know I don't mean to hurt you, but you've got to stop moping about like this."

"And what else am I supposed to do?" she asked dryly, turning to face her cousin. "The Velazquez family were not exactly thrilled to have me back on their doorstep."

Judith looked away from Deborah's steady gaze. "I know. I can't understand why Uncle John has not . . . didn't . . ."

"Didn't want me back, you mean?" Deborah laughed shortly. "He's not the kind of man to want to invite a *well-used* woman, even his daughter, back into a society he's trying to impress with his wealth and position. No, he's quite satisfied to leave me to the Velazquez family and let them worry about public opinion."

"I don't think it's quite that bad," Judith said in a wretched voice that made Deborah sigh.

189

"Perhaps not. Maybe it just seems that way." She turned back to gaze out at the flowering vines and lush garden shading the tiled patio.

Nothing had been as she had once envisioned it. The Velazquez family had politely accepted Deborah into their home, but it was plain that they did not want her. She had been Miguel's wife so briefly, that she was of use only to tie them to American citizenship. If not for that, the embarrassment of her stay with the Comanche would have prompted her immediate return to John Hamilton whether he wanted her or not.

It was to be expected, she supposed. After all, the horror of the raid and Don Francisco's slow recovery from the wounds he'd suffered during that horrible time had left marks on all of them. He was bound to be resentful.

So she remained, an unwanted guest, living on the fringes of life. But it was worse, she sometimes thought, for Judith. Her cousin had the same stigma, and no position to save her. At least, as Miguel's widow, Deborah was entitled to a certain grudging respect.

"Why don't we ride into town?" Judith suggested, her tone forced. "If we're to be ostracized, we should at least be able to shop."

Deborah laughed. "There must be some benefits to this situation, is that it?"

"Exactly." Some of Judith's former humor surfaced in her quick smile. "My generous cousin will be more than glad to buy me some new cloth for a dress so that I can add it to my collection of other unused dresses."

"Of course. And we can wear them when we sit on the patio at night with Don Francisco."

Judith grimaced. "That charmer."

"Isn't he? And so delicate when he repeats that if not

190

for the family, I would have met the fate of most women when captured by Comanche."

"As if he personally was responsible for our return. I don't think he bothered to look for us at all."

Deborah thought the same. Of course, after the brutal attack, there had been other worries. The army had been notified, and there had been a brief, cursory search. But the search had not continued after the first week.

She felt a pang. If not for her escape attempt, she and Judith would probably have remained with Hawk forever. *Usúni.*

But she was being selfish. Judith had hated it there, and she had, too. Only her love for Hawk had made it bearable, and that realization had come late, so late.

She thought of him often. And on the nights of a full moon, when it rode high in the sky and she could hear the lonely, distant wail of a coyote, she felt an unbearable loneliness that threatened to consume her.

Deborah turned abruptly, unable to bear her own thoughts any longer. "Let's go now. It's still early, and I want to get out for a while."

"Shall we check with our jailer first?" Judith asked with a slight lift of her brow. "Don Francisco has the notion that we should not breathe without his permission."

"I refuse to be treated as a prisoner. Since he has what he needs by my presence here as Miguel's widow, I should be allowed my freedom."

"Let's hope he remembers that."

Deborah didn't reply. There had been a few sharp words with Don Francisco; the patriarch of the Velazquez family did not take kindly to her professed independence. She was a member of his family, and the women did not rebel. They obeyed. She would remember that or suffer the consequences.

If not for her experience in the Comanche village, Deborah would have quietly acquiesced to his demands. But her experience had strengthened her and given her a dislike of being forced to comply. She'd emerged from that ordeal a much stronger woman than before.

"Shall we ask Tía Dolores to accompany us?" Judith suggested. "For convention's sake, of course."

"And to appease Don Francisco." Deborah smiled. "Of course. She is always agreeable to going into Sirocco."

Green humps of mountain fringed the horizon and made a stark contrast to the burning blue of the sky. Tucked in the shadow of a chewed gray line of ridge, Sirocco lay sleepy and quiet in the early spring sun.

A few soldiers from nearby Fort Bliss roamed the wooden walkways in front of weathered gray storefronts, and here and there a horse stood tied to a rail with head down and eyes closed. Music drifted on brisk wind currents, faint accompaniment from some off-key piano unable to drown out the warbling voice of a woman commonly known as a soiled dove.

Deborah, Judith, and Tía Dolores stepped up onto the safety of a wooden walkway outside a small store.

"Shocking," Tía Dolores clucked. "They should not allow such women to sing."

"Because of their voice, or their profession?" Deborah couldn't help teasing, and smiled at Tía Dolores's grimace.

"Both. It is bad, I tell you."

Deborah and Judith exchanged amused glances at the stout, good-natured disapproval of the chaperon. Tía Dolores made life more bearable at the sprawling Velazquez hacienda, her simple approach to life a mixture of strict discipline and generous spirit. Today, in spite of the warm sun, Tía Dolores wore a high-necked black dress, lacy veil, and long sleeves. Her gray-streaked dark hair was pulled back in a severe style from her face, somehow making her austere features softer instead of harsh.

Now, her mouth pursed with disapproval. "A woman who sings so badly should be stopped."

"Shall we go tell her?" Judith asked with an innocent smile.

Tía Dolores shook her head. "No, no, of course not. We can do nothing like that." Her dark eyes narrowed. "You are teasing me again, *niña*. I shall reprimand you."

Judith laughed and tucked her hand into the older woman's bent arm. "Yes, I admit it. But you are so easy to tease."

A faint, reluctant smile curved Tía Dolores's mouth, and she patted Judith's hand. "It is good to see you smile so often now. I will suffer gladly."

The three women paused in the shade of an over-hanging porch. Dust blew down the middle of the street like a small storm cloud, stinging their eyes and making them cough.

"I don't think I'll ever get used to the constant wind," Deborah remarked. "Or the dust."

"Sí, you will," Dolores assured them. "One can adjust to anything." She looked up the street, where the music had gotten louder. "There are too many cantinas here, too many lawless men."

Deborah followed her glance. In the small town, there were more than a dozen saloons. And armed men lounged in shady doorways and strutted the walkways at leisure. They looked dangerous, with low-slung pistols and an air of restless menace.

That much was true, Deborah thought. She shifted

from one foot to the other, then glanced at the storefront window behind them. "Shall we go in and see what Mr. Potter has in that's new?"

The store held a delicious variety of fragrances, all tempting. There was the sharp smell of spices, the rich scent of tobacco, and the pungent odor of newly-cured hides. A little of everything lined Mr. Potter's shelves and filled glass-topped cases scattered over the floor and filling the aisles so that it was difficult to move without bumping into something or someone.

Deborah moved down an aisle, engrossed in the prettily-arranged knick knacks in a glass case, and did not see the man blocking her progress. She bumped into him, and startled them both.

"Oh!" she exclaimed. "Excuse me, please sir."

The man turned, a tall, blond, muscular man in a dark frock coat and starched white shirt. He smiled slowly, and his lazy drawl was appreciative.

"Any time you want to bump into me, ma'am, feel free," he said, grinning down at her.

Deborah flushed. "I apologize, sir."

"No need, ma'am. I kinda liked it." Brown eyes narrowed on her. "I don't think I know you, ma'am. Have we met before?"

"No," Deborah said stiffly, "we have not. Now, if you will please excuse me, I must join my companions."

"Wee—oo! I can feel the ice from here," the man said with an unabashed grin.

Deborah could not push past without rubbing up against him, so she turned and marched back down the way she had come. She didn't like the way his eyes followed her, or the frank speculation she'd seen in his gaze.

And when he approached the three women, Deborah

didn't like the way he kept his gaze on her while he engaged Tía Dolores in conversation.

"Señora Velazquez," he said easily, "it is good to see you again."

"And you also, Señor Diamond," she replied courteously. "I trust you have been well."

"Well enough." His gaze remained on Deborah. "Is this a friend of yours, señora? I don't believe we've been properly introduced."

There was a brief, noticeable hesitation, then Tía Dolores said politely, "This is Señorita Hamilton, our houseguest. And this is my poor nephew's widow, Doña Velazquez."

The brown gaze sharpened slightly, "Ah, I had heard she was rescued."

Deborah's cheeks flamed, but she refused to act ashamed or embarrassed. Her chin tilted higher, and she met his gaze with a steady regard that made him smile.

"I am very pleased to make your acquaintances, ladies," he said politely. "I hope I have not intruded. I'm not known for my manners, I'm afraid."

"So I see," she replied icily. Her chilly reply only seemed to delight him instead of quell his overtures, and Deborah felt a rising sense of dismay as he turned to Tía Dolores and began asking questions about the Velazquez family. It was obvious that this man knew them well, and was on a familiar enough basis to be treated as a neighbor instead of a stranger.

The rigid social structure of the Velazquez family would not have allowed her to converse with a stranger, but as an approved neighbor, this man would be accepted.

"Well now," he was drawling, "runnin' in to you today saves me some time, Señora. I was gonna come out to your place and invite you and your brother to join me in a little party I'm throwin' next week. Won't do you no good to tell me no. I've invited the entire county, and if you folks don't come, I'll be insulted. That won't help neighborly relations, now will it?"

His gruff congeniality did not conceal his determination, and Tía Dolores floundered helplessly until Deborah intervened.

"I'm not at all certain it would be proper for us to attend a party, Mr. Diamond. It—"

"Dexter," he interrupted. "You can call me Dexter."

"No, I cannot." She inhaled deeply. "It has not yet been a year since the . . . the tragedy. I'm afraid that our mourning is not yet ended."

"Mourning?" He looked incredulous. "Out here, ma'am, if you don't mind me sayin' so, there ain't much time for things like mourning. Life goes on. And time is short. No, I won't take a refusal. I'll see you folks next Thursday. Until then, it's been nice meeting you ladies."

He brushed a finger over the brim of the hat he hadn't bothered to remove, then strode to the door. "Come on, Braden," he said over his shoulder. Deborah then noticed the man ranging close behind him, a dangerous looking man wearing a low-slung pistol strapped around his waist.

Tía Dolores was nervous and fluttery. "Ah, *Díos!* What will Francisco say?"

"Who was he?" Judith asked. "He certainly doesn't seem like a man to take no for an answer."

"He is not." Tía Dolores brushed nervously at her skirt and readjusted the veil atop her head. "That is Señor Dexter Diamond, and he owns the Double D, a huge rancho near here. He has tried many times to persuade Francisco to sell him our land, but of course, we have not. Señor Diamond says we have more water and

196

he needs it for his cattle." She made a face. "He also has a need for more land, it seems, and more cattle. He has said he will be the biggest landowner in Texas one day, and I believe he means it."

"But if Don Francisco has refused to sell, then there is nothing he can do," Deborah said soothingly. "And I am certain Don Francisco will not want to attend this party."

She was wrong.

Stroking his neatly trimmed goatee, Don Francisco considered gravely for several minutes before he said, "We will attend."

Shocked, Tía Dolores burst out, "Why?"

"Because I wish to see for myself the size of his ranch and how well-defended it is." He formed a steeple of his fingers and gazed back at the three surprised women. "And a little party will not make you unhappy, eh? Especially the lovely Señorita Hamilton, who needs diversion as any young woman does."

Judith shifted uncomfortably beneath Don Francisco's intent gaze. She looked away when he stood up and stroked the top of her bright, golden head.

"American women are accustomed to more freedom than our young women, so it is not unexpected that you would want to dance, is it not so?"

Edging away from his hand, Judith nodded. "I do like to dance. I've missed it."

"*Bueno!* Then we shall go, and you shall have your dance, *chica.*"

Deborah and Judith exchanged helpless glances with Tía Dolores after Don Francisco left the room.

"This is going to be fun, in spite of everything, I think," Judith whispered to Deborah as they stepped down from the Velazquez carriage and entered the house with Tía Dolores close behind. Sounds of revelry floated out from the rambling adobe house, and guitars and horns soared with music. Servants glided between the guests with loaded trays of food and drink.

Deborah shrugged. "Perhaps."

"Oh, Deborah. Give yourself a chance to enjoy life again. You're still young, not even twenty-two yet. And I know that you . . . think of things at times, but don't. Just relax and enjoy yourself for a while."

Deborah glanced at the guests already milling on the huge patio and in the house, and nodded. "You're right. I should forget everything. It's over. I have to go on from here."

Judith gave her arm a comforting squeeze. "Right. And I think—I *know*—that Dexter Diamond has taken a fancy to you. It was evident that day we met him."

"He's too brash. I don't like him that much."

"Well," Judith said practically, "you don't have to like him to eat his food and dance at his party."

Laughing, Deborah admonished, "You are impossible!"

"Yes. Now come along, and help me avoid Don Francisco," she leaned close to whisper. "I think he wants me to dance with him." She gave her blue taffeta skirts a final pat, then took Deborah firmly by the arm to pull her along.

They had not progressed very far before their host saw them. He switched direction immediately, and descended upon Deborah before she could escape.

"Miss Hamilton," he said with a wide grin that didn't fade when she corrected him coldly.

"Señora Velazquez."

"I hardly think a few hours with poor Miguel qualifies you as his widow, but if you prefer—Señora

198

Velazquez. Why don't I just make it easy and call you Deborah?"

"That's a bit too familiar, thank you."

Deborah swallowed a quick gasp of dismay when he deftly removed her from Tía Dolores with the promise that he would guard her well, and escorted her across the crowded room. She could feel Tía Dolores's shocked gaze following her.

Jerking her arm from his warm gasp, Deborah glared up at Diamond. "That was a very high-handed, ungentlemanly thing to do, sir. I do not need any more gossip directed at me!"

He grinned down at her, and Deborah felt a wave of irritation. Dressed in a starched white shirt, dark pants, vest, and a coat, he was handsome in a rough sort of way, she supposed, but entirely too autocratic. And bold.

Chuckling, Diamond said, "You're every inch a lady, aren't you? Right down to your lace drawers, I'll bet." Ignoring her angry gasp, he continued, "What kind of accent is that? It ain't just Southern. It sounds foreign, kinda, all clipped and cool. But all you Southern women are prissy. I like that. A woman who tries to be as tough as a man needs to be ridin' herd on cattle, not dancin'. Now, sugar, I'll bet you can dance better than any woman in Texas, can't ya?"

"I'm certain I can," she said when she recovered from her fury, "but I don't intend to do so. And I'll thank you not to discuss my ... underclothing ... in public."

Throwing back his shaggy blond head, Diamond roared with laughter, catching the attention of several guests. Still chuckling, he grabbed Deborah's hand and bellowed to the musicians to play a waltz.

"For me and my lovely lady!" he added with a possessive grin that made Deborah yearn to refuse.

But with all the smiling gazes turned toward them, she knew that to protest would only cause more gossip. So she smiled in what she hoped was a remote, cool way and put her hand daintily in his huge, outstretched palm.

"Thank you, Mister Diamond," she said coolly. There. If anyone wanted to read anything into her response, all they could see was ingrained courtesy.

But it was hard to keep her composure when Dexter Diamond held her close to him in the dance, his sturdy body a solid wall of heat and muscle. And it was obvious he liked having her that close to him. To her chagrin, she felt his male response to holding her, and it made her want to run.

Her head tilted back, and she felt the brush of her carefully coiled hair against her neck. Though she wore black, her throat was bare, and the slender black velvet ribbon circling it boasted a single cameo in its center to provide her only touch of jewelry. The gown was simply cut, with a cinched-in waist and straight skirt pulled snugly over her hips to flounce down the back in ruffles.

Fixing a smile on her face, Deborah looked up at Dexter and said softly, "Do not hold me so tightly, Mr. Diamond, or I will manage to stomp on your feet."

He looked startled, then grinned and loosened his hold. "Yep. I was right. In spite of everything, you're a lady through and through."

Anger sparked her eyes. "In spite of everything?"

He shrugged. "You know what I mean. Everyone heard about it. It happens out here. You were lucky."

"And you aren't repelled by knowing we were held captive for two months?" Deborah shot back stiffly.

Dark brown eyes roved her face boldly. "No. It happens. It wasn't your fault."

Deborah looked away, her throat tightening. No censure here, when she'd found it everywhere else. Sly whispers behind cupped hands, smirks glimpsed as she passed, and the inevitable curious gazes from the men—she'd seen and heard enough of them in the past six months.

"Thank you, Mr. Diamond," she said softly, and he squeezed her hand.

"Dexter."

She managed a smile. "All right. Dexter."

"Good." He grinned, a bold, possessive grin. "I think you and me are gonna get along fine, sugar."

"Perhaps. As long as you don't hold me too tightly and keep calling me sugar."

His loud laugh burst out again, delighted and attention drawing. "Miss Deborah—is it all right if I call you that? I think me and you are gonna get along great."

Tucking her hand into the crook of his bent arm when the music ended, Dexter Diamond kept Deborah at his side as he introduced her to other guests. She had the distinct feeling that he was laying claim to her, and wondered if she was the only one who noticed.

She wasn't.

Across the room, leaning against a raised window frame that served as a doorway to the patio, one of Dexter Diamond's hired guns noticed his attentiveness. He shifted, his broad shoulders scraping against the wooden frame. The butt of a pistol hanging low on his lean thigh made a clunking noise as it bumped against the wood, but he didn't notice.

He'd noticed Deborah the moment she came into the

room, and it hit him with all the force of a stampeding buffalo. She was beautiful, more beautiful than he'd dreamed a woman could be.

The sleek auburn hair was drawn up into an intricate mass of curls and held with ribbons and sparkling Spanish combs, and the black gown that might have looked dowdy on another, flattered her slender curves. Creamy skin, regal demeanor, cool amber eyes—yes, she was definitely the most beautiful woman there. She outshone her blond, vivacious cousin, simply with her quiet composure and dignity.

Not that Judith Hamilton lacked for admirers. Men flocked around her, drawn by her wit and beauty. But to Zack Banning, the only woman in the room was Deborah.

He knew he should leave the room and not watch, but the shock of seeing her had robbed him of the will to follow his common sense. So he stayed, and he watched as she danced with Dexter Diamond, slowly thawing to the blond rancher's avid attention. And he felt the slow burn of anger ignite deep in his gut.

It was late when Diamond escorted Deborah from the stuffy confines of the main room to the cool air of the patio. Lanterns hung from latticework and trees, shedding wavering light over stone tiles.

As he passed, Diamond noticed the newest addition to his huge force of hired gunmen, and paused.

"Banning. Everything quiet?"

Zack shrugged. "Quiet enough." His gaze shifted to the woman on Diamond's arm, and she turned politely toward him. He saw her stiffen, heard her gasp with shock, and wondered with a faint twinge of malice what she would do.

Deborah stared at him, shock making her wide hazel eyes almost black. "Hawk," she breathed.

Chapter 15

"It's him, I tell you," Deborah said with a nervous flick of one hand that gained her Judith's frowning attention. "Hawk. Here. At the Double D. Dear God, what am I going to do?"

"Well . . ." Judith sounded uncertain, swinging a bare foot back and forth as she perched on the edge of their wide bed in a second story guest room. A brisk breeze blew in the open window, tossing the curtains and her hair. "Are you certain it was him?"

"Am I certain?" Deborah stopped her pacing to turn to her cousin. "I knew him very well. It's Hawk. His hair is a little shorter, and he's wearing real clothes and looks just like every other disreputable gunslinger I've seen, but it's him. It's Hawk."

"What is he calling himself?"

"Zack Banning. Dexter introduced me." A burble of nervous laughter welled up, and she put a hand over her mouth. "Oh, Judith—I just stood there looking at him, and when I said *Hawk!* and he said so cool and remote—'No ma'am. Zack. Zack Banning,' I thought I would faint."

"What did *Dexter* have to say? And how did you two get on a first-name basis so quickly?"

"He insisted, and it seemed the lesser of two evils. I hate being publicly embarrassed. He also said Banning was the best gun he had, and that no one could make trouble when he was around. Then he laughed, as if it was funny."

"This is totally beyond the realm of imagination. It seems strange that Hawk would be here unless he knew it was you."

"Yes. So I thought. But he seemed surprised when Dexter introduced me as Señora Velazquez. Maybe it is just a coincidence, though it doesn't seem likely."

"Does Diamond know that Hawk—does he know who he is?"

"No. I'm sure he doesn't. He kept referring to him as a 'damn good gunny,' whatever that's supposed to mean." Deborah shivered. "I could hardly speak when Hawk—Zack—said it was nice to meet me and just kind of walked away. This must be what be meant when he talked about his other life in the white man's world. He's a *gunfighter*, Judith."

"Do you want to go back home in the morning?" Judith lay back on the bed. "If you feel uncomfortable staying here with Hawk so close by, we can make some sort of excuse."

"Yes. No. I don't know."

Judith laughed. "You sound so certain. All right. I think maybe we should talk about this again in the morning."

"Yes. After a good night's rest, maybe I'll find out this was all an unpleasant dream."

"Don't count on that."

Deborah made a face. "Thanks. If you're trying to comfort me, it's not working."

"Sorry." Judith slipped from the bed to the floor and bent to retrieve her shoes and stockings. "I danced so much my feet have blisters," she said with a happy sigh. As she straightened, there came a knock on the closed door and they exchanged quick glances.

"Let me get it," Judith said firmly. "And if it's . . . a person we don't want to see, I'll send him away."

Tía Dolores stood in the doorway, her plump face creased in a worried frown. "You must come with me, Judith. Don Francisco wishes to speak to you."

"To me?" Judith hesitated. "Why? It's late, and I was about to go to sleep."

"He has had an offer of marriage for you."

Judith's jaw sagged, and the glance she shot her cousin was astonished. "My God, these Westerners work fast! Who?"

Tía Dolores gave a nervous flap of her hands. "This is so irregular, so impulsive. These Texans, they have no sense of propriety at all, but the man is very insistent and Don Francisco said you would tell him yourself he must wait." She rolled her eyes. "Our host seems to find it quite amusing, but I am so outraged!"

Deborah laughed. "Well, Judith, you seem to have made a very good impression on someone."

"Probably that gouty old gentleman with no hair and bad breath," Judith muttered as she pulled on her stockings and shoes. "Just my luck."

"If I'm asleep when you get back, wake me," Deborah said, laughing at the face her cousin made. "I'm dying to hear all the details."

"Grim as they may be, I assure you that you will." As she gave a final pat to her hair, Judith followed Tía Dolores out the door, waggling her fingers at Deborah. "Lock the door behind me."

Deborah hesitated, then crossed to the door and locked it. The key clicked loudly. She leaned back against the door for a moment, then began undressing.

205

The events of the evening had left her tense and restless, and she jerked impatiently at the hooks on her gown. She heard a rip, and gave a sigh.

"More mending," she groaned.

When she had the dress off, she draped it over a chair and looked for the rip. It was small, and would be easily repaired. Her petticoats brushed against her legs in a soft rustle of cotton. She untied the tapes around her waist and hung the undergarments from a hook on the wall.

Clad in her chemise, pantalets and hose, she padded in her bare feet to the dressing table and began removing the pins from her hair. It cascaded around her shoulders as she took them out, and she carefully untied the satin ribbons that had been wound among the curls and combs.

Her thoughts were as jumbled as the box of hairpins, tangled and impossible to sort. Hawk. *Zack*. Here. After six long, agonizing months with no word of him—if he was dead or alive or captured by Colonel Mackenzie in his deadly sweep across the Texas plains into New Mexico—he turned up here right under her nose. And no one seemed to have equated the dangerous gunslinger with the half-breed renegade Comanche, Hawk. It was crazy. It was daring. It was suicidal.

"God!" she burst out, clenching her fists and staring at her reflection in the smoky glass of the mirror. "What can he be thinking!"

"Probably about how fickle women are," came a deep, lazy voice from her right, and she whirled with a gasp to see Hawk—Zack—standing by the open window.

The first flush of joy was quickly replaced by uneasiness. He didn't come toward her, but stood with one thumb hooked in his gunbelt, a lean leg bent at the knee, his stance wary and somehow dangerous. His other hand was braced above his head on the window frame, and the curtains blew out with the breeze, riffling his dark hair.

He looked so familiar, yet at the same time, so different. The difference was in more than the clothes he wore, the snug pants, red shirt, and leather vest. No, this was a difference he wore more easily. It fit him, fit him much more comfortably than the breechcloth and leggings had done. For the first time, she felt as if she were seeing the true man. Even his speech was less stilted.

But it was his eyes that had changed, the wary expression in them altering to something else, something cold and assessing—and unforgiving.

Deborah felt suddenly exposed, and shivered. She crossed her arms over her chest. Her voice came out in a strangled croak. "Get out of here!"

"Aren't you glad to see me?" His dark brow shot up at a slant. "Somehow, I thought you might be. Guess I was wrong."

"Hawk—if anyone finds you in here, you'll be shot!"

He straightened slowly, arms falling to his sides. "You locked the door. And besides, your new sweetheart wouldn't risk your reputation that way. He'd drag me out back to shoot me, so no one would know."

She reached blindly for something to pull over her, acutely aware of her lack of clothing. But when she grabbed a thin muslin wrapper, he moved swiftly as a striking snake. That was something that hadn't changed. He still moved with the lightning-quick reflexes of a Comanche brave, smooth and graceful and predatory. Too bad she'd forgotten how quickly he could move until his hand shot out to grasp her wrist and hold it.

"I've seen you without your clothes," he said tersely. "Or have you managed to forget that, too?"

"Of course I haven't forgotten." Her cheeks burned. "But I see no sense in—"

"In teasing me? Good point." He released her wrist with a shove, his eyes glittering and cold.

Deborah backed away, a little afraid. He was Hawk, but he wasn't Hawk. Now he looked angry and unfamiliar. Her chin lifted. She wouldn't give him the satisfaction of knowing that he made her nervous.

"What do you want?"

Dark blue eyes raked over her, and she felt naked. His gaze was hot and insulting, and she felt her flush warm her throat and chest. He laughed, a short, harsh sound.

"Diamond says he's going to marry you. Funny, but I never dreamed Señora Velazquez was the same person as Deborah Hamilton." He shrugged. "Guess you didn't think it was important to tell me the truth."

Her temper flared. "And why should I? I was a captive, remember? A slave. And when you asked my name I had been wed and widowed in a very short time. I owed you nothing. You were so intent on raping me, that I find it difficult to believe you cared about my true name!"

He glared at her. "Did I rape you?"

"Not then."

"Damn you," he snarled, grabbing her when she took a step back and away from him. "You wanted me as much as I wanted you. Don't deny it."

"I was curious," she began, but he put his hands on her shoulders and gave her a rough shake that sent her hair flying over her face and into her eyes.

"Curious? Is that what you're calling it? It was more than curiosity."

His voice vibrated with an intensity that shook her to the core, and Deborah couldn't form an answer for a

208

moment. There was anger, yes, but something else, a raw emotion she couldn't identify. She put a hand up as if to ward off a blow, and saw his eyes change.

Swearing softly, he released her. "I shouldn't have come up here," he said after a moment, his voice flat and emotionless. "I can see that you're able to land on your feet, just like a cat. I shouldn't have wasted any time worrying about you."

"Did you?" She rubbed at her wrist where his grip had bit into her tender flesh. "Did you worry about me, Hawk?"

The look he gave her was unreadable. "Zack. Zack Banning. If you haven't heard anything about me before, I'm sure you will. Remember—I told you what it was like for me in the white man's world."

She was puzzled. "I already know you're a gunslinger. You were hired to guard Dexter."

"Dexter?" His mouth curled into a hateful smile. "How cozy. Yes, I was hired to guard him, and this ranch, and anything else he thinks needs guarding."

"You kill for money."

"If it's called for," he replied in a cool tone that sent shivers down her back.

Deborah was quiet for a moment. "Why are you here?"

The question hung in the air between them for a long, sizzling moment. Then he looked away, thick lashes lowering over the intense blue of his eyes.

"I need the money."

"Where have you been? You just disappeared. We heard rumors about the Comanche under White Eagle, but no one knows where they went . . ." Her voice trailed off at the hot glance he flung her.

"And I intend for it to stay that way. Do you think I'd tell anyone where they're hiding? Not by a long shot. It was hard enough finding a secure place, and God only knows how long it will be safe with Mackenzie riding herd on the Comanche like a crazed cowhand."

She'd never heard this tone from him, the bitter irony in his voice. He looked at her, then turned away with a quick downward drift of his lashes and a careless shrug.

"Hawk—Zack—I do care what happens to them. And I care that you've obviously suffered for them."

"Don't."

Her throat tightened with emotion. He looked furious and sad at the same time, his mouth set into a straight line and his thoughts hidden.

"If you're so upset at being apart from them, why didn't you stay with them?"

"Why?" He turned around in a quick move that made her jump. "Because if I hadn't left, Mrs. Velazquez, Mackenzie would have pursued them to the gates of hell, that's why! I was the one identified by the soldiers and the Comancheros who came to camp and saw you there—*I* am the one those scouts saw the day you tried to escape. If I hadn't left and let it be known I'd left, they'd have burned down the entire mountain range just to get at me. I couldn't risk the others that way." His mouth tightened. "Spirit Talker was right, it seems."

"So you left them because of me."

He made an impatient gesture. "No, not entirely. I'd have probably left one day anyway. I didn't fit in there either. I'm too white to be a Comanche, too Comanche to be a white. So I live by the gun." His eyes were mocking, blue ice in a dark face as he leaned back against the dresser and raked her with a slow, insolent gaze.

"How's Sunflower?" she asked when the silence grew too thick.

210

"Still alive, the last time I saw her."

Deborah didn't dare ask any more questions. For some reason, he looked so—bleak. She put out a hand, and he looked at it, then his gaze shifted to her face. Slowly, he took her hand, pulling her to him.

Muttering something in Comanche, he buried his face in the curve of her neck and shoulder, his fingers tangling in her hair. His mouth moved across her bare skin in a fiery trail that made her shiver, up to her jaw, her cheek, then her parted lips.

He kissed her, gently at first, then deeply, his tongue sliding into her mouth and coaxing a moan from deep in her throat. Cradling her face in his palms, he moved his mouth over hers until she had to hold onto him to keep from falling to her knees. His hands curved over her shoulders, fingers sliding under the straps of her chemise and pulling them down.

With a groan, he cupped his palms over her bare breasts and raked his thumbs over her taut nipples. A shudder ran through her. Bending, he lent the heat of his mouth to her cool, pale breast. She cried out again, soft and wordless, and clutched at him with both hands. Her nails raked his back, sliding over his cotton shirt, and she could feel the flex of his strong muscles as he shifted to hold her.

When he lifted his head to stare at her, she saw the same glaze of desire that she knew must be in her own eyes. He was breathing raggedly, but she felt his withdrawal from her. He straightened slowly, and set her on her feet.

"Just curious, huh?"

Deborah blinked at him, then flushed. Her hands shook as she dragged her chemise back up to cover her breasts.

"Obviously, I lied," she said in a voice that she barely

recognized as her own. It sounded too calm, when she was raging inside with longing and confusion.

"At least you're being honest about that." He looked at her for a long moment, then said softly, "Your cousin's coming. I can hear her. I better leave."

The desolation was back, swift and cold and invasive. She couldn't let him leave her behind again. *Not again.*

"Hawk—Zack—wait. I . . . I missed you. And I worried about you."

"Did you?" He paused. "I'll keep that in mind next time I see Diamond rubbing all over you while you smile at him. It wouldn't look good if I was to pay you any attention where folks could see, anyway." His mouth twisted. "If you don't understand now, someone will be sure to tell you why soon enough."

Before she could ask him anything, he was gone, stepping back out the open window. She heard his light steps on the porch roof, then a soft plop as if he had jumped to the ground.

Deborah sagged to a chair, and heard Judith's voice in the hallway. She must be insane. She should have screamed, and had him dragged out to be shot. Instead, she had all but given him permission to assault her. All but begged to go with him.

The expected knock rattled the door, and she got up to let Judith in.

"You're awfully quiet," Judith said. They were sitting in the shaded courtyard of the Velazquez hacienda. It was warm, and sunlight heated the patio tiles to a blinding glow.

"Just thinking."

"About Zack Banning?" When Deborah looked up at her, Judith gave an impatient sound. "I don't understand

212

you. A man like Dexter Diamond is courting you, yet you won't give him the time of day. He's going to give up soon if you don't give him some encouragement."

"Good. I was beginning to think he was completely stupid."

"Deborah!"

"Well? And who said I was thinking about Zack Banning, or Hawk, or whatever name he goes by."

"I should hope not. He's dangerous, a real killer from what I heard."

"And what did you hear?" Deborah put her mending down and met her cousin's blue gaze calmly.

Judith flushed. "Well, for one thing, I heard that he's the kind of gunman that attracts challenges. That's how he met Dexter Diamond. He was in some sort of gunfight in El Paso a few months ago, and Mr. Diamond saw him. He was so quick and brutal, that Diamond figured he'd be able to take care of anything that came up here." She dragged in a deep breath. "And everyone knows he's a 'breed,' and they're supposed to be more ruthless than white men. People are scared of him, even if they do whisper about him and act as if he's famous."

"And where did you hear all this?" Deborah asked coolly.

"Hank Warfield."

"Ah—the impetuous suitor who proposes marriage at first sight." Deborah looked back down at the torn dress she was mending. Judith's voice was defensive.

"Well, he was a little drunk that night. Anyway, that was a month ago, and he's been a perfect gentleman since."

"He's managed to gossip a lot, too."

Exasperated, Judith snapped, "You just won't listen to anything about that savage, will you! Even if it's the

213

truth. He has done something to you, and I knew it before we were ever rescued."

"Maybe you'll recall that *the savage* took us to a fort while you're at it," Deborah retorted. "No one had to come after us."

"He *had* to free us! The Comancheros had seen us, and told the army, and then when that patrol saw us, they knew where we were. Oh, Deborah," she begged, her eyes anxious, "I know that he ... he forced you. Don't feel you must protect him, for God only knows what reason."

Deborah covered her face with one hand. "I don't know why I feel the way I do," she said miserably. "Sometimes I think he's everything people say, but if you talked to him, I mean *really* talked to him, I think you'd feel as I do. He has been caught up in something he didn't create and he can't fix, and he's just trying to survive."

"By gunning down men in the middle of the street? He's no better a white man than he was a Comanche."

Deborah's head snapped up, and she whispered tautly, "I don't ever want to hear that again. Perhaps I'm wrong about his reasons, but he's not as bad as you think. And remember your promise."

An unhappy expression settled on her face, but Judith nodded. "I will. I won't tell anyone who he is, but I don't think it matters. He's bad enough as Zack Banning, killer extraordinaire."

"Thanks. I feel so much better."

Deborah's dry tone didn't escape Judith, and she rose to fling herself on her knees by her cousin's chair. "I know you hate me for talking so badly to you."

"No, I don't hate you. I'm confused. And I haven't seen or heard from him since that first night, so he's probably forgotten me already."

"Do you really believe that?"

Deborah looked beyond the hacienda to the range of mountains gnawing at the horizon. "I don't know."

"I hope he has!" Judith said fiercely. "I hope he goes away and never, never comes back!"

Startled by her vehemence, Deborah asked slowly, "Why do you hate him so?"

"I hate all of them, not just him." Judith's fingers dug into the bent wood of Deborah's chair. Her throat was corded with strain, her voice a hoarse whisper. "They're savages, all of them. Brutal, torturing fiends. I'll never forget that old hag and her vicious treatment of me. I'll never forget—" She broke off abruptly, her eyes a wide, glazed blue.

"Judith?" Deborah touched her cheek gently. "Tell me what happened to you. I know that something very bad was done, but I can't help you unless I know. Won't you tell me?"

For a moment, Judith's lips trembled. She seemed about to speak, but then paused. "You'll hate me. It's so sordid and wicked, and at least you were wanted by—" Breaking off, she shook her head. "No. Nothing happened. Not like you may think. I told you. They were just mean to me. It was a nightmare, but it's over now." She cleared her throat and shrugged. "I'm sorry," she said calmly. "I just can't forgive them as easily as you."

Deborah stroked back her soft blond hair. "I'm sorry, too. I keep forgetting how badly they treated you, using you as a slave. You have a right to feel the way you do."

Judith buried her face in the length of the dress Deborah was mending. Her voice muffled. "I wish I could be like you. You always seem so calm and unruffled. Even when you're upset. You don't let anything truly affect you."

Amazed, Deborah said, "You know that's not true. You were with me the first night I saw him again. I was a bundle of nerves."

Judith lifted her head, a hint of amusement in her eyes. "I would have been hysterical. You were so nervous you actually giggled, but other than that, you could have been talking about a bad rainstorm."

"Maybe there's something wrong with me," Deborah said ruefully.

"If there is, it isn't lack of control." Judith pushed back a tangle of hair and sat back on her heels. "I think that is what attracts Diamond. Your cool poise."

"If I throw a temper tantrum or two, do you think he will leave me alone?"

Their good humor restored, the two laughed softly at the mental image of her throwing a tantrum.

When Dexter Diamond came calling that afternoon, Deborah was tempted to do just that.

Chapter 16

Big, blond, boisterous, it was obvious that Dexter Diamond was a man accustomed to getting his own way. He sat with his hat in his hands and his elbows resting on his thighs, gazing at Deborah with narrowed, frustrated eyes.

"I came to take you ridin', Miss Deborah, and that's what I intend to do," he said gruffly. "You're stubborn as a mule, and that's a fact."

She took another neat stitch in the square of embroidery she'd been working on. "What's your point?"

He growled an oath, and added when she looked up with a frown, "Miss Deborah, it's a fine day. We don't get many of those before the heat makes it too hot to get out. I'd like it a lot if you'd go riding with me."

Deborah laid her embroidery down and looked up at him. His rugged face was tight with exasperation when she said, "I understand you have told Don Francisco you intend to marry me."

He flushed and looked away, twirling his hat between his fingers. "Yeah. Guess I got carried away."

"I'd say so. Normally, a man asks the lady first."

"Didn't figure you'd say yes yet."

"And did Don Francisco?"

Grinning, he shook his head. "No. But that won't matter none when you agree to it."

Despite his outward hearty good humor, Deborah felt pressured and uneasy. There was a steely undercurrent to his attention that made her wary.

"If I agreed, which I am not inclined to do. It is nothing personal, Dexter, but I'm not ready to get married again. To anyone."

"Aw hell—heck, Miss Deborah, you'll get over that. Out here, there just ain't much time to waste. And you hardly knew Miguel. It was a marriage of convenience. You can't be that tore up over it."

"That has nothing to do with it," she said stiffly.

"Is it the other? Has anyone said anything to you about it?" His shoulders hunched forward, and he said softly, "I won't let no one bother you about that."

For all her irritation, Deborah couldn't help thinking how delicate he could be for a blustering man. She thawed slightly.

"That's very kind of you. But I—"

Standing, Diamond reached down to lift her. "No more excuses. If you want your cousin to go along or Señora Velazquez, or even Don Francisco, I don't care. They can all ride along, just so you enjoy yourself."

It was an appeal that was hard to resist, and Deborah smiled. "All right! You're too persistent to refuse any longer. I'll go this time."

He didn't seem to hear the qualifying *this time,* as he grinned and swirled her around with both arms around her waist.

"Damn woman, you like to hear a man beg, don't you?" he said when she protested his grip. His arms tightened, and Deborah looked up at him.

"Put me down, or I won't go."

218

He released her, still grinning. "A lady. Yep. All the way to—"

"Don't say it!"

When Deborah had gathered Judith and they met Diamond on the front patio, he gestured to the saddled horses. "All ready to go, ladies." He tugged at the brim of his hat and surveyed Deborah closely. "You look like a ray of sunshine in that yellow outfit, honey. Good enough to eat."

She felt her cheeks grow warm. "I'm afraid I don't have a riding habit in black."

"I ain't complainin', am I? Hell no." He put a possessive arm around Deborah's waist. "Come on. We'll help you mount up."

The *we,* Deborah discovered, was Diamond and his hired gunman. Zack Banning.

Her heart lurched when she saw him lounging under the shade of a scrubby tree, his back and the sole of one boot pressed against the trunk. He was smoking, and when they came out into the bright sunlight, he stood up slowly and ground his cigarette out under his heel.

He walked toward them with that languid grace and easy, loose-hipped stride, lethal and fascinating at the same time.

"You remember Banning, don't you?" Diamond asked with a careless wave of his hand at him. "He's our guard. Crack shot. Ought to make you feel a lot safer havin' two of us."

She couldn't say anything. She nodded, and saw that Judith had come to a quick halt. Zack watched Judith, his eyes cool and wary. She looked so pinched and frozen, that Deborah thought for a moment she would go back inside.

But then she said stiffly, "I can mount by myself, thank you."

Diamond seemed not to notice. He was looking at Deborah and paying no attention to Judith. "Come on, honey. I'll lift you up."

She had no time to offer a protest before Diamond had his hands around her waist and was lifting her onto the broad back of a docile bay mare. She felt Zack's amused gaze on her, and wondered if he was remembering her escape from his camp atop a lively Comanche pony.

When Diamond's hands lingered on her waist after she was seated, Deborah said tartly, "I can manage from here."

Still grinning, he drawled, "You ever see such a touchy woman, Banning?"

There was a moment of silence before Zack said, "Not often."

It was going to be a very uncomfortable ride, Deborah thought as she kept her eyes away from Zack. *Zack.* It was odd thinking of him like that. To her, he would always be Hawk—strong, arrogant, proud. A Comanche. It occurred to her to wonder if he had as much trouble adjusting to his dual identities as she did.

They cantered away from the hacienda and up into the low foothills, where spring flowers put on a brilliant display. Swaying in the wind, bluebonnets and Indian paintbrush vied with the hardier blossoms of strawberry cactus, and the creamy sprays of yucca dancing tall and gracefully on long stalks. A recent rain had caused a frenzied eruption of brief color across the hills and drier plains.

The sun was a warm caress on her face, the wind a constant urge at her back, whipping her yellow riding skirts around her legs and tugging at the ribbons of her stylish hat. She was suddenly glad she had come, despite everything.

Nudging his prancing mount close, Diamond asked, "Now, aren't you glad you came ridin', sugar?"

She flashed him a quelling stare, and he amended, "I mean, Miss Deborah."

"It's a very nice afternoon."

"I guess that means yes," Diamond said after a moment. A white hat shaded his eyes, but she felt him watching her. "You seem to be makin' it hard for me to know you on purpose. Why is that?"

Aware that Judith was riding on her other side, and Zack not far behind, Deborah said, "Do you mean I'm making it deliberately difficult for you to force me into marriage? If so, that is correct."

"Force—!" The word exploded from him, and he swore a moment before calming down. His horse tossed its head so that he had to soothe it, then he turned to Deborah. "I ain't tryin' to force you into nothin'. I've never had to ask so blamed much before a woman decided she'd even go ridin' with me. If you're playin' a game, I'm gettin' tired of your rules."

Deborah kept her attention on her gloved hands and the rhythmic motion of her horse, the gentle jogging that made the feather atop her hat sway back and forth. "I'm not playing a game, nor am I likely to be persuaded into doing something I don't want to do. I've been in that situation once, and I did not like it at all."

Her voice was loud enough to carry to Zack, and she wondered if he heard and understood.

He did.

Intolerable. Riding behind Diamond and Deborah, eating their dust and being subjected to Judith Hamilton's frequent murderous glances. He didn't blame Judith. At least she was being honest in her hatred. He had no idea what Deborah really thought.

He wondered what he was doing here at all. The moment he'd seen her, he should have ridden out. He didn't owe Diamond anything. The man had offered him a job when he needed one and was tired of drifting. He'd taken it. But there would be another job when this one ended. Men like Diamond hired gunfighters to enhance their own reputation anyway. They liked having dangerous men around them, men people feared and avoided. It caused a sensation, and he'd seen enough of Dexter Diamond to know that he was a man who always wanted the biggest, best, and loudest.

And now he wanted Deborah Hamilton Velazquez, but Zack couldn't figure out why. Besides the obvious. Deborah was being so cool, that could be part of the reason. She was a challenge, something he couldn't have. But there was an underlying current to his enthusiastic courting that made Zack uneasy. Nothing he could put his finger on, but an odd intensity that didn't ring quite true. Beneath that gruff, hearty exterior, Dexter Diamond had a driving ambition.

Maybe Deborah did too. Maybe he'd been wrong about her. Diamond was a powerful man, after all. He had money and position, and could give her anything she wanted. If that was her goal. Zack realized he didn't know what she wanted, really wanted.

When he was with her, touching her, she yielded despite protests, her body surrendering to his caresses. But that was a thing apart from ambition. The starched, reserved lady hid a wealth of emotions beneath her cool exterior. Maybe she hid a compelling ambition, too. Either way, there was no place in her world for him.

He had nothing to offer her, beyond passion.

The knowledge kept him from going to her when he wanted to, when he lay awake at night and thought about her, could almost feel her soft skin beneath his

222

hands and taste the sweet honey of her. And that denial ate at him.

"Let's stop here," Diamond said, and without waiting for a reply, reined in his horse and swung down. He reached up for Deborah, his hands again lingering around her waist when he stood her on the ground. "We'll rest the horses a little while before we go on."

Disentangling herself from his hold, Deborah murmured an agreement, fully aware of Hawk—no, Zack—watching them. Though he wore a low-crowned tan hat shading his face, she could feel the heat of his searing blue eyes on her. She shivered.

Diamond put an arm around her shoulders. "Cold, honey?"

"No. I have a name, you know."

"Yeah, I know. Deborah. But you're starched so stiff I thought maybe you might unbend a little if I called you somethin' sweet."

"Did you?"

He grinned. "Yeah. Is it workin'?"

Tilting her head back, she stared up at him with a mixture of exasperation and amusement. He was pushy. He was arrogant. But he had a certain rough charm.

"Not yet," she replied with a reluctant smile. "But keep trying. You're entertaining, at least."

"Guess I should say thanks, ma'am."

Taking her hand, Diamond drew her to a flat rock nearby and brushed it off with his hat before seating her, a broad, gallant gesture that made her laugh. When Judith approached, her blond hair shining gold and bright in the sun and her blue skirts the same bright color as her eyes, Deborah made room for her on the surface of the rock. She saw Diamond frown slightly, as if disgruntled by Judith's presence, and hid a smile.

"It's beautiful out here," Judith said, spreading her skirts over her crossed legs with a dainty motion. "Somehow, I thought this part of Texas was always dry and dusty."

Diamond shrugged. "It is. But even ugly has its moments, I reckon." He pointed toward a line of rocky ridge. "There in Heuco Mountains and the Diablo Basin, you'll find mule deer and pronghorn antelope, mountain cats, grouse, just about any kind of game you want. There's trees and green grass and ice cold streams. As well as enough Comanche or Apache to give you hell." He paused, hearing Judith's strangled sound, and grimaced. "Sorry." He flicked a glance toward Zack, and seemed to consider for a moment.

Deborah saw Zack stare back at him with opaque eyes, no sign of reaction, and Diamond shifted uncomfortably.

"I didn't mean no offense there, Banning."

"Why would I take offense?" No emotion, no indication of anger. Or absolution.

Diamond cleared his throat. "Well, uh, you bein' part Injun and all, I don't want you to think I meant somethin' by it."

"Like what?"

Deborah could see Diamond mentally squirm, and almost felt sorry for him. He wasn't a man accustomed to thinking about other people's feelings, but it was obvious he didn't want Zack Banning angry with him. And it was just as obvious Zack didn't intend to let him off easy.

Irritated, but trying not to show it, Diamond growled, "Like anything at all, dammit. It was just a comment."

Zack shifted his feet, resting one hand on his hip and

224

shrugging carelessly, his leg bent at the knee and his pose casual and unconcerned. The butt of his holstered pistol gleamed dully in the bright sunshine.

"Did I say anything, Mr. Diamond?"

Looking thoroughly put out now, and slightly embarrassed, Diamond snapped, "No."

"Then it didn't bother me. It's no secret that I'm a half-breed."

"Yeah, and it's no secret you don't cotton to bein' reminded of it." Diamond stared at him narrowly. "You shoot quick enough when you don't like a man's comments."

"Isn't that why you hired me? Because of my reputation for being quick to shoot?"

"Quick and deadly. You're the best, and I can afford the best." Diamond shrugged, and glanced at Deborah. Some of his arrogance returned as he said with a grin, "Like this little lady here."

Deborah colored when Zack's gaze shifted to her, and she felt it almost like a physical blow. "Yes," she heard him say quietly, "She's the best."

It was too much for her. She rose as quickly as if the rock had grown too hot, said the first thing that came into her mind.

"What kind of bird is that?"

Diamond turned to look up at the sky, squinting against the light. "A hawk. Red-tailed, I think. Right, Banning?"

Deborah wished she'd chosen another diversion, especially when she heard Zack's agreement.

"Yeah, it's a red-tailed hawk." He stepped close, so close she could almost feel his body heat. "Comanche regard them as great hunters. The braves wear hawk feathers in their hair, or make decorations of them."

His words conjured up an entire range of images

225

she'd tried to forget—Hawk with his ebony hair long and free, a hawk's feather dangling against his cheek. Hawk, pointing out the regal bird of prey circling lazily above them, saying the name in a husky voice, the imprint of his lips still warming her mouth.

Feeling stifled by his proximity, Deborah took a few steps away. Her voice sounded strained to her as she tried to say calmly, "Yes, so I understand."

Judith was staring at Zack, a strange, glazed look in her eyes. Deborah thought for a moment she would reveal his identity, tell Diamond he was the Comanche who'd kept Deborah captive. But she didn't. But her voice was unnatural, high-pitched when she said, "Hawks are dangerous. They kill things."

"Kill things?" Diamond echoed. "Reckon they do, Miss Judith." He smiled indulgently at her. "Just to survive, though. Animals don't kill for sport. Man is the only animal who does that."

Deborah shuddered, and Diamond looked down at her. He frowned. "A bad choice of conversation, I think. Look, why don't we ride over to that ridge? You can see halfway to Arizona from there."

Grateful for the diversion, Deborah avoided Zack's eyes as she remounted. Her mare snorted and pranced sideways just enough to make her grip the reins a little tighter and give her an excuse to concentrate on something except him. Judith nudged her sorrel mare close to Deborah, her voice faintly shaken.

"I didn't mean to upset everyone."

"Are you all right?"

"Yes. I just—remembered things."

"It's all right," Deborah said softly. "No one here will think less of you for what has happened. Dexter told me that he has only sympathy for women who were taken captive."

"He did?" Judith's eyes widened, capturing sunlight like a mirror. "Do you think he actually feels that way, even knowing—thinking—what could have happened?"

"I'm certain he does. And you know that Zack would not judge you."

Judith threw Zack a fierce glance. "He'd better not."

Deborah glanced at Judith's pale face. Lately, she'd been different, either a whirlwind of vivacity, or so quiet it was unusual. Their months of captivity had had its effect on her, too. Maybe more so. There had been no one for Judith to turn to. She'd been starved, beaten, worked hard. Their release couldn't have come too soon for her, while Deborah had been treated gently.

They rode quietly for a while, horses stirring up dust behind them in small clouds that drifted on the wind. Diamond spurred his mount between Deborah and Judith. He reined in, then pointed to a clump of sage and rocks.

"Look. There. In the shade of that rock. See the bird?"

It took a moment, but Deborah finally saw the bronze-green bird with a sharp-pointed beak and bristle of bluish feathers atop its crown. Long tail feathers jutted out behind as it moved with quick, brisk movements.

"What's it doing?" she asked, watching as the bird broke off small clumps of cactus with its sharp beak. It was making a small ring of sorts, it seemed, scurrying from the cactus to a chosen spot, carefully placing a snip of cactus, then retreating with swift, long strides.

Diamond chuckled. "Roundin' up a rattler."

"What?"

"Watch. See that dun-colored pile by the rock? That's a young rattler. Can't be an old one. Old ones are too smart to sleep out like that. This one may wake up inside that chaparral cock. Or road runner, whatever you want to call it. Mexicans call 'em *paisano,* or friend, because they eat snakes and mice. Watch it eat this snake."

Deborah stared in disbelief at the small bird. "Is this a joke?"

"No joke, honey. Watch a minute."

The bird scurried about soundlessly, seeming to glide above the ground. It busily surrounded the young snake with pieces of prickly cactus, then darted behind it. Lunging forward, the bird dove at the sleeping rattler and missed. The near miss alerted the snake, and its head snapped up, the tip of its tail twitching furiously.

Every time the agile bird darted in, the snake struck, and every time, it missed. Deborah could hear the *chi chi chi chi* of the rattles clacking together. It was a duel to the death, and for some reason, she felt sorry for the snake. Was there a double meaning in there somewhere, she wondered. She glanced at Zack, but his attention was on the struggle.

When she glanced back, it was just in time to see the nimble bird dart forward and impale the snake just behind its head with the sharp-pointed beak. In spite of herself, she jerked and cried out.

"Oh no!"

The sound startled Judith, who had been watching with intense concentration, and she gave a yank on her horse's reins. The sorrel spooked, snorting and half-rearing, then executed a few crow-hops across the ground before anyone could react. It stumbled, and Judith tumbled off backward in a flurry of blue riding skirt and white-stockinged legs.

Deborah cried out again even as she tried to dismount, and before she knew it, she was at Judith's side. Stunned, her cousin lay sprawled on the ground pushing dazedly at her skirts to cover her legs, her hair tumbling over her shoulders in a golden mass.

"My leg," she moaned, biting her lower lip and wincing.

"Judith! Are you all right?" Deborah anxiously felt her arms and legs, but found no sign of broken bones. "Here. Let me help you up."

Judith accepted her help, clinging to her arm as she rose to her feet, then cried out and sagged earthward again.

"My ankle! Oh, I think it's broken!"

"Are you certain?" Deborah checked again. Her ankle was already swelling inside the high-top boots she wore, and she looked up at her. "I think it's just sprained, but I can't be sure until we take off your boot. Does it hurt too badly?"

"Bad enough," Judith muttered, wincing.

She felt someone kneel beside her, and looked up to see Zack. His knife was in his hand, sunlight glittering along the sharp edge.

When he reached for Judith's foot, she screamed, a high, shrill sound that shocked Deborah and made Zack freeze in place. Runnels of light splintered from the blade, and Judith screamed again before Deborah recovered.

"Judith, Judith—he's just going to cut off your boot," she said calmly, but felt a tightening in her throat at the look of terror on her cousin's face.

"No, no, I don't want him anywhere near me!" Judith cried out, shuddering. "Please—make him go away!"

Distressed, Deborah looked at Zack. He gave her an understanding nod, and said, "Diamond can do this. I'll try to catch your horse."

"Catch my horse?"

His mouth twisted. "It took off when you did. Dia-

229

mond went after it." He rose to his feet and sheathed his knife, glancing at Judith. "Calm her down while I go after him."

Deborah shifted, smoothing back Judith's hair and wiping tears from her face. "It's all right," she repeated in a litany of comfort. "He was only trying to help."

"I know," Judith whispered. "Or, part of me does. But he looks so fierce, so—*savage*—that he makes me think of them. I keep seeing all those Indians, screaming, yelling—I'm sorry."

"It's all right." Deborah pushed her hair out of her eyes and tried to smile reassuringly. "We'll get you back to the house so you can put your foot up. In a few days, you'll be out dancing again."

She heard cursing behind them, and half-turned to see Diamond dismounting and stalking toward them. He looked angry and frustrated, and she cleared her throat.

"What's the matter?"

"Damn bad luck, that's what. Your bobtailed nag is halfway to Arizona by now, and your cousin's horse broke its leg in a snake hole."

Deborah stared up at him. "What are we going to do?"

"Reckon we can double up. We'll have to. She can ride with Banning, and you can ride with me." He grinned suddenly, his eyes raking her boldly. "Might be kinda worth all this at that."

Rising, Deborah said softly, "May I speak with you a moment privately?"

"Sure thing, sugar. Miss Deborah," he corrected at her quick frown.

They stepped away from where Judith huddled miserably. Putting her hand on his arm, Deborah said, "She won't ride with Mr. Banning, I'm afraid."

Diamond looked surprised. "Why not? Has he—?"

230

"No, no," she said hastily. "It's just that she's afraid of him. See, he reminds her of . . . of our ordeal. He looks a lot like a Comanche, you must admit."

"Yeah, guess he does. Didn't think of it that way. Must be why she's so skittish around him. Sorry. I wouldn't have had him come with me today. Just thought he'd be the best to have around."

"I know you meant well." Deborah managed a smile. "You'll have to let Judith ride with you."

Slapping the ends of his reins against his thigh, Diamond regarded her for a long moment. "Banning doesn't scare you?"

She met his gaze steadily. "Not like he does her. I wasn't treated as badly as she was."

"Right." Sweeping off his hat, he ran a hand through his thick blond hair, then tugged the hat back on and adjusted the brim to shade his eyes. "All right, sugar. I'll take your little cousin back to the hacienda. You wait here on Banning. Doubt if he catches that spooked hoss of yours, so he ought to circle back soon."

"You're going to leave me alone out here?"

Irritated, Diamond pointed. "See Banning? He's circling back already. Besides, your cousin don't look like she's doing too well."

That much was true. Deborah nodded. "You're right. I'll wait on Mr. Banning. You just take care of Judith."

He grunted. "This wasn't exactly what I had in mind when I asked you to go ridin' today."

"Nor I. I'm certain you'll forgive me if I say that you seem to have your priorities confused. My cousin's welfare should come ahead of your desire for a pleasant afternoon."

Swearing softly, Diamond grabbed her by the shoulders before she realized what he was going to do, and yanked her to him, kissing her full on the mouth. He

231

tasted hot and wet and salty; it wasn't unpleasant, but it left her cold. When he lifted his head, his brown eyes were narrowed.

"You taste good, sugar." His voice was rough, guttural. He cleared his throat and grinned. "I'm gonna taste you again soon, when we can be alone."

Deborah shivered at the heat in his tone, and managed to free herself from his grasp. "Please," she murmured. "This isn't the time or place. Not here."

"No, not here, that's for sure." His palm slid down her arm to grasp her hand, and when Zack rode up behind them, he was still holding it. "Banning, I'm gonna take the little lady back before her leg swells too bad. You take care of my woman for me."

Zack stared at him for a moment without dismounting. "I can catch her horse, but I'll need your rope. Won't be any need in us splitting up." He flicked a glance at the horse standing with head down and foreleg quivering. It snuffled softly, obviously in pain. "You going to put it down, or you want me to?"

Diamond sliced the suffering animal an indifferent look and shrugged. "Just get the gear off it. Let the damn thing die on its own for all I care. Stupid nag, stepping in a hole in the first place."

Appalled, Deborah must have made some sound, because he turned to look at her, a frown creasing his tawny brow. "Ah, sugar, I don't mean to be as hard as I sound. I just don't want you to see it, that's all."

"I assure you, that I would much rather see the poor thing put out of its misery than I would see it left to die slowly, Mr. Diamond."

"Didn't I say that?" he shot back irritably, and looked at Zack. "Cut its throat, Banning. Quick and easy."

Throwing a leg over his mount's neck, Zack slid to the ground and crossed to the injured horse. He unsad-

232

dled it while Diamond gathered Judith up in his arms and put her in front of him on his own horse. Deborah was almost in tears when Diamond handed her a coil of rope for Zack and mounted behind Judith. She tossed the rope to the ground and looked up at them.

"I'll be there soon after you," she told her cousin. "You just let Tía Dolores take care of your ankle until I get there, all right?"

Pain creased her pale features, but Judith managed a grimace that passed for a smile. "I will. I'll be drinking lemonade on the patio when you get there."

Deborah watched them ride away at a slow lope, crossing her arms over her chest as she stood with the wind whipping her riding skirt and tossing the feather on her hat. Then she turned to see Zack talking softly to the horse.

He'd unsaddled it, and poured water from his canteen into his hat to let the animal drink. He rubbed the sweaty back, crooning Comanche words the entire time, soft, liquid sounds that soothed the trembling animal. It nuzzled him in an affectionate gesture.

Deborah watched silently. There was a gentleness in Zack's movements, and respect for the animal. He stroked it and talked to it, and she felt her throat tighten as he drew his pistol from its holster and put the barrel against the mare's head. The horse seemed half-asleep, head lowered and pressed against Zack's chest. He scratched it between the ears, then pulled the trigger of his pistol.

The report made Deborah jump. For a moment, the animal seemed unhurt, then it sagged slowly to the ground and gave a last shudder before the eyes began to glaze. Deborah buried her face in her palms and wept. She didn't know why. She had felt no special affection for the animal, but she hated the necessity of killing it.

233

She sank to the ground, unable to stand a moment longer. With her head bent and her face still cupped in her hands, she didn't see Zack approach, but she heard his light step. He knelt beside her. She felt him, his warmth, his sympathy.

"It was kinder than the knife," he said after a moment. "Though if I had killed the horse in the Comanche way, I would have slit its throat as Diamond said, and honored it as a brave and faithful friend."

She didn't say anything. She couldn't look in that direction, and Zack seemed to know it. He crouched there beside her without speaking for a few minutes, and she was grateful. Then he rose to his feet with languid grace and held out his hand.

"Come on. I'll catch your horse, but you need to wait in the shade. I remember what happened last time you were out in the sun too long."

Startled, Deborah's gaze flew to his, and she saw the slight crinkling of his eyes as he smiled at her. She relaxed and nodded. "Yes, I do burn easily."

When she put her hand in his offered palm, shock waves shuddered up her arm and she caught her breath. The touch brought back a storm of memories. Pine trees, soft breezes, a hawk winging overhead. She shut her eyes, and when she opened them, Zack was staring at her.

"Are you Diamond's woman?"

For an instant, his question made no sense. Then she realized what he was asking at the same time as the more recent memory of his rejection slashed at her.

"I'm no one's woman," she said tartly, and tried to pull her hand from his grasp. He held it firmly, and a slow smile curved the erotic line of his mouth.

"That's what you think."

Chapter 17

"Kiss me," he muttered, and cupped her chin in his warm palm.

Shivering in spite of the searing sun, Deborah could not offer a word. Zack saw her eyes widen, sunlight captured in the dark centers and reflecting like gold, her long lashes making shadows on her pale cheeks. He was crazy. He had to be. He knew better than to begin anything. Hadn't he stayed away from her this long?

But there was something drawing him to her, some invisible tug, whether of heart or body was immaterial at this point. He just knew he had to taste her again, had to hear her soft, sensuous cries in his ear.

He didn't care what Dexter Diamond thought, what Judith thought, what anyone thought but Deborah. She was the only one whose opinion mattered.

His head bent, and he brushed his lips across her mouth in a light kiss. Her breath came in short, feathery pants for air, whispering over his face when he drew back a little to look at her. He saw her swallow, her throat rippling with a silky movement.

"I shouldn't do this."

"No," he agreed, because she was right. "You shouldn't do this." He kissed the corner of her mouth, then her cheek above the bronzed curve of his hand where he held her, then her closed eyelids. She quivered. He felt it, the faint tremors that told him more than her words could have done.

A hot wind blew over them, dry and rustling, scattering dust like dead leaves. He felt it beat against his legs, and pepper his bare skin in a fine mist, almost like rain. The air shimmered with intensity.

Her lashes trembled, lifted, her eyes huge and flecked with gold lights. She seemed slightly dazed.

It took a concerted effort, but he lifted his head after a moment. Her skin was warm, sun-heated, soft beneath his fingers. He drew in a deep breath to steady the raging blood pounding through him, and managed a faint smile. At least, it *felt* like a smile. From the widening of her eyes, he wasn't sure what it looked like. His voice was so hoarse it was barely recognizable to him, sounding more like a harsh croak.

"Deborah."

"Yes?"

"We can't stand out here in the sun and . . . and do this."

"No."

She wasn't going to help him, he saw that at once. He was on his own here; she looked too confused, too distressed by everything.

He suppressed the urge to draw her into him, to keep kissing her out here in the sun and heat where anyone who might wander by would see them. Not that this area was a highly traveled region. But he was a man who rarely took anything for granted, and he didn't intend to risk what was left of her reputation by subjecting her to more gossip. A ranch hand could pass, or Diamond could send someone back for them.

Zack set her back and away with a firm hand, regretting the necessity and his awakened hunger. "I'll take you to a shady spot, then catch your horse."

She looked at him solemnly. "Yes."

He wanted to groan aloud. There was something so wistful in the way she looked at him, so *needy*. He wondered if he had the same dazed look, as if he'd been knocked down by a wild bull. He figured he did, since he certainly felt like it.

Zack mounted his gray, then held out a hand to her to mount behind him. He saw her brief hesitation before she put her hand in his outstretched palm, then he lifted her and she swung up to perch with both legs on one side of the horse.

"You're going to have to straddle," he said. "Otherwise you'll fall off. And hold on to me. I don't have time to play the gentleman if I want to catch your horse before dark."

There was a brief silence, then he felt her shrug. "All right. Not that I thought you would play a gentleman anway."

It was maddening, having her legs nudging his, knowing her riding skirt was pushed up to her knees, feeling the soft press of her breasts against his back when she put her arms around his waist as gingerly as if he was a cactus. It certainly didn't cool the heat rising in him.

"Hold on," he said, and nudged the gray into a canter. The motion of the horse made her clutch him more tightly, and her breasts rubbed in a tantalizing scrape over his back as she held on. Her hands knotted at his waist, just above his belt buckle, nudging his belly with every jolt. He was in torment. He should have let her walk. He should have walked. He should have let her wait there in the sun while he went to find her horse. If he had to ride all the way back to the ranch with her like this, he'd be in trouble.

No. If he had to ride all the way back to the ranch with her rubbing up against him, he corrected himself, he'd be *inside* her. And that wouldn't do.

At the first grove of trees, Zack reined in. "Here," he said tersely. "You ought to be comfortable until I catch your horse."

Her hands moved away from his stomach, and the pressure of her breasts against him was gone as she dismounted. When she stood beside the horse, the feather atop her hat bobbed in the wind and he had to restrain the gray from bolting.

"Take that damned hat off," he said when he got the horse under control. "I don't know why white women have to wear such foolery."

The oblique reminder of what he was, their mutual past, made her look up at him. He felt the burn of her eyes, and it seared into him. The shade of the scrub trees dappled her face in light and shadow, and the wind pressed her skirts against her slender legs as she stared at him.

"To catch the attention of white men," she said, the cool, clipped tones reminding him again of his mother, as they had that first day he'd seen her.

Zack leaned on his saddle horn, his eyes narrowed. "And what white man's attention are you trying to catch, Miss Hamilton?"

"Mrs. Velazquez."

"That's a crock, and you know it. He was never your husband but in name." Temper made his words sharp. He wasn't certain why it bothered him that she laid claim to the title of wife to Miguel Velazquez, but it did. Just like it angered him when she let Dexter Diamond put his hands on her with that damned proprietary air, and kiss her.

Deborah shrugged. "But the marriage is legal, nonetheless."

"And that suits you just fine, doesn't it?" He scowled. "I never figured you for being so greedy, but it looks like I was wrong. You've got your hooks in the Velazquez land and you don't intend to let go, do you?"

"It is not exactly a matter of my *letting go*. I've been asked to remain because it profits the family interests, according to Don Francisco." She looked away from him, her eyes distant. She untied the ribbons to her hat and removed it before looking back at him. "Once the government changed the boundary lines, the necessity of their being American citizens precipitated my marriage. I am a wife of convenience, Mister Banning."

"Mister Banning." Zack fought his rising temper. "In case you don't remember, we've been a bit too *close* for you to be so formal."

"And you don't mind me making that fact public? Somehow I had the impression that you wanted to keep that fact a secret as much as I do. After all, if the authorities find out it was you who kept me prisoner in a Comanche village, your life—or at the very least, your freedom—will be jeopardized. I hardly think you want me publicizing such information."

"There's no one around to hear you right now."

"I'm not as good at leading a double life as you seem to be," Deborah returned coolly.

"Maybe you need more practice."

Her eyes flashed. "I hardly think so."

For a moment he didn't say anything. What was it about this one woman that made him lose control? She did. And it wasn't anything he could put his finger on that caused it.

"I'll be back," he said finally, wheeling his gray around and riding away without looking back.

By the time he found her bay, roped it, and rode back to her, the sun was a fiery ball in the sky. He dismounted under the scrub trees and squatted in the shade beside Deborah, feeling her curious gaze on him.

"You caught it."

He shrugged. "Yeah. Did you think I wouldn't?"

"Oh no, I realize that you are a man who always gets what he goes after."

His eyes slid to hers, narrowed and irritable. "What's that supposed to mean?"

She looked away. She'd removed her gloves, and was slowing waving her hat to stir up a cool breeze. "Nothing."

"No, you meant something by it, all right. Are you talking about the two of us? I'd be interested in knowing if you're gonna claim rape again."

Her cheeks suffused with color that had nothing to do with the heat or sunburn. She grew still, her voice cool.

"What would you call it?"

"Seduction, maybe. Coaxing. You wanted it, too. I may have removed your social objections for you with a bit of handy bartering, but you can't deny you didn't feel anything for me, Miss Deborah Hamilton."

Frustration made his voice tight, edgy, and he pulled his hat off and raked a hand through his hair. It was damp with sweat, and fell across his forehead.

"No, I won't deny that." Her eyes came back to his, and he could see the shadows in them. He wondered what made her sound so—hurt.

He studied her face for a long moment, the pure cameo beauty of her eyes, nose, mouth, chin, and felt a peculiar tightening in his chest. He pivoted slightly on the balls of his feet, still in a crouch.

"Good," he muttered, half-ashamed of himself for forcing her to an admission, half-glad she hadn't denied it. He needed to hear that she'd wanted him, that he hadn't been the only one to feel that raging desire. The same desire that pressed him so hard now.

Hugging her knees to her chest, Deborah began again the slow motion with her hat, the feather waving gently back and forth and back and forth, creating a cool breeze. The horses stood with heads lowered, resting, eyes half-closed in the shade where he'd tied them.

After a moment's hesitation, Zack said gruffly, "We'll go back as soon as the horses rest a little."

She nodded. "I thought as much. That's all right. I'm comfortable here in the shade. And I'm certain Judith is being well-cared for by Tía Dolores."

"And your sweetheart."

"Dexter isn't my sweetheart."

He glared at her balefully. "Just what is *Dexter*, if he's not your sweetheart?"

"What could it possibly matter to you? I believe you made it perfectly clear that you have no interest in me beyond a possible threat to your identity."

"What the hell are you talking about?"

Her steady gaze held his. "I'm talking about the fact that I have not seen you since that first night I discovered you were anywhere near. Your absence is an evident statement of your disinterest."

"What it is," he said evenly, "is knowing when to quit while I'm ahead."

"And your comment of earlier? What am I supposed to think when you say one thing and act like another?"

Baffled, he shook his head. "I don't know what you mean."

"I mean," she whispered, "your saying I was your woman, yet pushing me away."

241

"When did I do that?"

"Just a little while ago. You asked if I was Dexter's woman, then said I was yours."

He raked a hand through his hair. It was already dry from the heat and wind. "I didn't exactly *say* you were my woman. Ah, God. I don't want ties, Deborah. I don't want to want you."

"I see."

"Do you? Damned if I do." Frustration balled his hands into fists, and he stared down at them before he opened his fingers slowly. The brim of his hat was creased, and he spent a moment straightening it before he could look at her. "I haven't forgotten how much I want you. But it won't work. You're not the kind of woman to live that way."

"What way?"

He gestured at the hills. "Drifting. Moving from one place to the other, no goal in mind, no home to hold me. I'm too much like the hawk. I just beat my wings against the air and never stay too long on the ground."

"You're right. I could not live that way." She put a hand on his arm, on the bare skin of his forearm where his shirt sleeves were rolled up. He felt her touch all the way to his toes. "Have you thought about it, then? About being with me?"

He sucked in a deep breath. "Yeah. But it would never work."

A smile trembled on her lips, and she slid her hand to the corded muscle of his biceps, where he was quivering with the effort to keep from grabbing her. "Hawk— Zack—I've thought about being with you, too."

He closed his eyes briefly. She was pushing his restraint to the limits. "Forget it. I said it wouldn't work and it won't."

"You don't know that."

Her voice was soft and low, as if she had to force out the words. When he opened his eyes to look at her, he saw what it cost her to make this overture. Somehow, it made him feel even worse.

"Look," he snarled, "I want to be inside you. I want to feel you around me and push myself up in you so deep that you can feel me against your throat, but that's all. Dammit, that's all. That's all it can ever be, don't you understand that?"

She looked wounded, stricken, her eyes reminding him of the injured horse he'd had to destroy—baffled by the pain. When a single tear slipped from one eye to track her cheek, he clenched his teeth.

And before he knew it, he was pulling her against him, his mouth hot and demanding against her lips, tasting the salt of her tears. Slowly, as he kissed her with all the pent-up frustration of the past weeks, he unbraided her hair until it fell in a silky tangle down her back. Then he put one hand in it, tunneling his fingers up to cradle the back of her head in his palm. His lips moved from her open, sweet mouth to the smooth curve of her throat, and he tugged on her hair to bend her head back further.

He concentrated on the tiny, swift pulse hammering in a creamy hollow while his fingers deftly unbuttoned the rows on her riding jacket. It fell open, and he slid a hand inside, frustrated by the thin silk of a blouse covering her. Lifting his head, he studied the situation for a brief moment before surrendering to temptation. His mouth covered the silken swell of a breast, wetting the cloth, his teeth nipping at the hard little bead of her nipple. She moaned, and he felt her hands curve over his shoulders. That small sound spurred his desire higher, and he paused.

"How quick can we get this thing off?" he muttered, plucking at the blouse.

She didn't answer, but sat back and slid her jacket down over her arms. He watched, as aroused by the sight of that simple action as he was the shadowy jiggle of her breasts beneath the sheer material of her blouse. She undid the single row of buttons, and let the blouse drift in a snowy pile to lay atop her discarded jacket.

Zack stared at her, at the smooth flow of soft skin only partially hidden by her chemise, the enticing shadows beneath the thin muslin. For a moment he couldn't move. His erection pushed so hard against the front of his pants that it was painful. He'd thought of her like this so many times, it was agony to consider restraint.

Then she looked up at him with desire glazing her eyes and he forgot all about restraint.

He reached for her, pulling her up against him, dropping from a crouch to his knees, his legs spreading as he pulled her between them. She fit him so well, her body tucked into the angle of his as if made for him. He groaned at the feel of her body pressing against his groin.

She helped him lift her skirts, her hands shaking but eager, their movements hungry. Zack swore mentally when his hand encountered the barrier of her pantalettes, and he hooked his fingers into the convenient open crotch and jerked. There was the rending sound of tearing cloth and Deborah's faint gasp, but he didn't care. All he could think of, could focus on, was his driving need to be inside her, to feel her heat close around him.

He stroked a hand over the gentle mound of her belly then lower, his fingers seeking and finding the source of her pleasure. She moaned softly and pressed her face into his shoulder, shuddering when his thumb grazed her. He held one arm around her back to keep her against him, his other hand moving with quick, erotic flicks that drew small cries from her. Her fingers dug into his biceps, clenching and unclenching, and her thighs parted as his hand moved with the certainty of satisfaction at his fingertips.

"Oh, *God,*" she said in a gasp, and he smiled against the fragrant mass of her hair that tumbled over his chest and smelled of lilac. When he slid a finger into her to test her readiness and she shuddered, then convulsed, he felt it, too. He couldn't wait any longer.

One hand moved to his gunbelt and unbuckled it, then unbuttoned his pants, freeing himself. He put his hands on her waist, lifted her, then brought her slowly down on him, groaning at the exquisite slide of pleasure. She was hot, so hot, heated silk and velvet rose petals, clenching around him like a supple glove.

For a moment he just held her there, unable to move for fear he would explode, then his arms flexed and he lifted her again, bringing her back down in another delicious stroke of pure sensation. She was panting for breath and so was he. He couldn't think beyond what they were doing. The need to fill her completely overwhelmed everything else.

He lifted his head from the curve of her neck and shoulder and caught her eyes. Desire glazed them, and made her lips part to show her small white teeth, the soft pink of her open mouth another temptation, as tantalizing as the feel of her around him. He kissed her, fingers digging into her waist as he lifted her again, then brought her hips down in a swift motion that made her cry out as he pushed deeply inside her. He stifled her cry with his mouth, fiercely determined to fill her with himself, a primitive, ancient compulsion that gripped him too hard to ignore.

245

Grinding her hips down against him, he wanted to consume her with the same passion that devoured him, that rose up so high and hot that he wouldn't have been surprised to collapse in a shower of ashes and sparks. Lifting her again and again, bringing her down hot and so hard he heard her gasp, Zack brought them both to release at almost the same moment. His muscles corded with the strain, and he wanted to wait for her, but didn't think he could. Then she made a high, keening sound and dug her nails into him as she exploded into a series of contractions that shattered his control. He groaned and stiffened as her body convulsed around him, then shook violently with the force of his own release.

Deborah sobbed softly, collapsing against his chest and wetting his shirt with her tears. He held her as he brought his breathing back to normal, then shifted her a bit to see her face.

"You all right?"

No answer, just an averted nod of her head. He felt a twinge of guilt. She was worth more than this, more than a roll in the dirt. But he had no promises in him, no heart for words he didn't mean. Promises he couldn't keep.

His hand closed on the back of her head, and he stroked her hair with gentle, soft motions that must have comforted her. After a moment, she sat up a little, still on his lap with his body inside her. He could feel himself getting hard again, and was amazed that he wanted more so soon.

"Zack . . ."

"Shhh." He kissed her, and began the slow, rhythmic motions of sex all over again. This time, there was no sense of urgency, but a calmer, deeper emotion that drove him. And he saw from the slumberous droop of her eyes and her slow, languid movements as she clasped her hands behind his neck and took control, that she felt it, too.

He hadn't thought it possible, but this time the act was even more satisfying than the last. Maybe it was because Deborah regulated their movements, lifting her body, then sliding slowly down, keeping her eyes on his face as if gauging his reaction, her lips curved in a slow, sensuous smile that mesmerized him. Her hair swayed with her movements, dark fire framing her pale face and naked breasts in a sultry invitation.

God. She was like a volcanic glacier—ice on the outside but raging fire at her core. Sensuous, passionate, Eve after eating the apple.

She leaned forward, her small pink tongue flicking out to tease his lips, tracing them with a damp heat that made his breath come faster, but when he tried to hold her still for a kiss, she evaded him.

"No," she murmured, kissing one corner of his mouth, then the other. He closed his eyes, and felt his body swell inside her, surging up and up in that close, damp heat. She kissed him finally, gently at first, then with an insistent urgency as she sucked on his bottom lip, drawing it into her mouth while his hands teased her breasts and made her hips rock harder and faster against him.

Then, curling her fingers around his biceps, she leaned back so that her hair swung free, her eyes closed as he sought the needy peaks of her breasts, first one and then the other. And when her soft internal muscles clenched around him in a shuddering grip, she cried his name, over and over, her voice echoing on the wind.

"Hawk . . . Zack . . ."

As he lost himself inside her, the searing knowledge that she accepted him as either man, branded into his soul.

Chapter 18

Dark shadows lay over the Velazquez hacienda when they returned. Deborah felt Zack's gaze on her, and shifted in her saddle. She was embarrassed by her lack of control, her wanton behavior, and he seemed too quiet. She wondered if she'd shocked him that badly. He hadn't said. He hadn't said much of anything on the ride back.

Now she was there, and lights blazed against the purple shrouds of dusk.

"Looks like they're waiting on us," Zack drawled, and she flicked him a quick glance.

"Yes."

"What do you want me to tell them?"

Startled, she half-turned, and saw that he was staring at her. "The truth—well, not all of it, of course."

His lips twisted. "Of course. I'm not eager to have a rope around my neck."

"Why do you say that?"

His brow slanted up at a mocking tilt. "Do you think Don Francisco would be glad to welcome me to the family? No, no more than he wants Diamond."

Deborah suspected that was true. "I guess it's in his best interests if I remain unmarried."

"He'll do anything to keep his lands. I'm surprised he hasn't been after you himself." Her shock must have shown in her eyes, because Zack gave a slight shrug. "It'd be one way of keeping you—and the Velazquez lands—in the family."

"How do you know so much about our business?"

"It's pretty common knowledge. Besides, Diamond has made it his business to find out the terms of the legal settlement. I think he has more than a casual interest in the lands."

"So Tía Dolores says."

"Watch yourself," he said softly, and when she just stared at him, he looked away from her. Saddle leather creaked as he shifted. His voice was rough. "I told you—no promises."

"Yes, I heard you." Pain closed her throat. He'd meant it, then. Even after . . . after what they'd done. It had meant no more to him than he'd warned her it would. She was indeed a fool.

Deborah kicked her horse into a faster pace, and they didn't speak again.

Dexter Diamond was waiting on them in front of the low, sprawling adobe hacienda, his face like a thundercloud. It was obvious from his saddled horse and the men with him, that he'd been about to set out in search of them.

" 'Bout gawddamned time you two got back," he growled, his dark gaze flicking from Zack to Deborah and back. "What took you so long, Banning?"

Lantern light brightened the dusk, and Deborah saw the tension in Diamond as he stood with feet planted apart and braced, his eyes narrowed. He reeked with hostility and suspicion.

Zack dismounted slowly, his posture sending out mixed signals of amusement and danger. "Got a burr in

249

your britches, Diamond? Don't be shy. Ask what you really want to know."

Diamond stiffened. "All right—you tryin' to steal my woman?"

"Really!" Deborah exploded, anger and fear making her bolder than usual. "In the first place, Mr. Diamond, I am not *your woman,* and in the second—I resent any insinuation that I would welcome his advances."

For a moment, Diamond bristled with disbelief, but then he slowly relaxed. "Let him answer," he said roughly, and Zack eyed him without speaking.

"You heard the lady," he said finally. "I don't know about the first, but even a fool can see she's too much of a lady to go around inviting attention from strangers."

That simple retort left Diamond with no choice but to accept it. To continue, would make it seem as if he thought Deborah was no lady, and she could see his frustration.

"Now," she said coldly,"if you are quite through insulting me, Mr. Diamond, I would appreciate being allowed to see my cousin. I assume you brought her back without molesting her in any way?"

Diamond flushed, a deep, ugly crimson that was readily evident even in the shadows. "Guess I deserve that," he said after a moment. His voice altered. "But I got worried, damn it all. You shoulda been back hours ago."

"If you were that worried," Deborah countered as she slid from her mount to the ground, "you should have left to find us hours ago. As it appears you did not, I can only assume that you have confidence in the man you hired to secure our safety."

Trapped again, Diamond muttered something under his breath, then moved as if to escort her inside.

"No," she said. "I'm tired. It's been a long, weary

day, so if you will excuse me, I wish to retire. Good evening, sir."

"Dammit," she heard him say as she turned and walked toward the house, "she's done gone and shut me out again!"

Don Francisco, who stood with his horse's reins in his hand, said softly, "Perhaps it is best if you go now. It has been so soon since the tragedy, that Señora Velazquez is understandably delicate. Though I do not wish to insult you, Señor Diamond, she is not ready for what you desire."

Deborah paused on the tiled veranda, and heard Diamond say roughly, "You can't stop me from seein' her if I want to, Velazquez."

"On the contrary, I not only can, I will." Don Francisco's smooth voice lowered to a menacing clip. "She is a part of our family, of which I am the patriarch. I rule here, and if you wish to press the matter, I will give orders that you not be allowed on my lands."

"The hell you will!"

Don Francisco gave a soft command, and men stepped out from the shadows with rifles leveled. There was a series of clicks as the weapons were cocked. No one moved. Tension vibrated in the air.

Diamond muttered a curse. Then he stepped to his horse and into his saddle. "Come on, Banning," he snarled.

Deborah watched from the hidden shadows of the doorway as Zack followed suit, moving with that slow, lazy precision that made him stand out from other men. There was none of the same haste that marked Diamond's retreat. The two men wheeled their mounts and kicked them into an unhurried lope.

She was still standing in the doorway when Don

251

Francisco approached. His face was grave, his black eyes fastened on her with a narrowed stare.

"You will not see him again," he said softly, and she turned to look at him.

"You are not my guardian, Don Francisco."

"You are wrong. I have allowed you to act on your own, and you see what comes of it. From now on, you will obey me or suffer the consequences."

Rigid with anger, Deborah said as coolly as possible, "I feel no need to discuss this further. I'm going in to see my cousin."

He caught her arm when she turned away, his fingers biting into her tender flesh. "This is your only warning. If you value your freedom, do not force me into action."

"A threat, Don Francisco?"

"A promise."

She felt a sudden chill, and swallowed the fear rising in her throat. He looked serious. And menacing.

"I will keep that in mind," she finally said, and looked pointedly at his grip on her. He released her, and she turned without another word and went inside the hacienda to find Judith.

"This is intolerable!" Deborah turned with an agitated click of her heels against the smooth tiles of the patio, blinking against the glare of the sun. "He is keeping us prisoners!"

"No, no," Tía Dolores said faintly. "You are wrong. He means well. Francisco is a bit highhanded, that is all."

"I call it more than highhanded to be followed wherever I go, and not allowed to go into town or even to church when I please!"

"He is concerned for your safety," Tía Dolores protested, then sighed. "And your reputation."

"I believe," Deborah said, "that my reputation was in shreds when I was returned by the Comanche. What else can harm it now?"

Judith shifted position on the lounge chair where she rested in the shade, her ankle propped on a pillow. "Are you sure that Don Francisco is not more concerned with the interest Mr. Diamond is showing in your lands?"

Tía Dolores looked distressed. "There are the rumors, of course."

"But it seems to me," Deborah said, "that if he does not wish to sell, there is no problem."

"Normally, that would be true. But Miguel's will left you a certain portion of the land, as required. Since there were no children to inherit the land, it reverts to you. No one thought, you see, that things would turn out as they have, and after it was presumed that you had been killed by those marauding savages, Francisco inherited."

Deborah fought back a wave of frustration. "I realize that my return was rather inconvenient for him. I have assured him that I have no intention of claiming your lands, nor do I want them." She lifted her hands. "I just have nowhere else to go."

The admission was painful. And she had offered to sign over whatever claim she had, but Don Francisco insisted that the Velazquez lands would then be vulnerable to American claimants, as no American would own a portion.

"You will remain here," he'd said, fixing his dark eyes on her, "so that our lands are inviolate." His mood had not invited argument, and she'd retreated into prudent silence.

She looked at Tía Dolores's distressed face and

sighed. "Why doesn't he marry an American? That would solve all his problems."

Biting her lower lip, Tía Dolores looked down at her clenched hands. "He says that no American woman is aristocratic enough to be his wife."

"He certainly had no compunction in marrying me to his nephew!" Deborah retorted.

Dolores could not look at her. "That was not his idea. It was my oldest brother's decision, Miguel's father. Poor, dead Luis did not have the same . . . aversion . . . to Americans."

"Aversion?" Judith laughed suddenly, a strange, choked sound. "I've seen Don Francisco look at me with anything but aversion. Are you sure your brother feels that way?"

Coloring, Dolores mumbled, "If he feels anything, it is an unwilling attraction. He would not offer you anything so honorable as marriage, *chica.*"

Her meaning was clear. Shock silenced both Deborah and Judith.

Zack leaned against a support post holding up the roof of the bunkhouse. It was hot. Waves of heat rose up from the ground, shimmering and distorting the landscape. Diamond owned two hundred eighty-six thousand acres of prime land, and was in the process of acquiring more. He ran cattle, had over two hundred cowhands working for him, and a small army of twenty professional gunmen. He'd come to Texas twelve years before, and bought the ranch from the government. It had once belonged to a Spanish family, but after the boundaries were changed, the United States had sold it to him.

Diamond liked to brag that he would soon own all of

254

West Texas, and Zack figured he meant it. In the two months he'd been with Diamond, he'd seen three families sell out to him. Only one of the families had done it for the money. The other two had sold out for survival. Water sources had dried up suddenly, and wells had gone bad. Cattle died. Diamond had stepped in with offers, and had walked away with thirteen thousand more acres from the three. At a tidy little profit.

Now, the Double D brand rode the rumps of over twenty thousand prime beeves. At approximately seven acres of decent grazing land to feed each animal, Diamond ran his herd on the open range. Inevitably, cows wandered, and the recent roundup had produced open hostilities when other brands had been rounded up with the Double D.

"If it's on my land eatin' my grass, it's mine," Diamond had told one angry rancher. And when the man had seen the armed men backing him, he'd ridden away without his cows.

"You feel that way about your beeves?" Zack had asked when the rancher left, and Diamond laughed.

"Naw. If it's got my brand on it, it's mine."

Zack had shrugged. It wasn't his problem. Living with the Comanche, he'd come to think, as they did, that animals were to feed all the people. If a man was a good hunter, his family ate well. If he wasn't, or it was a lean year, they went hungry. There was no *owning* land or cattle for them. It avoided many unnecessary squabbles, as far as Zack was concerned.

He squinted against the bright prick of sunlight as he saw Diamond walking toward him. Since that day with Deborah, he'd felt a difference in the way Diamond viewed him. There had been speculation in his eyes when he looked at Zack, as if he knew there was something between him and Deborah.

255

Zack flipped his cigarette to the ground and waited.

"Banning," Diamond said, stepping up to the porch, "hot enough to melt iron out here, ain't it."

"Yeah."

Diamond's brow lifted slightly, and his mouth set in a straight line. "Not very talkative, are you?"

"I don't have anything to say." He leaned back against the post again, eyes level with Diamond's. "If you do, I'm listening."

"Kinda surly, ain't ya?" Diamond asked with a grunt, then lifted his hand palm-out. "Don't get me wrong. I don't give a damn. Some of the other boys are kinda nervous about you, though."

Zack didn't say anything, just waited. He kept his eyes on Diamond, all the while aware of what went on around him. A horse snorted and stomped its foot in the nearby corral, and he saw shadows ranging along one wall of the bunkhouse that he knew were some of the hands. Listening at the open windows, no doubt.

"Look, Banning," Diamond said finally when he realized that Zack wasn't going to ask, "I heard that you're the one who broke Charlie Raymond's arm. That right?"

"Sounds right."

"Damn, man. Why?"

"Raymond doesn't know when to keep his mouth shut, and when to talk. I gave him a lesson in deportment."

Frustration heated Diamond's brown eyes. "You also took one of my cowhands out of commission for a while. I don't give a damn about fightin' among my men. Hell, you can't get a bunch of men together in one place without some kinda trouble once in a while, but I don't like doin' without one of my wranglers for few weeks."

Zack met his gaze. "I could have made it permanent."

Diamond grunted. "I know that. And I told Charlie he's a fool to prod you, but he's just a kid."

"If he wants to grow up, he'd better learn to keep quiet at the right times. It's a hard lesson for some."

Diamond eyed him silently for a long moment. Then he said, "You're probably the best gun I've got. I want to keep you on, but I don't want to lose any more ranch hands. If I get more land like I'm plannin' on, it's gonna take all I've got to run it. Think you can just bruise the loudmouths, and not break' em?"

Irritated, Zack shrugged. "I didn't hire on as a wet nurse for a bunch of yahoos. I can ride away just as easy as I rode in. If you don't want trouble, you're talking to the wrong man."

"I don't want you ridin' out yet. Hell, this is just gettin' started. Things are gonna get a lot hotter soon, and I need you."

"I don't make war on women and children," Zack said flatly, and saw Diamond's brow lift. "If you've got in mind that I'm going to help run off any families, you're wrong."

"Did I say that?"

"I'm just going by what I've seen."

Diamond flushed. "None of that would have happened if old Ledbetter hadn't drawn a bead on Albright. Frank had to shoot."

"Old Ledbetter was a mite put out that Albright said he intended to hump his daughter, the way I heard it," Zack drawled. He noted that Diamond's flush deepened. "Now, those are fighting words where I come from."

"I admit Frank spoke out of turn, but he didn't hurt the girl. I gave orders they were just to be put off the land, not hurt." His brow crowded his eyes as he stared at Zack. "You with me, Banning? If you're not, say so now."

"I'm with you as long as you stay legal, Diamond."

"Yeah, that's your reputation. You've done more legal shootin's in the middle of the street than most men do in the middle of a war."

"It's just worked out that way."

Diamond scraped a thumb over the half-grown beard shadowing his jaw, studying Zack for a moment as if trying to figure him out. "You're cold, I'll say that for you. But I ain't never seen anybody as fast or accurate as you, either."

Zack settled his spine against the rough wood of the post and shrugged again. "There's always someone faster."

"Maybe. Look, just do me a personal favor and ignore the hotheads, will you? I'll say something to 'em, but I'd consider it a real favor if you overlook a few of the green ones."

"I generally try to."

"Yeah, I know. Charlie Raymond said things he shouldn't have. He's young and stupid."

"And that can get you killed out here," Zack said so softly Diamond tensed. Zack saw the doubt cloud his eyes, the faint, curious flicker of not knowing how far he could push. Then it faded.

"I know that," Diamond said. "And now Charlie knows it. Just go easy on the rest of 'em, okay?"

"As long as they keep their distance."

"I can almost guarantee that now." Diamond shifted from one foot to the other. "I'm gonna need you to go into town for me tomorrow."

Again, Zack waited. Diamond shook his head and pushed his hat back. "Since you're so curious," he drawled with a look halfway between irritation and amusement, "I'll tell you what I want you to do. There's a man comin' in on the noon stage that I need to see before he gets busy elsewhere. I want you and Jeb Braden to bring him out here."

"Braden and I don't get along."

"Hell, you don't get along with anyone here. You stick to yourself too much. The others don't trust you."

Zack eyed him coldly. "Did you hire me to be friendly to the rest of your gunnies?"

Frustration marked Diamond's face again. "No, but gawddamit, Banning, it'd help if you'd at least be civil!"

"I'm civil."

"Barely. You and Braden are my two best men, and I want you to do a job for me. Do you think you can get this guy here like I want?"

"Is he going to come willingly?"

Diamond took an envelope out of his vest pocket. "He will if you give him this. Watch your backs, though. There are some other people around here who'd like to talk to him before I do."

Zack took the envelope, glanced at the name on front, then tucked it into his vest pocket. "I can get him here."

"You sound damn certain," Diamond commented.

"I'm certain I can do my part. The rest is up to him."

"Do you ever screw up, Banning? Lose a fight? Catch a bullet?"

A faint smile curled Zack's mouth, and he nodded. "Sure I do. You just don't hear me bragging about it."

Diamond relaxed, and grinned. "Glad to hear it. I was beginnin' to think you ain't human like the rest of us."

The faint smile faded, and Zack looked away. "I just hide it better."

"Must be the Injun in ya." Diamond intercepted Zack's icy glance, and added, "No offense."

When Zack didn't reply, Diamond obviously decided the conversation was over. He stepped down from the porch and into the sunlight, then said over his shoulder, "I'm countin' on you to get Macklin here, Banning."

Macklin. The name on the envelope. Obviously, a pretty important man to Diamond. It occurred to Zack to wonder why.

Jeremiah Macklin frowned as he ripped open the envelope and read the contents, then looked up at Zack. "Tell your employer that I'm not interested."

Jeb Braden, standing beside Zack on the wooden sidewalk and looking bored up to that point, snapped to attention. "He said to bring you back with us."

Macklin stiffened. "And I said, I'm not interested. You will have to convey my regrets to Mr. Diamond for me, I'm afraid."

Sneering, Braden let his right arm fall to his side, a scant few inches from the butt of his pistol. "And *I* said, he's expecting you."

"That's too bad." Macklin paled a little, his beefy face creasing with anger, but stood his ground. His clear gaze shifted between Zack and Braden. "My services were already retained by another, and I cannot violate my client's rights or confidentiality."

"Looky here," Braden snarled, "maybe you don't understand something—Mr. Diamond wants to see you first. You can tell him whatever you damn well please, but I ain't gonna go back without you."

When Braden took a step forward and Macklin took two back, Zack moved between them.

"Leave it alone, Braden."

Surprised, Braden shot him a narrowed glance. "You're supposed to work for Diamond, Banning."

"I never agreed to kidnapping, and that's what it will be if you force him to go with us. Back off."

260

Jeb Braden had been on edge ever since they'd left the Double D that morning, making caustic comments designed to draw Zack's anger. So far, he hadn't been able to get so much as the flicker of an eyelash from him. Until now.

Now Braden turned his anger on Zack, moving away from the stunned Macklin a few steps, his posture tense. People on the sidewalk scattered, and a few shop doors slammed shut behind them. Braden rocked back on his heels, hands hovering over the holsters strapped to each thigh.

"You've been a rock in my craw since you stepped onto the Double D. All I heard was how fast you are, how good you are, and the only damn thing I've seen you do is break a kid's arm for callin' you a half-breed. You don't seem so hot to me, Banning."

"Care to test my temperature?" Zack drawled softly, and saw Braden's eyes thin.

"You callin' me out, Banning?"

"No. But I won't walk away if you feel frisky."

He could see Braden thinking, considering his chances. The world had narrowed down to the two of them, everything and everyone else forgotten. All sounds of wagons and dogs and horses and gawking townsmen faded into a distant, indistinct rumble. Zack waited, and watched.

A trickle of sweat slid down Braden's face, and his mouth tightened. His leather vest hung open and double gunbelts gleamed dully in reflected light from the hot, dusty street. Zack could almost taste the dust. And Braden's fear.

He wasn't surprised when Braden's hand whisked down for his gun. And he wasn't surprised when Braden pitched backward from the force of Zack's bullet, then slid down the wooden storefront to sprawl bonelessly on

261

the sidewalk. The shot still echoed in the air. It had taken only seconds.

Straightening from his half-crouch, Zack punched out the empty shell and replaced it with a bullet from his belt, listening to the pounding of running feet. He knew what to expect. He'd been through this before. As he slid his pistol back into the leather holster, he heard a gun click behind him.

Zack turned slowly to face the sheriff, and was stunned to see Deborah Hamilton only a few yards away. She looked shocked. And terrified. She must have seen the whole thing, and he regretted the loss of his temper. He shouldn't have let Braden's needling push him into a showdown, not here in town, anyway. But experience had always taught him that the best way to settle with an enemy was in front of witnesses, and he had acted on that. Now Deborah had seen it.

"Sheriff," Macklin was saying shakily, "this man acted in self-defense. I saw the whole thing."

Sheriff Roy Carpenter snarled, "And just who the hell are you?"

"Jeremiah Macklin, attorney at law."

Zack's gaze snapped back to him. He wasn't surprised to hear Macklin explain that he had been hired by a local rancher, and just arrived from Abilene. And Zack had a good idea who the local rancher might be when he saw Don Francisco Velazquez standing just behind Deborah. It was beginning to form a pattern.

"Come along, Mister Macklin," the sheriff said, then held out his hand for Zack's pistol. "You too, mister. I'm gonna check and see if there are any posters out on you before I let you go free on this one."

Zack slowly slid his pistol from the holster and held it out butt first. As the sheriff motioned for him to walk ahead of him, Zack saw Deborah's face again, a pale cameo of worry. It made him feel good that she seemed to care.

"Did you see that?" Judith whispered in Deborah's ear, her fingers digging into her cousin's arm. "I told you he was little more than a bloodthirsty savage."

Deborah shook free, irritated by Judith's remark and still reeling from what she'd seen. Zack, faced by a man intent on killing him. She'd watched from only a few yards away, and had not been able to tear her eyes from the chilling spectacle.

Everything had happened so quickly, almost a blur, though at one point when they had faced each other in tense silence, it had seemed to stretch for hours. She'd heard of gunfights being glamorized, but she'd not seen any glamour in this, only the ugly reality of death. So much that had been romanticized by the dime novels had turned out to be harsh and dirty instead of exciting. The novels had not made mention of the constant dust, the monotony of endless chores just to exist, the long days that melded into one another without change. Nor had they managed to convey the horror that ofttimes awaited on moon-bright nights.

"Deborah," Judith said, and Deborah realized that she must have been saying her name before, because there was a tension in her tone that made her aware. "Don Francisco asked if we would like to await him in the hotel lobby while he sees to his business."

"Yes. Of course."

Tía Dolores clutched at their arms, her face pasty and pale beneath the yards of stifling black lace mantilla. "Do come along. I must get out of this heat. I must sit down before I faint."

"By all means, sit in the lobby," Don Francisco was

263

saying with obvious annoyance. "But go nowhere else. When I return, you may do your shopping. *Comprendé?*"

"Sí, sí," Tía Dolores moaned. "We wait."

Even in the cool shade of the hotel lobby with a glass of lemonade in her hand, Deborah could not forget that frozen moment in time when she'd thought Zack was about to be killed. It had terrified her, and she didn't know why.

In the past weeks without seeing him, she'd convinced herself that he truly was the savage Judith named him. It would seem that witnessing the brutal act that had just occurred would only seal that impression. Yet somehow, the sight of his tall, lean body and animal grace had only made her realize how much she'd missed him. She was definitely mad. A lunatic. And she ached to hold him again. To hear the husky rasp of his voice in her ear, to see his face hard with passion above her, to smell the musky male scent of him and to taste his mouth on hers.

A flush heated her face, and she looked up from the small slices of lemon in her glass to see Judith watching her.

"Isn't that right, Deborah?"

"What? I'm—sorry. I wasn't listening."

"Tía Dolores said that it was a shame Mr. Diamond has such vicious men working for him."

"Did she." Deborah sipped her lemonade, silently sighing.

"Yes. I agree. It can only mean trouble to have men like that running around loose. See what's happened already? And they're supposed to be working together, from what I heard."

"Who?"

"Zack Banning and the man he killed. That's what a

264

man behind me said. Said they both worked for the Double D. They were friends."

"If there is any evidence of wrongdoing, I am certain Sheriff Carpenter will take care of it," Deborah said with more assurance than she felt. She hoped that Zack would not be charged with anything, and did not see how he could be. Too many people had seen the other man draw first, but then again, only Mr. Macklin had been close enough to hear the words exchanged between the two men. Zack's life hinged on Jeremiah Macklin's account of what happened.

Deborah fought back a rising sense of dismay. Macklin had been hired by Don Francisco, which was the reason they had come into Sirocco today.

"Here," Tía Dolores said, thrusting a small plate of cakes at her, "eat and you will feel better."

Deborah managed a smile. "I feel fine. Just hot and tired. And glad to be away from the hacienda."

"Sí, so am I. When Francisco arrives, we shall see what new things Mr. Potter has in his shop, eh?"

The thought of shopping was far from what Deborah really wanted to do, but she nodded quietly as Dolores began reeling off a list of items she'd needed for some time. Her days had begun to meld into one another without change, so that this outing was a real treat. Though she and Judith both had been brought up to be familiar with the running of a household, Don Francisco had his own retinue of servants, and did not want Deborah's help. The only release she had was reading and sewing and visiting with her cousin, and lately Judith had been acting very strange.

Their stay in the Comanche camp had been much harder on her than Deborah, and as time passed, she'd noticed Judith's increasing anxiety. Judith had seemed content to allow Hank Warfield to visit, even to court her, but when the young man mentioned marriage, she had refused to see him again.

"I'm just not interested," she'd said in answer to Deborah's puzzled query.

Several young men from neighboring ranches had visited, and though outwardly pleased at first, Judith had found fault with every one of them. Don Francisco still gazed at her with hot, interested eyes, but nothing had been done or said since the evening Tía Dolores had confessed his real interest. The atmosphere in the hacienda had become one of tension and expectancy, as if waiting for an inevitable explosion.

This excursion into Sirocco should have eased the tensions, but now Deborah wondered if they would only increase. She certainly felt worse.

The image of Zack standing there so calmly, with a faint, amused smile touching the corners of his mouth, his eyes a deep, icy blue, haunted her. She'd seen him as soon as she'd stepped out of the carriage, recognized his easy grace and lethal stride, and had watched as he and the man with him approached Macklin. Don Francisco had sworn softly in Spanish and begun walking toward them. Then the man with Zack had backed off in a peculiar, lazy glide that made Don Francisco swear again.

How strange, to watch with the blood pounding so loudly in her ears she heard only a roar, to see their mouths move but hear nothing said, and all that followed seemed to move as slowly as molasses in winter. And all the time, her fear for Zack had been almost a tangible thing, alive and curling inside her like a ravenous beast.

Would he even care?

She doubted it. He'd made it plain enough that he would use her, but never love her. *No promises.*

No, no promises. Only heartache.

She felt betrayed by his desertion of her, the way he'd made love to her then taken her back to the hacienda without so much as a hint of a future together. Once she'd thought a future impossible, but that was when he was Hawk and lived with the Comanche. Knowing she couldn't live in his world, she'd assumed he'd never live in hers.

Yet he did.

Perhaps not in the same social structure, but then, she no longer lived in the same society she'd been accustomed to in pre-war Natchez, either. Her entire life had been changed by the war, as had everyone's. Only her father seemed to have escaped the radical changes, and from his last letter, he was doing better than ever.

The Hamilton Shipping Lines were doing a booming business, and the money he'd received from the Velazquez estate had been invested in diverse businesses. Don Francisco was reaping some of the profits from those ventures too, she'd learned.

It was the way of the world, Deborah told herself, for a young woman to be given in marriage to seal family ties. Yet it rankled still that John Hamilton had not cared enough about her to ask her opinion, give her a choice, or even try to rescue her after she'd been taken by the Comanche. No, he'd stayed in his safe home in Natchez and written Don Francisco of his displeasure in his daughter's kidnapping, and contacted a few influential military acquaintances, but that was that. It was disconcerting to realize that the only person who truly cared about her was her cousin Judith.

And since Deborah had fallen in love with Zack, Judith had withdrawn from her. She was alone, truly alone.

Deborah looked up, blinking when she realized that Tía Dolores was speaking to her in an agitated voice.

"Señora, señora, do not allow that man to compromise you by publicly accosting you—oh *Madré Díos!*"

Judith's voice came out in a hoarse whisper. "Don't turn around!"

Faintly puzzled, Deborah half-turned, and dropped her glass of lemonade when she saw Zack Banning striding toward her across the hotel lobby. It splattered with a loud crash and sent sticky liquid over her dress and that of Tía Dolores, who was mumbling something in Spanish that sounded like a prayer. Deborah stood up.

"I want to talk to you," Zack said without preamble, and took her by the arm to lead her to a window alcove framed with potted plants and faded draperies. He turned so that he stood with his back to the light streaming in from the windows, facing the room.

"You're not in jail," Deborah said, then felt foolish for stating the obvious.

His mouth quirked. "No, I'm not. It was a fair fight. Macklin swore to it."

She stood, afraid to look at him yet aching to memorize every line of his face. Tension vibrated in the air between them, a different kind of tension than that which she'd become accustomed to in the last weeks. This was sexual, a strong, driving attraction that made her pulses race and her throat tighten and her heart pound so hard she felt she would shatter with the force of it. Zack had to notice; he had to feel it. She couldn't be the only one affected.

Deborah cleared her throat with an effort. She was aware of Judith's hostile glare and Tía Dolores moaning in her chair and gazing at them helplessly.

"What do you want, Zack?"

"I want you to be careful."

The blunt warning startled her. She thought of herself in danger only in connection with him. Was that what he meant?

Apparently her confusion showed on her face, because he growled, "There's liable to be trouble—shooting kind of trouble—and I want you to guard yourself."

"What on earth are you talking about?" Deborah's confusion was being rapidly replaced by irritation. He was so abrupt, and if anyone should be warned of trouble, surely it should be him. Hadn't he just shot a man?

"Deborah, take this at face value. I don't mean anything other than there's going to be trouble between Don Francisco and Diamond before too long. You're liable to get caught in the crossfire. Do you understand?"

His voice was rough, quick, as if he wanted to say what he'd come to say and leave. She had no intention of letting him get away that easy.

"No, I don't understand. Why should they have trouble?"

"Diamond wants the Velazquez lands. I'm sure of it. He's made Don Francisco an offer, but it was refused. He's liable to try something else next."

She stared at him incredulously. "And you're working for a man like that?"

"Can you think of a better way to find out what he's doing?" Zack snapped impatiently. "I don't think he'd want to spread his intentions around unless they're good, and I can promise you, they're not."

"So you do make promises after all," Deborah heard herself say, then froze. That was not at all what she'd intended. She'd had no intentions of letting him know how he'd hurt her.

He looked surprised, then his eyes narrowed, dark and hot and blue, shadowed by his lashes.

"On occasion," he drawled. His gaze dropped, and in spite of the sunlight behind him, she saw the way his eyes lingered on her mouth. "If half of Sirocco wasn't watching right now," he husked, "I'd kiss you silly."

Deborah didn't say anything. It wouldn't have taken much kissing to get her to silly, she decided. She was almost giddy now just at the thought of it.

Zack hesitated, and for one, heart-stopping moment, she thought he intended to throw common sense and caution to the wind and kiss her, but he didn't. Instead, he said softly, "Braden drew first. I just want you to know that."

"Yes. I know."

He slid a palm down her arm to her wrist, then turned her and walked her back to the chair next to Tía Dolores as if they were at a dance and he was returning her to her chaperon.

"Ladies," he said, his gaze flicking to Judith for an instant before moving back to Deborah. "I hope you have a more peaceful afternoon."

With that bit of mocking gallantry, he was gone, back out the double doors of the hotel and into the hot sunshine before anyone else could speak. Deborah felt both her cousin and Tía Dolores looking at her, but did not offer a comment. She was afraid her voice would crack, or that she would burst into unrestrained tears.

Silly. She was a fool. If he wanted her, he would have said so. He would seek her out, not give oblique warnings whenever he chanced to run into her.

Not once since her return had he sought her out for himself. Not once. She was a fool to think he ever would.

But she couldn't help hoping he would come for her.

270

Chapter 19

In the week since the gunfight in Sirocco, Deborah had found herself more closely watched than before. She hadn't thought it possible, but apparently, it was. The continued surveillance precipitated a disagreement between her and Don Francisco, and she had not emerged the victor.

Restless, angry, and frightened, Deborah prowled the small adobe-walled patio off her bedroom and watched the moon rise in the eastern sky. It hung, a silver ball in the dark sky, silvering the ground around her. Her nightgown swayed gently in the soft breeze that made the heat more bearable, and she breathed deeply of sweet-scented blossoms. Night-blooming flowers looked like small white moons against the dark backdrop of foliage clinging to adobe walls.

Deborah plucked one of the blossoms and tucked it into her hair over her ear, gazing into the night. She could hear the low moan of cattle, and in the distance, the laughter of the ranch hands, or *vaqueros* Don Francisco employed. Lately, he had hired men from Mexico, men who wore crossed bandoliers and carried guns and made her think of Dexter Diamond's hired gunmen. She and Don Francisco had quarreled over that.

"Do not presume to tell me what to do, woman," he'd snapped when she said it was only inviting trouble to hire men who would fight too easily. "I will not risk the land that my family has had for generations. There have been too many risks already."

Deborah had stared at him, at his slender, wiry build and darkly handsome features. "Why don't you marry and secure your claim, if that's what you're worried about?"

"I hired Mister Macklin to secure my claim for me, but even he will be useless against loaded weapons." A sneer warped his mouth as he glared at her. "You know, that if you think to escape me by marrying another, I will see that you suffer for it."

"Please explain that remark, Don Francisco."

"It is simple—Señor Diamond made an offer of marriage for you. I refused, of course. He wants what you will bring to the marriage, not you. But he will never have one rock of Velazquez land, not one! Not if I have to lock you up for the rest of your life."

He'd sounded so fiercely determined, that Deborah had not bothered to point out what was obvious to her—she did not want to marry Dexter Diamond. Don Francisco's threat to lock her up sounded too much like a warning, and Deborah retreated into silence.

Now, she paced and fretted. Life was growing more intolerable by the day. Judith was too withdrawn, and Tía Dolores too upset by her brother's fury at her for allowing Zack Banning to confront Deborah in the hotel lobby, for either of them to listen to her fears. So Deborah worried alone.

Or as alone as she could be, when an armed guard stood outside even the walls of her patio. To guard her? Or to keep her prisoner? She suspected the latter. Someone always seemed to be outside her hallway door, and there was the soft scurrying of feet at night. She also heard it during the day each time she left Tía Dolores's side.

She was becoming accustomed to the furtive noises.

Perhaps that was why she didn't hear the noise of a man climbing over the adobe walls of her patio. There was a scrape, a rustle of leaves, then a soft *plop,* and when she turned with a gasp, her eyes widened.

A man was outlined against the white adobe wall laced with vines, his silhouette large and familiar.

"Hawk," she whispered, and he reached her side in two graceful strides.

"Zack," he muttered, glancing warily around the patio. He looked back at her, his gaze raking over her nightgown. "Nice. Do you wear that often?"

She swallowed. "Every night."

He looked up at her face and a faint smile curled his mouth. "Sounds inviting."

"Where is your invitation for tonight?" she asked tightly, remembering her resolve to resist him.

"Right here." He stepped forward before she could react and pulled her to him, crushing her lips beneath his. His mouth was hot, the invasion of his tongue swift and sensual, and she yielded. Deborah welcomed the penetration by opening wider for him, curling her tongue around his. She felt him tense, heard his muffled groan, then he pulled away.

"This is too crazy even for us," he said softly, and moved to stand in the shadows. "Go put out the lamp in your room."

She trembled with indecision, and he must have sensed it. "I need to talk to you, Deborah."

When the lamp was doused, she turned and felt him beside her, his arms moving around her in a warm, comforting embrace. His gunbelt pressed into her side, and he shifted.

"What are you doing here?" she murmured. "I mean, how did you get in?"

His breath stirred the top of her hair. "It's easy for a man who knows how. Don Francisco's guards are not as vigilant as he thinks."

"Did you—"

"Kill them?" he finished when she hesitated. "No. It would attract too much attention."

"Then what—?"

"Don't worry about it," he cut her off, his arms tightening around her waist as he lifted her up and against him. "I don't have a lot of time, and I don't want to waste what I do have."

Her heart was beating rapidly, and her breath came in short drags of air. "You came to tell me something?"

"Yeah. You and your cousin need to go back home. Get out of here."

"Go home?" Dazed as much by his proximity as by his words, Deborah shook her head. "We can't."

"You have to. It's dangerous for you here. Go back to wherever it is you came from." He gave her arm a quick shake. "You can do that, can't you?"

"No, we can't." Her words stuck, and she had to force them out. "My ... my father doesn't want us back."

There was a moment of tense silence, and she felt the muscles in his arms contract. "Damn."

"Zack, what's the matter? Why do you sound so worried?"

"Because I am. All hell's going to break loose around here soon, and I want you where you can't be hurt."

"You're scaring me."

"Maybe I should," he said when she shivered. His

hands stroked down her back, fingers spread wide, the heels of his palms massaging her. "You need to get your cousin and get away from here."

"Just where do we go?" she drew back to demand. "I have no money of my own, just what Don Francisco has allotted. All my assets are on paper. My entire life is ruled by him."

"And your cousin?"

"I have more than she does."

Zack swore softly beneath his breath, then shifted so that the moonlight fell across his face. "Would you let me take you somewhere for safety?"

"Back to your father's village?"

"No. That's more dangerous than here. Mackenzie has run them down pretty close." He raked a hand through his hair in a frustrated gesture, and moonlight streaming through the open patio door silvered his features with a softening glow.

When he said, "I'll take you to my mother," she gasped with surprise.

"Your *mother?*"

"Yes."

"I didn't know . . . I mean, I assumed she must be dead. You never mentioned her."

His mouth twisted slightly. "We didn't do much talking before you left. My mother is alive, but I haven't seen her since I was fourteen."

Deborah studied his face, the opaque eyes, the slash of his mouth, and the corded muscles in his throat. She felt his tension, and began to understand his feelings, if not the details.

"I see."

His eyes flicked to her and paused. "There's not time now, but I'll explain later. Give me a day or two, and I'll come back for you. Tell your cousin, and be ready."

275

Deborah shook her head. "Judith won't go."

"Why not?"

"I'm not certain, but I know it has to do with our capture and you. You're part of it, whether you ever hurt her or not."

"Then you'll have to go alone."

"I can't leave Judith."

"Dammit, Deborah," he snarled, "I don't intend to let you get hurt."

"Zack, please—tell me what's got you so concerned. I don't understand. And I can't guard against shadows."

He led her to the wide bed, and sat her down on the mattress so that he could see her face. Hatless, in his black shirt, pants, and knee-high moccasins, he looked dark and forbidding in the shadows. Deborah couldn't suppress another shiver.

Kneeling, he took her hands in his and looked up at her. "Don Francisco's attorney may be smart in legal matters, but he's made Diamond so damn mad he can't see straight. He intends to use some pretty basic tactics, and I know Don Francisco will figure it out pretty quick. There will be some shooting before it's over with."

"And you? Are you still going to fight on Diamond's side?"

"For right now. Look," he said when she tried to jerk away, anger edging his voice, "I told you that it's the only way I can keep current on what Diamond intends to do."

"I'll keep that in mind when your bullets are flying."

"Don't," he said sharply, the one word reminding her of how often he'd said the same thing in Comanche. *Keta.*

He rose to his feet in a fluid motion that made her

276

shrink away, and he saw her movement and frowned. "You can't still be scared of me."

"No," she said, pride lifting her chin. "I just don't know what your true intentions are. I don't see or hear from you, and then you just show up here in the middle of the night like a thief, and tell me I have to leave. What am I supposed to think?"

"You're supposed to have enough sense to know that if I showed up here in daylight, Don Francisco would tack my hide to a wall with bullets." Irritation made his voice rough. "Why would I bother, if I didn't want to keep you safe?"

"That's a good question. Why are you bothering?" When he didn't say anything, Deborah gave an angry shrug to hide her pain. "I wish I knew why I allow you to do this to me, but I don't." She felt his stare, glimpsed his quick, impatient step away.

"I should leave here and not bother with you again."

"I suppose you should," she returned coolly, despite the burn of pain in her throat.

Turning back to her, he was a lethal silhouette of anger as he took the one step back to the bed and grabbed her, his hands hard on her wrists.

"Just once," he ground out, "it would be nice to hear how you really feel. You make me so damn mad, always prim and proper and cool, even when your eyes say the opposite of what your mouth is trying to tell me."

"And just what do my eyes say?" she shot back. "That you aren't exactly honest with your feelings, maybe?"

"Dammit." This time when he kissed her, he wasn't soft or tender. His lips were hard, almost hurtful, but there was a driving intensity that made Deborah lean into him and seek out that wildness. Despite her pain, despite her anger, she felt a certain satisfaction in being able to provoke Zack to passion. It seemed only fair that he should feel the same hot need he made her feel.

When his hands spread over her back, Deborah's arms rose to wind around his neck, and she pressed closer to him. She could feel the thunder of his heart against her breasts, hear his ragged breathing when he lifted his mouth from hers and stared down at her in the shadows.

"You make me do the craziest things," he muttered in a low, rough voice. He shifted to hold her breast in his palm, his thumb raking across her nipple and making it tighten. A hot jolt shot through her at his touch. When his mouth came down over her breast, wetting her gown and making her grab his hair to hold his head still, she shivered with the intensity.

It was obvious to her that he wasn't the only one doing crazy things. If she had any sense, she would insist that he leave immediately before someone found him in her room. It would be a complete catastrophe for both of them if he was caught there.

But it was hard to think of that—hard to think of anything but what his hands and mouth were doing. All her self-discipline vanished at his touch. The lessons she'd learned as a child and a young woman, the strictures that had ruled her life for so long, had blown away with the west wind when she'd met this man. He violated every principle she had, yet she surrendered to him easily. There had to be something wrong, but it was difficult to remember what.

"Someone might come," she finally found the strength to murmur when his hands were inside her gown and stroking her bare skin. "We need to stop before it's too late."

"Too late for who?" His voice was rough and gut-

278

tural, and she shuddered when he captured her nipple between his thumb and forefinger and rolled it gently.

His mouth was so hot, yet she was shivering. With his hands on her breasts and his lips moving to take her mouth again, she was fast losing any control she still had. Her hands dug into the muscles of his arms, and she dragged her lips away.

"You've got to stop ..."

"I will. I will."

The coiling fire deep in her belly made her squirm, and her hips brushed against his, her gown catching on the buckle of his gunbelt. He made another rough sound and moved to pull her up against him, tucking her between his legs and hard against his rigid body.

Then he was backing her across the room until she felt the bed at her knees, and his body leaned so that his weight pushed her back and down. The mattress sagged beneath her, feathers and quilt cushioning her as he stood between her legs.

Somehow, Zack had his hand beneath her nightgown and his palm was cupping the mount between her thighs. The touch was hot and alarming and enticing, and she didn't know whether to push him away or surrender all. It seemed as if she always surrendered when she knew she should resist, and part of her wondered why she was so weak where he was concerned.

Then it didn't matter anymore, because he was unbuckling his gunbelt and unbuttoning his pants, and there was not time for anything else but an ease to the driving urgency she felt. He kissed her fiercely while he undid his buttons, and then he was pulling her up with his hands on her hips, fitting her to him. When he slid into her she gasped, arching up to take him, her legs lifting. There was something primitive and arousing about him taking her like this, with her on the bed and him standing between her legs.

Beyond him, moonlight poured in through the open door. A full moon. A Comanche moon, he'd once told her. It seemed fitting that he should come to her like this on a night when even the moon heralded his presence.

He stood with feet apart and braced, looking down at her, the moonlight behind him and his outline blurred with silver. It was almost as if she was dreaming it again, as if he were an impossible god, a pagan symbol of the intangibles in life.

Bending, he kissed her again, hot, sweet and wild; they were both breathing raggedly, soft pants for air laced with steamy sensuality. The summer night pressed down outside, and the cool light of the moon washed them as Zack took from her and gave to her, all of him.

He shuddered, absorbed her shattering cry with his mouth, then relaxed his big body across hers. He leaned there, braced with one hand on the mattress and one foot still on the floor.

Finally he lifted his head to gaze down at her, and she felt it. Opening her eyes, she smiled as she traced a finger over the erotic outline of his mouth. He bit the tip gently, then took her hand and turned it over, kissing her palm.

Propped up on one hand and a knee, he curled his fingers over her hand and said, "I'll come back for you."

"I can't go."

An oath ripped from him, but it was more resigned than vicious. He pushed up and away from her, then stood. As he buttoned his pants and reached for the gunbelt he'd laid within easy reach on the mattress, he eyed her carefully as she sat up and smoothed her nightgown down around her bare legs.

"Deborah, I know you are loyal to your cousin. I admire that. But it won't do her any good if you both die. Let her make her own choice, but don't let her make yours."

"You don't understand," she began, but his steady stare stopped her.

"It's not understanding that's needed now. It's caution. Don't take risks because of some misguided notion of loyalty."

"Misguided?" Deborah stared at him uneasily. "Judith is my cousin."

"And old enough to make her own choices."

"I suppose you wouldn't risk your life for someone you care about," Deborah said with a trace of bitterness, though she saw the truth in what he said. She turned her face away, chewing on her lower lip with anxiety.

"I'm here, aren't I?"

Her head jerked back around at his soft words. It was the closest he'd ever come to admitting he cared. Zack was tucking his shirttail into the waistband of his pants, and he looked up at her as coolly as if he had not just set her world in a whirl.

"Yes," she whispered. "You're here."

"Then listen to me."

"I'm listening."

He crouched down in front of her, taking her bare feet in his hands. "Give me two days. I'll come back like I did tonight. Be ready. Take only what's necessary."

"What if—" She paused and licked suddenly dry lips. "What if something goes wrong?"

"Send me a message."

A shaky laugh erupted from her. "I don't think Don Francisco will allow me to just send over a man with a note for you, Zack!"

"Then I'll be here."

Deborah toyed with an eggshell thin cup of strong coffee and tried to avoid Don Francisco's irate gaze. The meals had been awkward enough since Macklin had arrived; now, with the news that Dexter Diamond had filed a claim against Velazquez lands in Sirocco, they were positively tense.

That must have been what Zack had meant.

As soon as Don Francisco had discovered it, he had ordered his men to post lines of armed riders along every road leading anywhere near the rancho. Then he had dammed up the river that flowed from Velazquez lands to the Double D, cutting off Dexter Diamond's most plentiful supply of water. With the summer sun drying up shallow water holes, Double D cattle would soon die of thirst. Battle lines had been drawn and a challenge issued. Now the place looked more like an armed military camp than a functioning cattle ranch.

"If there is a confrontation, Don Francisco," Jeremiah Macklin was saying, "I suggest you allow the authorities to handle it. Mr. Diamond cannot win. This is only an aggravation tactic."

"And we are more aggravating, no?" Don Francisco asked smoothly. He smiled, and the flickering light made the smile look positively evil. A heavy, silver-branched candelabrum graced the center of the long table. Elegant wax tapers shed light across the table in wavering patterns as servants served the meal.

Macklin frowned. "I cannot condone illegal actions, Don Francisco. And I will not participate in anything remotely against the law."

"Is it against the law to protect one's property?" Don Francisco shook his head. "I do not think so. I have a right to place a dam on my property where I wish it, sí?"

Clasping his hands together around his coffee cup, Macklin said heavily, "Yes, legally that is true. Morally, it can get sticky. There is a fine line that cannot be crossed. I suggest that if you are expecting trouble, you send for the sheriff."

"I value your suggestions, señor, but Sirocco is too far away for the sheriff to be of any help. We are the law out here."

Macklin sighed. "I find that to be true in many remote areas of Texas, but the end results are always regrettable."

Don Francisco's voice vibrated with intensity. "Here, we are fighting for our homes, our very lives. I will not let that *hombre* steal what has been in the Velazquez family for over a hundred years. He is arrogant and greedy, and he will swallow up other lands without remorse. But I, Don Francisco Hernando Velazquez y Aguilar, will not allow him to take what is mine."

Deborah heard the undercurrent of tension in his voice and shivered. He meant it. And if what Zack said was true, Dexter Diamond meant to try and take the Velazquez lands. There would be a bloody range war, and she would be in the middle of it.

Her glance moved to Judith, who was looking at Jeremiah Macklin. The brawny attorney occasionally cast her furtive glances, obviously admiring Judith's golden beauty. In the time he'd spent at the Velazquez hacienda, he had made more than one effort to draw her into conversation. Judith had avoided him so far.

Deborah looked down at her still-full plate. It was hard to think of food when she knew what was just ahead. She had to talk to Judith shortly. Zack might return before they were ready if she did not.

283

Once the uncomfortable meal ended, Deborah managed to get Judith alone for a few moments before Tía Dolores joined them. She caught her by the back of her dress, a mint green organdie that billowed out like a fluffy cloud around her.

"Judith—I must speak with you."

They stepped into an alcove near the veranda where the men had gone to smoke cigars and have after dinner drinks. Judith smiled, and put a hand on Deborah's arm.

"Everything will be all right," she said softly.

"No, Judith, I don't think so. At least, not for a while. There's going to be trouble." As Judith's smile faded, Deborah rushed on, "We have to be careful. And we need to get away from here before the trouble begins."

Judith stared at her, blue eyes widening. "I don't know what you mean."

"You heard Don Francisco and Mister Macklin. There is going to be trouble. Do you understand what that can mean?"

Judith's hand tightened on Deborah's arm. "No," she whispered.

"Shooting. And they won't be careful. We could end up as hostages if things turn out very badly." She watched Judith carefully. Her lips worked soundlessly for a moment as she digested what Deborah had said, and then she began to shake her head.

"No. I can't go through this again. Not again. Not guns and shooting and men screaming—"

"No, no, we don't have to," Deborah said quickly. "Listen to me—we can leave here before it gets worse."

"Leave?" Judith's face paled. "But how? And where would we go?"

Inhaling deeply and praying Judith would hear her out, Deborah said softly, "Please don't say anything until I've finished. I know how you feel about Zack Banning, but right now he may be our only hope. He has offered to take us to safety if we—Judith!"

Jerking her arm free, Judith spun on her heel and pushed from the alcove. Deborah caught her arm.

"You've at least got to listen! Please!"

"Listen?" Judith shook her head, blond hair falling into her eyes in small wisps. "No. He's bewitched you or something. I know he has. Besides, we haven't seen him since the day he shot that man. His friend. If he'd do that, do you think he would help us?"

"You're getting things mixed up, Judith. Braden was not his friend, and Zack does want to help us."

Judith's eyes narrowed. "How do you know that? Have you heard from him?"

Not quite trusting Judith not to be angry if she found out he'd come to her room, Deborah said slowly, "He's contacted me. He's trying to warn us."

"I'm sure he is." Judith's tone was dry. "What makes you think we'd be any safer with him than we are with Don Francisco? Does he intend to take us to live with savages again?"

"No. Will you come?"

Agitated, Judith clasped and unclasped her hands. She whirled away, shuddering. "I don't know," she finally said in a quivering voice.

"Judith. You have to decide. I know it's frightening, but you need to take this chance."

"How," Judith asked huskily, "can you *trust* that man after everything that's happened?" She turned back to look at Deborah, her blue eyes swimming with tears. "Don't you remember what he did to us?"

"Yes. I remember. I also remember that he released us as he promised me he would. Now he promises to help us. Can you not trust me?"

"Oh Deborah, I trust you. But you're asking me to

trust a savage, a man with no morals or conscience. If we trust him we're liable to end up in a Comanche village again."

"No, we won't." Footsteps sounded in the tile hall behind them, and Deborah added in a quick whisper, "Say you will go, please!"

"When?"

"Tonight or tomorrow night."

"But how?"

"He'll come for us. Are you going?"

Judith stared down at her still-clasped hands for a long moment. "Yes," she said, her voice a whisper.

Relief washed through Deborah, and she tucked her hand through her cousin's arm. "Oh, thank God. You can't know how anxious I've been."

"Anxious?" Tía Dolores echoed as she sailed into view. "About what?"

"About our safety," Deborah said quickly. "We are very concerned, of course."

"Sí, sí," Tía Dolores said. "We all are. Horrible man, that Señor Diamond. I regret ever allowing him to call on us here. We should have had him sent away the first time."

"Perhaps he will not actually do anything," Judith said softly. "This could all be for nothing."

"I hope so, *chica,*" Tía Dolores said. "I hope so." Her brow furrowed. "But I don't think so."

Chapter 20

A howl sliced through the hot night air, seeming to hang suspended in time before it faded away. Coyotes.

"You sure this is gonna work, Banning?"

Zack slanted Diamond a quick glance. "Yeah. Sure as I can be, anyway. If nothing else, the dam will be gone for a few days before they can rebuild it. Long enough to water your cattle."

"Good." Diamond gave a grunt of satisfaction. "Blowing it up was so simple, I wonder why I didn't think of it."

"Probably because it was so damn hard to get near it."

Diamond dropped to his knees beside Zack and stared out over the ridge. The river glittered below; a huge earthen dam had been built, and above it, a vast pool spread over the banks and ran in newly dug ditches to watering holes. Below it, not even a trickle of water escaped.

"This better work," Diamond muttered after a moment. He peered at Zack in the press of moonlight when he didn't reply. "Tell me somethin', Banning."

Zack shifted on the balls of his feet and lifted a brow. "What?"

"What did happen between you and Braden?"

"You already know what happened."

"I heard what Carpenter said when he told me to pay for the burial. I never heard your version."

Zack's voice was cool. "There's only one version, and you already heard it, Diamond. We disagreed and he went for his gun. Plain and simple."

There was an irritated grunt, and Diamond looked away again. "You already set the dynamite?" he asked after a moment, and Zack nodded.

"Yeah. Had to kill one of the guards. With any luck, they won't find out he's missing until the charges blow."

"Where are you gonna be when it goes off?"

Zack stood up. "I told you. I've got something else to see to."

"I heard you say that, but it kinda bothers me that you won't be around if there's shootin' goin' on." Diamond stared at him narrowly in the moonlight. "You scared?"

Turning in a smooth, unhurried motion, Zack looked at Diamond with narrowed eyes. "What'd you say?"

His mouth twisted, and Diamond looked away. "Hell, Nothin' worth repeatin', I guess. Just can't help wonderin' what you got up your sleeve, that's all."

"If you don't trust me—"

"Naw, naw, that ain't it. I trust you to do what you say. It's what you don't say that bothers me."

"You're paying me, Diamond, and as long as you are, I'm on your side. If I decide to change sides, I won't mind telling you."

"Did I say anything about that? I know your reputation and I know you don't mince words none."

Shrugging, Zack didn't reply. He had absolutely no intention of telling Dexter Diamond what he planned.

The man would either object or insist upon helping, and he didn't want to take the time to argue.

After a half hour had passed, Zack said, "I'm leaving."

Diamond didn't argue, but he stood with his thumbs snagged in his belt loops and his face dark with irritation as Zack left on foot. He could feel Diamond staring at him, and he had the thought that he might have him followed.

After several minutes of running, Zack heard the faint chip of a hoof against rock and smiled to himself. He'd been right. Diamond wasn't a fool, but he didn't like to have a man buck him, either. Laughing softly, Zack promptly lost the man following him.

It was close to midnight when Zack got within the boundaries of the Velazquez hacienda. He waited, watching as the guards changed. Don Francisco was taking no chances. He had armed men strung all along the perimeters of his ranch, as well as around the house. It had been a lot harder to get close this time than the last, but any self-respecting Comanche could manage it.

There was a trick to it, he'd learned. One had to think of themselves as part of the landscape to blend into it. It had taken him years to learn the patience of waiting, watching, and waiting some more. If a man allowed himself to get in too big a hurry, he failed.

So Zack waited. He wore dark clothes, so that not even the ragged moonlight could reflect from bare skin, and his moccasins were soundless in the dirt and dust. His pistol was stuck in his belt beneath his shirt, and he carried a knife in one hand, still sheathed so that no chance runnel of light along the shiny blade would betray him.

He wished he'd warned Deborah to wear dark clothing, but he hadn't thought about it. Too late now. He'd make her change if she was foolish enough to wear white. And her cousin too, though he doubted that Judith would go with them. He knew how terrified she was of him, and regretted it for Deborah's sake.

Sometimes it happened that way. A white woman rescued after years of Indian captivity, even if she had been treated as an honored wife, often denied that she had been shown any kindness or decency at all. Sometimes she was right. And sometimes she'd been so brutalized that she reacted with hatred and terror to any Indian. Like Judith.

Judith's fear could make things difficult for them if she hesitated because of it. This would be dangerous enough without worrying about her reaction, and Zack hoped she refused to go.

Crouched behind a clump of bluethorn and cactus at the corner of an outbuilding, Zack waited until the men who were on guard duty crossed to one of the bunkhouses. It would take them maybe five minutes to exchange places, not exactly as efficient as a military post.

He seized his chance when they went inside, and he could hear their faint discussion and laughter. Running in a low, half-crouch, Zack crossed the open yard to the house, keeping to shadows when he could. Tonight, his purposes would have been served much better by no moonlight.

The adobe wall of the courtyard around Deborah's patio was cool against his back as he edged around it. Vines tugged at him, and he had to go slowly. Everything depended on time. If he was off even by a minute or two, it would be too dangerous to continue. When the explosion distracted Don Francisco's guards, he would have only a very few minutes to get Deborah out of there. It was the best he'd been able to come up with. Don Francisco had covered all details pretty well.

A sound came from his left, and Zack froze. A vine stirred in the breeze, brushing against his cheek, and he could hear the scrape of something moving. He waited, but when no other sound followed, he moved cautiously forward.

It wasn't hard to leap up and grasp the top of the adobe wall, and he hauled himself up and over, landing with a soft thud on the other side. Deborah had left only a small lamp burning in her room; she sat in a chair with a book in her lap, easily visible from the patio. It appeared as if she was ready and waiting, but something made him pause.

He didn't know what it was. Deborah was alone. It was quiet. Maybe that was it. It had grown too quiet. There should have been some noise, the sounds of a ranch at night. Instead, a hush seemed to have fallen.

For a long moment he just stood there, pressed up against the wall with the vines curling around him. Leaves quivered in the wind. A sweet-scented blossom brushed his cheek. The fragrance reminded him of the last time he'd come here, and the blossom Deborah had tucked behind her ear. It had fallen unnoticed by her, but he had picked it up and tucked it into his shirt pocket for some reason. He thought of that briefly before turning his attention back to the quiet night.

He could see Deborah, her head still bent, the lamplight making her hair shine with deep fire. He moved from the wall, taking cautious steps around the edge of the patio and toward the open door. Bending, he picked up a small pebble and tossed it so that it rolled and bounced over the floor toward her. She looked up, her eyes wide and dark in the dim light.

She shut the book and stood up, smoothing the skirt

of her black dress. A faint smile curled his mouth. He was glad she'd had enough sense to wear dark clothing.

When Deborah stepped out onto the patio, he was waiting at the side, and touched her gently on the shoulder. She drew in a sharp breath, but didn't scream.

"Zack?" she whispered.

"Yeah." He slid his hand to her elbow. "You alone?"

"Yes. Judith will be here soon."

"How soon?"

She turned, eyes finding him in the shadows. "I don't know. I told her to be ready, and she said she would."

He made an impatient sound. "We can't afford to wait too long. I've arranged a distraction, and we'll have to go then or not at all."

"A distraction?" He hadn't thought it possible for her eyes to get any larger, but they did. "What kind of distraction?"

"Don't worry, nothing deadly, only loud." He pulled her against him. "Got your gear ready?"

"I have a small carpetbag and that's all."

He nodded his satisfaction. Deborah was not a woman to insist on frivolities, and he was glad. She was sensible and level-headed.

"Can you go get your cousin?" he asked after a moment. He wanted to keep holding her, but there would be time enough for that later. Now, he had to focus on getting her to safety.

"I suppose I can." Deborah leaned into him for a moment as if needing reassurance, and he felt a peculiar tightening in his chest. He couldn't remember ever having felt so drawn to a woman, so connected. And he'd never felt this overpowering need to protect a woman.

He tilted her face toward him with a finger under her chin. "Be careful," he murmured. He wanted to say more, but the words wouldn't come. He didn't know how to say more, or what to say. When he bent his head, she lifted her mouth willingly to his, and he kissed her gently, then drew back. "I'll wait here."

Deborah nodded. He watched her glide back into her room and pass through the square of light thrown by the lamp, then go into the hall. Still uneasy, Zack melted back into the shadows of the patio, trying to dispel that sense of unease. Nothing seemed amiss. It was quiet, and no alarm had been given.

When Deborah returned, she slipped through her bedroom door with Judith in tow, both women obviously nervous. Zack watched them through the open patio door, his eyes narrowing slightly. They were alone, but Judith kept looking over her shoulder as if they were being followed.

He waited until Deborah stepped out on the patio, then said quietly, "Over here."

She came to him swiftly. "We're ready."

"Then we need to go now." His hand closed around her wrist, and he pulled her to him. When he glanced up, he saw Judith staring at him, her eyes wide and dilated, her face pinched with hatred. Her expression shot through him like a lightning bolt, and he instinctively pulled Deborah closer. "Are you ready to go?" he asked Judith warily, and she gave him a strange look.

"Yes. I'm ready."

Zack shot Deborah another guarded look. She was looking at Judith with concern.

"Judith darling, you don't look well. Are you nervous?"

Judith pushed at her hair, and her hand was trembling. "A little."

Deborah went to her and put her arm around her. "Don't be. Zack will take care of us. He'll get us to safety."

"She needs to wear something dark over her gown," Zack pointed out. "That pale color will show up at night."

"I'll get her my cloak."

When Deborah stepped back into the bedroom, Judith turned to Zack. Her eyes were bright, and her mouth curved in a slight smile.

"You can't have her."

Zack stared at her with narrowed eyes. "What?"

"You can't have her. She's too good for you. I won't let you hurt her anymore."

"I don't want to hurt her. I want to help her." He took a step back, sensing she was near hysteria. *Damn.* Just what he needed. A hysterical woman. Why hadn't Deborah left her behind? It would have been a lot better than trying to calm her down, and he flicked a glance up to see if Deborah was hurrying. Something needed to be done before Judith caused a scene.

But when he glanced up, Zack caught a glimpse of motion to his left and behind him, and he reacted instinctively. With a swift twist of his body, he wrenched to one side and reached for his pistol all in the same motion. The shadows became solid figures, and before he could get back to the wall, four armed men faced him.

"You are caught, señor," one of them said softly. "Do not force us to shoot."

A glance showed him Deborah being held several yards away by Don Francisco, her lovely face contorted with anger and despair.

"Let me go," she said calmly, and Zack felt a wave of admiration for her poise under duress. "I refuse to be handled like an animal."

"Patience, *niña,*" Don Francisco growled. "We only wish to talk with this *muy malo hombré,* eh?"

294

"Do you think me fool enough to believe that?" Deborah snapped.

Don Francisco laughed. "It does not matter what you may believe at this point. We just wish to ask him a few questions about his presence here."

"And then you'll let him go?" Deborah asked after a moment.

"Of course. As soon as he tells us how he got here and why. And who sent him, naturally."

During this exchange Zack had not moved nor spoken. He stood stiff and still, wary and tense. He expected what came next, Deborah's soft voice telling him not to make them shoot him.

"Please, Zack."

Zack had no illusions. These men had no intention of scolding him and letting him go. He moved swiftly, taking a step forward as if to surrender, and bringing up one foot in a smooth, almost casual motion that caught the closest man between his legs. There was a shocked exclamation that changed into a retching sound, but Zack had turned in the same motion and aimed another kick at the shadow next to him, sending his weapon flying from his hand. He heard it clatter, and somehow he had his knife in his other hand and his pistol cocked and aimed.

Shots shattered the night air, and he felt something tug at his sleeve. A hot wind zipped past his head, leaving a burning trail. His pistol bucked in his hand, and one of the shadows fell. He could hear, as if from a great distance away, women screaming. It set his teeth on edge.

There was the stinging smell of gunpowder and the rusty smell of blood, and he tried to turn to find Deborah but for some reason he couldn't. His body would not obey his command to turn.

Zack stared down in disbelief as his knees buckled and he crumpled to the ground. He managed to get one leg up under him and stand, but some force stronger than he kept pushing him back down, and he couldn't even see anyone near him. He heard, vaguely, Deborah crying out his name over and over, but he couldn't answer.

And then there was an explosion, a shuddering roar that made the earth vibrate and the walls tremble. He knew it was too late then, that he'd gambled and lost. Regret surged up in him, but the regret was for Deborah, not himself.

"How could you!"

Judith looked away from Deborah's accusing gaze. "He'll hurt you. You just won't believe it."

A lump clogged her throat so that she could barely breathe, and Deborah couldn't say anything else. She watched as Don Francisco had two of his men lift Zack and carry him inside. They tossed him carelessly on her bed, and she saw the bright strings of blood flowing behind him. She closed her eyes.

"If he dies, I'll never forgive you, Judith," she said tonelessly, and heard her cousin's soft sob. It was true. If Zack died—her imagination failed her at that point. He could not die. She wouldn't let him.

Turning, Deborah faced Don Francisco. "I insist that you allow me to see to his injuries."

"And I already told you, I will see to them." His voice was brisk and impatient, and he turned to snap out an order in Spanish to one of the men behind him. Then he turned back to Deborah. "I worried about the wrong man, I see. I thought Señor Diamond had your favor. Apparently, your taste runs to gunmen instead."

"My tastes, as you so quaintly put it, Don Francisco, are none of your business. And that is not the reason Zack Banning is here."

"No? How curious." Don Francisco smiled, flicking a glance toward Judith. "That is not the explanation I heard."

Deborah felt another spur of betrayal. She inhaled deeply and said, "None of this matters at the moment. Zack is hurt and needs medical attention. If you will not give it to him, then I will."

When she took a step toward her bed, her gaze shifting to Zack, Don Francisco stopped her. His hand caught her arm and he jerked roughly.

"If you wish him to die," he said softly, "you will go to him. I'll have him staked out on the desert and left there."

Whitening, Deborah felt a cold flash rip through her. He meant it. She saw his determination in his eyes, in the icy sneer twisting his mouth.

"No," she got out in a breathy whisper, "don't. Please. I won't—go near him."

"Bueno. I thought you might change your mind if I explained it properly."

Deborah stood only a few feet from where Zack lay on her bed, unconscious and wounded, and she couldn't help him. It was the most frustrating, helpless feeling she'd ever had in her life.

When Don Francisco had his men drag Zack from the room as if he was a sack of meal, she heard him groan as they treated him roughly. It tore at her, that mutter of pain, even though he wasn't conscious. She couldn't help it. Tears spilled from her eyes and down her cheeks, and she shut her eyes against Don Francisco's malicious smirk.

"Oh please," she heard herself whisper, "don't hurt him."

Don Francisco only laughed.

Zack already knew all about pain. He'd learned at an early age. Pain could control a man, or a man could control pain. It wasn't easy. And there was a trick to it that had taken him a long time to master. But he had, and the lesson helped him endure.

"Tell me, Señor Banning," Don Francisco said, facing him. "Did Diamond send you for her? Why?"

Zack refused to look at him. He could taste blood in his mouth from where he'd been hit. One eye was closed from the fists that had plowed into his face, and he thought his nose might be broken. He kept silent. And waited.

The next blow sent him reeling back, and the chair in which he was tied toppled over so that he crashed to the floor. Lights exploded in his eyes, bright and blinding, spiralling to pinpoints. He heard a roar, like the rush of wind in his ears as pain splintered throughout his entire frame. He lay there and waited. They'd pick him up again. It had become an endless cycle in the past hours, the questions and fists and falling to be picked up for it to begin again.

Rough hands dragged him up with the chair. His arms were bent back behind him and tied around the back, putting pressure on his shoulders and the wound he'd suffered. It still bled, the bullet hole high in the fleshy part of his left arm. The bullet crease on his scalp had stopped bleeding for the most part. He thought so, anyway. It was hard to tell which bled now, since they opened up new cuts and gashes on his face.

The sharp pain had subsided into a dull ache, a throb

that seemed to renew with each beat of his heart. He tried to focus, and finally Don Francisco's face swam into view again, a little blurred, but recognizable.

"Señor," he heard him say as if he was far away, "I can do this much longer than you can suffer it, I am certain. Will you not tell me what I wish to know? Diamond is behind the blowing up of my dam—a waste of his time since I will only rebuild—but why send you? Does he intend to steal Señora Velazquez to hold her hostage?" He leaned closer, and there was a soft menace in his voice that caught Zack's undivided attention. "She has agreed to this, has she not? I wish to know. I *must* know. Tell me, and I will set you free. No harm will come to you if you will confess to her part in this."

Zack must have looked doubtful, because Don Francisco gave him a wolfish smile. "Don't be a hero, señor. It will cause me an irritating delay, and you a great deal of pain."

For a long moment, Zack considered his options. There was no question of admitting that Deborah had known he was to come for her. He'd never risk her that way. But telling Don Francisco some trivial fact might help his situation and save him more bruises. He dragged in a punishing breath that made his ribs ache, and blinked to clear what little vision he still had.

That was when he saw the paper Don Francisco held, a neat white piece of parchment that had writing scrawled on it. He didn't have to read it to know what it said, and he felt a sense of impending doom.

"I would greatly like for you to sign this paper." Don Francisco's smile was encouraging. "A confession, of such, you see."

Zack blinked. His eyes stung. Blood. Or sweat, maybe. He wasn't certain. His mouth was sore and his lips were puffy and split. Even if he wanted to talk, he wasn't sure he could. So he settled for staring at Don Francisco without speaking, blithely ignoring the paper he held out.

The slender Mexican sighed dramatically. "Ah, you are so stupid. What difference does it make if you tell me or if I wait and find out myself? The outcome will not change. And if you cooperate, perhaps I will let you go free, heh?"

When he didn't say anything, Don Francisco shrugged. Zack braced himself for the next blow. This one was aimed at his belly, and the pain radiated outward in intense waves that took his breath. He barely felt the chair go backward, or the sensation of falling. Then the floor slammed into him and he heard something crack. He wondered if it was one of his bones.

Slowly, he regained his breath. It came in short little pants for air, each one painful and feeling as if his chest was in a vise. The air seemed thick, like soup. He dragged in another short breath. His ribs hurt. Maybe that was what he'd heard crack.

But then he heard Don Francisco's companion— Alfredo?—cursing in Spanish, and realized the chair had broken. He was hauled upward again and untied. The rush of blood back into his hands made him suck in a sharp breath between his teeth. He flexed his fingers, relieved to find they still functioned. He'd wondered.

His relief was short-lived.

"Did Señora Velazquez know about this?" Don Francisco was asking again, idly, as if the answer did not matter. Zack felt a wave of renewed doom. He blinked again, heard the question come at him—"Were you supposed to take her to Señor Diamond?" and tensed, waiting.

He wasn't disappointed. The fist crashed into his midsection again, doubling him over to meet the fist coming at his face. He managed to duck that one, and heard a curse.

"*Madre Díos*—hold him!"

Someone grabbed his arms. His muscles seemed numb, from lack of circulation and the pain that slowed his reflexes. He tried to shake off the grip, but couldn't. There was barely enough time to brace himself before the next blow came, and he had the vague thought that it shouldn't matter so much to Velazquez who had sent him, as who might try to get Deborah. Not that anyone would, but Francisco did not know that. Maybe he feared an attempt would be made.

When he was finally released to slide to the floor in an aching sprawl, he heard a man's sharp voice. "What in the hell are you doing, Velazquez? I cannot condone this!"

The voice was familiar. It took him a moment, but Zack placed it when the man spoke again.

"Dammit, this is against the law!"

Macklin.

"It is more illegal to kidnap than it is to beat the truth from a man, señor," Don Francisco retorted. "I am trying to get him to sign a confession that he came here on Diamond's command to kidnap Señora Velazquez in order to hold her as a hostage until I remove my dam."

There was a short silence. Zack opened the one eye still able to focus, peering up at Macklin. The attorney was staring down at him with a frown.

"There are better ways," Macklin said finally. "If you continue with this, you will have to find a new attorney."

Zack shifted to get a better look. The movement almost wrenched a groan from him as his tortured body protested, but he clenched his teeth against it. Don Francisco looked angry. Macklin looked angry. He

301

turned his attention to his surroundings, his first chance since waking up to hell.

The room was small, furnished with a table, the broken chair, and another chair. A high window bisected one wall, and the door was opposite. It wasn't the best of conditions. Two men stood behind Don Francisco, one of them the man called Alfredo. Both were armed and looked capable of murder if called for. Right now, Zack realized, Macklin was all that stood between him and death.

Cursing, Don Francisco argued with Macklin, but the attorney was adamant. Either the beating stopped, or he would leave the hacienda and withdraw his legal advice. With a faint sense of dazed relief, Zack heard Velazquez reluctantly agree to stop.

"But I will find another way to the truth about this," he added.

Zack smothered an oath. He needed time to gather his wits and strength and focus on escape. And he needed to know where Deborah was and if she was all right.

"Tie him up," Don Francisco ordered tersely, and Zack braced himself. Alfredo and the other man jerked him to his feet to retie him. He crossed his arms behind him wrist to wrist when they spun him around. Alfredo wrapped a length of rope around them, then bent to tie his feet at the ankles.

Zack didn't resist. He willed his aching muscles to a taut stretch, and ignored the taunts directed at him in Spanish. He understood them, but chose to act as if he did not. He half-stumbled as they pushed him back to the floor, only partially because of his bruised condition.

Chest heaving, his breath still coming in strangled pants, Zack tried to keep his attention on what Velazquez and Macklin were saying instead of his own

302

body's screaming demands. Waves of pain receded slowly, and he shoved himself up against the wall.

"Dammit, Don Francisco," Macklin was grating, "I didn't count on any of this. You hired me to establish your undisputed claim to these lands, and I've established it fairly well. I never anticipated this."

"Neither did I," Don Francisco shot back, "but Señor Diamond forced my hand. What am I to do?"

"I told you—fight it in court."

"Bah! I know about courts. No, I will fight him my way, but I will listen to you."

"Good. Then come with me, and release this man."

"He is a spy."

"And if you kill him, you will be a murderer."

Don Francisco paused, then said something softly in Spanish.

"Excuse me?" Macklin asked. Don Francisco smiled.

"Sorry—I said, you are right. I will comply." He turned to Alfredo and rattled off a command in Spanish, then turned back to the attorney. "I've given orders to release him. Now come with me. We will discuss what can be done."

Zack felt his gut tighten with anticipation. He had understood Don Francisco's order quite clearly: "Take him to the desert and kill him."

Chapter 21

Deborah paced back and forth, her nerves stretched tautly. It was almost daylight. In the east, the dark sky bore a trace of gray that signalled the rising sun. She was alone. Don Francisco had not returned, and Judith had gone to her own chamber.

A lump clogged her throat. Judith. Perhaps she'd truly meant well, but it was hard for Deborah to think of that now. Not now. Not when Zack was suffering, maybe even dead. If he was . . .

Her mind shrank from the thought. No. She could not bear it if he was. Thank God Jeremiah Macklin had listened to her. If anyone could stop Don Francisco, it would be he.

Deborah crossed to the patio, and stared at the guards lounging just outside the door. More guards were stationed at her hall door. Did they think her a dangerous criminal? If she hadn't believed Zack before, she definitely did now. He was right about the danger, and right about Don Francisco stopping at nothing to keep his land. Now she was truly frightened, whereas before, she'd only been concerned about the possibility of danger in an all-out range war.

Her fear for Zack escalated in spite of Macklin's intercession. Perhaps he would not be able to help. After all, if Don Francisco was determined to keep his land at all cost then he would hardly listen to an outsider, even an attorney he'd had come all the way from Abilene.

"You must stay inside, señora," one of the men at the door told her when Deborah paused at the threshold, and she flashed him a cool look.

"I have no intention of coming out. I merely wished to feel the breeze. Are you staying here all night?'

"Sí."

Irritable at the lack of privacy, Deborah turned away from the patio doors and went back to the chair where she'd sat waiting on Zack to arrive. Dear God, she wished she knew what was happening to him. It was terrifying and agonizing, not to know anything.

By the time Don Francisco swung open her door, it was almost daylight. Deborah's nerves were raw, and she leaped up from the chair to face him.

"What have you done to Zack Banning?"

"He's been taken care of," was the smooth reply, and Deborah shuddered at the look of malice on Don Francisco's face.

"You've killed him." Her tone was flat, and she felt a dull ache begin in her chest. "Haven't you?"

"No, no, I have been right here. I admit that I did question your gallant *caballero,* but that is all that *I* have done."

Deborah searched his face for a sign that he was lying, but saw nothing. She wanted to believe him, but couldn't. It would be so much easier, so much kinder, if he was telling the truth.

"Then where is he?"

"Ah, that I cannot tell you." A faint smile still curved his mouth, and he leaned back against a heavy carved table and toyed with the sculpted figure on it. Deborah watched him silently. His long fingers smoothed over the bronze horseman and horse as if memorizing it, and she knew he was waiting on her to ask again. She inhaled sharply.

"I would like to know where he is now."

"Would you?" Don Francisco lifted a brow, and his hooded eyes focused on her face. "I'm not at all certain about that."

Deborah fought the urge to leap forward and throttle him. It amazed her, that rush of blood through her veins, the sudden, fierce desire to choke the life from a man. She'd never thought she could feel such a horrifying emotion about a human being, had never thought she would truly wish to kill someone as much as she wished now she could destroy Don Francisco.

"You're toying with me," she said when she could speak without screaming. "If you wish me to beg you for information about him, I will do so. All you have to do is explain what you want."

"Señora, you take all the fun out of this," he complained with a shrug. He shoved away from the table and stepped close to her, staring impassively at her face. "I do not know what Diamond sees in you. You have no fire, no passion to share. You are cold, too cool and collected to be a real woman." His mouth twisted. "But there must be something, for your gallant *caballero* would not betray you with words. I did my best to get a confession from him, a confirmation that you were to run off with Diamond, or with him. But he refused. A brave man, if a bit stupid. Too bad."

"So, now you've decided that it is my idea to leave? I thought you held to the theory that Dexter Diamond wished to kidnap me as a hostage."

Don Francisco shrugged again. "It does not matter, in the end, what the reasons are. They failed. You are still

306

here and will be watched more carefully. And I will not take another chance that you can be used in any way against me."

"Am I to fear for my life from you, Don Francisco?" She shook back the hair from her face, chin lifted defiantly. "If you kill me, then you lose the leverage you had to keep these lands."

"Perhaps. And perhaps the attorney will be able to take care of that for me. I do not wish to be saddled with you for the rest of my life, *chica.*"

"Don't you think the law will frown on murder?"

"Definitely." His smile made her shiver. "But an accident would be so sad, once my claim has been established. I will grieve for you, have masses said for your soul, and on your feast day there will be candles lit in the chapel."

"Why do I have the feeling that Mister Macklin is unaware of your—goal?"

"He has no foresight, and a singularly innocent nature in some ways. But that is of no matter, either. I expect you to stay in this room, and to speak with no one."

"Not even Judith?"

"Ah, the lovely Judith. She thinks she has done the right thing. I do not wish for her to know differently." His eyes almost glowed with unholy glee. "And I will tell her, of course, that you are so angry at her treachery you do not wish to see her again. Ever."

Deborah stared at him hopelessly. "It won't do you any good. None of this will. Do you think Dexter Diamond will stop his efforts to force you to sell to him? I don't. And if you think I won't be missed, you're wrong."

"But my dear—haven't you heard? You met with a very unpleasant time at the hands of the gunman sent to take you. You are so unwell in light of your recent experience, that you have become unhinged. Until it is convenient for me to hasten your demise, you will be kept under guard and away from everyone else."

Drawing herself up into what she hoped looked like a dignified, unworried pose, Deborah said slowly, "I hope that you are so confident when the authorities are brought in. But I do not think you will be."

"There will be no authorities. Señor Macklin has been told of your—infirmity—and so has my tender-hearted sister. Of course, the final blow to your poor, bruised mind was discovering the death of your latest lover."

"Latest lover?" Deborah stared at him blankly, unable to comprehend what he must mean. It simply would not penetrate the haze of confusion that rose up in her.

"Sí—oh, I forget. I have not yet told you. Señor Banning has met with an unfortunate accident. He is dead."

Deborah did not speak. A rush filled her ears, like the sound of the sea. She heard someone screaming, saw through a blur Don Francisco's shocked face, then, mercifully, fainted for the first time in her life.

Summer had melded into a dry autumn. The glorious flowers on the hillside were gone. The sky was still a bright burning blue that reminded her sometimes of Zack's eyes, and how deep a blue they could be, with gold flecks dusting them. She thought of him often in the long, lonely hours.

No one came.

She was alone, locked in the small, cheerless room where Don Francisco had imprisoned her. She saw no one but the rigid, taciturn guards who brought her meals, and a Mexican woman who was mute. It wouldn't have been so bad, she supposed, if not for her memories.

For a while, she'd not wanted to see anyone. Then, as the days passed and the pain eased enough for her to bear, she knew everyone must believe the story Don Francisco had put about. That he had been so close to being right, no longer had the power to distress her.

Nothing distressed her. She was beyond emotion.

Emotions were for the living. She, for all practical purposes, had died the day Zack had. Perhaps her body still functioned, but the essence of her, the spirit that had kept her alive during the aftermath of the Civil War, that had changed her life, kept her alive during the arranged marriage to a stranger, kept her alive during a Comanche raid, then kept her alive when she'd been terrified and alone in a village of hostile strangers, had deserted her.

She was adrift now, uncaring.

She read sometimes, but mostly she sat in a chair and stared out over the high walls of the hacienda at the sky and ridged hills. And tried not to think at all.

It had been almost six weeks. Six weeks since the dam had been destroyed and along with it, her illusions about the future. She'd dared to hope for love, when she should have realized that it was too dangerous.

Zack had tried to tell her.

He'd said no promises, and she should have listened to him. He'd known how it could shatter a soul to lose someone beloved, and she had been too stubborn to listen. She'd thought that it would be different, that she could somehow make a difference in his life.

And in the end, that stubbornness had cost her the man she loved.

If she'd only been strong enough to refuse his offer to protect her, he would still be alive. She should have.

And she should have listened to his reservations about Judith. Poor Judith. Tortured soul, trying to save Deborah, but in the end she'd destroyed her. She should have seen that too.

So now she just sat and waited, and she didn't know if she would recognize her fate when it came.

In the Hueco hills high above the Velazquez hacienda, light touched the rocky rim of a cave. It lingered, warming the mouth, not reaching the shadowed interior. Inside, it was cool and dank. Water seeped down the sides in a slow trickle and formed a small pool in a cleft, cool and clear.

Below, stretching for miles, the flat plains yielded an infinite variety of edible plants for someone who knew how to find them. In the rocks, the dry weather had withered the vegetation dependent upon infrequent rains.

Hunger was a constant; water could not fill the void. It was that dull, empty ache that finally lured Zack Banning from the safety of the cave.

He was wobbly, almost too wobbly. His injuries had left him unable to do more the first two days than drag himself into the rocks to hide. They'd left him for dead after two more bullets had been put into him, but he had survived. He wasn't quite certain why, except that it had been dark and they had been careless. Another man would have died.

The man taught to survive as a Comanche, had not.

No, he had survived, but barely. It had taken him long, painful hours to crawl from that burning desert up into the shelter of the rocks. Longer still to find the cave. He'd been disoriented by his injuries, weakness, and the pain that he'd kept at bay only with a fierce concentration. He had not given in to it until he'd curled up on the cool rock floor of the cave and dipped his hand into the tiny pool of water. His reflection had startled him into awareness, and he'd begun to feel it then.

He wasn't certain how long he'd drifted in and out of consciousness. It could have been days, or weeks. His wounds had begun to heal slowly, but the bullets were still in him. He was surprised he wasn't dead or crippled; as it was, he could barely move his left arm, and the fleshy part of his right side bore an angry red streak.

If he had his knife, he would cut the bullet out himself, but they had taken it. And they had taken his pistol, as well. Left him to die, left him for the buzzards to finish, and his bones to bleach in the sear of the sun. When he was whole again, they would pay for that. As would Don Francisco.

But now he had to concentrate on living to see justice done, to go back for Deborah.

That drive took him from the safety of the cave and down into the desert, a distance that should have been easy but was torturous and slow. Yet when he returned to the cave, he had gathered enough edible plants to give him some strength. Roots, yucca stalks, wild prairie turnips—raw but life-sustaining. He ate, and then he slept. And when he woke, he ate some more.

His dreams were feverish and restless, and there were times he woke in a sweat, certain he'd heard Deborah call his name. He didn't think about Diamond or the struggle between the ranchers; he thought about Deborah, about her soft, cultured voice and the graceful sway of her hips when she walked. And sometimes, as he lay between sleep and awareness, he got Deborah mixed up with his mother.

It was Amelia Banning Miles's voice he heard, soft and smooth with the clipped accent of her heritage. And

311

it was his mother's hand on his brow, coolly efficient, her touch loving and gentle.

He was burning up, even lying in the cool gloom of the cave. The fever scored through his body like a flame, making him feel as if he was standing over an open fire. In his delirium he saw the wagon train driver again, chained to a wagon tongue and being roasted over a fire, and he thought he was beside him, chained next to him with the flames licking his flesh.

And then he saw the cavalry riding down, shooting and yelling and riding their horses over fleeing women and children, swords slashing high in the sunlight and coming down in swift, lethal slices to kill and maim. They had killed many before White Eagle could rally his warriors into a line and fend off the attack. After the cavalry rode away with their dead, the air was shrill with the songs of mourning for the dead.

He kept seeing them, faces he'd known, people familiar to him, and his father's grim sorrow. Sunflower had wept and helped to bury Old Grandmother, slashing her young arms with grief. Blood flowed red, swirling around him in a tide that he'd never be able to wash away.

And Spirit Talker's warning rose above all the keening sounds of sorrow, reminding them how he'd predicted what would happen if Hawk kept the white woman. His own sorrow was not eased by knowing he was right, that the soldiers had found their camp because of Deborah's flight and his pursuit of her.

He was alone again, with that empty, hollow feeling that had always been such a part of his life. Until he'd found Deborah again, had seen the joy in her eyes at seeing him and dared to hope against all reason that he would find a welcome somewhere. He'd dared too much.

Pain made his body spasm, and he tried to focus on something else. He remembered his name dream, and how he had spent time alone in the hills to wait for the vision that would give him his Comanche name. He had come late to the People, and his father had said he must find his own path. He had done so, and had followed the instructions of the old shaman and suffered deprivation to prepare himself, to make himself worthy.

At the end of three days, he had watched as a full-grown hawk landed on a fallen tree only a few feet away. It had sat there, looking at him, and when he had spoken to the bird, it had not flown away. He'd known, then, that this was a sign. This was his name. And when the bird had finally darted up into the air, three feathers had floated back to earth near him, and he had put them into a pouch and taken them back with him.

As he clawed his way up out of the red mist of pain, Zack heard the lilting cry of a hunting hawk, and knew he would survive. He would recover, and he would go back for Deborah. And this time, he would kill anyone who tried to stop him from taking her. This time, he would be ready.

The hawk came again. Deborah saw it, gliding on wind currents, wild and graceful and free. She shaded her eyes with one hand, looking up at the sky. Its wings beat down in a drift of feathers, up and down, making it rise higher and higher until she felt a pang of regret that she couldn't go with it.

Her throat closed, and she fought the sharp edges of emotion that tore at her. She wanted to retreat back into the welcoming void where nothing could hurt her, but the hawk had surprised her. It made her think, made her remember things she didn't want to remember.

313

She shut her eyes against the glare of the sun and the wild beauty of the hawk, and gripped the arms of her chair with both hands. Her book fell from her lap to the smooth tiles of the patio, and she didn't move. She sat there, her heart beginning to thud and her mouth dry. There was the whirring of wings, a soft thudding sound that made her eyes open, and she saw the hawk land atop the thick adobe wall that enclosed her patio.

Frozen, she sat in silence as the hawk settled its wings and perched alertly. Its head was lifted and cocked to one side, eyes bright. She saw the sharp talons grip the wall, saw the curved beak shine in the light. White-tipped feathers fanned out as the hawk spread its wings in a quick, fluttering motion.

Afraid to move for fear of startling it away, Deborah sat and watched the predatory bird for a long time. It seemed not to mind that she was there, or indeed, to be alarmed by anything. And she felt strangely comforted by its presence, as if it had come to watch over her.

For the first time in a long while, Deborah felt the easing of the tight knot in her chest. It loosened ever so slightly, and she took a deep breath.

When the hawk left, rising into the air with a whirring of wings and a piercing cry, Deborah rose to her feet and went to the wall. She bent, and lifted a single white-tipped feather from the tiles where it had fallen. Her fingers closed around it, and she felt a fierce surge of anguish that dissolved slowly into acceptance. Life went on. There was loss and pain, but to give up was to refute the cycle. There was no answer in surrender.

Her head lifted, and she watched the hawk disappear, a tiny dark speck in the sky. A faint smile curved her mouth, and a militant gleam lit her amber eyes with gold.

Dexter Diamond faced Don Francisco with angry belligerence. He sat his horse stiffly, glaring down at the slender Mexican. "I don't believe you, Velazquez."

A faint shrug accompanied Don Francisco's soft, "I do not care, señor."

"Where is she? Word has it you locked her up."

"Rumor also has it that she ran away with your famous gunman," Velazquez returned in a silky purr. "Ah, I see that you do not like that suggestion."

Fury radiated from Diamond, making his huge frame tense and his jaw clench tightly. Deborah could see it, even from where she stood in the shadows of her patio and watched the two men. Dexter had ridden boldly up to the hacienda with the sheriff in tow. She'd heard him shout for Velazquez to come out, and had managed to pull herself up to peer over the top of the adobe wall encircling her patio. She had no idea where her guards were, but knew they wouldn't be gone long.

Deborah didn't hesitate. She'd kept up her weak, fragile appearance for Don Francisco's guards, awaiting a chance for escape. This looked as if it would be her only real hope for success.

"Dexter!" she screamed, hoping her voice would carry and the sheriff would at least investigate. "Help me!"

Before she could utter another plea, hard hands seized her and dragged her down from the wall. A sweaty palm clamped down over her mouth, and she heard Spanish curses in her ear as she was hauled backward and into her room. The man who was her guard swore viciously as he pressed her onto the mattress of her bed, holding her while another man bound her arms behind her.

Deborah tried to fight, but her struggles were useless against the two determined men. She was taken quickly from her room and half-carried down the dimly lit hallway and out of the hacienda by a back door. Despair filled her. She wasn't even certain she'd been heard, and now she would be killed. Francisco could not afford to risk her release.

Thrust into a dark, small room that must have been a storeroom at one time, Deborah cried out as the door was slammed shut. Even in the autumn, the heat inside the closed room was stifling. At least they'd untied her hands before dumping her in here. She felt her way around the room, her palms scraping on rough adobe. As her eyes grew accustomed to the dimness, she could make out faint shadows and the thin shaft of light coming through a high, narrow window at the top of the wall near the ceiling.

Fear throbbed in her, real fear. The weeks of apathy had left her too vulnerable. She had little strength to resist this raw an emotion.

She pressed back against the wall and took a deep, steadying breath. Slowly, as she stood there, the fear subsided into a thread of determination. She would not allow Don Francisco to win. Perhaps she would lose, but he would not win all. Not this way.

The only form of furniture in the cell was a straw pallet on the floor, and it didn't look very inviting. Deborah thought she heard furtive rustlings in it, and didn't dare investigate too closely. There was a musty, dank smell to the room, and she began to explore gingerly, half-afraid of what she might find in the deep shadows.

By the end of her search, she had gathered a rotting scrap of leather, a single spur with sharp rowels, and

316

half a chair leg. Sliding down the wall with her back to it, Deborah faced the door and waited. They would come for her eventually, whether to kill her or hide her, didn't matter. When they came, she would be ready.

Chapter 22

Dust blew high and hard behind him. Zack paused at the edge of the yard where a small split rail fence leaned drunkenly around a few goats. A neat frame house stood beneath a wind-twisted cottonwood. A woman hung clothes out to dry on scraggly bushes, her skirt flapping in the wind. He put a hand to his face, wondering what her reaction would be if he just walked up to her without warning. In his dark beard and torn shirt and pants, he probably looked frightening.

After a brief hesitation, he moved toward her. He had little choice, and perhaps he could form an explanation before she screamed for her husband to come running with a rifle.

"Excuse me, ma'am," he said when he got close enough for her to hear him.

She whirled around with a gasp, reaching for a rifle propped in the bushes. She had it up and levelled at him before he could lift his hands high enough for her to see he was not armed.

"Who are you?" the woman demanded. "What do you want?"

Zack eyed her closely. She was startled, but not afraid. There was no fear in the calm green eyes watchng him. "I want food," he said slowly. His voice was rough from disuse, and his throat felt thick.

"Food." She kept the rifle on him, assessing him with a steady gaze.

The wind blew around him, kicking up dust devils and peppering him with grit. His stomach growled as the wind brought a faint whiff of roasted meat. It was what had lured him to this house, that tantalizing odor and the hope of help. He was still so weak, his body aching and unable to answer the demands he put on it. It had taken him three days just to get down out of the hills.

He swayed slightly, and managed to stay on his feet, though his arms drooped from where he held them over his head. She was still watching him closely, and Zack closed his eyes. He was near the end of his endurance, but his body was too stubborn to surrender just yet.

Zack felt a rising dismay when his knees buckled and he sagged slowly to the ground. His eyes snapped open. He saw a faint flicker in the woman's face, and the muzzle of the rifle lowered slightly. The clothes on the bush snapped in the wind, a flutter of muslin and cotton that punctuated the tense silence. He heard the rattle of a windmill turning slowly, and a faint creak of chains. Goats milled and bleated harshly.

"Ma'am," he croaked, "I won't hurt you. I just need some food and water . . ."

His voice trailed into silence, and he felt the terrible weakness steal over him. He clung desperately to consciousness, but a numbing weariness sapped him of the strength to continue talking. He just gazed at her mutely, and saw her take a step toward him.

"Try anything funny, mister, and I'll shoot you between the eyes," she said finally. Her voice was firm, but soft.

He wanted to assure her he wasn't capable of trying anything funny, but couldn't summon the energy. His head nodded once, and the rifle barrel lowered to point at the ground. He knelt there in the sun and wind on his knees with his hands spread on his thighs and waited as she crossed to the house, looking back every so often as if expecting him to leap after her. If he hadn't been so tired, he would have laughed. Never in his life had he been so helpless, and it wasn't a good feeling.

Here he was, on his knees in the dirt, begging for food from a stranger. It was certainly humbling.

She returned. He smelled the bowl of food she carried, and it snapped his head up.

"Here," she said. "I brought you some stew. Come eat in the shade where it's not so warm."

Zack noticed the small table set up under a scrub oak with twisted branches and dusty leaves. He pushed painfully to his feet, staggered a step, and jerked away when she put out a hand to help him.

"I'll get there," he muttered, realizing he was being ungrateful, but too proud to take her hand. It was bad enough asking for her food. To allow a woman to offer him her strong shoulder, was too much.

She seemed to understand, and watched as he crossed the few yards to the table under the tree. The chair creaked loudly as he sank into it, and the woman put the bowl of stew down in front of him.

"There's bread and stewed apples. I'll get them." She came back with the rest, bringing her own bowl of stew. By that time, Zack had eaten most of his, feeling his belly knot at the unexpected bounty. He chewed slowly, and washed it down with cool well water. Then he looked up to find his hostess watching him.

"Thank you," he said simply. There weren't words

enough to convey how much he appreciated the food. He had the thought it had literally saved his life, and wondered if she guessed that already.

"You're welcome." She smiled faintly, and tucked a strand of dark blond hair behind her ear. It fluttered in loose curls around her face. "My name is Sally Martin."

He hesitated. Zack Banning was well known in some places. Hawk might frighten her. He looked away.

"My mother named me Zachary, but most folks call me Zack."

"Well, Zack, you look pretty tired. If you like, I can offer you a bed of straw in my barn and a good break-fast in the morning."

His gaze shifted back to her. "I have no way to pay you."

"I am not asking for payment. I made the offer. You may accept it or not, as you like."

She stood up and cleared the small table, piling the dishes with slow, unhurried movements. Sally was sturdy, with capable hands and a slender frame.

"What will your husband say?" he asked, and she paused with one hand hovering over an empty plate still smeared with the sticky juices of stewed apples.

"Nothing. He'd dead."

"I'm sorry."

Her eyes met his, a clear, cool green, direct and un-shadowed. "So am I. He was a good man and I miss him."

Zack stayed in the chair under the oak for a while, and saw her come back out of the house and go back to the basket of wash she was spreading on bushes. Then she fed the goats and chickens and went into the barn. He saw a clump of hay come sailing out into a small corral, and a rangy horse ambled over to munch.

With a pained grimace, he heaved himself out of the

chair and hobbled to the barn. She had her skirts hiked up a little and tucked into her waistband while she forked hay out the side door of the barn.

"I'll do that," he said.

Sally turned to look at him. "No. You don't look like you can do much of anything. My guess is, those are bullet holes in that shirt."

It was more a statement than a question, and Zack grew still. "Yes."

"Thought so." She studied his face in the dusty gloom of the barn for a long moment. "Rest today. If you want to help me tomorrow or the next day, I'll be glad of it."

The dizziness made him reel slightly, and though pride nudged him to insist on helping, common sense won out.

She left him alone in the barn, and returned only to bring him a few blankets. Zack managed to stay upright until she left again, then made up a bed in the straw and rolled up in the blankets. Through the open door, he could see the sun sliding into a crimson and gold thread of sky. As it disappeared, the last fiery rays shot up in splinters of light that made him think of the firelight in Deborah's hair. Dark fire, glowing and shimmering with radiance.

"Who's Deborah?"

Zack looked up in surprise, eyes narrowing slightly. A brisk wind blew as he leaned on the fence. "Why?"

"Because sometimes at night I hear you say her name." Sally shrugged. "Just curious. Your wife?"

"No." Zack looked away from her. He'd been at her ranch for a month, slowly recuperating from his injuries. The day after he'd arrived, she'd come into the

322

barn to wake him for breakfast and found him delirious and raving. His wound had suppurated during the night. If not for Sally, he would have died. She'd removed that bullet, tended his wound, and even removed the bullet still in his arm.

Sally Martin was a very capable, undemanding woman. He'd never known anyone like her. She asked for nothing, not even help. She offered quiet companionship and gentle humor, and in exchange, he did what little he could to help her. He had learned that she was very self-sufficient, and content to remain on her small ranch.

"It suits me," she said in reply to his question about the suitability of her living out here all alone. "After Marty died, I just went on. At first, because it was the only thing I could do, and it helped me focus on the everyday things that make up life. And then, I realized that even alone, I could enjoy sunsets, the flight of an eagle, the smell of freshly baked bread." Her mouth had curved into a smile. "I just have to admire them with the goats."

As Zack slowly regained his strength, he began practicing with a pistol again. Sally gave him the Colt that had belonged to her husband, along with a worn leather holster for it. Sometimes, in the evenings when the chores were done and before the sun set, she came to watch him draw and shoot tin cans balanced on the top rail of a fence.

"You're good," she said once, her eyes shrewd. "Even with that sore arm."

"It's a good thing I'm right-handed."

"Can you shoot with your left?"

His eyes crinkled with amusement. "Passably well."

"If I were you, I'd work on that one too."

He turned to look at her as she leaned against the

trunk of a cottonwood that slanted over a small trickle of water. As he shoved more bullets into the cylinder of the Colt, he asked, "Why?"

"A man like you can't afford not to be the best."

He knew, then, that she must know who he was. She'd never said. Nor asked. He felt a spurt of warmth for this quiet woman with calm green eyes and a peace that lent him strength.

"You'll be going soon, won't you?" she asked quietly.

He felt her eyes on him as he focused on the pistol. "I think so." He slid the last bullet into an empty chamber and clicked the cylinder into place. "I'm almost ready."

Unanswered questions hung in the air between them, and he knew she wouldn't ask. He looked up at her. He owed her the truth. She'd given much, and asked nothing of him.

"My name is Zack Banning. The men who shot me and left me to die in the desert work for the man who has Deborah. She . . ." He paused, not knowing how to put it into words. She what? She was his woman? She was his life? He didn't know. He didn't know how to explain to anyone else what he'd never been able to explain to himself.

"She's important to you," Sally finished for him, and he flashed her a grateful glance.

"Yes. And I think she may be in danger."

"Then you have to help her."

"Yes."

Zack turned back to the fence and the cans neatly arranged in a row. He felt a spurt of impatience. It was taking too long. He had to regain his complete strength and ability with a gun. Every day put Deborah in more danger, and he had no idea what had happened in his absence. He only hoped she was all right.

His legs bent slightly at the knee and his hand flashed down to the holstered gun tied low on his thigh, sweeping it up and out in a blur of movement. The air was filled with the sharp rattle of gunfire and the *ping* of tin cans flying off a fence rail.

He straightened and reloaded without looking at Sally. He could feel her gaze on him. His muscles were working again. Only traces of the stiffness remained. He looked up finally, and was startled by the slight sheen of tears in Sally Martin's eyes. She cleared her throat.

"You're ready to go."

"Tomorrow."

She nodded. "Take the horse. No, don't protest. You can't very well walk. And you can bring him back when you get another one."

Zack thought of his gray, and hoped the stallion was still at the Double D. "We can take the wagon into town," he said, and saw a flash of relief in her eyes.

"Yes. We can do that."

He lay in his bed in the barn that night, and thought about Deborah. She was so different from Sally, with her cool poise and elegance of features. Sally was sturdy, a sensible woman with no frills or elegance to her. Yet she was as precious in her way as Deborah, and he felt a pang of regret that he would be leaving her behind. There had been nothing between them but a quiet companionship, but it had been healing and peaceful and he'd needed that.

A faint smile curved his mouth as he had the thought that Deborah and Sally would probably be friends if they met under the right circumstances.

The wagon rolled to a halt in front of the general store and Sally looked around. "It sure is busy here.

I've never seen so many wagons unless it's a Saturday."

"Must be something going on. A funeral, maybe."

She laughed. "Or an election."

"Sometimes that's the same thing." He set the brake on the buckboard, and glanced at the crowded streets. He didn't see anyone he knew yet.

"I usually go into San Ysabel," Sally said when he looked back at her. "Sirocco is a little farther away from my ranch."

"I appreciate your bringing me here."

Her smile was wry. "I might need to hang around to haul you out again."

He leaped lightly from the buckboard, leaning in to tie the reins to the brake he'd set. "Let's hope not. Come on. I'll help you down."

Sally stood and leaned over, bracing herself with her hands on his muscled forearms as he lifted her down and swung her to the wooden sidewalk. She wore a sensible sunbonnet to shade her face, and the brim kept her eyes in shadow.

"Not only handsome," she said with a forced laugh, "but a gentleman. I'm going to miss you, Zack."

"Handsome?" He laughed ruefully, touching his face with one hand. "I doubt my own mother would recognize me now."

She eyed him speculatively. "With your beard gone and a little meat on your bones, you've changed. I didn't know you before, but if you looked as dangerous as you do now, it's a wonder people didn't avoid you."

"They did," he said grimly.

People passed them, and wagons rolled down the middle of the dusty street with noisy rattles. Sally studied him for a moment, then smiled.

"Would you like to help me with my shopping before you leave me? I could use a little advice."

"Sure. As long as you aren't talking about female gewgaws, I'm game."

She laughed, and tucked her hand over his forearm. "I would not dream of asking you for any advice on those. Not only would it be useless, but it would be embarrassing for both of us."

Zack laughed with her, and let her draw him along toward Potter's General Store. Sally had been generous and open with him and he could tell that she didn't want him to leave. He also knew she'd never admit it. She was not a woman to try to keep a man by tears and pleas. But it hurt him, nonetheless, to know that she'd come to depend upon him for companionship and would truly miss him.

Sometimes he'd seen her looking at him wistfully, a soft expression on her face and her lips trembling slightly. She would have been mortified if she'd known he recognized her emotions, and neither of them had mentioned it or allowed any awkwardness to mar their friendship.

Reaching around her, Zack pushed open the door to the General Store and held it for Sally. He let it close behind him with a jangle of the bell that announced new customers.

"Potter's probably in the back," he said as Sally began pricing a copper kettle. "I'll see if I can find him."

"Zack."

He turned, brow lifted. She was holding out some greenbacks, and he stiffened. She colored hotly, and her voice was defensive.

"You earned it, helping me and all."

"You fed me and gave me a place to sleep. Keep it. I don't want your money."

327

"Well, you should buy some new clothes. Marty's don't fit you that well. You're taller. And leaner."

"They'll do." He relaxed slightly. "I appreciate it, but I can't take your money."

She sighed and slipped it back into her reticule. "I had forgotten how stubborn you can be."

Grinning, he leaned down and kissed her smooth cheek. "A disastrous mistake."

Sally tilted back her head, her sweet face lighting. "Yes. I'll know better next time. I'll trick you."

He laughed, and was still smiling when Mr. Potter came out from the back. The older man jerked to a halt, and his eyes grew big.

"Banning?" he whispered hoarsely, fixing Zack with a frightened stare. "I heard you were dead."

"Looks like you heard wrong," Zack said coolly, letting his hand fall away from Sally's arm.

Potter eyed him for a long moment. "You look different, somehow."

"A couple of months older, maybe."

A rusty laugh echoed, but Potter didn't look truly amused. He kept staring at Zack, and it was obvious he was uncomfortable.

"You still working for Diamond?" he asked after a moment of tense silence.

"Maybe." Zack didn't elaborate, and Potter didn't ask. For a brief moment, he considered asking the older man what had happened between Diamond and Velazquez, and if Deborah was all right, but didn't. He could find that out from the sheriff. He had every intention of pressing charges for attempted murder against Don Francisco, but he wanted to wait until the right time. If there was a chance Deborah would be hurt by it, he'd handle it another way.

"What can I do for you?" Potter asked finally and Zack gestured to Sally.

"She's buying. I'm just looking."

"Certainly. What may I help you with, ma'am?"

Potter bent to help Sally with her purchases, and the murmur of their voices discussed the merits of different copper kettles.

Restless, and filled with a growing impatience, Zack moved to the store window and stared out at the street. He saw carriages roll past, and heard a burst of laughter from down the street. Even on Saturdays, Sirocco had never been this busy. He massaged his right arm, flexing and unflexing his fingers as he watched people pass.

Frank Albright rode past, his hat pulled low over his face, but unmistakable. Zack stiffened. Albright, the man Diamond used to run off squatters and even legal homesteaders. If he was in town, odds were, so was Diamond.

"What's going on?" Zack asked when Potter had loaded Sally's purchases into the newly purchased copper kettle and a cloth bag. He gestured to the street. "Town's crawling with folks."

"Most of them came to the wedding, I guess," Potter said as he swung open the door and the bell jangled loudly. "It's a big to-do."

"Wedding, huh." Zack frowned. "Must be someone pretty important to make all this fuss."

Potter was shoving the kettle into the buckboard, and he turned to Sally. "Ma'am, if you want to drive your wagon around back, I'll load up that other stuff for you."

Zack broke in when Sally started to climb onto the seat. "I'll do it. You go back in there and pick you out a new hat or a scarf, or something. You can't come into town and not buy something pretty for yourself."

"I'd rather you have the money."

His mouth curved into a smile. "Spend the money you were going to pay me." He chucked her under the chin as if she was Sunflower. "Get me some candy, if you just have to buy me something frivolous."

Zack climbed onto the seat, took up the reins, and released the brake. Then he clucked to the horse and the buckboard jerked forward. He drove to the end of the street to go behind the stores, and was turning the corner when a burst of organ music caught his attention.

Glancing up, Zack saw the flurry of motion as people streamed down the shallow steps of the church on the corner and formed a double line. The bride and groom emerged from the old stone church and started down the steps. Zack pulled the wagon to a halt and stared.

Dexter Diamond, garbed in a dark suit and grinning ear to ear, had a possessive hand on the bride's arm. She was dressed in a flowing yellow gown that billowed around her legs as she demurely descended the wide stairs.

Zack's hands tightened around the leather reins, and he felt as if someone had just plunged a knife into his belly.

The bride looked up at her husband, her hair shimmering like dark fire in the press of sunlight, her pure, perfect face as pale and cool as a cameo. She turned gracefully, and with a gentle swing of her arm, she tossed a small bouquet of flowers into the air. There were squeals of surprise and delight, and then laughter when it was caught by a blond girl in the front.

Zack burned, but shivered with the effort to restrain himself. When the bride turned back, smiling, Diamond took her hand again to escort her down the last few steps. She lifted her skirts in one hand, and glanced up when someone called out to her.

330

Zack wasn't surprised when she looked directly at him. The force of his gaze should have seared into her fickle, faithless soul. He met her gaze, saw her eyes widen with shock and her mouth open. It was the second time she'd had that reaction to seeing him, and he had the grim thought that it would be the last.

He saw her lips move to form the word *Zack*, then she slumped into a faint.

Chapter 23

A clock ticked loudly. Soft breezes lifted the curtains from the open window in a billowing cloud that caught Deborah's attention. She sat stiffly, her hands twisting in her lap. She could hear Dexter ranging behind her like an angry lion, pacing the floor of his ranch house parlor.

He stopped behind her, and put a hand on the back of her chair. "You married me," he said flatly.

"Yes."

"In a church before witnesses."

She looked up at him. "Before God. Yes, Dexter, I married you."

He spread his arms and gave her a baffled glare. "Then why? Why are you puttin' me off?"

Deborah inhaled, her hands knotting into small fists in her lap. She looked down, saw that she'd wadded up her skirt and relaxed her hands.

"You agreed before we married that you would not rush me. You know what—what I've been through lately."

"Is it Banning? Is he the reason?"

Her gaze was clear and direct, her voice only slightly unsteady. "I did not know he was alive until after we were married. You know that."

Diamond's hand gripped her shoulder. "And if you had? Would you still have married me?"

She stood up, and his hand fell away. "Did you marry me for love, Dexter? Because you cannot live without me?"

He flushed, and his mouth tightened. "No," he said roughly. "I was honest with you about that."

"To a point. You said you wanted to marry me to gain part of the Velazquez lands, yes. But you also said you wanted me."

"I do." The look he gave her was unmistakable, and her eyes widened. "And marryin' you is the only way I can get you. You made that clear when you said you wouldn't live in my house without vows."

She looked away from him. "There has been enough trouble. I'm grateful to you for rescuing me from Don Francisco. He would have killed me eventually, I'm certain of it."

"Grateful." Diamond said the word as if it soured his tongue. She looked back at him.

"I never hinted there was more. You said it was enough."

"I thought it was." His mouth tightened. "Ain't no woman ever kept me at bay like you, Deborah. You may have married me, but I'm not the man you want."

She waited, expecting him to bring up Zack again. Since seeing Zack watching her with that look of stunned disbelief she had gone over everything again and again, and had come to the same conclusion: She'd thought him dead, and had done what was necessary to survive.

"Just what was between you and Banning, anyway?" Diamond asked roughly.

Deborah didn't reply for a moment. She couldn't tell him everything. No one knew that Zack and Hawk were

333

the same man, that she'd lived with him in the mountains and been his woman. She might have told Dexter about it before marrying him if not for the fact that just mentioning his name was so painful for her. Now it was too late. Now, she would look as if she had done something wrong if she told the truth, and in spite of everything, she could not think that her love for the man the Comanche called Hawk was wrong. But how did she explain that to Dexter, who was owed some kind of explanation? After all, he'd rescued her, and even brought Judith to his home at Deborah's request.

And perhaps she could have found a certain peace and contentment with him if not for Zack. Deborah closed her eyes. Seeing Zack alive had freshened her pain, left it raw and agonizing. She wondered where he'd been, and if he had thought of her at all and what she must be going through.

No promises.

No, he'd never made promises, and she supposed that he'd thought it more important to keep out of Don Francisco's way than to get word to her that he'd survived. He wouldn't think of how she suffered over him, perhaps had not even thought she would. But neither had he come to rescue her, and she found that it was hard to forgive him that.

"Well?" Diamond demanded. "What does Banning mean to you, Deborah?"

She took a deep breath. "He's a man from my past, Dexter. You are my present. And my future."

"Maybe you need to tell him that."

Deborah grew very still. She felt the color receded from her face, and an icy chill made her hands tremble.

"What do you mean?"

"I mean," Diamond drawled, "that he's comin' out to

the ranch to get his horse and gear, and he sent word he wants to talk to you."

She stood up without realizing it. "I can't talk to him."

"Does he mean that damned much to you?" Diamond grabbed her by the shoulders, his grip harsh. "By God, I don't share what's mine!"

Her eyes flew to his. "I have no intention of being shared."

"No shadows. I don't want him comin' between us even when he ain't around. You tell him, you hear?"

Deborah nodded. "I'll tell him."

A week passed and he hadn't come. Every rider who approached the Double D immediately made Deborah's heart lurch and her throat tighten, but none of them were Zack. Judith watched her, her face drawn and shuttered.

"You still love him," she said quietly, her voice noncommittal.

Deborah glanced at her. "Yes."

"It's not fair to Dexter."

"No, but I never promised him love. He didn't expect it."

Judith stared out the window of the parlor, her hands folded in her lap. She was quiet and reserved now, her blue eyes haunted. She'd wept and begged Deborah's forgiveness for what she'd done at first, then retreated into a shell of silence that made Deborah think of the long days she'd spent locked in her own anguish.

There had been no question of forgiving her; Judith had acted out of love, not spite, and had truly thought she was saving Deborah from a man who would harm her.

"Why do you hate him so much?" Deborah asked after a moment, and felt Judith's start of surprise.

"It's what he represents," she said slowly. "He never did anything to me personally, but his kind did."

"His kind?"

Judith's face flushed. "Yes—Comanche. I hate them. I wish . . . I wish they'd all be rounded up and put on government reservations forever. Or killed like cattle. I don't care."

Deborah was quiet, startled by Judith's ferocity. She thought of gentle Sunflower, and White Eagle's aristocratic features and innate dignity. She also recalled the brutal woman who'd tormented Judith, and thought she understood.

"There are brutal, uncaring people in every race," she said after a moment. "Color doesn't make a person nice or bad."

"You can say that because you fell in love with your captor," Judith shot back. "I didn't!" She took a deep breath and asked, "Does Dexter know about Hawk and Zack?"

"No. I see no reason to tell him now. It would only make things more difficult for me. He's already angry because Zack said he wanted to speak with me when he came for his gear."

"You should refuse."

Deborah looked at her. "I can't. I want to know why he never came back for me, why he stayed away so long. He could have sent word that he was alive somehow. But no one knew. I died inside, and he could have eased it."

"You wouldn't have married Dexter if you'd known."

"I don't know." Deborah shook her head. "I don't think I would have, but none of us will ever know now."

336

Judith rose from her chair and wandered around the parlor, running her fingers over the smooth surfaces of the scattered tables. Since their occupation of it, the Double D's main house had taken on a softer appearance with the addition of a few stuffed pillows and lace doilies. It was mostly Judith's idea. Deborah hadn't cared.

"I always wanted a house like this," Judith murmured as she fingered the soft drape of a curtain. "Once, I thought I would have it."

"You still will." Deborah came to stand beside her. "If you want, you can have your pick of men out here. Many have tried to court you."

Judith shrugged. "They're weaklings. None of them have accomplished what Dexter has. He's strong and ambitious, and has the intelligence to succeed." She looked at Deborah with accusing eyes. "He deserves a loving wife. You know he said he didn't care . . . didn't care what happened with the Comanche. Not many men would feel that way. Dexter's special, and I hate to think he's not appreciated as he should be."

Deborah didn't say anything for a moment. This wasn't the first time Judith had praised Dexter. It was obvious she admired him very much.

"You're right, Judith. I should appreciate his good qualities, I suppose, and not dwell on those that disturb me. It's just that it's so hard at times, when he says things or does things."

Judith stared down at a lace doily. "He's better than any other man I've met."

"Are you happy here, Judith?"

"Very." A smile curved her mouth, and the sad blue eyes lightened some. "I don't feel afraid here. There are so many men to protect us, and Dexter is not the kind of man who will let his guard down. He's shown that by the number of gunmen he's hired."

"That's true." Deborah leaned against the windowsill and pulled back the curtain to look out. Bunkhouses dotted the grounds, filled with men who could and would shoot. There was a small army of them, as well as men who worked the cattle. The Double D was like a small town, with most of its needs provided for.

That was, perhaps, the main reason Don Francisco had not retaliated when Dexter blew up his dam. He'd simply rebuilt it, along with others, slowly drying up the water sources that fed the Double D's streams. The only water now was from wells or the occasional stream that did not cross Velazquez land first.

Cattle rustling in the area was growing rampant, and the sheriff had been forced to call in Texas Rangers as well as the Federal Marshal for help. Tempers were taut, the tensions strained to the breaking point. Sirocco was being divided, with some adhering to Diamond, and some to the Velazquez faction. Men from both sides turned up dead on occasion, always with the opposite side taking the blame.

Dexter Diamond had filed another claim, this one on part of the Velazquez land, citing his new wife's inheritance from her dead husband, and the battle raged in court as well as in the hills and flat plains. Even John Hamilton had become involved, firing off a letter to his daughter condemning her for taking sides with the enemy. Of course, Hamilton had a personal interest, as Velazquez money backed his thriving shipping firm.

"It's all so sordid and confusing," Deborah murmured, and Judith turned to look at her.

"Don Francisco deserves whatever Dexter does. He lied and cheated and killed."

Deborah's smile was wry. "Dexter hasn't exactly been a saint."

"No. But he'll win."

"You seem awfully certain of that." Deborah leaned back against the wall, idly watching the curtains flutter out with the breeze.

Shrugging, Judith said, "I suppose so. He's hired an attorney from Forth Worth, and what he can't get done legally, he'll resort to doing as Don Francisco does."

"And that doesn't bother you?"

"Why should it? I haven't noticed anyone else paying close attention to ethics when it comes to land and cattle and power. Out here, it seems as if only the strong survive."

"Yes." Deborah pushed away from the wall and walked back to her chair, disturbed by both the conversation's subject and Judith's words. Her cousin had changed, but then again, so had she.

"Deborah."

She looked up, and Judith turned away from the window. "Zack Banning is here."

Diamond stepped down off the front porch, his bootheels stirring up puffs of dust as he walked toward Zack. Zack saw him coming, but continued his leisurely inspection of the gray, running his hand down the horse's forelegs and over his chest, letting the stallion nudge him affectionately.

"Banning."

Straightening, Zack turned and met Diamond's hostile gaze. "Yeah?"

"You owe me an explanation."

"For what?"

Diamond's jaw clenched, and he glared at him from

beneath the brim of his tan hat. "For goin' off and almost gettin' yourself as well as Deborah killed, for one thing."

"I'm not responsible to you for that. I worked for you. You didn't own me."

"Why'd you do it? Why'd you go after her?"

Zack studied him for a moment. If Deborah hadn't told him the truth, he had no intention of doing so. He shrugged.

"She needed rescuing. I gave it a try."

"And where were you going to take her, dammit?"

Zack threaded a hand through his gray's mane, then began to bridle him. "Somewhere safe. It hardly matters now, does it? I didn't make it."

"Why haven't you filed charges against Velazquez for tryin' to kill you?"

"Haven't decided yet if that's the way I want to go with it," Zack returned coolly. He buckled the throat latch with deft fingers, then let the reins drop to the ground as he reached for his saddle blanket. He could feel Diamond's gaze hard on him, and ignored it as he slung the blanket over the gray's back and smoothed it. "What do I owe you for feeding my horse while I was gone?"

"Nothing. A little feed ain't gonna hurt me. Besides, I owe you some back wages."

"I'll collect before I leave." He hefted his saddle to the gray's back and pulled the leather girth free, then reached under the belly and grabbed the dangling girth to pull it through the cinch ring and knot it. Finished, he turned and leaned back against the gray, meeting Diamond's expectant gaze. "I'd like to see Deborah now."

Diamond's jaw knotted. "She's my wife."

"I know that. I only want to talk to her a few minutes, see how she's doing." Pride wouldn't let him say more, and finally Diamond nodded.

"She's in the house."

Lifting up the gray's reins, Zack walked to the house set under a grove of trees. Diamond remained by the corral, but he felt him watching as he flipped the reins over a hitching rail and stepped up onto the porch. His sharp eyes caught the flutter of movement inside, and he knew Deborah had seen him.

The door swung open before he could knock, and Judith took a step back to let him in. "She's in the front parlor. Try not to stay too long."

Zack's mouth twisted. "You're as congenial as usual. Nice to see you again, too."

When Judith didn't reply, but gave him a murderous glare, Zack paused. He studied her for a moment, trying to see the resemblance between this golden-haired, icy-eyed woman and her cousin. Any resemblance faded when she opened her mouth.

"You can dress in civilized clothes, but underneath you're still a savage. A heathen. I can see through you."

His steady gaze made her blue eyes narrow. "I wasn't the one who raped you, Judith."

"You're part of them!" she shot back, her voice low and filled with venom. "You look like them—evil and all dark as sin. Maybe you didn't hurt me, but you did Deborah. You did the same thing to her that—"

She stopped suddenly, and her eyes grew big. With a soft cry of anguish, she turned and fled. Zack watched her, and heard a muffled sound. He turned to see Deborah standing in a doorway, her face pale with shock.

"I never knew," she said slowly when he didn't speak or move. "She never told me." She looked at him. "You knew."

"Yes."

341

"Why didn't you tell me? Perhaps I could have—"

"There was nothing you could do." His voice was harsher than he intended, and he took a deep breath. "I want to talk to you."

He could see Deborah gathering her poise around her like a shield, and felt another wave of admiration. Her cool control made him realize how close he came to losing his when he was around her, and he hooked his thumbs into his belt loops to keep from reaching her. She was too tempting.

Deborah led the way to the parlor, her hips swaying gently and her full skirts drifting gracefully around her ankles. Zack looked around at the house, the carpets and wallpaper, and fine furnishings. It was a fine setting for Deborah, a bed of velvet for a pearl beyond price. Some of his anger faded, and he recognized that Dexter Diamond could give her everything he could not.

When she shut the parlor door and turned to face him, Zack couldn't speak for a moment. His throat ached, and he felt suddenly awkward. She was so beautiful. So damn lovely. He tried not to think of how soft her skin was, or how sweet her lips were. She was looking at him as if wondering why he had come, and he was beginning to wonder that himself.

Before he knew it, he asked, "Why, Deborah? Why did you marry him?"

The question startled her. He could see the quick widening of her eyes, the flash of gold sparks before her lashes veiled them and she looked away.

"You have no right to ask."

"No right?" He couldn't help a blaze of anger. "Dammit, I think I have a right to an answer, at least. I end up in a desert with four bullet wounds because I try to save you, and you want to tell me I have no right to ask?"

Her face paled, and he saw her chin quiver. "Zack, they told me you were dead. I believed them."

"So you mourned me for what? A month? Two?"

"It wasn't like that!"

"No? How was it?" He shoved away from the wall where he'd leaned to keep from going near her, and took a step closer. "Tell me, Deborah. I want to know. How was it you get married two months after my supposed death? *Christ!* I may not believe in a long mourning period, but you don't seem to believe in any."

"What was I supposed to do?" she asked calmly, and her poise was suddenly more maddening than endearing. "Don Francisco kept me under guard for weeks. At first I didn't care. Then, when I began to think about survival again, it was Dexter who was there for me. You weren't. I was grateful to him for rescuing me from Don Francisco. He asked me to marry him and I said yes." She looked down at her lightly clasped hands and said softly, "He was willing to make promises."

He stared at her, feeling as if he'd been kicked in the belly. It felt as if the world had suddenly dropped away from beneath his feet and left him suspended. His words came back to haunt him, those denials of how he felt even to himself. She was right. He had taken her, kept her from her family, and offered nothing in return, not even the comfort of promises. She'd had nothing to hold to, yet she'd loved him until death. Could he really blame her for surviving the best way she knew how?

Zack leaned back against the wall again, suddenly tired. "I need to go."

He felt her eyes on him, heard her sound of distress, and looked up. Tears made her hazel eyes gleam softly, like muted gold, and he straightened. He knew he couldn't stand this another moment. Emotion ripped at him, feelings he'd thought he'd lost or could control threatening to overwhelm him.

He turned and yanked at the doorknob, slung the door open and crossed the hallway. His boots echoed loudly on the smooth, polished floors. Squares of light made the wood gleam and blurred his vision, and he reached the front porch without knowing how he got there. He crossed it in two long strides, grabbed the gray's reins and vaulted into the saddle without bothering with stirrups.

The gray bounded forward eagerly, and he thundered from the yard in a cloud of dust and regrets, hearing Deborah's soft voice call his name once, then twice. Then nothing. She was behind him, and there was nothing before him, nothing but dust and broken dreams, and emptiness.

Zack didn't look back. He couldn't.

Chapter 24

Dusk seamed the horizon with purple and gold shadows. Deborah stared out her bedroom window without seeing it, her mind tortured with visions of Zack riding away. No tears came, but she hurt too badly to weep.

His pain had been real, and she'd known then what she'd only hoped before—he loved her. He loved her, and she was married to another.

There had been such a stricken look in his eyes, those clear blue eyes that haunted her dreams. God, would she ever be able to forget it? No, no more than she'd ever be able to forget him. He was part of her, part of her past, part of her heart, part of her soul.

She'd wanted to tell him that, watching him stand there against the door, his thick dark hair brushing down over his ears to his collar and shining like a raven's wing in the gloom of the parlor. She might have, if she had not seen his eyes. Then she'd known, she'd known she could not say the words that would make it even worse. It would destroy them both. It was kinder for him to think she didn't care, that she'd chosen the easier path.

But oh, dear God, how very hard it was for her to watch him leave. She'd been weak enough to cry his name, but the echoes of it ringing through the air had stopped her. And she had stood in the open doorway while he had ridden away, remembering that night at Fort Richardson when he had paused on the crest of a ridge and wheeled around to salute her and shout *Usúni!* Forever. He would remember her forever, he'd said, and she had not realized how short that could be.

Or how long.

A knock on her door startled her, and she turned as it swung open. Dexter stood in the opening, his brawny frame blocking the hall as he gazed at her.

"You all right?"

She cleared her throat. "Yes. I'm fine." *Just dying inside.*

He looked uncomfortable. "Mind if I come in?"

Deborah forced a smile. "No, not at all." She indicated a chair to one side, and he gave it a dubious glance and shook his head.

"No thanks." He shut the door behind him, and came to her and put a hand under her chin, tilting up her face. "No tears?"

"Am I supposed to weep?"

"That's what I was wonderin'." He released her chin, and gazed down at her with a baffled expression. "How long are we gonna sleep in separate beds?"

"I told you, until—"

"I know," he cut in with an irritated growl, raking a hand through his tawny hair. His eyes were narrowed to dark brown slits, his mouth tight. "Did Banning kiss you?"

Deborah stiffened. "Really, Dexter, that question is insulting."

"I don't give a damn." His voice was hard. "Did he? Did he kiss you, gawddamit?"

Deborah's chin lifted, and her face was pale. "No, he

did not come within two feet of me, if you must know. Do you think me so dishonorable that I would already break my vows to you?"

He turned away, pacing with frustrated steps around the spacious bedroom. "No," he said finally. "But I know that you thought he was dead when you agreed to marry me. Does his being alive change that?"

After a hesitation, Deborah said, "No. I made vows in front of God. I'll keep them."

Diamond's shoulders relaxed slightly, and his eyes grew warmer. "You're quite a woman." When she didn't respond, he stepped close, and lifted her face to his again, this time with a different emotion.

Her eyes closed as he set his mouth over hers, and she felt his hunger. He kissed her long and slow, and when he drew back to look at her he was breathing raggedly. She felt the tension in his corded arms, the muscles bunched beneath rolled-up shirt sleeves. His forearm was coated with thick, golden hair, and his hands were broad and possessive.

A faint shudder tickled her spine, and he swore softly and let her go. "Dammit, Deborah. Why won't you let me close to you?"

She looked away, then forced herself to look back at him. "If you want . . . want me, I won't refuse to do my duty."

He stepped back as if she'd slapped him, and anger made his voice rough. "Duty! Is that what you call it? I'll bet you didn't feel that way with that damn 'breed, did you?"

Deborah's face went white, and she clasped her hands together in front of her. Diamond groaned.

"Deborah—I'm sorry. I don't know why I said that. I won't bring him up again, I promise. If you say there's nothing there, then I believe you." He sucked in a deep

347

breath. "After today, when Banning rode out of here like all the hounds of hell were after him, not even stopping to pick up his pay or the horse he rode in, I figured that . . . that something had happened between the two of you."

"Nothing happened today."

He nodded acceptance. "Fine."

An awkward silence fell, but Deborah couldn't think of a single thing to say to ease it. All her early years of training in the social graces and self-discipline had not given her the words she needed now, and she stood with her hands quietly folded and her face a polite mask, and waited.

Finally Diamond said gruffly, "Guess I'll let you go to bed. Unless you want to join me and Judith in the parlor for a while."

"I . . . I'm rather tired. If you don't mind, I'd like to wait until another night."

"Sure. Sure." He flicked her a glance, then gave a careless shrug. "My lawyer says we got Velazquez on the run, in case you're interested. Says we can win in court, and those lands will be mine." Some of the confidence came back into his voice as he said, "Once I get him where I want him, I'm goin' to crush him like a bug. That bastard will know he's lost, by God."

Deborah eyed him. "Is that what this is all about? Ruining Don Francisco?"

"Hell, sugar, don't you want to?" He sounded amazed. "Look what the man did to you. And would have done to you if I hadn't shown up."

"Yes, he was wrong. But you put him in a position he must defend. If he does not want to sell his land, why are you trying to force him into it? Those lands have been in his family for generations."

Sparks of anger lit his eyes, and Diamond shook his

348

head. "I don't understand you, woman. No, I surely don't. I thought you'd want revenge. Hell, he almost killed Banning when he tried to help you, and would have if those men of his weren't so damn careless."

Deborah had paled again, and Diamond's eyes narrowed.

"Dammit, Deborah, I can't even say his name without you lookin' like I hit you." He grabbed her shoulders and shook her until her hair tumbled free of the neat coil and fell around her shoulders and into her face. "I told you I won't have him between us, you hear? If I have to kill him myself, I won't live my life with a gawddammed half-breed gunman lyin' between us in bed at night!" He gave her a shove that sent her stumbling backward, and she came up against the edge of the bed.

Instinctively, she put her hands behind her to catch herself, and saw Diamond staring at her with a return of heat in his eyes. She froze, unable to move as he walked toward the bed with determined strides.

His broad hand pushed her the rest of the way back, and Deborah bit back a scream as he lowered his weight atop her. He pulled at her skirts and unbuttoned her blouse, and when she remained still and quiet he began kissing her. She could not force a pretense of response, but she did not resist him. This was her husband. She'd married him of her own free will, and if he chose to ignore her request to wait until she was ready, she would not struggle.

But neither would she participate.

Diamond kissed her and fondled her breasts and caressed her until he was panting and ready, his body hard against her. He pushed her skirts up and tore aside her pantalettes, then wedged between her thighs. She felt

349

him, and closed her eyes, steeling herself for what came next.

He lifted to his knees and she heard the metallic click of his belt being unbuckled, then the snap of a button as he unfastened his pants. Deborah turned her head to one side and waited.

After a long, tense moment, she heard him curse harshly before he pushed away from her. "Dammit, you're lyin' there like a friggin' sacrifice! I don't need to rape a woman to find one willin', do you hear?"

Deborah opened her eyes, aware of her skirts up around her waist and her blouse open and Dexter Diamond angrily buttoning up his pants. She wanted to say that she was sorry, but knew that it wouldn't make any difference. Not to him. Not to her.

When the door slammed behind him, she rolled over on her side and stared dry-eyed at the far wall. Her throat ached with the unshed tears, and she gazed down the long years ahead without Zack. She could understand his loneliness now, the emptiness he'd spoken of so long ago.

Sunlight poured into the bedroom and glinted off the porcelain chamber pot. Deborah's shoulders shook with retching spasms. She didn't hear the door open but suddenly Judith knelt down beside her.

"Are you ill?" she asked anxiously. "Deborah, what's the matter?"

"I'm . . . not sure . . . what it is." Deborah shook her head slowly, unwilling to move too quickly for fear the world would spin alarmingly again.

Judith's cool hand cupped her brow. "No fever," she said after a moment. "Maybe it's something you've eaten."

"Not eaten," Deborah muttered. She looked up at her. "I've lost my appetite the past few months."

"Here. I'll help you back to the bed." Judith lifted her, cradling an elbow in her palm as she urged her toward the wide bed. She helped Deborah into the bed and pulled the covers over her, then stood there for a long moment. "I wish Tía Dolores were here. She would know what to do."

Deborah managed a faint smile. "It's nothing, really."

"Shall I tell Dexter? He could send for someone . . ."

"No!" Deborah's eyes opened wide with panic. "Don't tell him. This is the third time this week, and I'm sure it will go away soon."

Judith perched on the edge of the bed, her blue eyes worried. "I don't like it. You could have something truly bad. I want to tell him. He's your husband, Deborah, even though you treat him as if he were your enemy," she added sharply, then sighed when Deborah flinched. "I'm sorry. But if you heard him talking about you every night—he should be with you, not playing cards with me at night."

Her hands clenched tightly together. "God knows, I enjoy his company, and he makes me laugh. I can't understand why you don't try to know him better. He's got so many good qualities, and I feel badly for him when you push him away."

"Please, Judith," Deborah said faintly. "Not now. I feel so weak."

The clock on the mantel ticked loudly. Outside the open window, there was the distant noise of men and cattle. The two women gazed at one another.

"Would you let me ask one of the women in the kitchen?" Judith asked finally. "There's Juana, who seems very nice and kind."

"Yes," Deborah replied. "But tell her not to mention

it to anyone else. Especially Dexter. I don't want him fussing over me."

Judith pressed her lips tightly together, but nodded. A short time later, she was back with the genial Mexican cook. Juana listened gravely to Deborah's symptoms, asked a simple question, then nodded wisely.

"You are to have a child, señora. If you will but think back to the time of your last courses, then add two hundred and sixty-five days, you will know the time of the birth."

Deborah just stared at her blankly, her thoughts chaotic. Pregnant? Impossible. Why, the last time had been with Zack, of course, and that had been three months before. She blanched. *Three months.*

Juana was smiling, her broad face creased with pleasure. "The señor will be so pleased! A child makes everyone happy, no?"

No, Deborah wanted to say sincerely, but Judith had recovered from her shock and was thanking Juana for coming to see about her.

"Don't tell anyone," she admonished the cook. "It must be a surprise, all right?"

"Sí, sí, I would not tell anyone," Juana said. "It is always the mother's privilege to do so."

When Judith shut the door, she leaned back against it, staring at her cousin. Deborah wondered if her face was as white as Judith's.

"What are you going to do?" Judith finally asked. "This will kill him."

Deborah buried her face in her palms. "Dear God, I don't know. Oh, why didn't I think? I should have known."

"If I remember correctly," Judith said dryly, "you have been a bit busy with other things the last three months. If not worrying about Don Francisco, you were half out of your mind with grief. And then, after the rescue—well, I imagine it just never occurred to you."

"Obviously." She took a deep breath. "Well, I'm certain Dexter will not want to remain married to me now. It won't matter about the Velazquez lands."

Judith looked down at the floor. When she looked up again, her eyes gleamed with blue lights. "This should suit your charming savage very well. Now he can take you back to the woods to live in primitive delight for the next forty years."

"That was cruel," Deborah said quietly, and Judith had the grace to flush.

"I'm sorry," she muttered. "When do you intend to tell Dexter?"

Gathering her courage, Deborah said, "As soon as possible. It's only fair."

Dexter Diamond shook with fury. "No. You're not going anywhere. You're married to me. When you throw the brat, you can send it somewhere, but you're staying."

Shocked, Deborah couldn't speak for a moment. Then she felt a wash of cold rage sweep over her. "I have no intention of doing any such thing. This is *my* child, no matter who the father. I am keeping my baby."

Diamond closed the distance between them in two steps, and he grabbed her by the shoulders, his voice rough. "I won't have no gawddammed Comanche's bastard on my land!"

Deborah glared up at him in spite of her sudden fear. "I told you, I will grant you a divorce or annulment or whatever you want. You can say what you like. I'll leave, and I won't ask you for anything."

He shook her until her hair tumbled free of the confining pins and tangled in her face. She fought a wave of dizziness and nausea. Her hands gripped his forearms for balance, and she cried out with distress. He stopped, his hands falling away. His chest rose and fell with quick, angry drags for air.

"You're mine, Deborah. You'll stay."

She pushed the hair from her eyes. "No. I won't. I won't bring a child into a home where it will be hated."

Without warning, Diamond's hand crashed against her face and sent her reeling. Lights exploded in front of her eyes, and she reached out for something to grab but nothing was there. Her head slammed against wood, and she heard the loud crack. As she slid down the wall to a crumpled heap on the floor, she heard Diamond repeat through clenched teeth, "You'll stay, all right."

Though the nights were chill, the days were still warm with sunshine and temperate breezes. Zack felt the heat on his bare shoulders as he loaded the buckboard for Sally.

She came out of the house with a basket over her arm, stumbling slightly when she saw him there beside the wagon. "Zack. Aren't you going with me?"

"No."

She didn't say anything for a moment, just gazed at him with her calm green eyes. He paused, and looked up at her. A faint flush stained her cheeks, and he lifted a brow.

"Did I say something wrong, Sal?"

She shook her head, and her voice came out in a rusty whisper. "No, you didn't. It's just that—silly, I know, but you reminded me suddenly of Marty. He used to chop wood without his shirt, and . . . and I guess it made me remember things, that's all."

Zack knew better than to ask what kind of things. He'd seen that look in her eyes, and knew what she felt. It was one of the reasons he'd decided to move on. He didn't want to hurt her by taking what would be given freely. It would mean more to her than to him, and she'd done enough for him already.

He finished loading the last bushel of apples she was taking into town to sell, then reached casually for his shirt and shrugged into it. "I won't be here when you get back," he said softly, and saw her hands curve tightly around the basket handle.

"When will you be back?"

"I won't."

"I see." She took a deep breath and met his gaze. "I wish you the very best, Zack. You deserve it."

"There are some folks who'd disagree with you," he said with a mocking twist of his mouth. She stepped forward and put a finger over his lips.

"Don't. There are always people who hate what they fear. You're a good, decent man. I don't know what I would have done without your help."

"I know what I would have done without yours. I would have died and the buzzards would be making nests with my bones out there somewhere." Zack leaned a shoulder against the side of the buckboard. "You need a husband, Sal. A man who can fix things for you and keep you company on cold nights. You need a man who'll be there for you."

"Do you have someone in mind?" she asked lightly. "I'm sure I could find the time to interview one or two." She smiled, shaking her head. "I did find out that I wasn't as content by myself as I thought."

"Maybe it's just the right time for you now. The Comanche say there's a season for everything, even love.

355

You can't grow something if it's not time for it, whether it's apples, corn, or love."

"Sage advice."

He rubbed his thumb over his jawline. "At times. Like everything else, you have to know when to listen. And how much to hear."

"When are you going to listen?"

His thumb stilled. "What do you mean?"

"Deborah. You love her. She only married that man because she thought you were dead. Go to her. Tell her you love her, Zack. I can't stand seeing that lost look in your eyes."

Straightening, he glared at her, and she took a step back at his fierce look and harsh growl. "You don't know Deborah. She's made vows, and she would never break them."

"I think you're wrong." Sally swallowed, and her chin came up defensively. "Look, I never said anything because it's not my place to give out unwanted advice, but you started it. And besides—I care about you. I'd like to see you happy."

"Happiness is for fools and children, not grown men."

"Don't be an ass, Zack Banning. Happiness is for whoever has the guts to grab at it. Don't tell me, I know. If you hadn't come into my life and shown me what I was missing, I probably would have stayed out here alone until I dried up and blew away. Now I know that's not what I want. I want more. I want a man at my side who loves me, and a man I can love."

"That's good for you, but it doesn't work that way for me."

"Bulldust. It will if you let it. You're good at taking care of yourself in other ways, Zack. Take care of yourself in the most important thing of your life."

356

He looked down and began buttoning his shirt, trying to keep his voice neutral. "I appreciate your advice, Sal. I'll keep it in mind."

"No, you won't. You're stubborn as a mule, and you think she's lost to you forever. Well, if you just sit back and sulk, she will be."

His head shot up, and his eyes narrowed ominously. "I think this discussion has gone far enough."

"So do I." Sally's green eyes were shiny with tears, and he felt a twist in his gut. "You're man enough to fight for men who pay you, but you're not man enough to fight for your woman. I misjudged you."

Clenching his hands, Zack stuffed them into his pockets before he gave in to the urge to pound the buckboard with frustration. He inhaled deeply, and looked away from her, to the hills where he'd lain for weeks halfway between life and death. Only the thoughts of Deborah had kept him going then, the driving urgency to survive and go after her.

Maybe Sally was right.

He looked back at her, and saw that the tears had spilled onto her cheeks. This was the first time she had ever spoken to him of Deborah. Before, she'd always listened when he'd wanted to talk about her. He wondered if it had hurt her to hear him. God, he was such a bastard at times. He knew how Sally felt, yet he'd stayed on because it was easy, because he was hurt and alone and miserable. It would have been even easier for Deborah to do the same thing.

Reaching out, Zack pulled Sally up against him and held her tightly. There was only affection in the embrace, and he patted her back with a comforting hand.

"I don't think there's anything I can do, Sal," he admitted finally. "Unless I kidnap her, and I don't think she'd want that."

She pulled away, slightly embarrassed, wiping her eyes with the cuff of her sleeve. "You won't know until you try it. Besides, if you love her, I'm willing to bet she'd get over it quick enough. She did before, didn't she?"

Zack smiled. He'd told Sally everything, everything she hadn't already heard when he was delirious in those first days.

"I didn't kidnap her. Spotted Pony did. I just bought her from him."

"Lucky girl. I think you need to do it yourself this time."

He cupped her chin in his palm. "I'm a lucky man to have a friend like you, Sally Martin."

"Yes," she said briskly, "you are. Now go after her. And invite me to your wedding. Or the christening of your first child."

Zack reached for his gunbelt and strapped it around his lean waist, then shrugged into his leather vest. When he had his hat on and tilted to shade his eyes, he untied the gray from the sturdy new fence that penned in the goats and swung to its back.

The stallion snorted, prancing eagerly in the early morning light. Zack controlled him with his knees, and gave Sally a slight smile.

"See you, Sal."

"Are you going for her?"

"Maybe someday. Right now, it's time I settled an old score."

Ignoring the sudden pinched look on Sally's face, Zack wheeled his gray in the direction of Don Francisco's hacienda. He didn't look back for a while, and when he did, he saw that Sally's buckboard had taken the fork in the road that led to Sirocco instead of San Ysabel.

"Damn," he muttered. What was she doing? Sirocco was filled with Velazquez men and Diamond men, and the town was a powder keg waiting to blow. He considered going after her and convincing her to go to San Ysabel, but recognized that he'd given up any rights to advise her by leaving. Sally was no fool. If she was headed to Sirocco, she had a good reason for it.

After a brief hesitation, he wheeled the gray down the slope and continued riding toward the Velazquez hacienda. He would figure out what he wanted to do and how on the way. He just knew that he intended to do *some*thing. Francisco Velazquez would not be allowed to get away with murder, and neither would the two men who had shot him and left him to die in the desert.

Chapter 25

Sheriff Roy Carpenter thumped a finger on his desk and frowned. "Two bodies were found a few days ago, Banning. You know anything about that?"

Zack's expression was bland. "Why do you ask me?"

Carpenter glanced up, his eyes shrewd beneath bushy gray brows. "Since they work for Velazquez, and have been known to boast they were responsible for killing Zack Banning, it occurred to me that you just might."

Zack shrugged. "Many men have died lately since Diamond decided he wanted Velazquez lands."

"Yeah, but none of them were killed like these were." He peered at Zack closely. "These two men were staked out like they'd been killed by Comanche. They didn't die easy, and since you're a 'breed—forgive me if I'm wrong."

Zack ignored his sarcasm. He stood up. "Forgiveness you'll have to get from a priest. I'm all out."

"So I understand." Carpenter didn't move, just gazed at Zack with assessing eyes that made him tense. "You know, Banning, you're not quite what I expected."

"I'm flattered."

"Don't be. When you came to town the first time, I thought you were gonna be like all the rest of 'em, looking to make a name for yourself and pick up some easy cash." He shrugged. And after you shot Braden, I was sure of it. Now, I don't know."

He leaned forward, elbows on his desk and his fingers forming a steeple. "Why are you still here? It ain't just Don Francisco."

Zack stared at him without replying. His cold gaze made Carpenter shake his head and sigh with resignation.

"Go on, Banning. If I find out you're even a hair into this trouble, I'll lock you up so quick your head will spin."

When Zack stepped out into the crisp sunshine, he tugged on his hat and nodded to the ranger who'd brought him in. The man gave a surly grunt, obviously displeased to see that his quarry was being released so quickly. Zack's mouth twitched in a faint smile. He felt better. Alfredo and his vicious *compadré* had paid for what they'd tried to do to him, and that left only Don Francisco.

He wondered if the ranger had been surprised that he'd come with him so easily. He shouldn't have been. Zack had left a trail a blind man could follow. Don Francisco would have heard about it by now, and would be expecting him. He could almost smell his fear from here.

A cruel smile curved his mouth, and he felt a fierce exultation. There were still some pleasures left in life after all.

"Here, Miz Diamond. A lady left this for you. Said I was to give it to you the next time I saw you."

Surprised, Deborah took the small square envelope Mr. Potter held out to her. "For me? Who was she?"

"I dunno. Only seen her oncet before. She came in with Zack Banning a little while back."

Deborah's hand shook, and she glanced over her shoulder to where Dexter stood talking with Frank Albright, one of his hired killers. He hadn't heard. Any mention of Zack made him furious, and she had no desire to provoke him again. The truce between them was uneasy enough as it was.

"Thank you, Mr. Potter," she said when it seemed as if he was waiting for something. She looked up, and saw Potter staring at her gravely.

"If I was you, Miz Diamond, I'd stay away from Zack Banning," he said after a moment, his voice low. "The man's a killer."

"There seems to be a lot of that going around," Deborah returned coldly.

Potter nodded. "Yeah. But not the way he done it. Took two of the Velazquez men and staked 'em out on the desert. I heard it wasn't very pretty, and they musta regretted they ever messed with him long afore they died. Banning's part Comanch, ya know."

"I heard. Thank you for my mail." Deborah stuffed the envelope into her reticule and turned away, fighting the nausea that rose in her throat. She could imagine how the men had died, and though she didn't blame Zack—in one way was glad—she still shuddered at the cold cruelty that could torture another human being. Another difference between them to think about, she supposed.

Zack would always battle between two very different cultures, between his white mother's upbringing, and his Comanche father's beliefs. He'd spent his first years at his mother's knee, but the last years had been spent learning to live as a Comanche. Would he ever be able to find peace in either world?

She hoped so. She loved him. And she loved the child they had created between them, the small life that grew inside her and warmed her heart. It was all she had of Zack. All she would ever have of him. When her child was old enough, she would tell it of its father, and hope her child did not have the same decisions to make.

"Where you goin'?"

Deborah stopped and looked up at Dexter. His eyes were cold and dark, and she stilled the nervous flutter of her hands. He'd only brought her into Sirocco to sign legal papers in the courthouse, and had kept a close eye on her every movement. He treated her with icy contempt now, but she felt his gaze resting on her frequently.

"I thought I would step outside and wait for you on the bench in front of the store," she said coolly. "I'd like to sit down."

Diamond grunted. "Go with her, Albright. See that nothin' happens to my sweet little wife."

His sarcasm warmed Deborah's cheeks, but she didn't comment as she opened the door to the jangling of the bell. Her nerves were stretched tautly, and she wished Judith had come with them. She would have served as a buffer between them. Dexter liked Judith, and there was an easy camaraderie between them that often made Deborah feel like an outsider. By her own choice, she realized.

She sank to the hard wooden comfort of the long bench stretched in front of the store, and blankly gazed at the dusty street. The letter in her purse felt heavy, and she wished she was alone so that she could read it. Was it from Zack? Potter had said the woman was with him.

A pang struck her, and she felt suddenly foolish. As if she had a right to be jealous of him being with another woman when she was married to someone else.

She closed her eyes, and leaned her head back against the front of the store. She could hear the jangle of Albright's spurs as he leaned against the wall beside her. Several minutes passed as she listened to the sounds of horses and wagons and people passing. Then Albright stirred, his spurs rattling as he straightened.

"Goddam," she heard him say softly, then laugh. She opened her eyes, looking up as the door bell jangled again and Albright stuck his head inside and called to Diamond. "Hey, boss—you might wanna come out here a minute."

When Dexter stepped onto the porch, Deborah looked away from his quick glance at her. And saw Zack Banning.

Her heart rose in her throat as she heard Dexter's low, vicious curse and saw Zack striding down the wooden sidewalk with that loose, easy stride she knew so well. His lean grace and dark good looks gathered more than one sidelong glance from feminine eyes, and Deborah felt her heartbeat escalate alarmingly.

However, feminine eyes weren't the only interested looks he got, and several of the men paused to look after him. Zack didn't look like most gunmen; his holster was worn and plain, the butt of his deadly revolver bore no notches on the smooth handle. He wore tan denims, a brown chambray shirt, and an open leather vest that had seen better days. The only detour from the norm was his boots—knee-high moccasins that made his step light and soundless. A dark brown hat shaded his eyes and covered the thick mane of glossy black hair. Deborah shut her eyes briefly, and prayed that he would not approach them.

Her prayer went unanswered.

"Banning." Diamond's voice rang out, and Deborah saw Zack switch direction. She looked down at her

364

hands, and saw that her knuckles were white as she clutched her purse with an almost frantic grip.

Zack stopped only a few feet away, his voice cool. "Yeah?"

Deborah could feel his eyes on her, and finally took a deep breath and lifted her head. She wasn't prepared for the shock of seeing him again. Pain vibrated through her body like a jolt of lightning, and she steeled herself against it. She barely heard Dexter's growling voice, or Zack's raspy reply.

"Heard two of Don Francisco's men got themselves kilt a few days ago," Dexter was saying.

"I heard the same thing."

"Reckon how that happened?"

"Sheriff Carpenter has some men working on it." Zack shifted slightly on the balls of his feet, his voice wary. "I got the feeling you aren't that interested in Velazquez's men, Diamond. What do you really want?"

Dexter took a step forward, and hatred scored his voice as he said softly, "I want you dead, Banning."

Zack shrugged. "You've got a lot of company."

A small sound escaped Deborah, and she surged to her feet. Her voice was choked. "Dexter, please—I'd like to go home now."

She felt his hand on her shoulder, then lower on her waist as he pulled her up against him. Diamond's voice was low and intimate.

"Sure thing, sugar. I just want to talk to your old friend here a minute." His hand shifted upward, his fingers grazing her breast, and Deborah stood there like stone as he fondled her. She could see Zack stiffen, and heard Albright laugh softly.

Zack expelled a short, angry breath. "I don't think we've got a lot to say to each other, Diamond. I don't work for you anymore."

"No. You never did collect your wages."

"You sent the other horse back. That was enough."

"Yeah, figured as how it was your lady-friend's horse and all, it was the least I could do."

"She appreciated it," Zack said after a short pause. His voice was flat. He flicked a glance at Deborah, and she felt it all the way to her toes. There was a message in those dark blue eyes that shook her, and she must have made some sound, because Dexter was pulling her even closer, his hand openly caressing her breast.

Shaken, she gathered her courage and pulled away a bit, turning to face Dexter, her voice cool and composed. "I'll wait for you in the wagon, if you like."

"Sure thing, sugar," he said easily, but his dark eyes burned with anger. "Albright will go along with you to make sure nobody bothers you."

"Thank you." She turned back to Zack and gave him a polite nod. "Good day, Mr. Banning."

As she walked away with Albright at her side, she could feel his gaze on her, and wondered if she'd make it all the way to the wagon. She was shaking, and her knees were so weak she stumbled. Albright caught her, his gloved hand grabbing her arm.

"You all right, ma'am?" he drawled, and she caught the sardonic inflection in his tone. That served to straighten her spine, and she pulled away.

"I'm fine, thank you."

Albright slid a sly glance back the way they'd come. "I hear Banning ain't as fast as he used to be."

Deborah didn't reply, and as Albright moved to help her up into the wagon, she shook away his hand. He stepped back and looked at her, this thin face angry.

"Any woman who hangs around with 'breeds shouldn't get too uppity. *Miz* Diamond."

"Is that so? Strange advice, coming from a man with your background, Mr. Albright." Her voice was cool, and she sat stiffly on the wagon seat, staring down at him.

He took a step closer, his eyes pinpoints of fury. "You ain't nothin' but a lightskirt, the way I see it. Diamond's my boss, but he done gone and got hisself hitched to a woman who likes lyin' under some buck's robes. It ain't nothin' but your claim to Velazquez lands that keeps you safe, and I reckon you know that."

"I'm certain my husband would appreciate the fact that his hired hands gossip so freely about his business," Deborah said in the same cool tone that seemed to infuriate him. "Perhaps I should tell him, so he can be sure to thank you properly."

She saw Albright flush. He knew as well as she did that Dexter Diamond's stiff pride wouldn't allow him to stomach men who laughed at him behind his back. And he was just as likely to send a man into an ambush as he was to fire him. It was one of the things she'd learned about her husband that distressed her most.

Albright backed off, his voice a low snarl. "Maybe I'll bring you back Banning's scalp when I'm done killin' him. I know a few Comanche tricks myself, and I can tell you, I'll enjoy every minute of it."

"I have the feeling that Zack Banning is not as easy to kill as you'd like to believe," Deborah said. "If he was, he'd already be dead."

"He ain't got much longer, I can promise you that."

Deborah just looked at him, then lifted her chin and turned away. She saw Dexter striding toward them, and from the look on his face, she was certain he would be very unpleasant on the ride back to the Double D.

* * *

There was no moonlight to betray him this night. He lay still and quiet on his belly. Not far away, lay one of the guards, his throat cut ear to ear. Zack had no intention of taking any chances this time. This time, Don Francisco would have no warning of what was to come.

Rising to his knees, he reached for the large sombrero he'd taken from the dead guard. Stuffed into the deep crown, he felt the rough wool of a serape. He pulled it out, slid it over his broad shoulders, then tugged the hat on over his head and reached for his knife. It shone dully in the absence of moonlight, long and lethal and ready.

With the knife in one fist and half-hidden beneath the long wool folds of the serape, he picked up the rifle the guard would never use again, and walked calmly into the main courtyard of the Velazquez hacienda. Other guards nodded or ignored him, and he continued on his way.

"*¿Quien es?*" someone growled at his side, and Zack half-turned.

"Pedro." A common enough name. There were probably a dozen Pedros employed by Velazquez. The man grunted acknowledgment, and peered closely at Zack.

"*¿Qué pasa?*"

"*Nada de particular.*" Zack shrugged carelessly and gestured with his stolen rifle. "*¡Yo soy hambriento!*"

A faint laugh was his answer, with the mocking reply, "*Allá haba—fríjoles.*"

"*¡Bueno!*"

After an instant's hesitation, the man moved on, and Zack continued walking toward the kitchens. It was a stroke of luck that he'd smelled the beans cooking, or he might have given himself away. With his dark hair and skin he could pass for a Mexican if no one got too close. And he didn't intend for anyone to get too close.

Around the next corner, Zack saw three guards lounging casually just inside a doorway. Behind them, a curved arch divided a long walkway from a main *sala*. He figured it was a safe bet that Don Francisco would be inside on a chilly night like this one, and walked leisurely in that direction.

"*¡Hola, compadres! Salir al encuentro de el jefe.*"

"*¿Hasta donde?*" one of them asked, and Zack shrugged.

"*Por allí.*" He pointed back the way he'd come, and the men grumbled, but moved in that direction. This was easier than he'd thought it would be, and Zack stepped to the arch and stood in the shadows. Don Francisco sat inside, a pewter goblet in one hand, a map in the other. He sat with his back to Zack, bent over his desk and concentrating on the large map spread out.

With a last glance over his shoulder, Zack slipped into the room. He pulled the open door closed behind him, shutting it so softly Don Francisco never turned around. He did not turn around until Zack was right behind him, and then he turned angrily.

"*¿Quin es?*"

"*Un amigo.*"

He saw Velazquez stiffen, and the goblet lowered to the table as he barked, "*¿Qué?*"

"I said, a friend. What's the matter, Velazquez, don't you have any friends?" Zack mocked. "Ah—that wouldn't be wise. If you try to shout for help, I'll have your throat slit before they get to the door." He gestured with his knife, and lamplight skittered along the razor-sharp blade with splinters of reflected light.

Don Francisco wheezed slightly, his face paling. "If you do, you'll never get out of here alive."

"I'm dead anyway. Remember? And if you think I care about your threats, you're wrong. Dead wrong.

Come on, nice and easy. You and I have some talking to do."

"What do you want with me, Banning?" Don Francisco was shaking. "You intend to kill me. I know you do. I will not die like you killed Alfredo and Javier."

"That's not your choice. Your choice is if you die here, or if you take the risk and live a little longer. Anything can happen before you die. *¿No es verdad?*"

"Sí," Don Francisco moaned, "that is so." He licked his lips, and at Zack's quick gesture with the gleaming knife, put trembling hands in the air. "It was a mistake. I never meant that you should truly die."

Zack's voice was hard. "In case you haven't noticed, my Spanish is excellent, Don Francisco. Now please— walk just ahead of me, so that none of your men will suspect anything. If you are asked a question and do not give an answer that I like, I will gut you like a dead pig and you can take the next three days to die. Think about it. Now, let's go."

Don Francisco shivered as they stepped out of his *sala*. His thin shirt and dark pants would provide little warmth in the night wind. Zack stayed close behind him, nudging him with the tip of his knife when he faltered.

"Por favor," Velazquez gasped once when the blade dug into his skin, "do not cut me!"

"No whining," Zack muttered. "And no talking. Just keep going, and I'll tell you when to turn and when to stop."

No one delayed their progress, and in a few minutes, they had reached the adobe wall at the back of the courtyard. A wooden door was cracked open, and Zack pushed it wide with one foot.

"After you, señor," he mocked, and Don Francisco hesitated briefly before the knife spurred him forward.

A creek ran behind the wall, and Zack forced him down into it. They walked for a mile, until the lights from the hacienda were behind them. In that time, no one had seen them, and Don Francisco was almost frothing with frustration, fear, and fury.

"My guards are not as vigilant as I was told," he said once, and Zack laughed.

"Some of them were. Those are dead."

Don Francisco shuddered, and didn't offer any more comments. He said nothing until Zack tied him to a horse, then mounted his own.

"Where are you taking me?"

Zack didn't bother to answer, but spurred their mounts into a hard gallop. He rode across the rolling hills and rocky ridges, leading Velazquez's horse, not caring how hard it was for the Mexican to stay on. He felt a grim sense of satisfaction. One lone man had done what an army of men could not have managed, and that was go into the sanctuary of the hacienda and take Don Francisco out without a single shot being fired. It was incredible, and had been so easy as to be laughable. He wondered why Diamond hadn't thought of it.

Finally, he reined in his horse and dismounted, walking back to the obviously nervous Don Francisco. He swept off the sombrero he wore, and shrugged out of the wool serape, then reached up to pull Don Francisco from his horse.

The Mexican shot nervous glances around him when Zack set him on his feet and untied his hands. "Where are we?"

"Doesn't matter." With a deft twist, Zack unsheathed his knife and threw it so that the blade sliced into the ground between Velazquez's feet.

He gave a sharp cry, and leaped back. "What are you doing?"

"Giving you a chance. That was more than you gave me."

Zack eyed him. There was very little light. Dark shadows surrounded them, and in the distance a coyote howled to the night sky. Don Francisco stared at him, the whites of his eyes gleaming in the murky light.

"I cannot fight you!"

"Let me explain it to you this way, then. You can go for that knife and have a chance, or you can wait for me to pick it up and start slicing you into pieces too small for the coyotes to find."

There was a thread of menace in Zack's tone that not even Velazquez could miss, and he quivered with fear. Zack saw him glance around desperately as if looking for help, then suck in a deep breath. Zack smiled, and knew from the sudden look of terror on Don Francisco's face that he must look at least as savage as he felt at this moment.

This was vengeance, pure and simple, and he relished every moment of it.

He waited, muscles relaxed, eyes intent, and when Don Francisco finally made a move for the knife, Zack took a step forward. His foot slashed through the air and caught the Mexican in the face, sending him staggering backward. The knife still jutted up from the gritty desert floor, the handle gleaming an invitation in the night. Zack didn't even glance at it. He waited for his quarry to get up and try again.

Groaning, Don Francisco lurched to his feet, one hand held to his face. He wiped his sleeve over his bleeding nose and straightened slowly. His eyes glittered with hate this time, and Zack smiled.

"Come. Try again. You are so fierce, no? You are

such a brave man, you hit others who are tied up and helpless, and you terrorize women. Come on, Don Francisco. Show me what a man you are. Show me how you can die bravely."

"You are a damned half-breed!" Velazquez spat. *"Mestizo bastardo!"*

"Yes," Zack answered coolly. "See if you can kill either half. I know I am not tied up, but you might manage to frighten me a little, eh?"

Velazquez dove for the knife, and again Zack kicked him back, his foot catching him in the throat and driving him to his knees, gasping and retching. When he got to his feet, Zack taunted him into trying again and again, each time kicking him away from the promise of the knife. Finally, Don Francisco lay bleeding and half-conscious in the dirt, his face battered almost beyond recognition.

Zack felt a sense of justice. Crouching down beside the dazed Velazquez, he jerked his head back by his hair and gazed at him dispassionately. He could only blink and gasp for breath as Zack studied him.

"You are a pathetic excuse for a man, Don Francisco," he said softly. "You prey on the weak and helpless, but cannot defend yourself." He drew the tip of the knife along the curve of Velazquez's cheek, watching him shudder and whimper at the blade that chilled but did not cut.

Velazquez began to sob, tears mixing with blood and running down his face, and Zack felt a surge of disgust.

"I should kill you, but you are not worth the trouble it would cause." With swift slash, he brought the blade through the air and buried it in the ground beside Don Francisco. "If you value your life," he said softly, "you will not be foolish enough to come near me again. Nor will you cause Deborah any more trouble. If I hear that you have—and I will—I will come after you. And this time, you will die by inches, do you understand?"

"Sí, sí! Do not kill me, and I will do anything you say to do, I swear it!"

Zack's lip curled slightly. "I am sure of it." He stood up and went to his horse, and when he stepped back to Don Francisco, he held a piece of paper in one hand. He hunkered down on his heels beside him. "I have something here for you to sign, Don Francisco. When you have signed it, I will put you on your horse."

Without bothering to read it or ask what it was, the Mexican signed with the pen Zack gave him, scrawling his name across the bottom of the paper. Then he looked up.

"Are you taking me back to my hacienda?"

Zack folded the paper and tucked it into his saddlebag before replying.

"No. I have a pleasant surprise for you, Don Francisco. I am sure you will like it."

Blanching, the Mexican babbled protests as Zack put him atop his horse, tying his hands again.

It was almost daylight when Zack left Velazquez behind, and a grim smile curled his mouth. When he reached the crest of a rocky ridge, he reined in the gray and looked back.

Don Francisco Hernando Velazquez y Aguilar was stripped and gagged and tied to a post like a sacrifice. He would be the first thing Dexter Diamond saw when he stepped out of his ranch house that morning. Zack wondered what the rancher would think—and what he would do with such unexpected bounty. It should be interesting to find out.

Laughing, Zack wheeled his gray and rode down the other side of the crest. What a temptation for Diamond to resist.

Chapter 26

"Dexter, you can't!"

"Why not?" His tawny brow rose, and a malicious smile curled his mouth. "It's a gift."

Deborah shook her head. "It's murder."

"It's too gawddammed good to be true, is what it is," he said gleefully, raking a hand through his hair and looking back at Don Francisco.

Velazquez cowered in a parlor chair, keeping a wary eye on Frank Albright's drawn pistol. "She's right you know," he dared to say. "If you kill me, you will be arrested for murder and probably hung."

"Damn, Velazquez, you're here on my property! Who in the hell do you think would arrest me for shootin' a man that's trespassin'? Carpenter? Naw, I don't think so."

"Aren't you curious about how I got here?" Velazquez licked dry, split lips and peered up at Diamond through his one good eye. Bruises and gashes distorted his once handsome face into an unrecognizable mess. Someone had given him a pair of trousers and a shirt, but they were too large and hung shapelessly.

Deborah shuddered and looked away. Part of her felt no sympathy for the man, but the humane part recognized that he should be dealt with by the authorities.

"Yeah, tell me who brought you here," Diamond was saying with a grin. "Must be a good friend to risk doin' this for me."

Velazquez gave a short, sardonic laugh. "Perhaps. And perhaps he is a better friend of your new wife."

"Just what the hell do you mean by that?" Diamond growled, and Deborah felt a chill trickle down her spine at the glitter in Don Francisco's eyes.

His gaze moved to her, malevolent, dark, and bruised. "I mean, señor, that Zack Banning was the *amigo* who thought you might like to be made a present of me. So you see, if you do what he intends that you do, it will get rid of me and you both. He is very diabolical, Señor Banning, no?"

Diamond swore horribly, and Deborah winced. When he slammed a fist against the wall and bellowed, "I'll get that damn 'breed if it's the last thing I do!" she stood up.

"I'm going to my room now," she said quietly, but he moved to stand in her way.

"Did you know about this?"

She met his angry glare calmly. "No, of course not. How would I? I'm not allowed more than a foot from any of your watchdogs."

For a moment she thought he intended to make her stay, but then he swore again and signalled to one of his men to go with her, and Deborah left the parlor. She was aware of the man behind her, following at a discreet distance. At least it wasn't Albright. She hated him. He made her feel dirty. This man was fairly young, but wore a well-used pistol slung low on his hip as so many of the other gunmen her husband employed.

She turned at her bedroom door, and he paused. A chair stood in the wide hallway, and she gestured to it.

"Make yourself comfortable. I intend to go back to bed."

"Yes, ma'am. I hope you rest easy."

Deborah had started into her room, but turned back. He sounded as if he meant it, and his voice was quiet and respectful. "What's your name?" she asked.

"Lonny King." He had his hat in his hands, and he bent the brim as he stood there watching her. Deborah smiled.

"Well, Mr. King, I thank you for being so polite. And I shall try to rest well indeed."

She shut the door softly behind her, and crossed to her bed. She'd dressed hastily that morning, hearing the commotion and not wanting to be left out. Judith had gone inside abruptly upon seeing Don Francisco, and she supposed she was still in her room. Hiding.

Poor Judith. It was obvious she was falling in love with Dexter, and he didn't seem to notice. Deborah sighed. She had never dreamed life could become so complicated when she was in Natchez, never thought beyond marriage and babies and long, lazy days. What a simple little fool she'd been.

Deborah knelt beside her bed and felt under her mattress for the letter she'd been given in Sirocco. She'd read it so many times she should have memorized it. Yet she still savored the words, reading them again and again as if they came from Zack.

The handwriting was neat and spare, feminine. Deborah wondered about the writer, and if she loved Zack. She must, or she would never have written a letter like this. The page crackled as she unfolded it, scanning the lines with an eager need for reassurance.

Mrs. Diamond,
You don't know me, but I'm a friend of Zack Ban-

ning's. He doesn't know I'm writing you, and I'd rather he didn't. I just want you to know, he has not forgotten you. If you truly care for him, you need to remember that. I cared for him when he was wounded, and he spoke your name over and over. He loves you. I do not want to see him ride off again without knowing how you feel. Please, if you care, tell him.

It was signed, *Sally Martin*. Deborah stared down at the words for a while, trying to envision the woman who cared enough about Zack to interfere. Then she folded the letter and tucked it back beneath her mattress for safekeeping. She could imagine Dexter's anger if he ever discovered it.

Deborah sat on the edge of her bed for a while, gazing out the window. In the distance, she could see the ridged hills that seamed the horizon. She thought of the Comanche camp sometimes when the wind blowing through the cottonwoods sounded like the music of tall pine trees. Had the people survived the effort of the government to put them on reservations? She hoped so. She was tired of killing and war and death.

Her hand moved to rest on the gentle swell of her abdomen, and she wondered if she should try to tell Zack of his child. He had a right to know, but it would only make more trouble. Dexter would not release her, and Zack would come for her. There would be shooting, and someone would be killed. No, she could not risk it. It was better if he left thinking she didn't love him, than to know she did and they could not be together.

Closing her eyes, Deborah sat on the edge of her bed for a long time, and thought of the way things might have been.

* * *

Judith stuck her head in the door. "Deborah. Dexter wants to see you."

It took a moment for her to wake. She hadn't realized she'd been sleeping, and glanced at the window. Afternoon shadows slanted across her bedroom walls.

Deborah sat up. "What does he want?"

A frown creased her brow, and Judith shook her head. "I don't know, but he seems pretty agitated. I think he's still mad about having to let Don Francisco go."

"Surely he's over that by now. It was a week ago." She pushed at the hair in her eyes, and tried to keep her eyes open. She slept so much now, as if her body was greedy for the rest.

"Maybe so," Judith was saying, "but he's been talking about it to some men out there."

Alarmed, Deborah burst out, "He's not planning on anything dangerous, is he?"

"Worried about him?"

"I'm worried about an all-out war," Deborah shot back, swinging her legs over the side of the bed and standing. "If you will remember, two more of our men were killed in a gunbattle yesterday."

"I remember, all right. I'm the one Dexter talks to at night while you hide here in your room."

Deborah looked up at her. "Censure, Judith? You must know how I feel."

"Yes," Judith said softly, "I know. But Deborah, you need to understand Dexter. He's not as harsh as he sounds to you, he's only hurt."

Deborah saw the distress in Judith's eyes, and realized that she had grown very fond of Dexter. Too fond. When had it happened? She'd not noticed because she hadn't cared, and she knew that her cousin would never want to admit it to her. It would be a betrayal, and though Judith had betrayed Hawk, she'd done it for love of Deborah. God, what a mess. She wished she could tell Judith to beware of Dexter, but she knew she wouldn't listen.

"I find it difficult to believe that Dexter Diamond is hurt because of me," she said slowly. "Worried about losing his claim to the Velazquez lands, yes, but not me."

Judith made an irritated sound. "Are you still angry because he hit you and said all that about getting rid of the baby?"

"Wouldn't you be?"

"Yes, for a while. But you have to understand, he was hurt and upset."

"I see." Deborah slid her feet into her slippers and crossed to the dresser. She tugged a brush through her hair, watching Judith in the mirror. "Just think—the next time he gets hurt and angry, he could hit me so hard I lose the baby. And I have the feeling that's just what he wants."

Judith flushed, and knotted her hands in front of her. "You wrong him, but I guess you won't see that."

"And you won't see the truth." Deborah clubbed her hair into a knot on her neck and tied it with a ribbon, then turned to her cousin. "I hope you don't end up hurt as well."

Tears trembled on Judith's lashes, and she wiped them away. "Please—forgive me. I say hateful things that I don't mean."

Deborah managed a smile. "I know. We're both caught in the middle of something that's like a runaway train. Neither of us knows how to get off and stop it."

"That's true enough."

"Who does Dexter want me to see out here?" Deborah asked as they left her room.

Judith shrugged. "I don't know. They just look like a bunch of scruffy buffalo hunters to me. Don't get downwind of them. You'll get the heaves again."

At first, the sun was in her eyes and Deborah didn't see the men, then one of them turned, grinning at her. She stared at him, and felt her heart do a flop. He was tall and thin, with lanky blond hair that hung to his shoulders. And he was smirking. She'd seen that leering grin before, high in the mountains when he had tried to buy her from White Eagle.

"Comancheros," she murmured. The man was gesturing to her and then looked at his companion. Deborah saw Frank Albright turn and look at her with a satisfied smirk. Beyond him, she saw Lonny King's young, troubled face, and felt the first premonition of danger.

"Deborah," Dexter was saying, "this man says he's met you before."

"Sure I have," the Comanchero said, stepping closer to her. "'Course, she was wearing buckskin and belonged to a handsome buck last time I saw her."

Diamond's face was a cold mask, and Deborah felt a wave of dizziness wash over her. She wasn't really surprised to hear the Comanchero's next words.

"Hear tell that Hawk is roamin' around here callin' hisself Zack Banning now. You better 'watch your woman, Diamond, or that Injun might steal her back."

Deborah felt Dexter's dark gaze pierce her, and knew he would make her pay for her mistake. Behind her, Judith was saying something, but her words were drowned out by the rising roar in her ears as she stared at the Comanchero and Frank Albright's smug expression.

* * *

"What do you mean?" Zack's eyes narrowed slightly, and he raked the sheriff with a quelling stare.

"Just what I said, Banning. After the stunt you pulled, you need to move on. You've got Velazquez after you as well as Diamond, and I'm getting tired of burying folks."

"Have I broken any laws?"

Carpenter blew out a heavy breath. "None I can pin on you, no. Velazquez won't press charges."

Zack smiled, and he could tell from the sudden tightening of the sheriff's mouth the effect it had on him. "Maybe he isn't, but I might."

"What's that supposed to mean?"

"Figure it out. Rumor had it for a while that I was dead, remember? Velazquez had me shot and left in the desert to die. He's lucky I didn't do the same to him."

"Maybe you're the lucky one. Dying from a bullet is a sight better than dying at the end of a rope."

"It's all relative," Zack shot back. "Dying is dying, and when it comes down to it, the way a man dies is usually a reflection of the way he lived. We all take chances. Don Francisco took a big one when he didn't make sure I was dead."

Carpenter's mouth twisted, and his gray brows lowered over his eyes. "That's indisputable. But if you kill him, you'll hang for murder. Simple as that. I got enough to worry about with him and Diamond making this county into nothing but a big war without wondering whether you'll shoot it out on the main street with one of his hired killers."

"So tell Diamond, not me."

"I'm telling all of you, by God!" Carpenter roared, slamming his fist down on his desk so hard papers flew to the floor. "Clear out of town, Banning! Dammit all, I don't want your death on my mind."

Zack straightened. "My life is my own, my death is my own. It should weigh on no man."

"I don't work that way." Carpenter glared at him. "You ain't in this world all by yourself. Your life touches a whole lot of folks, and if you get yourself killed, there's going to be some repercussions. I think you can figure out what I mean if you think about it."

For a moment Zack didn't say anything. Then he drew in a deep breath and nodded. "I have thought about it. But she is taken care of, and there's nothing I can do."

"Yes there is. Save her a little bit of damn pain and clear out before she has to attend your funeral." Carpenter shot him a frustrated glance, then shrugged. "Can't figure women out, but there you have it. She's a fine woman and doesn't deserve being hurt. She's been through enough."

"So how did you know?"

"Hell, I ain't stupid, Banning. Just because I'm dumb enough to get elected to sheriff and get myself mixed up in a frigging range war, doesn't mean I can't see or hear. There aren't too many people in Sirocco who hasn't heard what went on out there at the Velazquez place, or that she thought you were dead and married Diamond to get away from that crazy-mad Mexican." His eyes narrowed under the shelf of brow. "If you care about her at all, you'll leave town."

"I'll keep that in mind," Zack said tightly. "Thanks for the heart-to-heart chat."

Carpenter grunted irritably. "Any time."

Zack slammed the door behind him, and stared down the wide main street for a moment before stepping off the porch. Damn. What did it take to get people to mind their own business? It would be Deborah who suffered, not him. He didn't care that much what people said. He'd listened to rumors and lies and truth for most of his life, and it no longer had the same power to hurt him. But Deborah—*Christ!* She didn't deserve to be the butt of gossip, to have people stare at her and whisper behind their hands. She deserved a lot more than that, and he knew what Carpenter had said was true.

If he left town, the gossip and rumors would die down soon enough. Something new would come along to replace it. Hell, Diamond and Velazquez might even kill each other off and give them that to talk about for a while. Too bad Diamond hadn't given in to the temptation to kill Velazquez. He would have enjoyed watching them both go down.

Zack stepped down off the porch and into the street. He needed a drink. Then he'd leave town, and leave Deborah to lead her own life. God, he hoped she found happiness. None of this was her fault.

A hush fell when he pushed open the double doors to the Six-Shooter Saloon and walked in. Unperturbed, he strode to the bar and ordered a beer. The bartender slid it across the wet surface and dunked the proffered coins in a dingy glass, then stepped back and away as if afraid. The tinkly music of the piano plinked out an erratic tune again. Zack felt eyes on him, and as he lifted his mug of beer, he glanced up into the mirrored shelves behind the bar.

A faint smile curled his mouth. Frank Albright sat at a table with his back to the wall, watching Zack from beneath the brim of his hat. Zack shifted slightly so that he had ready access to the pistol on his thigh, then leaned one elbow on the bar as he sipped his beer. He waited.

Of all the saloons in Sirocco, he had come into this one. This confrontation would be inevitable, and he knew by instinct that Albright would provoke it.

It took Albright only ten minutes to make up his mind, and he rose from the table while a younger man grabbed at his arm and said softly, "Don't, Albright! Just leave it alone, will ya?"

Apparently, Albright had no intention of leaving it alone. He shook off the younger man's arm and walked toward the bar, while the music stopped abruptly and several chairs scraped back from tables as patrons decided to abandon half-finished drinks in the interest of safety.

"Hey, Banning."

Zack ignored him for a minute, sliding a glance up at the reflection in the smoky mirror to keep an eye on his movements. Albright spoke again, belligerent this time, his tone sharp.

"Banning, I'm talkin' to you."

"I heard you."

Zack didn't bother looking up or turning around, as if Albright made no difference to him whatsoever. He dragged his sweating mug across the surface of the bar idly, streaking the wet rings. Then he took another sip, still watching Frank Albright's reflection.

The younger man stood up, his voice insistent. "The boss ain't gonna like it if you make trouble and get folks to talking, Albright."

"Shut up, Lonny," Albright said without looking at him. "This ain't none of your concern. Me and Banning got some unfinished business between us."

Zack turned slowly, lounging back against the bar with his elbows braced on the edge. He rested his heel on the footrail and eyed Albright coldly.

"You got me mixed up with someone else. I don't do business with snakes."

Albright stiffened. "That right? You're awful damn cocky for a stinkin' breed. Ain't that what you Coman-

385

che call yerself? Snakes? You ought to feel right at home with a whole nest of 'em, the way I hear it."

There was the clunking noise of overturned tables and the creak of the saloon doors as Zack slowly straightened. Men scattered, the music came to an abrupt halt, and there was a feminine squeal as one of the saloon whores fled.

"You're right, Albright," he said slowly, and saw the surprise in the other man's eyes. "I feel a lot more at home with snakes than I do with men like you. You'd put any self-respecting rattler to shame."

Anger flared in Albright's eyes, and his face flushed an ugly red. He kicked a chair out of the way, and took two steps forward before stopping.

"Care to talk about that outside?"

"I'm not interested in dodging cow piles just to stand in the middle of the street and watch you die, Albright."

Zack turned back to the bar as Albright made a sound somewhere between a snarl and a sputter.

"Goddam you, Banning," he finally got out. "Turn around and fight!"

Zack ignored him. A mutter ran through the men watching, but he didn't care. Let them think what they wanted. He had no intention of letting Albright force him into stepping outside if he could avoid it.

The jangle of Albright's spurs set his teeth on edge, and he tensed. With deliberate, slow movements, he lifted his beer mug and took a long drink. The bartender had moved down to the far end of the bar and was watching him with an incredulous stare, and he heard someone cough.

A grim smile curled his mouth, and he knew what people had to be thinking: He'd lost his edge since he'd come back; he was afraid to fight. They were right and they were wrong. He *had* lost his edge as far as feeling that constant pressure to prove himself to be as much man as any other. But he wasn't afraid. Death would be welcome when he thought of the alternative, the long years ahead that were empty and mocking.

"Banning," Albright snarled again, and this time Zack saw the quick movement of his reflection in the mirror and turned, his hand flashing down in a blur as he spun on his heels in a half-crouch, pistol bucking in his hand.

The shots seemed to roll on top of one another in a loud explosion that was deafening in the saloon. Someone yelled, and there was the sound of boots thudding on wood and the bang of the saloon doors being shoved open. Zack stayed in his half-crouch a moment longer, eyes narrowed against the acrid curl of smoke and gunpowder.

Albright had been knocked backward by the force of the bullet that hit him, and lay groaning on the floor, his pistol still clutched in his hand. The young man with him stared down at the gunman for a moment, then looked up at Zack.

"You want in on this?" Zack asked tersely, and the youth shook his head.

"No. I told him not to do it."

Zack gave a single nod, and when no one else moved or seemed inclined to, he straightened slowly. Albright's shot had seared across his right shirt sleeve, wide of the mark. He reloaded, shoved his pistol back in his holster, then leaned back against the bar and watched as men came forward to lift the groaning gunman up to take him to the doctor.

"That was good shooting, mister," Albright's companion said slowly. He held the felled man's hat in one hand and his pistol in the other. "But Mr. Diamond ain't never gonna believe that you didn't provoke it."

"Diamond is not my problem."

"No, but he might make himself one."

Zack looked at him coolly. The young man was nervous, but earnest. Some of his irritation eased a little

"Is this a threat?" he asked lightly.

"No, sir. A warning."

A spurt of surprise made Zack look at the youth more closely. "I'll keep that in mind," he said finally.

The young man stood there a moment longer, looking as if he wanted to say something, and Zack wondered what. Advice on how to be a gunslinger? He hoped not. More than one youth had been rudely disappointed when brave enough to ask Zack Banning how to get as fast as he was. Zack took no pleasure or pride in recommending it as a career.

He returned the youth's stare coolly, and sipped his beer. If he knew Carpenter, the sheriff would be there to arrest him very shortly.

He was right.

Sheriff Carpenter shook his head and took Zack's pistol before he took him into custody, saying grimly, "I warned you to leave town, Banning."

"Yeah. I got delayed."

"You just might end up getting delayed for a long time, in case you've forgotten that men get hung for murder."

"Maybe murder, but not self-defense."

Carpenter snorted. "Too bad I don't buy that. You and Albright been at each other's throats before, the way I hear it. If he dies, you'll swing."

The young man who'd been with Albright cleared his throat. "Excuse me, sheriff. Frank Albright drew first. If you ask around, you'll find that out."

"Dammit, boy, ain't you his partn

388

The youth's chin tilted. "We worked together. That's all."

"Well, you go tell Diamond that I got one of his men dying over at the doc's office. And tell him I said stay out of town and let the law handle it. If Albright dies, there will be a fair trial. A jury can decide if it was self-defense or not.

"A fair trial in this town, sheriff?" Zack mocked when Carpenter shoved him into an empty cell and slammed shut the barred door. "You're dreaming."

"Probably." Carpenter stared at him, then shook his head. "I told you to leave, dammit. Why didn't you listen to me?"

Zack pressed his face against the cold bars and grinned at him. "I'm listening now."

"It's too late, my friend."

When Carpenter walked back into his front office, Zack had the sinking feeling that he was right. It was too late. It was always too late.

Chapter 27

"You whoring bitch."

Deborah sat stiffly in the parlor chair, trying not to let Dexter see how frightened she was. She heard Judith's quick protest through the fear pounding in her ears.

"Dexter, please! It wasn't like that."

"This is between me and her, Judy," he growled. "Keep out of it."

"I can't." Judith took a step toward him, hand held up as if pleading. "Deborah would never be dishonorable, but it was forced on her. At first, she was so terrified, and then he was so persuasive, so gentle—I guess she did what any woman in those circumstances would do. She began to love the only comfort she had." Judith broke off in a small sob. "If I had been shown the same kindness," she said a moment later, "I would have grabbed at it, too."

Diamond glanced at her. "I know. You told me. I'm sorry about what happened to both of you, but gawddammit, at least you didn't fall in love with the friggin' Injun who raped you!"

Deborah winced. Judith had discussed it with Dexter, but not with her. She wondered why. Why would her cousin feel more comfortable talking about such things with a man like Dexter Diamond?

Raking a hand through his hair, Dexter paced the floor furiously, pausing to glare at Deborah every few moments. He looked trapped between fury and disgust, and Deborah sat in stiff silence and waited.

When he paused in front of her, she kept her gaze riveted on the far wall, willing herself not to react to anything he might say.

"I'm not gonna divorce you," he said after a moment. "I won't have everyone sayin' you prefer that gawdammed 'breed to me. But I'll be damned if you're gonna keep his brat. I mean it. I won't bash its head against the wall like I want to, but it's leavin' as soon as it's born. The only choice you've got, is how. If you fight me on this, I swear I'll kill it, you hear me, Deborah?"

Despite her vow of silence, Deborah tilted back her head, her eyes blazing. "Is that what this is about, Dexter? Pride?"

He shot her a look of loathing. "No. Not just pride. There's a lot more at stake here, and you know it."

She stood up. "What? The Velazquez lands that you want so badly you're willing to murder for them? Let me assure you that you can have them. I don't want them."

"No court will let me keep them if you leave. You're staying here."

Deborah took a step closer, and her voice was soft. "I do not intend to give up my child, Dexter Diamond. If you so much as *act* like you're going to harm it, I'll kill you. Do I make myself perfectly clear?"

He looked astounded. His eyes opened wider, and his jaw sagged with shock. "Have you gone crazy?' he finally sputtered.

391

"No. I think, that for the first time in months, I am finally quite rational. I married you, Dexter, and if you insist that I stay with you, I will. But so help me, God, if you try to harm my child, there will be no place on earth that you can go to escape. I'll see to it."

"And how do you think you'll manage that?" Diamond demanded angrily, some of his shock fading.

"I'll help her," Judith spoke up quietly, and Diamond pivoted on his heel to stare at her. "She's been through enough. Don't threaten her anymore, Dexter. Please."

His face darkened. "So you're turnin' against me, too. I thought you understood me, Judy."

Her mouth trembled with emotion, but she said stubbornly, "I do, but I can't let you hurt her. I love her. She's my cousin. Don't make me choose between you, please."

Clenching and unclenching his big hands, Diamond finally growled, "I don't make any promises. If I have to look at Zack Banning's bastard every day of my life, I'll feel like killin' somethin' all the time."

He spun around and stomped out of the parlor, slamming the door behind him so hard that Deborah jumped. Her leap seemed to startle her unborn child, and for the first time, she felt it move within her. Deborah stood still, her hands moving to the swell of her stomach. A wave of protectiveness washed through her, and a strange sense of peace.

This was her child, hers and Zack's, and she thought suddenly of his face when he'd told her how he'd had to live with hate. It had driven him from his home, driven him from his mother, and she knew that she couldn't do that to her child. She did not want it to learn to live with hatred. And she did not want to wake up one day as Zack's mother had done, and see her child vanish from her life.

She hadn't realized she'd closed her eyes until she opened them and saw Judith gazing at her curiously.

"I can't do it, Judith," she said, and Judith nodded.

"I meant it. I'll help you. I just don't know what to do."

Deborah's smile was wry. "Neither do I."

Judith moved to her and put her arms around her. "We'll think of something," she whispered, and Deborah nodded.

"Yes. We'll think of something."

Sunlight streaming through the bars overhead made a striped pattern on the floor of Zack's cell. He'd never been locked up in jail before. At first the walls had seemed to close in around him, and he'd spent his time pacing. And waiting for Frank Albright to die.

Now, he'd grown resigned. He wished the bastard would either die or survive, but do one or the other. Even a rope and a short drop would be better than this.

So he lay drowsing in the warmth, arms folded behind his head. His lean body was relaxed, and he deliberately cleared his mind of any worries. He imagined blue skies and the wind in his face, and a strong horse beneath him. If he let himself, he could almost hear Deborah's soft, clipped tones, and see her dark fiery hair gleaming in the sunlight.

God, he could make himself crazy thinking about her. He tried not to. It was torture to remember her, to recall her soft skin and gold-flecked hazel eyes, the sweet taste of her mouth and her cool grace and poise. An almost physical pain made his stomach twist, and he sat up abruptly.

"Banning," he heard Carpenter say, and turned his head. "You got a visitor."

393

Surprised, Zack just stared at him. No one would visit him. He had no friends, no family to care.

Carpenter was beckoning to someone, grumbling, "You got just five minutes, young feller."

Zack rose slowly, his curiosity pricking him. When the young man came down the narrow hallway and stood in front of his cell, he felt another wave of surprise. It was the youth who had been with Albright in the saloon. He waited silently for him to say why he'd come.

"Mr. Banning," the young man said, stepping forward to press his face against the bars. "My name's Lonny King. I hope you don't mind me coming here."

Zack shrugged. "I'm not too busy right now."

"Yeah, I noticed." He paused, then said softly, "I know you're wondering why I came. I've got a message from someone for you."

Zack's eyes narrowed warily. "A message?"

Nodding, Lonny said, "Yeah. She said you'd know what it meant."

Not moving, Zack watched as Lonny King unbuttoned the top two buttons of his shirt and tugged at something knotted around his neck. When he freed it, Zack stiffened. Even before King held it out to him, he knew what it was.

Zack moved slowly to the barred door and held out his hand for the bone and eagle feather amulet. It nested there, the leather thong spilling from his palm to sway gently in the air.

Splinters of memory came back to him, flashing through his mind in disjointed fragments. He saw Deborah, the full moon shining in her hair like moonfire, her eyes fastened on him with a mixture of pain and bewilderment. Behind him, the restless murmur of armed, painted warriors cut across the soft sweep of wind over the Texas plains. Below, lay Fort Richardson and the end of his hopes. And he could hear his own voice, sounding cool and indifferent even though it cost him pain with every word.

"This was my father's. He left it with my mother should she ever wish to find him. When I was old enough, I searched for him with it. You may do the same if you should ever need me."

He looked up at Lonny King. "You said this was a message?"

"Yes. Mrs. Diamond said you would understand."

Zack's hand closed around the amulet. "Yes. I do."

A brisk wind blew the curtains back from the bedroom window, and Judith crossed to shut it. "It's gotten cold."

Deborah roused from her reverie, and looked away from the cheery fire. "As cold as it gets here, I suppose."

"It gets cold," Judith said when she returned to her chair by the fire. "Just not like at home."

"Yes. Not like at home. Natchez can have the wettest, most bone-deep chills I've seen."

A log in the fire popped and broke, sending up showers of sparks, and Deborah stared at it as if mesmerized. She tried to think about Natchez, and days when she'd been happy and innocent, but it all seemed so long ago. So long ago.

Sometimes, when she closed her eyes, she could see Zack as she'd first met him. He'd been terrifying then, with his bronzed face and cold blue eyes, the long sweep of raven hair brushing against his broad shoulders. How had he become less frightening and more comforting in such a short time? It didn't seem as if it should be possible, but it was.

Her hands moved, as they often did now, to the swell of her belly. The child moved frequently. It was active, and she reveled in each energetic kick and prod of the tiny life inside her. Zack's child. *Hawk's child.* God, how closely the two were entwined.

She hoped ... she hoped, she hoped, for miracles. For the sweet promise that had once been, but was now denied. And she hoped for the liberation of the man she loved. He deserved more than life had given him.

"Do you think he'll come?" Judith asked, startling her.

Deborah looked at her. "He'll come."

"He's in jail, Deborah. For shooting Frank Albright." Judith made a frustrated gesture. "Even if Albright lives—which I doubt, since he has lead poisoning—they might find a reason to hang Zack. After all, he's not exactly popular. People are afraid of him."

"He'll come."

Judith put a hand on her arm and said softly, "I hope so. And I hope you made the right decision."

"I think I have. Dexter will never accept Zack's child, especially now that he knows that Zack was the man who kept me in the Comanche camp. I'm not quite certain why it made such a difference, but it did."

"I think," Judith said slowly, "it was because he felt you had made a fool of him. Remember the day I sprained my ankle and he took me back to Don Francisco's?"

"Yes."

"He talked about how fine you were, how honest and good and all the things he thought he wanted. "Then, when it took you so long to get back, he worried that Banning had somehow tarnished you."

"And I told him I was insulted by his suggestions," Deborah said quietly. "Yes, I can understand why he would feel betrayed and foolish."

"He has a lot of pride."

Deborah thought of Zack, of how arrogant and proud he could be, and how he'd ignored that pride to come to Dexter Diamond's house and ask to see his new wife. She closed her eyes. So many mistakes. So much pain.

The fire popped again, and snapped with the collapse of a log. Deborah opened her eyes. The heat warmed her face and feet, but her back felt chilled by a brisk breeze. She turned and frowned at the open window.

"Judith, did you—?"

"I opened it," came a husky, familiar voice and Deborah rose to her feet with a soft cry.

"Hush," Judith said quickly. She crossed to the window and shut it, then threw Zack a narrow glance. "Are you sure no one saw you?"

He didn't answer for a moment, standing back in the shadows and blending in so well it took Deborah several seconds to see him. She moved across the room toward him, and when he pulled her into his warm embrace, she felt as if she'd been granted the key to paradise.

"You're here," she said against his broad chest. "You came for me."

"Yes. Did you think I wouldn't?"

It was such a typical reply, that Deborah laughed, the sound halfway between amusement and a sob, and Zack folded her more tightly in his arms. Her voice came out in a choked whisper.

"I hoped so. God, how I hoped you would."

"You sent me my father's amulet. I could not fail."

Tilting back her head, she looked up at him, and her breath caught at the blaze in his eyes, the blue lights that seared into her soul. She traced the outline of his mouth with a gentle finger.

"How did you get out of jail, Zack?"

His arms flexed, and then he set her back from him. "We can talk about that later. All I'll tell you, is that the sheriff will have a very bad headache when he wakes up."

"If he hasn't already," Judith cut in, her voice curt. "I hate to bring this up, but you two are in trouble if Dexter finds you together. I suggest you leave quickly."

Deborah turned, still in the circle of Zack's arms. "You are coming with us, aren't you?"

After a hesitation, Judith said, "It might be better if I stay here to distract Dexter. I can delay him a little, maybe."

"No, I don't want you to suffer because of me," Deborah protested, but Judith smiled.

"He won't hurt me. Dexter and I have an understanding."

When Deborah would have protested more, Zack growled, "Listen to her. It will be hard enough just getting you out of here." He put her back a step and looked down at her face in the shadows. "You do want to come with me?"

It was hard to talk around the sudden lump in her throat, but Deborah whispered, "More than I want anything."

A faint smile curled the erotic lines of his mouth, and he gave a satisfied nod. There was an exultant light in his eyes.

"Then we will go. Together. *Nahma?ai.*"

"Yes," she whispered, "together."

His head bent, and he gave her a swift, hard kiss that

set her pulses racing and made her knees weak. Then he tucked her into the angle of his body and moved with her to the window.

"We don't have much time. If anyone finds the guard I left out back, there'll be hell to pay," he muttered as he bent and peered out from the side of the window. He turned to Judith. "Blow out that lamp."

The light was extinguished, and as darkness flooded the room, Deborah blinked against it. Slowly, her eyes became adjusted to the absence of lamplight, and she noted the pale silver light that streamed in through the open window. Zack seemed to adjust more quickly, because he was pulling her to the window and stepping through it, reaching back for her.

Without hesitating, she put her hand in his. Then she felt Judith at her back, and turned.

"You love him, don't you?" Judith stared at her, and Deborah grabbed her hand. "Don't be timid now, Judith. If you love Dexter, go to him. You're right. He'll need you, and God knows, there's little enough love in this world to deny anyone what they can find."

Tears welled in Judith's eyes, and she bit her lip as she met Deborah's loving gaze. "You know?"

"I'd have to be blind not to know. Yes, and I don't mind. I only wish he was more worthy of you, but I suppose you think the same." She managed a smile, and felt Zack give her a gentle nudge.

"Go. Be careful," Judith whispered. "And be happy."

Deborah couldn't speak for a moment. She felt Zack's strong tug on her hand, and his impatience, and knew the time was too short.

"I'll send word."

"Godspeed."

Zack lifted her through the window and set her down

on the porch, pushing her gently back against the wall. His breath feathered over her cheek as he whispered, "Wait here while I check things out."

She pressed back against the wall, shivering with cold and fear and anticipation. Zack moved silently across the porch, a dark shadow against the brighter light from a full moon. She saw him go to the far end of the porch and blend into the shadows, then he was back within moments.

"Come on," he muttered, taking her cold hand in his and pulling her with him. She tried to move as quietly as Zack, but could hear her own footsteps echoing on the wood.

Perhaps surprise would keep their flight secret. No one would expect him to boldly walk into an armed camp for her, especially as he was supposed to be in jail. Deborah felt a wave of admiration for Zack, despite her shivering fear of discovery. He moved as silently as the wind, seeming to drift above the ground while she stumbled along like a blind mare.

He vaulted over the porch rail and landed lightly on the other side, then reached up to lift her over. It was dark on this side of the house, and the bunkhouses stretched beyond them in a wide arc, and beyond those, the corrals just off the barn. Zack knew the ranch well, having lived there for several months, and he used that knowledge to his advantage now.

Moonlight brightened the grounds and drew long, distorted shadows. A dog barked in the distance, and she could hear the muted murmur of men in the bunkhouses. A light burned inside, and a figure was silhouetted against the window.

Deborah was breathing heavily now, her lungs aching from the unaccustomed strain as she tried to keep up with Zack. She felt as if a faulty bellows was pumping air into her body. Her side throbbed, and a pain stitched her ribs.

"You all right?" Zack murmured against her ear when they paused in the shadow of an outbuilding. She nodded, and he swore softly. "Damn. You're shaking so bad I can hear your teeth chattering."

"I can make it," she managed to say, and he kissed her.

"It's not much farther," he said when he lifted his head to peer at her in the light. "My horse is just beyond that second ridge. It's the closest I could get without being seen by the men near the house."

Deborah didn't ask what had happened to the guards assigned to the perimeters. She didn't want to know.

"Deborah—it's clear between here and that ridge, and the moon is full. We're going to have to go as fast as we can, do you understand?"

She swallowed a surge of fear. "Yes."

A Comanche moon. The night sun gives good light for our warriors to see, he'd said, his voice mocking.

If only it was dark tonight.

He tucked her hand into his broad palm and held it for a moment, his smile encouraging. "I'll help you," he said softly, and her fear faded. He eased away from the security of the shadows, and they began running.

They were halfway across when the alarm was given. She never knew if they had been seen, or someone had discovered one of the dead guards. But a man shouted, a gun was fired, and all hell broke loose.

Panic set in, but Deborah refused to give in to it as she tried to keep up with Zack. When she fell, he stopped and pulled her to her feet, urging her forward again. The stitch in her side grew worse, and she was gasping for breath with each terrified step. Shouts sounded behind them, and then the thunder of hooves against the ground.

Deborah's legs felt too heavy to move, but she forced them on, one foot in front of the other, desperation coming from somewhere to give her the strength to keep going. Zack caught her when she stumbled over a clump of brush, his arms strong and capable, and she knew, suddenly, that she was only slowing him down. She sagged to the ground.

"Go on," she managed to say in between pants for air. "He'll kill you if he catches you. Leave me."

Zack picked her up. "If I leave you again, I'd rather he kill me," he said in her ear.

She caught at his arms, harsh breath hurting her throat. "Please—I could not bear it if he hurt you. Go. I am only slowing you down."

"No!" he said fiercely, and lifted her into his arms and began running with her. She felt his chest heaving with effort, his feet hitting the ground as he ran in long, smooth strides, and pressed her face against his shoulder.

"Banning!" a voice shouted from close behind them, and Deborah stifled a scream as Dexter Diamond pounded toward them on his horse. They could not outrun horses.

Apparently, Zack realized it, too, because he halted and put her down, shoving her away from him as he turned to face Diamond. Four men flanked the rancher, and they were all mounted astride unsaddled horses.

Zack waited, feet apart and legs braced, and Deborah saw with anguish that he would not ask for mercy. She sank to the ground and closed her eyes, burying her face in her palms.

When Diamond slid from his horse and walked toward them, Deborah took a deep breath and stood up. If Zack could meet his fate head-on, so could she.

Chapter 28

"Step aside, Deborah," Diamond said coldly, eyeing Zack with pure hatred.

Her chin lifted defiantly. "No. If you kill him, you're going to have to kill me, too."

"Don't tempt me," came the growling reply.

"Go back to the house," Zack told her. He kept his eyes on Diamond warily, his posture stiff and tense. "You cannot help either of us now."

"No! Zack, I won't leave you again."

"Listen to your lover," Diamond said. "Or stay here and watch him die. I don't give a damn, but whatever you do, get out of my way."

Frantic, Deborah put herself in Dexter's path as he took another step toward Zack. She saw the armed men behind him, and knew that any one of them was capable of shooting.

Zack shoved her aside. His tone was contemptuous. "He's made it plain he doesn't mind shooting you. Go into the house as you were told."

Shaking her head, Deborah said, "No. I won't hide anymore. He's going to have to shoot both of us."

Diamond swore softly. "Gawddammit, woman, get out of the way!"

Deborah sought Zack's eyes, and saw the determination in him, the pride that would not allow him to bargain with Dexter Diamond or risk her life.

"If you shoot me, Dexter," she said, keeping her gaze on Zack's taut face, "what will you tell the sheriff? He might let you get by with shooting Zack, but how about me? How will he feel about your shooting a pregnant woman?"

She saw the quick look of disbelief Zack gave her, and the dawning doubt. His mouth tightened, and she prayed that he would understand.

Some of the men with Diamond swore, and one of them took a step back and away. Deborah continued desperately, turning toward Dexter as she said, "I've wronged you, and I'm sorry, truly I am, but I did not betray you. Never that. I made you no promises because I didn't want to break them, and you must know that. You only married me to get the rights to Velazquez lands, and if you like, I'll sign them over to you. But please, Dexter, no more killing. There's been enough."

Diamond's jaw tightened. "You made a fool of me, you and that half-breed bastard. You pretended you didn't know him, when you'd just spent months in a damned Comanche camp with him under his robes. Hell, I knew you weren't no innocent young thing anymore, but I was willin' to overlook that. A woman can't help some things, but you acted as if you were too damn good for me after you'd been layin' under that 'breed."

"It wasn't that," Deborah said faintly. She could feel Zack's murderous glare on her. "I love him. I loved him before I ever knew you, Dexter. Don't do this, please."

He shook his head, moonlight mixing in the pale strands and making it gleam. "Too late, sugar. Banning's shot up too many of my men and put himself in

405

my way once too often. Now step out of the way, or I'll have you dragged out of the way."

"No," she said, shaking her head desperately. She heard Zack mutter something in Comanche to her, and she half-turned to look at him.

"Miaru. Unu nu kamakunu?"

Tears blurred her eyes. *"Haa. Deborah kamakuru Tosa Nakaai."*

Clear blue eyes softened, and a faint smile curved his mouth at her admission of love. *"Miaru,"* he repeated softly.

Her throat ached, and she knew he did not want her to see him die. "Please—I can't," she started to say, when a hand descended on her shoulder and spun her around.

"Gawwdammed bitch, jabberin' in that Comanche tongue like you was raised to it!" Dexter's face was furious, and before she could avoid it, he'd drawn back his other hand and slammed it across her face.

Lights exploded in front of her eyes and the ground came up to meet her. Rocks dug into her skin and she tried to move but Dexter had her by the front of her blouse and was shaking her like a rag doll. Everything was a blur, the ground and men and the full moon sliding past at an alarming rate of speed, and she tried to speak but couldn't.

Then there was an explosion of sound and she fell back, suddenly released to sprawl on the ground. Dazed and shaking with fear and pain, Deborah rolled to her stomach to protect her child, arms folded over her body. She could hear men yelling. A sharp, acrid smell stung her nose, and she recognized it as gunpowder.

Looking up through the tangled veil of her loose hair, Deborah caught a painful breath, her eyes widening.

Zack stood in the bent-knee posture of a gunfighter,

his pistol levelled and a curl of smoke drifting up from the barrel. He looked as cold and deadly as she had ever seen him, and the faint, cruel smile that she'd seen once before curved his mouth.

"Which one of you boys wants to give it a try?" he was asking coolly. Four men shuffled in the dirt and exchanged glances. "I can get two of you before I go down. Who's willing to take a chance?"

Deborah's gaze shifted, and she gasped as she saw Dexter Diamond sprawled on the ground and groaning. Blood spurted from a wound high in his shoulder, and he was panting for breath.

"Gawdammit, one of you shoot him!" he got out between pants. "Kill that half-breed bastard . . ."

"Let 'em go, Mr. Diamond," one of the men spoke up, and Deborah saw Lonny King step forward. "Nobody wants to take him on. We all know him, and we didn't sign on to take that kind of risk. Not for a man who hits pregnant women."

No one else spoke for a moment, and Diamond rolled over to peer up at King blearily. "You're the only one I hear talkin'," he snarled, his eyes moving to the other three men behind Lonny. He gave a grunt of pain at his movements, then laughed harshly when none of the men spoke. "Guess that's an answer then."

"Reckon so," King said softly. He stepped over to Deborah and helped her to her feet, keeping a wary eye on Zack and his lethal pistol. Moonlight shimmered over them as he looked down at her. "You all right, ma'am?"

"Yes." She drew in a shaky breath, wondering what would happen if she were to go to Zack. He hadn't moved or spoken since shooting Diamond. Menace vibrated in his stance and his eyes, and the other men stood still as if afraid to move and provoke him. She supposed that the drawn gun was enough of a deterrent to any man familiar with Zack's accuracy.

Deborah had taken a step toward Zack when she heard a soft scream and paused, looking behind her. Judith ran toward them, her long golden hair streaming behind her as she skimmed over the ground.

Half-sobbing, she flung herself to the ground beside Dexter. "Oh sweetheart, Dexter love—you're hurt! Oh God, I couldn't stand it if you died . . ."

"Hush, sugar," Diamond muttered, giving her a clumsy pat that made his face contort with pain. "I ain't dyin' yet." He shot his hired guns a furious glare. "No thanks to any of them."

Judith cradled his head in her lap, smoothing back his blond hair and weeping softly. She rocked back and forth, murmuring soft words to him, oblivious of everything else. Deborah saw Dexter grimace at the pain as he tried to offer her comfort, and let her breath out in a soft rush of air.

She moved to stand just behind Zack, feeling his tension as he kept a guarded watch on the men around Diamond. "I think we can go now," she said softly, and he hooked an arm around her waist to pull her closer. His pistol was still aimed and ready.

"Go on, Banning," Lonny King said. "Get her out of here before it's too late."

For a suspended moment of time, Deborah wondered if Zack had heard him, then he nodded. Keeping his pistol up, he took several steps backward, taking her with him.

Deborah looked back at Judith and called softly, "Do you want to come?"

Her cousin looked up, there were tears on her cheeks but a faint smile curved her mouth. Blue eyes glistened

408

as she shook her head. "No. I want to stay here with Dexter."

Deborah had expected no other answer. "Be happy," she whispered, and then there was no time to say more because Zack was pulling her with him, his long strides taking them to the next ridge and his horse.

He threw her atop, then vaulted up behind her and reached around her for the reins. His pistol nudged her side as he wheeled the horse around and kicked it into a run. The sound of hoofbeats on hard-packed ground echoed in her ears, and she leaned back against Zack's muscled chest and closed her eyes.

The rhythmic motion of the horse and the strain of the past weeks left her drained, and she was barely aware of her surroundings. All that mattered was Zack, and that she was with him.

"Notsa?ka," Zack whispered as he pulled Deborah from his horse and shook her gently awake. "No one can find us here. You need to rest for a while."

Her eyes opened slowly, and a faint smile curved her mouth as she leaned back against his sturdy strength. "What does that mean?"

"What?"

"Notsa?ka."

He grinned, tracing a finger over her cheek and down to her mouth. His voice was husky. "Sweetheart."

Her eyes opened wide. "Am I?"

"My sweetheart? Yes. My only heart." His arms closed around her tightly, and he dragged in a deep breath and let it out slowly, so that it stirred the deep fiery tendrils of her hair.

For a moment she didn't say anything. Then she asked, "Where are we?"

Zack's head lifted, and he shrugged. "The Hueco Mountains."

"Where are we going?"

"Presidio County."

Turning in his embrace, she looked up at him with puzzled eyes. "What's there?"

"My mother."

"Your mother." There was a short pause, then she said, "You were going to tell me about her."

"Yes. I will. First, let's build a fire and eat something, then I'll tell you."

Deborah sat on a flat rock and held her hands out to the blaze Zack started with swift efficiency. In just a short time, he'd fashioned a shelter from brush and rock, and spread blankets and a serape on the ground for them.

"You came prepared," she commented, and he looked up at her, firelight making his bronzed features glow. A faint smile touched the corners of his mouth.

"Yes."

"Are you ever unprepared for the unexpected?"

White teeth flashed as he grinned at her. "I wasn't prepared for you."

"Complaining already?"

The shadows in his eyes altered subtly, taking on a different light, and Deborah caught her breath. He looked at her with the same intensity he had the first time he'd seen her, and she felt the familiar clutch of her heart.

A pulse began throbbing between her thighs, warm and strong and insistent, and she vibrated with the same longing she could sense in him.

"No," he said softly, "I'm not complaining."

He rose to his feet in a lithe motion and crossed to her, reaching down to pull her up against him. Deborah

410

felt the thud of his heart beneath the palm she put on his chest, and his muscles flexed as he folded her into his embrace.

"I want you to know something," he said in a husky, strained voice that made her tense. He sounded reluctant, as if it was an effort for him to speak.

"What is it, Zack?"

"I didn't kill Dexter because I did not want to kill your child's father. It would be too much of a burden. No," he said when she opened her mouth to speak, "let me finish. Your child will never know hatred from me. I will keep it as my own, and love it. The father doesn't matter. I will be the father."

Hot tears sprang to her eyes, and emotion choked her so that she couldn't speak for a moment. He thought the child was Dexter's, yet he was willing to love it anyway. His own painful betrayal still hurt him after all these years. She buried her face in the warmth of his shoulder and held back a sob.

When his arms closed around her more tightly and he leaned back to tilt her chin up for his kiss, Deborah wondered if he could see the love shining in her eyes.

"Zack—oh, my love—the child is yours. Ours. When early spring comes, you will have a child of our love to hold in your arms. We'll be a family."

For a long moment, he didn't say anything. His face was impassive, emotionless. Only his eyes showed any emotion, and the shadows were slowly replaced with growing peace.

There were no words to express what he felt, and he sank slowly to his knees on the blankets he'd spread, taking Deborah with him. He held her hard against him, breathing in deep, regulated rhythm.

"You are sure of this?" he finally asked, and there was no censure in his voice.

411

Deborah nodded. "Dexter never touched me. He wanted to at first, but then—he didn't."

Zack's mouth smothered anything else she might have said, and he pushed her gently back into the blankets with the weight of his body. She tingled everywhere he touched her, thrills of flame racing along her nerve-endings and starting blazes. This time, there were no shadows between them, no reservations.

Moonlight shimmered around them. Zack slowly undressed her, pausing to put a warm palm on the mound of her belly and gaze at her with love and wonder and raw emotion flickering over his features. He knelt with his bent legs between hers, his hands exploring the soft contours of her body.

"I love you," he said hoarsely, and Deborah reached up to pull his shirt off his shoulders.

"I love you, Zack," she murmured. "Hawk—my beautiful, arrogant lover. Did you know that the hawk came to me when I was alone and lost and hurting, and I knew it had to be you. It brought me back when I thought I'd never want to live again."

He pulled her skirt free of her hips, sliding his warm palms down her thighs to her knees, lifting her legs to pull them around his waist. He was still wearing his pants, and she could feel the rough texture of the denim material against her tender skin. His lashes lifted, and she saw the smoky gleam of his eyes as he gazed at her with love and a male hunger that made her breath come a little faster.

Slowly drawing his fingers down from the rapid beat of a pulse in the hollow of her throat to the firm thrust of her breasts, he shaped the creamy mounds with his palms, his eyes half-closing. "You're so beautiful," he murmured, his voice a little hoarse and his breathing ragged. "I used to dream about you . . . doing this . . . touching you and just learning you."

His thumbs dragged over the taut, aching peaks of her breasts in a tantalizing caress, and Deborah felt the heat in her belly rise and curl and flush her entire body. When his knees pressed her thighs a little wider, he spread a hand from her breast to the obvious swell of her belly. He looked up at her, eyes darkening to a blue so deep it was almost black.

At that moment, he made her think of a savage again, fierce and brutal with pleasure. The exultant light in his eyes was a deep, steady flame.

"We are one, Deborah. You have my heart. And I have yours. There will be no more misunderstandings between us."

"No," she whispered. Her fingers trailed down the strong curve of his arms to his wrists where he held his hand on her stomach. "One—together."

Spreading his fingers across her stomach, he looked startled, and Deborah laughed softly.

"Our child wants to remind us that we will be three together."

A strange look stole over his features, and Zack sat quietly for several minutes, feeling the strong thumps against his palm as the child moved. She saw his throat work for air, and his expression blurred as he closed his eyes as if in pain. When his lashes lifted again, thick and shadowing his eyes, she saw his mouth flatten and curve into a smile.

"I hope he does not mind if I share his mother for a while."

Deborah held her breath when his hands moved lower, grazing the tender curve of her inner thighs, stroking her with leisurely caresses that made her tremble. His weight and the gentle pressure of his knees

413

holding her legs apart made her feel hot and restless with growing excitement.

He bent his head, his hands dark against her pale skin as he watched her reaction to what his hands were doing. In between drags of heated air, Deborah saw the smooth, muscled curve of his broad shoulders shudder slightly as he stroked her, his fingers moving to the pulsing warmth between her legs.

When she pressed up into his hand with a ragged moan, he muttered something in Comanche and sat back. He fumbled at the buttons of his pants, rose to his knees to push them down, then kicked them away. Deborah stared at him with appreciation, the lean hard strength of him, the bronzed muscle that roped his body and flexed with his movements, and then he was back over her, his knees wedging between her thighs again.

Her breath came in short, tortured pants for air, the need for him rising so strong and demanding that she reached out. "Zack ... please."

The renewed pressure of his body against her damp, hot center made her shudder, and her fingers caught at his long hair and pulled his head down to hers. She caught his lower lip between her teeth, nibbling with tiny, fevered bites that made him groan, and he thrust his tongue between her lips. The exploration of her mouth made the heat rise to a fever-pitch, and when his hands found her taut nipples, she cried out.

Zack didn't try to smother her cries, but instead, seemed to take a fierce pleasure in them. His breath came harsh and fast, and his braced arms trembled with strain as he held himself over her. He raked his lower body up and over her sensitive folds of flesh in an erotic rhythm that made her squirm and shudder and strain toward him.

On fire with need, Deborah moaned again, "Please, Zack, oh please love me . . ."

This time he answered with a shift of his body so that the hard heat of him pressed into her. Her hips lifted in an automatic move to accept him. She felt his throb and shudder as he hesitated, then the hot, delicious slide of him into her that made the world spin around her in a blur of moonlight and sensation.

Zack made a sound somewhere between pain and pleasure, and his breath feathered over her cheek as he bent his head. Soft moans escaped her, tangled in his hair, brushed against his ear. His invasion filled her, hard and strong and powerful and making her arch upward into his thrusts until she felt as if she was sailing above the earth.

Before, Deborah had always felt as if he'd held something back from her, some part of himself that he could not share as easily as he did his body. Not this time. This time he lost himself in her, driving into her with mindless passion and whispered words of love, some of them she understood and some she didn't. His heat and the smells of their lovemaking drove her to match his fierce thrusts.

Her hands slid with almost frantic urgency over the glistening curve of his shoulders, down the ridged bend of his ribs to his lean, hard waist, then moved to cup and hold his buttocks in her palms. She could feel the flex of muscle as he moved, the thrust and drag of him inside her, the almost unbearable friction growing higher and hotter until she thought she would explode with it.

When the release came, it washed over her in endless waves that spun her up so high she thought she was touching the moon. Light everywhere, flashes behind her eyes, bathing her in warmth and love.

415

Spiralling slowly back to earth, she grew more aware of Zack, his body heavy atop her, some of his weight braced on his bent arms, his breath harsh and ragged in her ear. She remembered his groan, the husky word he had muttered when he had exploded inside her.

"Usúni."

Forever. Yes. Forever.

Epilogue

Pecos River, Texas 1873

"I got a letter from Judith." Deborah held out the page, and Zack took it, his eyes scanning the neat scrawl. He handed it back to her after a moment.

"She seems happy enough since they got married."

"Yes." Deborah folded the paper and tucked it back into the envelope, smiling at her husband as he held their child in the strong cradle of his arms. "It's a good thing my divorce came through. She and Dexter are expecting a child next spring."

A faint smile curved the hard line of his mouth, and Zack muttered, "Poor child."

Deborah pressed a hand over her mouth, and her voice was reproving when she said, "That's not fair. Judith only wanted someone to love her, and Dexter—" She paused, and he lifted a brow and grinned wickedly.

"Yes? You were going to say something nice about poor Dexter? I'm waiting." When she gave him a glance of reproof, he couldn't help laughing. "Sweetheart, you know he's too damned mean and ambitious for his own good. I just hope your cousin knows what she's got herself in for."

Sighing, Deborah said, "I think she does. She loves him, and that's all that matters."

Zack felt something raw and still painful move in his chest, the memory of the years without love clawing at him. Thank God those memories were slowly fading now. He had Deborah, and he had his son, an armful of active baby that chose that moment to wet his napkin and his father's lap.

Holding him with an expression of chagrin and disgust, Zack heard the front door open and his mother laugh.

"Zachary dear, you should know that these things happen on occasion."

Amelia Banning Miles moved onto the porch with a twinkle lighting blue eyes remarkably like her son's.

She bent over and lifted the squirming child from his father's arms, tucking him into the angle of her arm and shoulder and cooing softly to him. Laughing, the baby waved chubby arms, staring up at his grandmother with thick-lashed golden eyes. His dark hair and tawny skin echoed his heritage, but the bright smile was a replica of his mother's. The eyes were strictly his own. Wolf eyes, Zack had named them, and that was what he called the child. Wolf.

Deborah had insisted upon a more proper name for their son, that decision echoed by Amelia. In the end they had settled on Caleb Hamilton Banning. Little Caleb answered just as readily to either name, Deborah and Amelia had noticed with dismay. Six months old and active, he literally ran the household.

Zack smiled at his mother, and saw her eyes cloud with shadow. She still regretted the lost years, he knew. Daniel Miles had died several years before, and the ranch belonged to Amelia and Danny now. His older half brother had asked him to remain and help out, but

418

Zack had still not made up his mind. At first, he'd not known what was going to happen to him if Albright died, but then the gunman had survived and all charges had been dropped. Then he'd just wanted to see Deborah settled somewhere safe, but the reunion with his mother had lured him into lingering until after the birth of his child.

Now he was restless, feeling the need to move on again. Old habits died hard, he supposed, but this time the urge to roam had an end goal in mind. He cleared his throat.

"I got a letter, too, you know," he said, and Deborah looked at him, her hazel eyes flecked with gold and shadow.

"I know. I was wondering if you would mention it."

Shrugging, Zack rose from the chair, plucking his damp pants away from his thighs with a mutter of disgust. Then he went to his wife and pulled her against him.

"Sally Martin wrote me. She has decided to put her ranch up for sale."

"Sally Martin—the woman who saved your life." Deborah nodded. There was no jealousy in her tone, only a profound gratitude to the woman who'd helped Zack and loved him.

"Yes. I invited her to come here for a while." He grinned when Deborah's head tilted back to look up at him. "I thought she and Danny might get along pretty good."

"Zack Banning, are you matchmaking?" Deborah demanded so incredulously that he could feel a slight flush rising.

"Well, she's lonely and so is Danny since his wife died a few years back," he defended himself. "I can't see any harm in it."

419

"Any harm in what?" a masculine voice asked, and they turned to see Danny Miles step up onto the porch. He was dusty and smiling, his light blue eyes raking his brother with affection. "Not another baby, I hope."

"Do you object to this one?" Amelia demanded so swiftly they all laughed.

Danny dragged a hand through his light brown hair and shook his head ruefully. "No, but he sure is a noisy thing at times. Yowled for an hour the other day after I took away the knife he found."

Zack felt a shudder run through Deborah, and curled his arms around her again. "He gets into trouble, that's for sure."

Leaning back against the porch post, Danny eyed him closely. "You're up to something," he guessed. "I can tell by your eyes."

Deborah smothered a laugh. "Zack has someone he wants you to meet, I'm afraid."

"Oh?"

"Yeah, I'm thinking about buying her ranch."

There was a moment of quiet, and they all heard Amelia Miles's quickly in-drawn breath. Young Caleb gave a squeal of protest at her tightening hug, and she soothed him with soft words in her cool, clipped tones.

"Where is it?" Danny asked after a moment.

"At the foot of the Hueco Mountains."

"Near the Velazquez and Diamond places?" Danny's surprise was evident.

"Not too near. But I'm not worried about it. I don't think Diamond will mess with me, not since he's married to Judith. And since Don Francisco lost any claim to his lands, he's certainly not a threat. I hear he's living in some adobe hut near Sirocco."

"Hardly the grande hacienda he once had, but it's his own fault."

Zack tilted a glance at Deborah. "You sorry you didn't get to keep any of it?"

"I could have, you know. After you produced the paper you had him sign, I could have claimed all of it." Deborah shook her head. "At least Tía Dolores is well taken care of. I think it's justice that Don Francisco lost everything, but I can't help feeling a certain sadness that she lost, too."

"Too bad the law didn't take care of Velazquez." Zack shrugged. "You'd think a signed confession of attempted murder, extortion, and various other crimes would have put him away for a while at worst, gotten him hung at best." Zack's voice hardened, and his eyes narrowed. "It would have suited me if he had dangled from the end of a rope, but I don't always get my way."

"No," Amelia said coolly, "you don't. I don't want you to move away."

Zack shifted slightly, leaning back against the wooden porch rail and pulling Deborah with him. "We need our own life. Our own place. Sally's offer is a good one. She has plenty of water, deep wells, and enough acreage to run a few cattle. I don't need more. Don't want more." His arm tightened around Deborah. "I have all I want now."

Danny cleared his throat, boot scraping against the porch as he bent one long leg and looked out over the land stretching beyond the house. "I sent that herd of cattle to market like you wanted."

"Did you cut out the beeves we agreed on?"

Danny nodded. "Yes. White Eagle's camp will have enough meat for the winter."

"This winter, anyway."

Silence fell. The Comanche had been relentlessly pursued by Mackenzie, and defeated in a bloody battle at North Fork. Shortly thereafter, a Comanche war chief,

Parra-a-coom, or Bull Bear, had gone to Fort Sill and asked that the women and children Mackenzie had taken be released in exchange for the surrender of the warriors. United States Agent Tatum had reservations. Release of the women and children being held as hostages would only free the men to make war again, he thought. Already, their imprisonment had secured the freedom of fourteen white captives and twelve Mexicans being held by the Comanche. He refused.

Sunflower was still among those being held by Mackenzie at Fort Richardson, and White Eagle had chosen to go on the warpath to affect his daughter's return. It was a tense situation.

"It will not end well," Zack said heavily. "There will have to be a Comanche leader who has the foresight to lead the people to peace instead of war. White Eagle is old and alone."

Later, as Zack and Deborah walked to the crest of a rolling swell of land, she asked softly, "Do you miss living with the Comanche?"

"At times," he answered honestly. "It was a simple way of life. And free. We followed the buffalo, or the wind."

"Freedom is costly," Deborah murmured.

Zack stopped and turned her into his arms. His eyes burned into her, and he felt a growing constriction in his chest. He knew his voice was hoarse, raw, but he couldn't help the emotion. His years of control vanished as if on the wind.

"All I need," he said, "is right here in my arms. I have found it with you. You are my wind, my freedom, my love."

He saw her eyes glaze with tears, and the polished sheen of her hair glowed under the setting sun with an underlying fire. Her arms came around him, and she fit

422

against him as if she had been created for just that purpose.

"I will always love you, Zack Banning," she said
softly. "You are as wild and free as the hawk for which
you were named, and I'll stay with you forever. *Usúni.*"

Bending his head, his dark hair brushed against her
cheek as he kissed her, and overhead the cry of a hawk
spiraled down in lilting waves.

To my readers—

This story was special to me, and I hope you found it to be special as well. Sometimes, characters seem to take over. I found that to be true with these. As I did my research for this story, I became quite involved with Hawk. He occupied my mind so much that I thought of him even when not writing. His situation was one a great many people of his time faced, and to some extent, may still face.

What intrigued me, was the fact that though I live in a busy suburb, I became host to a hawk. This beautiful bird has shown up at my house on numerous occasions since I began this story, and I never knew when it would arrive or how long it would stay. I thought it unusual, and sometimes would begin my day wondering if the hawk would come today. I took it as a symbol, and when the hawk came to perch on my fence or in a tree in my backyard, I felt as if it would be a special day. And a special story.

I hope you think so, too. If you enjoyed Hawk and Deborah's story and want to tell me about it, please write to me in care of

ZEBRA BOOKS
475 Park Avenue South
New York, N.Y. 10016

For a prompt reply, please include a self-addressed, stamped envelope, and I will put you on my mailing list for newsletters about future releases.

Virginia Brown